Matthew's D

E.M. Phill

To all members of the Forest Writers' Group
with thanks for your support, your friendship
and all the tea and chocolate biscuits

Cover design: Diana Durant

Matthew's Daughter

E.M. Phillips

The second book in a Cornish Trilogy

Matthew's Daughter

Published 2007 by Sagittarius Publications
62 Jacklyns Lane, Alresford, Hampshire SO24 9LH
Tel: 01962 734322

Typeset by John Owen Smith

ISBN 978-0-9555778-2-6

Printed and bound by CPI Antony Rowe, Eastbourne

Part 1

Prologue

If you looked carefully at those Newsreels taken outside the Admiralty in Whitehall on VE day, and if your eyesight is very good, you might have noticed on the third lamp post down from Big Ben myself in WAAF uniform accompanied by a Canadian pilot, both of us perched on the crosspiece below the lantern. Not conduct becoming an officer and gentlewoman but who cared, the war, or at least my part in it, was almost over. I can't speak for the Canadian pilot because I never saw him again, nor needed to. For an hour or so, perched high above cheering, dancing crowds, to each other we were just Caro and Jake; two of the thousands of lunatics celebrating after five long years of war.

Four months later I called another woman ma'am for the last time, dumped my uniform into the bottom of my suitcase and sallied forth to begin life over again; ex-Squadron Officer Caroline Penrose, twenty-three; unattached (for longer than was comfortable and through no fault of my own), and with little faith or immediate wish that Fate might be about to dish up a second chance.

The battered but functional old Standard, purchased for a tenner from a USAAF medic leaving for Texas, carried me on the long road to the West Country, to Trewlyn's and the flower meadows high on the cliffs above Penmarrion Cove.

I sang as I drove, loudly if not always tunefully. Cheerful songs, vulgar songs and some downright dirty songs, but somewhere along the way they turned into a haunting Auld Lang Syne, played in slow waltz time and danced to on the wooden floor of an Air Force mess, with Stefan's arms about me and the certainty of parting in the dull light of morning.

'When we finish this war; then I come back to you and we shall never again part.'

The smile I had loved, the beautiful voice, the body still ached for, all gone in a few brief moments, in a thousand fragments falling from the sky over a Normandy beach.

Nothing left. Not even a grave to sit beside.

'Sod you, Stefan!' I thumped my fist on the steering wheel. 'You had no right to clear off like that and leave me to go it alone…and not even a proper goodbye…what am I supposed to do with the rest of my life, you bastard?'

But I knew there was no answer to my question, no magic wand to wave and bring him back. I drove on into the September day, grateful for the old familiar lift of the heart as I headed for Penzance and the coast road to Penmarrion and home.

1

The rattle of enamel bowls as the dogs rooted for the last scraps of their breakfasts woke me; then the sudden raucous clatter of the chickens that told me my father was on his way with their morning feed. Still only half awake, I pulled on my old pre-war dressing gown and leaned from the open casement window to let my gaze wander slowly over the familiar landscape.

Immediately beneath me was the cobbled yard, dotted with half-barrels spilling over with bright flowers; to the left the stable built for the pony I'd long outgrown and passed on to a small cousin. Stepping away into the distance, almost hidden by the early morning mist were the fruit cage, the chicken run, the pond with the six comical Indian Runner ducks, the packing shed and glasshouses. Beyond the confines of house and farm buildings the flower meadows swept down toward the sea, some thick with the dull green foliage of wallflower and sweet william, some soon to be showing the first green spikes of daffodil thrusting through the rich brown earth.

I could hear the waves break in the cove below the cliffs where the big black backed gulls drifted, breaking now and again to dive and take a fish from the sea, or snatch some edible morsel stranded on the shore. Later, as the day warmed, the seals would gather to bob on the water, snouts lifted to the breeze, round liquid eyes scanning the beach for convenient rocks on which to bask in the late September sun.

Nothing, I thought with satisfaction had changed all that much, it was almost as it had been: timeless and a world away from war.

Trewlyns had been my grandfather's pride, now it was my father's and he I knew hoped that it would one day be mine. But one could never be too sure of anything in this life and I couldn't look that far ahead. The decision to put on hold for the present all thought of any future career had been dictated purely by instinct and the need to lick my wounds in familiar surroundings.

The door opened and Grace crossed the room to place two cups of tea on the bedside table. ''Morning, Grace,' I stretched and yawned then returned to snuggle back under the covers as she took her own cup and sat on the end of the bed to gossip, just as she had from the time I was ten years old.

I studied her while she chatted and I drank my tea, thinking that here was something else that hadn't changed at all. Ever since she'd come to housekeep for my father Matthew and me after my mother died, she'd looked exactly the same. Around five feet nothing; the long reddish hair piled on top of her head still secured with a tortoiseshell comb and a battalion of hairpins, most of which she would lose as the day progressed, never any trace of make-up on her freckled mischievously puckered face. When I was a child I'd thought her a hobgoblin sort of figure; a changeling, an elderly child who aged slower than mere mortals. Whatever she was I loved her and couldn't imagine Trewlyns without her busy-bodying, presence.

* * * * *

When later I went downstairs, comfortable in old slacks, shirt and jersey, I stood for a few moments to look around and run my hand along the sofa that stood before the fire, a multicoloured blanket thrown over the back to hide the wear I'd made as a child; using it as a spirited horse, riding furiously to bring the good news from Aix to Ghent or triumphantly winning the Grand National.

A driftwood fire was laid in the brick hearth, ready to be lighted against the chill of evening; the leather corner seats of the brass fender, like almost every other flat surface in the room covered in papers, seed packets and catalogues, Several boxes of matches and a couple of my father's pipes lay around, handy to be picked up as the mood took him. It was all comfortingly sane and familiar, a kind of easy order in what might appear to a stranger as a haphazard arrangement of well-worn furniture.

Uneven footsteps sounded in the passageway and Matthew limped into the room, untidy straw-coloured hair flopping across his forehead. My father was not a handsome man, his face too weather beaten and craggy for that, but his eyes were blue as the cornflowers that grew in our meadows and he had a wonderful, one hundred watt beam of a smile. Crossing the room he put his hands on my shoulders and kissed my cheek.

'Hello you, you get more like your beautiful mother every time I see you!' he exclaimed and I laughed.

'Huh, like most fathers you see only what you want to see.'

'Nonsense, there is nothing wrong with my eyesight, but it *is* nice to have my daughter back. Come and have breakfast, but watch out for Brahms and Liszt. They've been in the pond again.'

Being jumped upon by a couple of wet Springer spaniels was no unusual event at Trewlyns; I ignored Grace's automatic grumble about muddy feet all over her kitchen floor and encouraged the dogs boisterous greetings, aware that they too were five years older since I had been a permanent part of this household, and beginning to show their age.

I studied my father as he craned to read the headlines on Grace's morning paper, comforted to see there was no grey showing yet on his well-covered head, nor any other obvious signs of ageing; in fact he was looking suspiciously young and vigorous: always a give-away that something, or more likely someone, was adding a little extra zest to his life.

I had been aware from an early age that over the years since my mother's death various women had come and gone, although none had stayed the course I wondered now if there was again someone else in the offing. An old jealousy I should have grown out of gnawed at my gut. Hell but I hoped bloody Barbara wasn't responsible for that youthful look on his face...but no, I thought, Paul was his closest friend and my father had too much integrity to be rolling around in the hay, or anywhere else, with Penmarrion's very own man-eater, Barbara Tremaine.

He began to slice open the morning post as Grace darted her way through the Daily Mail, grumbling audibly about Attlee, Bevan and 'that shower – what are they going to use for money for all their high falutin' ideas; that's what *I'd* like to know!'

Although it was all comfortingly sane and familiar, I reminded myself that the transition from efficient Squadron Officer back to being Matthew's daughter would not be easy. I had left this place at eighteen and straight from school. A hell of a lot of things had happened to change all of us since then.

Later, doing the rounds of glasshouses and fields with my father and breathing in the heady scent of clean sea air, I was glad I'd turned down an offer of a promising career in an Ordnance Survey office full of bright young things. Three years of map making and a further two reading aerial photographs, first in a bunker deep in the Kentish countryside, later at Oxford preparing for the Normandy invasions, had kept me too busy for many home visits. Now, I thought dreamily, there would be time to pick up the threads, time to know my father all over again, to walk the cliff paths, to take off my shoes and walk barefoot along the shoreline as the tide went out...

'Are you quite sure you are going to stay? You've grown away from this life over the past few years.' I came back to the present as Matthew stooped for a moment to tap his pipe out on his boot. 'Helping out on the odd long leave is one thing, living back here and slogging away on a permanent basis quite another. Next month we'll be on the run-up to Christmas, and barring any freak weather, should be bang on target with next year's daff harvest. If you're thinking of sticking around you won't get much chance to adjust slowly to the rigors of Civvy Street.'

'Sitting on my backside all day never was my favourite occupation,' I avoided the question of whether or not I might stay. 'I've done enough of that in the last few years to last a lifetime. How much other help will you have to see you through until the spring?'

'Well, young Kate is here full-time for the present...certainly until way past the big rush, and Betty Trescoe says if we can stable and spare a bit of hay for that knock-kneed nag of hers, she'll ride over and work most days.' He gave me a sideways look. 'Then, of course, there's Charles de la Tour...'

'Who's he? Not one of your lame ducks, I hope.' In the past Matthew had been famous for taking on for a few days or weeks anyone who spun him a hard-luck story, and they invariably turned out to be useless. 'Who's this one – some nut that came for a summer holiday and fell in love with Cornwall?' I laughed. 'He'll soon buzz off once winter sets in!'

He leaned against a packing bench; unscrewing the bowl from his pipe he blew down the stem. 'You're jumping the gun a bit, aren't you? Charles de la Tour is an extremely intelligent, very able Frenchman who was unlucky enough to get too close to a mortar shell in Normandy...I have a fellow-feeling for him.' He tapped his right leg, the knee shattered in an earlier war.

Caught off guard by a sudden wave of vertigo I sat down on the slatted bench and holding my head between my hands battled against a threatening wave of nausea. Immediately my father was beside me, his arm about my shoulders. As though from a great distance I heard his voice urging me, 'Steady. Take a deep breath...'

I opened my eyes but the shed continued to spin and I put my head down again, screwing my eyes tight shut until the ground ceased to tilt beneath my feet. 'Sorry...' I mumbled, 'I'm OK. Really.'

'We'll go back to the house when you feel like it,' he kept his arm about me. 'You should have had a lie-in after driving such a distance yesterday.'

'It isn't that...just you talking about Charles de la what's-his-name getting blown up in Normandy.'

I hadn't meant to tell him about Stefan. At least, not for a very long time, but it was such a comfort to have that familiar arm about my shoulders, the rough tweed of his old jacket against my cheek, that suddenly and without any real volition on my part, all the grief and anger I had kept festering inside for so long poured out in an unstoppable stream.

When I finished he stayed silent for a minute or so, then said with gentle exasperation, 'My dear idiot child, why on earth have you kept all this bottled up for so long?' He gave my shoulder a brisk shake. 'Don't you know the only way to cope with grief is to share it – and who better to share it with than me?'

It was too much; I burst into great blubbering sobs all down the front of his Guernsey, so that he had to fish for a handkerchief with his free hand and mop me dry as he had when I was a child.

We sat for a long time in the warmth of the packing shed while I told him of our plans to marry as soon as Stefan returned from North Africa and could ask if he minded having a Polish son-in-law; only when he had arrived back in Oxford we were both caught up in the run-up to Overlord and there had been no long leave to spend together in Cornwall, or anywhere else for that matter.

'I would have got married at any time and anywhere,' I said earnestly, 'the day after we first met, or any of the days in between then and when he went overseas, but he was quite old-fashioned about marriage and wanted to do everything by the book. You know, father's consent and the Wedding March and all that, but we never had time; he came back from North Africa only a few weeks before D Day and then it was too late.'

'I presume he was going to whisk you off to Poland as soon as the war ended?'

'No, he wasn't planning to go back; he was half-Jewish and I don't think any of his immediate family survived. He said the Russians would fall on his country like wolves as soon as the war was over, and that they loved Jews no more than the Germans did.'

'Well, he was right about them hanging on to their middle European conquests, and God knows they've had enough Pogroms of their own over the years. I wish with all my heart your dreams might have come true darling, and I would like to have known your Stefan,' he shook his head slightly, smiling, but his eyes were troubled. 'Don't shut him away, Caro. If you let him he will walk alongside you for as long as you need him.'

'That's how it was when mother died; you never shut her away, did you? You made it easier for me, but it must have been hell for you.'

'One survives. Hearts don't really break, you know. Bruise pretty badly, but not break.'

13

'But I loved him so much...' I blurted vehemently, 'I can't even think straight any more, I just feel so dreadfully sad and dreary inside and it never lets up.' My hands felt cold and I rubbed them on my knees. 'Now it's like being in a theatre when the curtain is down and the audience gone and there is nothing but this great, black void...'

'I know. But it will get better. Perhaps not for a long time, but eventually it will. I promise you.'

'I'd like to believe you, although even all this time later I still can't see it that way. But somehow I have to, or grow into a crazy old woman.'

He smiled again then stood and pulled me to my feet, suddenly brisk and businesslike. 'Not yet, you won't – I'm only just getting used to you as a crazy *young* woman. Now let's see if Kate has arrived. Its time to start getting the bedding plants up. We need eighty boxes for tomorrow's flower train.'

'OK,' I followed him as he turned back towards the sheds, 'but while we work you can tell me all about your tame Frenchman and how he ended up here in Cornwall. I like to know about people I'm going to work with,' I forced a smile, 'but I warn you, if he's the bottom-pinching kind, either he goes or I do!'

* * * * *

By the time we reached the packing shed to collect our boxes Kate had arrived. She was a luscious, dark haired Cornish beauty, who, if Grace was to be believed, had half the male population of Poltreven hanging about for the chance to try their luck with her in the back row of the local fleapit. With so many to choose from she flitted, Grace reported with disapproval in every syllable, from one to another like a pollen-gathering honeybee.

As we three began work on adjacent rows of plants, I nudged my father's mind towards the so far unknown and not particularly welcome Frenchman. I'd come home to rediscover familiar faces and places and I resented having a stranger on what I saw as my own private territory.

'Tell me about this Charles what's-its, then,' I invited. 'Who is he and exactly what does he do around here?'.

'He was a Major with the Free French and came down to recuperate earlier this year when he finally left hospital.' Matthew explained patiently. 'He was still in a pretty bad way when they released him from the convalescent home...you remember, the one near Penzance? Paul met him when he and Barbara were hosting some fund-raising bash for the place, took a fancy to him and invited him to stay for a while until he was ready to go back to France.'

'Sure it wasn't Barbara who took the fancy?' put in Kate, with a mischievous grin. 'He's quite a dish.'

'"Here she comes, and looking for anything in trousers!"' I quoted Grace's invariable comment at the sound of Barbara's: 'Coo-ee, is anyone at home?' and we both relapsed into giggles.

Matthew looked at me with raised brows and a pained expression. 'D'you want to hear the rest of the story or not?'

'Yes, sorry; please go on,' I said meekly, reaching for another plant tray. 'I'm sure we all know Barbara wouldn't go for anyone who wasn't fighting fit and she always likes her men well matured...or is he already knocking on a bit?'

'Certainly not, thirty at the most, I should say. Very quiet sort of chap; keeps himself to himself.'

'Unfortunately,' Kate sighed, 'Charles Boyer being unavailable, *I* wouldn't mind jollying him up a bit!'.

'Hard luck,' Matthew returned, 'because he doesn't seem to want to socialise very much with women. He was an Army photographer during the war, now he spends most of his free time wandering around the place taking photographs for a couple of Nature Magazines.'

I sniggered. '*Nature* Magazines? Nudists playing ping-pong and tap-dancing and what have you? Is there a nudist camp around here I don't know about?'

Kate sat back on her heels, braying like an ass as Matthew rolled his eyes heavenward. '*Mother* Nature, you fool,' he said witheringly, 'animals, flowers, birds – the glorious Cornish countryside.'

'Oh, I *see*.' I tore my thoughts away from the mind numbing vision of the buxom Barbara leaping naked through the churchyard pursued by a stage Frenchman with camera and tripod. 'So how's he surviving the vicarage? With Barbara around I shouldn't think he's getting much peace and quiet there.'

'I took pity on him,' Matthew grunted, resting a moment from his labours, 'I've let him have Tyndals Cottage until he goes back to France. He's been very useful all through this summer... keeps my books like a professional and doesn't mind mucking in with the packing and bunching either – and he won't take a penny in wages.'

I scowled and dug my spade deep into the earth. As I heaved a large wedge of wallflowers into my box I thought nastily that the bloody man sounded too good to be true...*and* he was taking it easy on what was rightfully my territory. Although I was happy for the present to be back under my father's roof, it could only be a temporary measure and I should soon need my own space. I thought as I had so many times before how easily Stefan, who had farmed before the war, would have fitted into this life and how comfortable and snug the cottage would have been for the two of *us*…

Grandfather Penrose had built Tyndals for my father when he and my mother were first married; built it of the same grey Cornish stone as the farmhouse, with deep sunk windows and strong oak beams. Now there was some bloody Frenchman occupying what was rightfully mine. Dishy or not, I hoped he'd soon bugger off and leave Tyndals for me.

Once a girl had left home she should stay left.

* * * * *

By the time Grace called us for lunch we had filled two-thirds of the boxes and were glad to sit at the long metal table in the yard and tuck into thick soup and hunks of freshly baked bread.

'I've dreamed of this bread for years; ours was pale khaki, you know – like wartime loo paper and army issue knickers.' I dipped a crust in my soup. 'Wonderful to find Pascoe's are still performing miracles despite the rationing.'

Grace sniffed. 'Aye, although I hear that young Davy of theirs is staying in the Navy – and his sister couldn't wait to get out of uniform and rush up to London…studying to be a doctor she is. You'd think one of them would have come home to help run the business, wouldn't you?'

'Why should they?' returned Matthew reasonably. 'Everyone has a right to live their own life.'

'Elizabeth was never likely to stay around at home anyway.' I grinned at Grace's indignant expression 'Even if there hadn't been a war she would have been off…much too clever and independent to stay behind any shop counter all her life. I wish I'd had a brain like hers when we were at school. Mind you we had to pay to pick it; she used to charge us a shilling a time to do our biology homework for us.'

Grace tut-tutted and Kate laughed. 'At least she's left the rest of us a clearer field with the blokes.' She turned to me. 'Josh Milton's back, did you know? He came to inoculate dad's heifers a couple of weeks back and was asking after you.'

'He'll keep, the big-head,' I scowled again, not caring to remember my calf-love for our local vet. If I hadn't taken off for the WAAF and Josh disappeared into the army as soon as war was

16

declared, I would probably have been daft enough to end up as one more scalp on his belt. When we'd met from time to time on long leaves I had been rather less eager to please, having by then had more experience of the Josh Milton's of this world.

Looking up now I caught Grace watching me with a thoughtful eye. She'd always had a soft spot for Josh, who could when it suited him charm any number of mature birds from the treetops to wash and darn his socks; the younger ones he just shook off the branches and straight into bed.

At this point in my life the very last thing I needed was Grace getting any ideas about Josh and me and I hurriedly changed the subject.

'When we're through with the wallflowers I'll take them in ready for tomorrow morning's train, if that's OK, dad.' I used the last piece of bread to mop my plate. 'I'd like to look in at the rectory and see if Jenny is there. You know, I never could see her sticking at nursing; she's much too classy to be doing with bedpans. I thought when she was finished with the Q.A's she'd be putting her feet up at home for a while.'

'Oh, you'll be lucky to catch Jenny; she's a busy girl – off-duty anyway.' Grace commented tartly. '*I've* not seen her for weeks past...even her parents only qualify for the occasional glimpse. We suppose she's with her latest conquest – whosoever *that* might be.'

Matthew said peaceably: 'She'll be home by the time you go over, Caro. I happen to know she's back for a day or two after a stint of night duty.'

Under her breath Grace gave a significant huff and suddenly the air was electric. I glanced quickly around the table. My father was eating industriously, a closed look on his face; Grace had folded her lips and was now feigning interest in the view, while Kate semaphored wildly with her eyes.

I asked crossly, 'Am I missing something important?'

'I don't think so,' My father reached for another piece of bread, 'unless Grace has anything to say.'

'Me?' She continued to gaze into the middle distance, 'Why expect *me* to know anything that goes on around here.'

There was a long uncomfortable silence. Matthew joined in the distance gazing and by now Kate's eyes were spinning like tops. Abruptly pushing back my chair I stood. 'If you've all been struck dumb,' I snapped, 'I might as well go back to the wallflowers.'

Kate leapt to her feet. 'I'll come with you.'.

'What in hell is the matter with those two stupid buggers?' I exploded when we were out of earshot, 'I could murder Grace when she gets that "I know something you don't" tone in her voice – and as for *dad*...'

'Don't ask me,' Kate picked up a box and flopped down amongst the plants. 'They've been sniping at each other on and off for weeks now and I'm keeping well out of it. Each time Matthew goes over to the rectory to see Paul, Grace starts.'

'She always did, being convinced that Barbara starts polishing her hormones the second he appears, which she does...but why be so bitchy about Jenny?'

'I think she may have sniffed out who her new chap is and doesn't approve. You know Grace; when she's fond of someone, nobody is ever good enough for them.'

'True,' I agreed, 'but all the same it's very odd. Who *is* the boy friend anyway and what the hell is it to do with dad? Don't kid me *you* haven't managed to find out.'

She shrugged. 'I've no idea, honestly Caro; nobody has. She's keeping this one under wraps. But you know your dad's always ready to lend a shoulder or give a helping hand, so he probably knows but won't tell. Mum reckons the boyfriend's married or something.' She pinched my arm. 'Bags you tell me first if you find anything out.'.

* * * * *

I couldn't wait to get over to the rectory for a good, all-girls-together with Jenny and dig all the juicy details of her latest, so once I'd unloaded the plants at Penzance station I drove back to Penmarrion, parked the van in the empty drive and hammered the knocker on the front door. The bangs echoed, resounding mightily throughout the building. It was a good old-fashioned stone-built rectory, with a door and knocker like the one on the Tower of London; none of your new brick and glass nonsense in this corner of Cornwall.

Jenny answered my summons; flinging open the door and enfolding me in an enormous hug.

'Oh, Caro...back again at last...come in, come in. I'm all alone and feeling blue. Have a beer...a gin and Ajax...a cup of mother's dire coffee!'

She towed me into the cavernous kitchen and began rattling glasses and bottles onto the big square table. 'Honestly,' she removed the cap from a beer bottle with her teeth, 'am I glad to see you...such a lot of time to make up.'

'Still the same disgusting habits, I see. One day all your bloody

18

teeth are going to fall out with a sickening crash – what *would* Miss Martingdale say if she could see you now?'

We sniggered like school kids, tilting back on our chairs and putting our feet on the table, chorusing: 'Girls, Pull your skirts down at *once*! Nobody wishes to see your knickers!' in passable imitation of Poltreven High School's headmistress. 'But the boys certainly did,' I reminded Jenny. 'One absolute swine of a little tyke from St-James had me off my bike one morning, yelling that he could see my pink frilly ones!'.

We had grown up together Jenny and I, firm friends since junior school, she the leggy longhaired blonde with stunning Cambridge blue eyes, me the rather less leggy curly-crop brunette, with eyes not quite blue and not quite green, but a sort of indeterminate shade rather like the sea. At least that's how some of the nicer men in my life described them, although Grace had once likened them to the muddy puddles that appeared in the yard after rain. But that was after she'd caught me practising my come-hither smile in the mirror when I was about fourteen and thought I needed taking down a peg or two.

'How do you manage all that hair when you're on the wards?' I eyed Jenny's flowing silky locks with the same old feeling of envy they always aroused. 'I bet Matron doesn't allow you to go around tickling all the chap's fancies with that lot every time you give a bed-bath!'

'You're damn' right she doesn't – it stays under my cap with the help of about fifty hairpins…God' she gulped on her beer, 'I'll end up looking like Grace, so I will.'

'That reminds me: Kate reckons Grace would like to put the mockers on your latest boyfriend.' I looked at her expectantly. 'Come on, tell: who is it; surely not that dishy old recluse M'sieur de la Tour I've heard so much about?'

She choked over her drink, spluttering, 'Nosy old bitch – not you – Grace!' Avoiding my eyes she reached for a handkerchief and began mopping at her face and dress. Odder and odder, I thought; whatever was going on around here?

'Look.' She spread the damp handkerchief to dry on the Rayburn, 'It's all a bit difficult. I don't want to talk about, um…*things* right now. I promise I'll give you all the grisly details sometime. It's just too difficult at the moment. I've got a lot to think about – Oh Caro – ' She seized my hands across the table, 'I'm in love, really in love, and it's all so *impossible*!'

'You mean he's married?'

'No, of course he isn't,' she laughed and let go my hands.

19

Recovering her poise she smoothed back her hair.

'Well don't keep me in suspense for too long,' I grumbled. Jenny being coy about any man was something new. 'I don't want to find myself fancying the same bloke then discover he's your mystery man.'

'Oh,' she was airily dismissive. 'I don't think he's at all your type.'

'Bitch, how would you know what my type is, you haven't seen me in action for the past five years. Come on, Jenny…give!'

But despite my best efforts I couldn't get another word out of her and I left an hour later, promising myself a return to the attack as soon as possible. After all, even the hardest nut will crack under repeated assaults, and I was nothing if not persistent.

2

I sat cross-legged on the cliff edge above the cove while beneath me a man who just had to be Charles de la Tour moved slowly along the rock strewn beach, peering into the rock pools, pausing occasionally to raise a professional looking camera to his eye. He was about six feet tall, I guessed, slim, but solidly built, crisp brown hair, a dark, strong face and one of those long mouths that tuck in at the corners…just for a moment I felt a definite twinge of something more than passing interest.

After a while he stopped taking pictures and for several minutes stood gazing out to sea, thumbs hooked in his belt and face raised to the early morning sun. I thought that in those dark green slacks and pale yellow shirt he looked nothing like any army photographer I'd ever met, and I'd met a few – and I'd certainly never come across one with the rank of major. Somehow I couldn't visualise this particular Frenchman following the battle with a camera in his hand. He looked more the type to be right out in front and carrying something rather more lethal.

Just my kind of man, I mused appreciatively; or rather, he might once have been, but it was still impossible to imagine having any kind of relationship with someone else; to think of arms other than Stefan's.

In the couple of days since my return it had been possible to forget for a while, to chat and laugh as we dug and picked and bunched our way through the hours of daylight. Even after work I had managed the evenings fairly well, but at night I slept fitfully, the dreams were still unkind and the sight of Grace bearing the ritual early morning tea always more than welcome.

Now I watched the long wispy clouds begin to come in from the sea and wondered if I should ever be able to remember just the good times I'd spent with Stefan. Rejoice in the laughter and the loving we had shared, escape the ever-recurring nightmare of that plane exploding in the sky and taking with it all our future hopes and dreams. Surely after all this time I should be over that loss and beginning to forget, or at least remember less vividly?

Drawing up my knees I rested my forehead on them, staying motionless for a long time until a slight sound warned me that I was no longer alone. I looked up sharply to find Charles de la Tour was no longer on the beach but standing a few feet away from where I sat, leaning on a walking stick and regarding me with a kind of mild curiosity.

Close up he was taller and looked older than I'd expected from Matthew's description and my foreshortened view of him on the beach. Two vertical frown lines were etched between curved dark brows and that long mouth looked just a little too sensually fashioned to belong to the kind of misogynistic recluse as hinted at by my father. The months I had spent in Oxford amid crowds of randy servicemen of many nationalities had taught me those sort of dark brooding good looks generally went hand in hand with an unfailingly devastating seduction technique.

Suddenly he smiled and his features lightened, taking years off his face. 'Excuse me, please. I did not know anyone was here.'.

I said, 'It's all right. I was just having a rest. You must be Charles,' I stood and held out my hand, 'I'm Caroline...Matthew's daughter.'

He took my hand, the dark brown eyes lively. 'Ah, yes! ...*Enchanté*, Caroline. Tomorrow I come to the farm and I think then I shall meet with you...but now, we are already acquainted, are we not?'

'Looks like it.'

I didn't mean to be brusque, but the deep, accented voice had shaken me for a moment, reminding me of Stefan. I gestured at the camera slung around his neck. 'Get some good photographs did you...down in the cove?' I asked, then flushed when I realised I'd let slip I'd been watching him.

His close-mouthed smile told me he'd noticed, but he only answered mildly, 'I hope so. I am supposed to be providing them for a magazine, but was getting a little bored. This morning there was a gentleman on the telephone much worried about the deadline and so, work I must, but I think that soon I shall stop taking the pictures for that so anxious man and have time to do other more enjoyable things.'

I had recovered enough to laugh and he gave an easy, relaxed grin. We began to walk along the cliff path towards Trewlyns, chatting about the farm and the rush of orders that Christmas would bring. He said that he hoped to be in France sometime after the holiday and I caught myself feeling rather sorry then that he would soon be moving on, until I remembered that his going would mean I could at last claim my right to Tyndals cottage. Still, I had to smile to myself when I remembered my remark apropos bottom-pinching Frenchmen. There was nothing like that about Charles de la Tour, I

22

thought, and it was refreshing to be with a man who didn't feel duty bound to strip off at least one layer of a girl's clothing with his eyes within minutes of meeting. However, I knew when I was face to face with a natural born charmer and found it hard to believe in the uninterested-in-women label Matthew had pinned on him.

When we came to the narrow cliff path he gestured for me to go ahead and I walked on at my usual steady pace. I was longing to ask him exactly when he thought he would return home, but couldn't think how to put the question without seeming rude, but until he left Tyndals I was well and truly stuck..... .

'Can we perhaps, go more slowly?'

Caught up in mulling over my own problems I had been unaware that he was lagging behind; now I turned at his words to find he was leaning heavily on his stick, his mouth twisted with pain. 'The path, it is rough and I cannot go too fast.'

'I'm terribly sorry, you should have said earlier...' I gestured to a low outcrop of flat rocks, 'why don't you sit down there until you feel like going on.'

He lowered himself gingerly, his face strained. 'It is difficult not still to be doing all the things one once took for granted.'

We sat for some minutes in silence as he slowly recovered and the colour began seeping back into his face. 'Better,' he said presently, 'much better. I think now that I should leave you.' Still with some difficulty, he stood up, holding out his hand, '*Au revoir*, Caroline.'

I smiled, taking the outstretched hand. 'My friends call me Caro.'

'Then *au revoir*, Caro. '

Leaning heavily on his stick he walked away from me towards the sunken lane that led to the cottage. I watched him out of sight then turned for home, quite pleased with myself in having made a step towards friendship with someone I had been prepared if not to dislike, at least to resent.

* * * * *

He arrived at Trewlyns the next morning, spending an hour or two in the office before joining us in the packing shed, where Mathew was bunching the tightly budded daffodils, and Kate and I fashioning Cornish posies from the glass-grown flowers. Engrossed in our work and gossiping happily we scarcely noticed the clouding skies until rain began to rattle on the corrugated iron roof.

'Damn and blast!' Matthew looked up with a frown. 'I wanted to walk over to the rectory later to save on petrol, now I shall have to drive.'

'Take my car,' I offered, 'it's less thirsty than the van, and if Jenny's around will you ask when she has her next free afternoon? All my civvies look positively ancient now and I want to drag her into Penzance for some shopping.'.

'Didn't you ask her yourself when you went over yesterday?'

'No, I forgot. We were too busy digging the dirt.'

He selected some flowers with care then picked up a length of raffia before giving me a sideways glance. 'Was there anything particularly interesting *to* dig, might one ask?'

'One might...but I can keep a secret.' I teased, and was astonished to see him fumble, scattering the blooms he had just taken up. Charles cleared his throat quietly and as I turned from Matthew to him, gave an almost imperceptible shake of the head before gazing pensively out of the window.

Annoyed and with my curiosity now thoroughly aroused, I glared first at him and then at my father, who with only the briefest glance at Charles had calmly picked up the scattered blossoms with an, 'Oops – butter-fingers!' then carried on as though nothing unusual had happened.

Now just what the hell I thought, is going on here.

* * * * *

'The plot thickens,' I hissed at Kate as we ran through the rain towards the house, where Grace stood in the open doorway swinging the old school bell with which she summoned us to meals. 'Did you *see* that little exchange of looks?.What *is* that daft tart Jenny getting up to that everyone knows about but you and me?'

She shrugged. 'Search me...I told you, I haven't a clue.'

'Don't worry.' I muttered, as we stood in the porch, shaking the rain from our hair. 'The next time I get Matthew alone I'm going to ask him outright; I'm fed to the back teeth with all this old cobblers about her phantom lover...and what the hell is it to do with our French friend? He knows something, so if I can't wring it out of dad, I'll just have to start on him...and yes,' I said as she went to open her mouth, 'you *will* be the first to know!'

* * * * *

Matthew returned late that evening after Grace had gone to bed and I seized my chance to tackle him about the mystery at the vicarage.

'What *is* it with Jenny?' I demanded. 'and why all the cloak and dagger stuff: you doing the understanding uncle bit, Grace sniffing like a bloodhound with sinus problems, Charles looking shifty, Jenny twittering on about it all being so difficult – and nobody prepared to say what the hell she's playing at. If I'm really as daft as you seem to think I am, try explaining the mystery to me in words of two syllables or less and I'll probably get the drift.'

He sat down and reached for a book. 'Even supposing there was a mystery I can't see it's anyone else's business but Jenny's.'

'But I'm not *anyone*, I'm her best friend.'

He began to leaf through his book. 'Then she will undoubtedly tell you herself when she is ready.'

'In that case, how come if it's so secret that you and Grace, Charles de la Tour and possibly Old Uncle Tom Cobley and all know?'

'Caro,' he said tiredly, 'just leave it, will you?'

'No, sod it!' Now I really was mad. 'If you won't cough, I'll be around first thing to Tyndals and choke it out of Charlie boy, just you see if I don't...or failing that I'll ask Paul. I'll bet he knows, and he won't be as bloody uncooperative as the rest of you.'

Rarely did my father lose his temper with anyone but now his eyes were positively flashing sparks of fury. 'Just keep your nose out of that girl's business,' he snarled. 'I will not have anyone in this house play silly-bugger's with someone else's life. Understand?' and he flung his book across the room.

There was one of those silences that one could cut with the proverbial knife. I sat staring at him, completely thrown by this outburst. Whatever Jenny was hiding I'd never hear about it from him, or from Charles de la Tour either, unless I was prepared to light the blue touch paper and retire immediately. Sneakily I contemplated the possibility of worming something out of Grace then met Matthew's smouldering gaze again and knocked that idea straight over the head. What a frigging awful end to my first week's homecoming...

'Well?' he challenged, 'It's unlike you to be lost for words.'

'I'm sorry.' I hesitated a moment, then picked up the book and crossed to sit on the arm of his chair. 'For one ghastly moment I thought time had back-peddled and you were about to take a hairbrush to me – like the time I was ten and called you a rotten bastard!'

He reached for his pipe and filled it, eyeing me sardonically over the flame of his match. 'You always did sound off before you thought about the consequences – and you're still the most pig-headed female I know.'

25

'I am not being pig headed. I'd just like to know why Jenny's love life is suddenly surrounded in mystery. After all, I've known about every other bloke she's been out with – even shared some of them. I'm damned if I can see what's so special about this one that makes you and Grace and Charles behave as though you're all guarding a state secret.'

He gave a wry grin. 'I know how much you must hate being on the outside, but Grace knows nothing, only guesses. Charles *is* involved, but only indirectly and I don't advise that you try to get any information from him, because when it comes to being secretive, he's a past master of the art.'

'Well, bully for him.' I stood and kicked a log on the fire. 'Frankly, I'm so pissed off with the lot of you that I'm tempted to clear off and leave you all to it.'

He gave an exasperated sigh. 'Oh, just leave it alone, Caro. Jenny really does have a problem that she needs time to work on. I'm sure she'll tell you when she's sorted things out in her own mind. That'll have to satisfy you for the present. OK?' And he cocked his head enquiringly.

'Not really.' I was still smarting from what I could only see as a snub and turned away, 'I'm going to bed. Goodnight.'

He caught at my hand. 'I'm sorry. You were a pain in the neck but I shouldn't have bawled you out like that.'

I shrugged. 'Don't bother yourself. My shoulders are broader than they used to be.'

Ignoring my irritable response to his attempt to make peace he gave my hand a squeeze. 'Are you all right, Caro...really all right? D'you need to talk...' he hesitated, 'about...anything. Is Jenny not the only one with secrets?'

I snapped, 'I don't have secrets, only regrets.'

He picked up his book again, stuck his pipe in his mouth and stretched out his long legs. 'OK. At least, I can take a hint and mind my own business, if no one else around here can.'

I sighed. 'Oh, sod it; I'm sorry. I suppose it's not your fault that you're such an aggravating, bad-tempered old man.'

'Bear with me,' he grinned down into his book, 'nobody's perfect!'

* * * * *

Matthew took himself off alone to church that Sunday. I'd never been quite sure what made him go each week as he never displayed any particular signs of piety at any other time. Jenny and I decided years ago that he most likely did so out of friendship and support for her father.

Certainly when Paul Tremaine had first appeared in Penmarrion some twenty years back, he'd needed all the support that he could get. Already in his forties, recently ordained and down from Oxford, enthusiastically trailing clouds of Keeble, Pusey, Newman and possibly Beverly Nichols as well, he'd turned the parish upside down. It was difficult to know which caused the most scandal, his High Church Anglicanism or his wife's habit of flirting outrageously with every likely looking man who crossed her path. With the passing of time his parishioners became more or less reconciled to the candles, incense, boat boys and genuflections, but never did quite come to terms with Barbara.

Jenny and I had bellowed in the choir in our younger days. Not so much out of love of or a talent for music, but rather in order to check out the least pimply choirboys in the opposite stalls, scribbling notes to each other during the sermon about which ones we fancied that particular week. I even continued going with Matthew long after I'd given up wearing a red robe and a pie frill around my neck, but that was done mostly for the pleasure I got from watching Grace squash her Sunday hat on her head while muttering darkly, and with a wonderful mix of metaphors, about our Popish practices and Heathenish goings-on, before departing to the Methodist chapel in Poltreven.

Now, after seeing both off to their different devotions I decided that a long walk would do me a world of good.

It was a splendid morning, the high blue sky broken only by occasional puffs of white cloud, thin and insubstantial as candyfloss. Calling Brahms and Liszt I set off along the coastal path towards Porthcurnow. Far below on the left of the narrow track, the sea creamed along the shore on the vast stretch of sand between Penmarrion and Tregenick; on the right cattle and sheep grazed in the fields and the occasional curious donkey peered over the hedges as we passed. After a pause to take a brief rest at the stile before the Coastguard station, we crossed the fields and walked down the narrow lane leading to Logan Cottage.

'If lover-boy Josh is home he just might need someone to help exercise those nags of his,' I told my companions and at the sound of Josh's name they began to yelp and run around in circles like a couple of headless chickens, or, I thought bitchily, any one of Josh's bird-brained tarts: there usually wasn't a lot to chose between them and the chickens.

He was in the yard when I arrived, leaning on the gate with folded arms, his back turned on the house and wilderness of a garden. The dogs raced ahead of me, flinging themselves through the bars of the gate to cavort madly around his feet, their frantic barks bringing his stolid old black Labrador out to see what all the fuss was about.

'Hi, Penrose, I wondered when you'd get around to gracing my humble acres,' he swung the gate wide, making a practised move to put an arm about my waist but I was ready and side stepped him smartly.

'Humble acres, my foot; more like Cold Comfort Farm…I shouldn't be at all surprised if you haven't something nasty in the wood shed.' I glanced disparagingly at the dock-strewn grass and overgrown bushes. 'You should try getting a few pigs in; they'd soon feel at home in this lot.'

'Flattery will get you nowhere, my girl. I know you've only come to do the weeding, but I won't hear of it. Now if you were to offer help with a spot of bedding-out…'

He stood grinning down at me from his six-foot-three-in-his-socks, curly brown head at the familiar, confident angle. He was not handsome in the way that Charles de la Tour was, but had the kind of rugged, zestful outdoor looks that most women found attractive; all combined with a massively unsubtle seduction technique that would leave a prize bull swooning with envy.

The odd thing was that so many women fell for it.

I sighed. 'Do stop being such a fatuous idiot, the only thing that lures me to even set foot in this midden is the possibility that you might still want someone to exercise Blondie alongside that other atrocious old nag of yours.'

'My…' he raised his brows with a look of comical dismay, 'we are waspish this morning, aren't we? Nero won't like you referring to him in that derogatory manner.'

In spite of myself I laughed. Somehow I just couldn't help liking Josh and providing one kept those roving hands at bay he could be good company. 'Come on,' I took his arm. 'How about a good long ride over the hills,' I urged. 'That should keep your pants aired!'

We left the dogs rooting happily in the overgrown garden and rode hard towards Porthcurnow, reigning in the horses to a walk for the last half-mile or so, before allowing them a drink at a stream. Turning again for home we rode side by side at an alternate walk and canter, chatting comfortably together; catching up on our news, talking Service slang, just skimming the surface with neither of us going too deeply into memories of war.

'Are you going to stay around Trewlyns, then?' Josh asked the inevitable question as we neared his cottage. 'I dare say Matthew will be relieved if you do...he's had a bit of a struggle from time to time this last year.'

'Well, he's not too badly off at the moment. Kate is brilliant, Betty will be on the strength soon and Charles is a great help in taking most of the paperwork off his shoulders. As for me,' I shrugged, 'I don't make plans anymore. I'm just glad to be back and happy doing what I'm doing for now...I dare say I shall stick around for a while.'

'I wish you would. We had a lot of fun on the odd leave together, didn't we? At least we did up until the last year or so when you seemed to vanish off the face of the earth, a bloody nuisance that was. When I was on sick leave after a sniper put a bullet in my bum I could have done with you there to kiss it better.'

I said obliquely. 'I had better things to do then than worry about your bum.'

'I've missed you since I came back,' he leaned to snick open the gate, 'nobody insults me quite as sexily as you...so how about I get you legless on the old vino then lure you up to view the etchings on my bedroom ceiling?'

'You never give up, do you?' I swung myself down from Blondie before he could get round and give a helping hand or two, 'I can't tell you how many line-shooters like you I've come across during the last five years, so give it a rest Josh, and just be a pal.'

He grinned unrepentantly, busying himself unbuckling his horse's girth, his bright, predatory eyes already down to my bra and pants. 'You need one of those, do you Caro?'

'Yes,' I said simply, 'I need one of those.'

'OK.' he pulled off Nero's saddle and bridle and turned the horse into his loose box. 'But I think it only fair to warn you I shall probably try it on once in a while...just to keep my hand in, as it were!'

He leered. I ignored the *double entendre.* 'That'll do...so long as you realise it still won't cut any ice with me.'

He took Blondie's saddle and bridle from me, hanging them alongside Nero's, smirking at me over his shoulder. 'Want to bet on that?'

'I'm not a betting woman.' I whistled to Brahms and Liszt and got myself safely to the other side of the gate. ''Bye, Josh, dream on by all means, for all the good it's likely to do you!'

'You know the Milton motto, Caro,' he said, and winked. '..."If

29

at first you don't succeed try, try again"…and I always do!'

* * * * *

When I returned to Trewlyns I spent the hour or so to Sunday lunch helping my father prune the raspberry canes back for the winter. We worked for a while in silence until fetching up at the end of a row together, he put down his knife to stretch lazily and ask, 'What d'you think about taking on a young apprentice?'

'Sounds all right – can you afford one?'

'Oh, I think so…I'm not sure how much longer Charles will be staying. I think he'll probably see us through until well after Christmas but I don't want you to be tied here day in and day out, until you're quite sure about how you see your long-term future. To be honest I'd quite like to take on this particular young chap.'

'Anyone I know?'

He shook his head. 'Shouldn't think so; his name's Willi Fischer: he's living in Poltreven at present. Old Father Con over at Tregenick asked Paul to put in a word for him. Apparently, he's very keen so I said to send him over.' He resumed his cutting and tying. 'Bye the way, Jenny say's she's free to go shopping Wednesday morning, if that's OK.'

'Fine…if you can spare me.' I laughed, 'Don't tell me she actually got roped into going to church?'

'No. I met her as I was walking back along the cliff path.'

'I wish I'd known she was around; she could have come out to Josh's place with me and deflected some of his dastardly attentions onto herself. He's been after her for simply years.'

'Correction: he's been after every woman for simply years. The man's a menace.'

Before I could ask him where Jenny had been walking to all alone on a Sunday morning instead of catching up on her beauty sleep after a hard week's nursing, Grace called us in to lunch, but I thought about it again that night as I was drifting off to sleep, chalking it up as just another instance of how someone I thought I knew so well had changed. In all the years I'd known her Jenny had been pathologically opposed to walking anywhere and would never willingly ramble around the countryside on a Sunday, or any other day.

It was odds on, I thought sleepily that she'd been mooching with her new man, but given that the only one within shagging distance was the supposedly uninterested-in-women Charles de la Tour….

Suddenly I was wide-awake and tingling with the excitement of

30

discovery. Of course; it *had* to be him, didn't it, because there just wasn't anyone else even remotely likely to take Jenny's fancy nearer at hand? Misogynist my foot – that was all a smokescreen; but why on earth all the mystery? Perhaps Betty's mother was right and the mystery man – aka Charles de la Tour, *was* married after all.

I thought about her mother's probable reaction when Jenny gathered the courage to tell Barbara her glad news, and.couldn't repress a snigger; French, married, and jumping her daughter. That, I thought, would create a stir at the vicarage all right.

* * * * *

Forced to put all discussion of Jenny's love life on the backburner I nobly refrained from bringing up the subject when we made our shopping expedition together in Penzance, returning instead to the safer subject of the lecherous Josh's less than subtle advances.

'That man's a menace,' she commented, echoing Matthew. 'Just make sure it's only the horse he wraps his legs around when you're out on those evening rides. I've more than once had to fight for my honour after parties.'

'I've sorted out bigger fish than him...the RAF had its fair share of Josh Milton's and as for some of them at Combined Ops in Oxford, well...' I rolled my eyes, 'I could tell a tale or two about a certain well-known Rear Admiral that would make your toes curl.'

She said reprovingly, 'What you need after the trials of service life is a nice, quiet old-fashioned gentleman...'

We were in a very posh department store, trying on hats, none of which we intended buying. Now she tilted her head this way and that, peering at me from beneath a sickening confection of pink tulle. 'I thought you might fancy Charles, although he's just the *tiniest* bit of a stuffed shirt, in which case I was going to warn you – '

'Warn me about what?' I pounced, and she raised her brows in a particularly irritating fashion.

'Hmm, well, on second thoughts, perhaps not...'

I said rudely, 'Don't fuss yourself. I'm not in the market anyway.'

'Why? What's up? Training to enter a nunnery are you?'

'Mind your own business,' I snapped, 'and you look absolutely God-awful in that hat.'.

She cast down the offending headgear and stood up. 'All right, all right, keep your hair on – you remind me of my mother; God, but she's bloody fit to be tied these last few weeks.'

'Her love life not going smoothly?' I steered her away from

31

another Ascot-type disaster. 'I've been expecting her round to have another go at getting into Matthew's pants, but not a sight of her.'

She stopped and gave me a considering look, 'D'you think she actually does? Get into bloke's pants, I mean; I've often wondered.'

'How would I know? She probably just enjoys stirring things up...or could I perhaps have phrased that better?'

We giggled and headed for the perfume department, where after trying every tester on the counter we were in danger of being coerced into actually buying something by a blue rinsed assistant with scarlet talons, who bore down upon us with a determined, 'May I help Modom to choose?' Which invitation sent both Modoms in hasty retreat to the Coffee Shop, smelling like a couple of refugees from a Mexican Bordello.

Eventually we managed to get on with the clothes hunting, returning home in the late afternoon with a modest assortment of sweaters, slacks, skirts and sufficient frillies to tide me over the winter months.

'Charles is here for dinner. Why not stay and join us?' Matthew invited Jenny as we hauled our loot from the old Standard. 'Grace has cooked enough for a regiment as usual.'

'Lovely. Thank you kindly...I'm famished.'

She put up her hands to sweep the hair back from her face, shaking it over her shoulders in a sexy gesture that I deemed to be for the benefit of Charles, if so it missed its mark as he was already following me towards the stairs.

'You have bought up the whole of Penzance, yes?'

I laughed. 'Just about...Used up all my de-mob coupons and some of Matthew's before I realised I hadn't anything left for a winter coat; still I can make do with my WAAF greatcoat and this old duffle. I'll just put these away before Jenny starts strewing them all over the place.'

'But please,' he began to take some of the bags and boxes from my arms. 'Let me assist...'

'Fast mover...' commented Jenny, *sotto voce*. I ignored her and led the way to my room, Charles following, peering rather anxiously over the mound of bags and packages as he climbed the narrow stairs. Placing his burdens on the bed he crossed to the window. 'But here you have a wonderful view,' he exclaimed, 'from Tyndal's I can see only the trees until the leaves fall; then I think the sea may be made more clear.'

I joined him where he leaned on the sill and for a few minutes we stayed there in companionable silence. His arm next to mine was comfortable but impersonal. I liked the feel of the warmth coming through his jacket sleeve and he smelled of sea air with a faint overlay of French tobacco, making a change from Josh's all pervading aroma of horseshit overlaid with disinfectant. A complete contrast to the ebullient, energetic Josh, he was altogether a most restful sort of person.

After a while he stirred, turning to smile at me. 'I think we should perhaps leave before your friend begins – how is it – the leg pulling!'

I was irritated again. For God's sake, why should they make such a big thing out of hiding their affair, if that's what it was…and why had Jenny said it was 'impossible'? I shrugged. 'She'll do that anyway.'

And of course she did, the artful cow.

But it was a good evening and when the meal finished Jenny and Matthew volunteered to help Grace to clear and wash-up while Charles and I took the dogs for their evening run through the meadows.

We strolled down as far as the cove and while the dogs hunted rabbits in the hedgerows we stood for a while in silence beneath a bright three-quarter moon, the sea spread at our feet like a blue-black carpet crested with silver,.

'I think I should like to live here in this country, at least for another year or so,' Charles observed eventually. 'I have to go to France early next year…there are some people I must see, some cousins to visit. But I think I should like to return and find somewhere here to stay for at least a while longer.'

'What about your parents? Won't they expect you to stay at home now?'

He shook his head. 'My father died when I was quite young, from the tuberculosis he contracted in the trenches during the first war, and my mother became ill soon after the outbreak of this last. Her heart you see was not strong and she feared how it would be if the Germans came.' He shrugged. 'I think I have been finding excuses not to go back, but one has a duty…there are things with which I must deal before I can really settle and think about the future.'

I was curious about someone who seemed so reluctant to return to his own country and earn a proper living. I said, 'Matthew told me you were an Army war photographer. I probably saw some of your shots on Pathé News. Was photography your peacetime job?'

He pointedly ignored this not very subtle probe into his past. 'Before the army I worked in Paris as an Architect and hope to continue designing buildings. Now I think there will be work everywhere, will there not? Here in England there is much to be planned for and re-built.'

Hmm, I thought, that put nosy old you in your place, my girl, but as he was obviously the secretive type I decided to let it rest. If shallow chit-chat was what he wanted then shallow chit-chat was what he would get…

When we returned to the house he stood back, allowing me to go first. Pushing open the door into the sitting room I stood blinking in the light from the lamps, taking a few seconds to register the sight of Matthew standing by the fire and speaking urgently to a tearful Jenny:.'But your parents will have to know soon, my dear, you simply can't – '

He broke off at our entrance and for a brief moment both of them froze. I stared in astonishment at the tears running down Jenny's cheeks then looked at my father. Recovering quickly he returned my gaze as though there was nothing out of the ordinary happening and said easily, 'Hello, you two. Had a good walk?'

All right, I thought, so it's nothing to do with me what advice you're dishing out now, but Charles had again made an involuntary move to put a cautionary hand on my arm and I was suddenly furious. How dared they all exclude me, and what was wrong with bloody Charles de la Tour that it all had to be kept under wraps? Jenny was hardly a vestal virgin and married or unmarried, I'd take a bet Charlie boy was no slouch when it came to jumping between the sheets.

Seething with anger I brushed Charles' hand from my sleeve, said an abrupt and barely civil goodnight and went straight upstairs, where I proceeded to run a very deep bath, taking a reprehensible childish pleasure in visualising Matthew's annoyance when he discovered later that I'd used all the hot water.

3

I came to breakfast the next morning determined to ignore all the intrigue simmering away beneath the surface at Trewlyns, but Matthew was cool with me and retreated behind Grace's Daily Mail. Whether this was because of my graceless departure the previous evening, or the fact that he'd had to put up with cold bath water, I neither knew nor cared. I was polite but distant, daring a curious Grace with a look to ask what was wrong.

It was an uncomfortable meal.

Leaving the house first, I went straight to the big field to start lifting plants, leaving my father to open up the sheds and start the bunching alone. While I had been well aware that returning to Trewlyns would present some difficulties and a period of adjustment, I had more than enough of my own troubles without all this tiptoeing around everyone else's problems. Resentment against Matthew, Jenny, Grace, Charles and anyone else who was a part of the circle that excluded me began to fester and I dug plants with a vicious intensity that did them and me no good at all.

'Busy so early?'

I glanced back over my shoulder to see Charles had made another of his silent approaches and now stood a few feet away, leaning on his stick and regarding me with his grave, charitable gaze.

I slammed a muddy wedge of Sweet Williams into the box. 'Someone needs to be.'

'Perhaps, like me, you have the difficulty to sleep,' he suggested.

'Perhaps.'

His mouth twitched. 'You should put up the red flag which says 'Danger', when like Miss Garbo you wish to be left alone!'

I wiped a muddy wrist across my forehead. 'Do you always go around telling people what they should say and do?'

'Quite often…but why do you frown so? When one is as lovely as you one always should smile.'

I gave him my best haughty glare. 'When one is so little acquainted with one as one's self, one should actually mind one's own bloody business.'

'Ah, *Mon Dieu,* would you like me to abase myself here in this muddy field?'

He was laughing at me. I felt my face flame and my temper with it. He stepped back a pace, raising peaceable hands. 'Please. I am sorry. You do not wish to be friends this morning...I should leave and not tease you so when you are *triste*...' The dark eyes were suddenly warm and understanding and I felt an absolute pig.

'It's all right. It isn't you. I've just had enough of everyone today.' To my horror I felt tears come into my eyes and I turned away with a brusque, 'If I were you I'd go and talk to Matthew; he'll be much better company than I am this morning...nothing much ever bothers *him* for long.'

He answered with light sarcasm, 'Such a fortunate man,' but as he still made no attempt to move I was faced with either grubbing again amid the plants to hide my emotions, or finding some quiet corner where I could snivel in peace. Deciding on the latter, I stepped past him and stalked toward the glasshouses, knowing without needing to turn my head that he was still watching me.

Cursing beneath my breath I reached the first glasshouse, wrenched open the door and bolted inside. Leaning back against the door I allowed myself to wallow in a relieving solitary grizzle.

It had been so good to return home, to be again with my father and Grace, to find at first that everything was pretty much the same as before: safe, and warm and loving – a place to heal my wounds and mend my heart. Now I felt terribly alone; so alone that I had very nearly burst into tears in front of a barely known French gentleman, simply because he had looked at me with warmth and understanding in his eyes.

* * * * *

When I was quite sure my own eyes were back to normal I went in search of Matthew to make my peace. If he wouldn't give, and I knew he wouldn't, I should have to, much as it went against the grain. I found him in the packing shed alone and as I shut the door behind me he looked up, pipe clenched between his teeth, his hands busy with the flowers, and grunted a non-committal, 'Hello.'

'Hello.' I looked at him forlornly. 'Are you still being a toffee-nosed sod or can anyone talk to you?'

'*You* can.' He patted the stool beside him. 'Sit down you idiot and do some work. I'm paying you at the end of the month so you might as well earn it.'

'How nice...I thought I was doing it for love.'

'There is that as well.'

He put an arm about my shoulders as I seated myself beside him and for a moment I laid my head against his before reaching for the raffia to begin bunching a posy. 'Sorry about the bath water.'

'It doesn't matter; in the circumstances I might have done the same.' He looked at me sideways. 'I promise there won't be any more such irritating scenes.'

'I don't give a damn about any of it. You may do and say as you please, just don't try to pretend nothing is happening.' I wasn't going to let him get away with it *that* easily. 'You might try to remember that for the past few years I've been responsible for telling hoards of young women what to do, whilst managing to do a far from unimportant job myself. Therefore I do not take kindly to being treated like a nosy child.'

'Hmm.' His mouth twitched. 'Someone else has already reminded me this morning that I seem to have overlooked that fact!'

'*Have* they?'

'Uh huh.'

'He does get around, doesn't he?' I asked dryly, 'it's no wonder you get on so well. You're just about the most irritating bloody pair of know-all's I've come across for some time.'

* * * * *

Willi Fischer arrived the following day; a lanky, darkly pleasant, rather shy young man. A Jewish refugee smuggled out of Germany during the war, his native accent was already beginning to fade beneath an acquired Cornish burr. Kate predictably made sheep's eyes at him, but getting no response other than a shy smile, soon gave up. For myself, I enjoyed his company and appreciated his hard work as he insisted on doing a great deal of the lifting and carrying that had formerly fallen to me.

Things began to settle down. Apart from the fact that Matthew now borrowed my car four evenings out of seven to play cards with Paul at the rectory, little had changed on the surface. Jenny's problems, whatever they were had been either solved or swept conveniently under the carpet; either way my father appeared no longer to be involved.

Jenny and I met occasionally in Penzance, when I was careful still to steer clear of any reference to her love life. Although she wasn't any more forthcoming, she looked happy and blooming and I assumed she now had everything under control. If it was Charles de la Tour with whom she was spending her time while she was in Penmarrion their assignations were relatively safe from prying eyes; Tyndals

Cottage was situated down a sunken lane and well away from the main road. Although the village gossips would eventually put two and two together, if the lovebirds were very discreet and confined their meetings to the hours of darkness their secret might remain just that for quite some time.

Josh kept his word and we had several rides through the early part of October without my having to parry too many passes. He was good company and I was grateful for the chance to spend time with someone whose thoughts and intentions, although mostly deplorable, were at least on view for all to see.

One evening when I had stayed at Logan Cottage for supper it began to rain heavily and he offered to drive me home in the Land Rover. Usually I enjoyed the walk back along the cliffs with the dogs, especially if the moon was bright, but on this occasion was grateful for the lift.

'Just as far as the rectory will do,' I directed as I shut the tailgate on Brahms and Liszt. 'Matthew's playing cards with Paul as usual. I'll go the rest of the way with him.'

'You won't, you know.' Josh laughed. 'Paul isn't at home tonight. In fact he's out most evenings now, what with the Cubs and Brownies, Choir practice and the Youth Club in full swing again.'

I said feebly and untruthfully, 'O-Oh, yes...I forgot.'

But if my father wasn't with Paul, I puzzled, then where and with whom *was* he spending his evenings? I finished the journey too distracted to do more than give a few monosyllabic grunts in answer to Josh's companionable chatter. Dodging a goodnight kiss I escaped into the house, thankful that Grace was over at her sister's in Poltreven for the night and I had the place to myself.

I heaped wood on the banked-up fire before going into the kitchen and raiding the larder for a sandwich; carrying this and a glass of whisky I returned to crouch before the blazing logs, my mind going deeper and deeper down just one alleyway. If Paul was out at his youth club then that left only one reason for Matthew spending all those evenings at the rectory.

Jumping Barbara, *that's* what he was doing. I could hardly contain my fury; downing my whisky in one I poured another and prowled around the room in silent rage. How could he have been so unbelievably stupid as to let the old cow get him into her bed at last!

Eventually I calmed and curling into a corner of the couch, watched the clock and waited for him to come home.

It was past midnight when he finally showed. He looked surprised to see me but greeted me with an amiable smile before sitting down to hunt his pockets for the inevitable pipe.

'Have a good game of cards?' I asked.

'Umm, fine…have you got my matches?'

'Here.' Uncurling myself from the couch I picked up a box from the table and walked across to where he sat, inhaling surreptitiously as I reached his side.

Perfume…

It was hard to contain my anger and revulsion. My father was no saint, I knew, but he had never before lied to me about any woman he might have been seeing, and I found it impossible to forgive his betrayal of Paul's friendship. However much he might be in need of a bunk-up he could surely have managed to have it with someone other than his best friend's wife. Not trusting myself to say other than a terse 'Goodnight' I escaped to my bedroom, where I lay staring at the ceiling for an hour or more before falling into a restless sleep.

* * * * *

For days I worried and wondered about this unwelcome revelation, often catching Matthew watching me watching him. Several times I was actually on the verge of asking him outright what the hell he thought he was playing at, but always drew back at the last moment. Perversely, I wanted my worst fears confirmed, but balked at the row that was bound to follow if they were.

Finally, I could bear it no longer. I had a desperate need to unload my problem on someone, but whom? Not my father, that was for sure. Jenny and Charles were out, even if they weren't doing what I thought they were; Grace absolutely a non-starter and Paul, in whom I might have confided, was quite definitely out of the running. Josh, it seemed, was the only one left to fill the rôle of confidante.

* * * * *

The next time we rode together I chose my time, waiting until we had tethered the horses and settled down for a short rest before the return ride.

'Josh, you've known Matthew all your life,' I strove to sound casual, 'do you think he'd ever do anything *really* low-down and dirty?'

He looked up from where he lounged on the rough grass above Lamorna Cove, his eyebrows practically disappearing into his hair. 'That's a damned odd question; how low-down and how dirty?'

'Swear you won't breathe a word…'

He sat up, mischief sparking in his eyes. 'God, this sounds like wonderfully old-fashioned scandal! Come on, Caro…what's the old devil been up to, groping the barmaid's bum in the Penmarrion Arms?'

'Look, I need you to *listen*.' I was beginning to regret the impulse to confide in the big idiot. Scowling repressively at his expectant grin I threatened, 'If you repeat one word of this, Josh Milton to anyone, anyone at all I shall seriously damage you. I mean it.'

'Never a word,' he raised two fingers, 'Scouts' honour…dib dib dib!'

'You were never *in* the Scouts.'

'Only because they wouldn't have me…honestly Penrose, you can trust me.'

I took a deep breath then blurted, 'I think Matthew is duffing up Barbara!'

For a moment he stared open mouthed then clutching his head in both hands began to rock back and forth, howling with laughter. Coldly I waited for him to stop guffawing and regain his speech.

'God Almighty, Caro; are you *completely* off your head? And what a disgusting way in which to describe one of life's greatest pleasures!' He was spluttering and mopping his eyes with his sleeve.

'When you've quite finished rolling around in your vulgar mirth and frightening the horses, we might as well ride back and I'll go home. I should have known better than to expect any understanding, let alone help, from you.'

'Don't get shirty,' he stood up, struggling with another explosion of laughter, 'but, really…Matthew and *Barbara*? For fuck's sake – if she'd been going to get his trousers round his ankles she'd have managed it years ago! Just what, may one ask, put that bloody silly idea into your head?'

'Dad told me he's been playing cards with Paul four evenings a week; *you* said Paul was out almost every night. Who else would he be at the rectory with but Barbara?' I played my trump card. 'Besides, he comes back smelling of perfume.'

'Lucky old him, but it isn't Barbara's because for the past five weeks she's been in Poltreven practically every evening with the Dramatic Society; according to her she's about to give Margaret Lockwood a run for her money!' He began to splutter with laughter again. 'Don't you hear *anything* from the outside world up at Trewlyns?

I was completely bewildered, gaping at him like the proverbial fish out of water. 'Well in that case what in hell is my father doing at the rectory all those evenings…and why tell me he's playing cards with Paul? It's all too bloody *stupid*. She must be there.'

'Why worry about it? Maybe its Jenny he's getting his leg over,' he grinned. 'Now that really would be flying into the realms of fantasy, wouldn't it?'

'Too damn' right it would. With all the men she's had flocking around her an old man like Matthew wouldn't stand a prayer; I suspect all she thinks he's good for is being some kind of buffer between whatever she's up to and mummy and daddy's undoubted disapproval.' I paused in the act of tightening Blondie's girth to look over my shoulder at him. 'I suppose you're not her secret lover?'

'What, Jenny and me? Never in a million years.'

'Liar – you've been trying to get into her knickers ever since we were in the fifth form.'

'But, Caro darling, surely you realise I do that with everyone.' Nonchalantly he let down Nero's stirrups, not bothering to hide the smirk that conveyed an unspoken conviction of his sexual prowess.

'And one day you'll come unstuck,' I retorted spitefully, pulling myself up into the saddle. 'Why don't you do all of us a favour and lay Barbara yourself some time? You'd make a great pair, you and Matthew…the local Bookie would probably take bets on who got whom into bed first.'

'Bitch!'

'Compared with Barbara I'm nowhere in the bitch stakes – and whatever you say I just know she's got her hooks into Matthew.' Brooding, I stared out over the sea. 'I'd like to know how many, and exactly which nights she's at the Am Dram. That may be the word she's putting around but I bet it wouldn't stand up to being looked at too closely.'

'You really are *the* most pig-headed ass…'

'Better that than being a randy sod like you.' I swiped at him with my crop, catching him a resounding *thwack* across his boot. 'Maybe you and Matthew could try alternate nights. That should keep the old cow satisfied – '

'Wow! You really are crackling today – I warn you, if you hit me again I'll scream 'Rape' and ruin *your* reputation!'

'Yes, well… I've had a hard time lately. I feel like lashing out at someone and you just happen to be handy.'

'So say "sorry" nicely,' he leaned over and caught my reins in one large hand, 'come on, kiss and make up.'

I dug my heel into Blondie's side and the mare shied away,

making him swear and loose his hold. I yelled, 'You'll have to try a lot harder than *that*,' and clapping both heels on her flanks shot across the headland with Josh in hot pursuit, alternately bellowing with laughter and threatening murder and mayhem at the full pitch of his lungs.

Dishevelled but exhilarated, I beat him back to the cottage and was out of the saddle, swinging open the gate and yelling 'Pax, Pax!' as he arrived in the yard a few seconds behind me.

Nero, who loved a chase was unwilling to stop and while he pranced and gyrated around the yard trying to unseat a swearing Josh, I seized my chance to lead Blondie into her box for a good rub down. 'Lovely girl,' I crooned, 'that showed 'em, didn't it?'

'Just you wait,' Josh threatened from behind the partition where he was calming a stamping snorting Nero, 'as soon as this nag of mine is comfortable and settled down, I'll be coming in there to have my way with you.'

'No you won't,' I popped my head over the partition, 'the lovely Amelia is in residence. You were too busy trying to stay in the saddle to notice her watching you through the window. If you don't go in she'll be out here after you.'

He swore, fluently and with feeling.

Amelia Bird was a cross he had to bear since inheriting her from his father, along with the Veterinary practice and Logan Cottage. Village rumour had it that she was well into her eighties, but Josh swore she'd never see ninety again. He firmly refused to continue allowing here to live there and had pensioned her off to a bungalow on the edge of the nearby village. But she loved him dearly and would pop up from time to time to disarrange his cupboards and cook him enormous meals, half of which usually ended up in his Labrador's ample stomach.

'I got a lovely bit o' mince without points this morning so you've beef and onion pie tonight, Mister Josh,' she greeted him as we crossed the threshold, 'and you've brought Miss Caroline to eat it with you...are you back from the war at last, m'dear?' and she cocked her bird-like head at me. Everything about Amelia was like her name. Long and bony as a heron with bright inquisitive eyes, all she lacked were the feathers.

'Yes, Amelia, I'm back for good.'

'Sorted that old Hitler out, didn't you...you and Mister Josh here?'

'Pretty well,' I agreed, 'but we had a bit of help from Winston.'

Josh gave the fragile shoulders a squeeze. 'You shouldn't be up here slaving over a hot stove, old dear. It's Saturday, remember?'

'Is it really?' her wrinkled brown face went into the spasm that indicated deep thought. 'You know, I think it is!' Talking all the while she began to gather together the accoutrements deemed necessary for the two-hundred yard walk between Logan cottage and her own dwelling: hat, string shopping bag, gloves, scarf, a man's black umbrella and a handbag the size of a cart horse's nose bag.

'Now just you eat up all your supper, Mister Josh. That old Tansey over Tregenick way phoned an hour ago and say's can you be up to see his heifer first light tomorrow, so get to bed early now...and you too, Miss Caroline – right tired you look m'dear. Just you eat some of that pie then slip between the sheets an' get your beauty sleep!'

Still chattering nineteen to the dozen and waving a vigorous goodbye, she trotted briskly across the yard to disappear, still waving, around the bend in the road.

We stood side by side in the doorway and watched her out of sight.

'Now then,' said Josh, 'you heard what she said,' and turned to put his arms about me.

For a moment I stood quite still as he smiled down, his brown eyes full of mischief, then took a deep breath as desire, sharp as a blade shot through me. Deliberately I moved closer, putting up my mouth and inviting his kiss. He made a thorough job of the kiss, holding me hard against him and as I felt his arousal my heart began an uneven thump. He slipped one hand under my sweater to curve around my breast. 'What, not going to do me actual bodily harm for trying it on?' he asked.

*This is all wrong. You don't love this man and what you're doing you are doing for all the worst possible reasons...*I closed my ears to conscience. 'No.' I said slowly, and locked my arms about his waist. 'I don't believe I am. Not this time.'

* * * * *

He was a generous lover and if he lacked a certain softness and delicacy of touch, he more than made up for that in the sheer energy and pleasure with which he made love, and I clung to him as though he were rescuing me from drowning, so wracked with sheer physical need that I wilfully chose not to heed the inner voice that asked *What about love?*

Only afterwards when we lay in the gathering darkness, I

remembered that this was the time when Stefan and I would talk; about our love and our future and how wonderful it all would be…

'You wouldn't I suppose, like to tell me just why you decided to end several years of snotty insults and come to bed with me tonight?' Josh asked, pushing his fingers through my tangled hair.

I kept my head turned into his shoulder. 'I expect I wanted to see if I'd forgotten what it was like…' He shifted his weight and I said, 'Don't move. I should like you to stay right where you are for at least another hour or so.'

His finger passed lightly to my neck. 'I'm not sure if I'm man enough for that although I'm perfectly willing to try. But it was wonderful. You were wonderful, and I care about you, Caro, I really do.'

'Don't give me the usual pillow talk. Tonight you wanted me, and I wanted you, because you are attractive and sexy and I needed very much to enjoy making love again. Also a good steamy bout of sex is a wonderful way to forget one's troubles.'

'Good and steamy, was it?'

'Positively earth-moving,' I returned dryly, 'but don't go getting ideas for the future; this is a damned uncomfortable bed.'

He said recklessly, 'I'll get a new one.'

'You said you'd be a pal.' I reminded him, 'no strings attached for either of us – promise that, Josh. This bed is just fine for the amount of time I'm likely to spend in it. Don't expect me to follow in the footsteps of your usual doxies and keep your back warm every night for weeks until the novelty wears off.'

'As you're nothing like my usual doxies I'll go along with that, but I am fond of you, Caro; very, very fond.'

'And I of you…pal.' I pulled his head down to mine. 'And I'm getting fonder by the minute.'

'Really – so soon?' he smiled down on me, 'we'll have to see what we can do about that…so what was it you said you felt move?'

* * * * *

Josh drove me home that night and I arrived back at Trewlyns just after midnight. Grace was, thank God in bed. Matthew lay dozing in his chair before the dying fire and looked sleepily up at me over the top of his Growers' Weekly.

''Lo,' he grunted a cautious greeting. 'Have a good evening?'

'It was very nice, thank you for asking.' I replied primly, and he made a face.

'Umm, I trust you put up your navigation lights on the horses.'

'We were off them long before dark,' I flopped into the opposite chair, draping my legs over the arm, 'and the next question is?'

'Not in any danger of getting hurt, are you?'

'Not the slightest.'

'Nothing to give you sleepless nights either?'

I grimaced. 'I manage those without any extra help.'

He smiled, that understanding, Matthew smile and suddenly I was overcome with sadness that he should be doing with Barbara what I had just been doing with Josh, feeling somehow that he was no longer the father I had known and trusted. Tired and confused by the events of the day I got up from my chair. 'I'm going to bed,' I said abruptly

'Caro...what's wrong?' His eyes were puzzled.

'Nothing,' I was moved suddenly to bend and kiss his cheek, 'goodnight, dad.'

He squeezed my hand then watched me until I was halfway up the stairs. 'Bye the way,' his voice was innocent; apparently devoid of guile, 'it might be a good idea to give Josh some decent hair oil for Christmas, that stuff he uses stinks to high heaven; it *almost* kills the smell of horse!'

In silence I returned to the living room, selected a large cushion and threw it at him, then resumed my journey up to my lonely bed.

Despite my weariness I stayed for a long time at the window, gazing over the moonlit fields, my body now at peace but my mind still in limbo.

Why has everything gone so horribly wrong, Stefan? I'm sorry about Josh, but it's your fault; you shouldn't have gone you know. Now Jenny has her chap and whatever Josh says, I'm sure Matthew has Barbara...I can't go on forever without having someone's arms around me. Please tell me you understand and that you are still out there.

I waited for an age before turning away and jerking the curtains across the window. Matthew, I thought bitterly, was wrong. He had known only the illusion of company. Stefan would never walk beside me because he wasn't there. Nobody was.

4

The run-up to Christmas was when Trewlyns went into over-drive and it was nothing for us all to be working a ten, or even twelve-hour day. Riding went out of the window, as did my occasional long gossipy meetings with Jenny in Penzance. Grace looked harassed and stomped around muttering under her breath when we were late for meals, and Charles spent most of his time in the office. Surrounded by order forms, bills, accounts and an ever-ringing telephone, he toiled like the rest of us to meet the deadline for local hotels and the early morning flower train to London.

Willi Fischer proved to be a tireless worker, never flagging and always helpful and good-humoured. Although not in the least interested in the pretty and vivacious Kate, from the first morning Betty rode through the gate and treated him to her open, happy smile he was immediately smitten with the quiet, and it had to be admitted plain daughter of Hector Trescoe, Penmarrion's butcher. Now they arrived together, riding side by side over the headland.

Love was certainly in the air down on the farm.

The increasing workload was a good excuse to keep myself from becoming too reliant on Josh's company, although there were occasions when I was beset by a periodic treacherous physical need for him, then, cursing my weakness, I'd drive to Logan Cottage when the day's work was finished, knowing he would be there, waiting to pull me into his arms, as desperate as me to make love. I think we had sex in every room of the house at this time, apart from the scullery, which was so cold and damp that it chilled even Josh's ardour.

Matthew still maintained his routine of several evenings a week away from the house, only now he left me the car and instead drove the laden van to Penzance station, seldom returning much before midnight. I rejoiced, thinking that for a while at least he was too busy to spend his time with Barbara, although from time to time I wondered uneasily what was keeping him so late in Penzance, a town not exactly famous for the quality of it's night-life.

Only once did I try a little diplomatic inquiry, only to be met by an expression of innocence that wouldn't have looked out of place on a Botticelli cherub, his only reply that as he asked no questions about my activities outside the environs of Trewlyns, I might try doing the same for him.

* * * * *

'Just leave him alone,' advised Josh, 'he's old enough to know what he's doing, you don't get to forty-five without learning not to make a fool of yourself.'

'Look, I don't want him turning up one day with some old hag and inviting me to call her Mother!' I glowered. 'There are times when I wish I'd stayed in the WAAF; at least I knew where I was there. Ever since I came back things have been going from bad to worse.'

'No they haven't, there's you and me...and this bed.' He snuggled closer, kissing my neck, running an exploratory finger down my spine. 'This just goes from good to better, doesn't it?'

'Umm, it has its moments...'

He grinned. 'Well then, what are you moaning about?'

'Oh, I dunno. I suppose I just hate all the undercurrents. Dad and Barbara or God-knows-who, Willi and Betty mooning at each other, Jenny and Charles de la Tour –'

'*WHAT!*'

He shot bolt upright, the exploration of my spine forgotten. 'Where in the name of all that's holy did you get that idea?'

'Why are you squawking like a bloody egg-bound chicken?' I snatched at the eiderdown, 'You're making a draught, lie down again will you.'

'Charles,' he almost shrieked, '*Charles*?'

'That *must* be who she's having it off with – she must be sneaking back whenever she gets the chance. It's obvious.'

'To you, maybe; look...' he started to laugh, 'it can't be de la Tour.'

'Why not?'

'Because...because he's...he's a *thingy.*'

'A thingy what?'

'One of *those*!'

I was mystified. 'One of those what?'

He exploded. 'Christ on a bicycle, Caro! How long were you in the forces? Do I *have* to spell it out?'

The penny dropped.

'Don't be so stupid.' I was too dumbfounded to be even annoyed. 'You've absolutely no grounds for saying that...not,' I added sarcastically, 'unless he has actually propositioned you, and if he has, he needs his eyes tested.'

47

'Dear God,' he fell back on the pillows, noisily grinding his teeth. 'Just get off your high horse and think, will you? Practically every day he spends at least a part of it closeted with three young women. Does he show the slightest interest? Did he ever flirt with *you*, even when you were wearing your shirts with the buttons undone to your navel....did he hell!' He gave a derisory snort. 'I'm telling you, he simply isn't interested in women, *per se,* and do you really imagine he could be getting his leg over anyone, let alone the vicar's daughter, without the whole of Penmarrion catching on?' He bellowed with laughter. 'They'd know if he entertained her to afternoon tea, never mind about spending the last umpteen weeks shagging her.'

'Bollocks. If they wanted to keep it under wraps they could. Anyway, perhaps they meet somewhere in Penzance...I tell you there just isn't anyone else that Jenny would be hopping into bed with every chance she gets.'

'Did she tell you that's what she was doing?' he demanded.

'No, but...'

'Oh, my God,' he rocked his head in his hands, 'first of all Matthew's bonking Barbara, now Jenny's having it off with that French pixie. You'll be telling me next that Paul's been nailing Grace's knickers to the vestry floor and having his way with her!'

'Don't be so disgusting. No matter what you say I still think I'm right about Jenny although I *may* have been wrong over Matthew.'

'Oh, bloody magnanimous of you, I'm sure.'

'Shut up...you're wrong about Charles, I'm sure you are, Josh. He's just a very nice bloke and I think you're an absolute cad to be spreading stories about him. Who else have you shared your stupid ideas with?'

'Only Jenny...and I didn't have to; she told me.'

'Oh.' I was silenced. I remembered Jenny's guarded comment about Charles and realised I'd jumped to the wrong conclusion – again.

'Oh, Oh, Oh!' he mimicked. 'You fat head – if you really want to know what a bloke's doing ask your Uncle Josh. I have a nose for these things.'

'Then get it to sniff out Matthew's bit on the side and Jenny's chap.'

'You persistent pest!'

He grabbed me and we rolled together, swept by gales of mirth until we lay exhausted and weak with laughter, grinning companionably at each other, still shattered by the occasional explosive giggle.

'Tell you what,' he said some time later, 'I think you and I should get married; that way we wouldn't have to keep interrupting our arguments, not to mention what we are doing right now, by your having to get up and go home.'

'Those are very poor reasons for getting married – and your record for fidelity to any one woman hardly inspires a girl to think of hitching herself to your particular wagon for life.'

'Think about it.'

I really didn't want this conversation. Fortunately there was always one way to silence Josh. 'Remember, you said you'd be a pal and no strings attached.' I moved against him, immediately achieving the required response.

'Strings, what strings?' he murmured, his mouth on mine, a sudden resurgence of lust driving all else from his mind. 'I don't need strings; I'll have you know I'm getting where I am quite unaided!'

* * * * *

'You didn't tell me you thought Charles was homosexual,' I challenged Jenny the next time we met.

'Well, when you really think about it it's obvious.' She peered at the bright yellow lump on her plate, dissecting it delicately with a knife. 'Surely I'm not actually meant to eat this?!'

'Careful, that's one of the more edible efforts.' I mimicked Miss Lucy's genteel whine. '"It's the War, Miss, we can't get the ingredients!"'

We were in Ye Piskey Tea Rooms in Poltreven, where the Misses Lucy and Pearl had been serving indigestible cakes and weak tea to the tolerant and iron constitution residents longer than anyone could remember. The war had been, and continued rationing still was, a wonderful excuse for their culinary shortcomings.

'Well, anyway, I think it would have been far better dropped on Krupps than eroding the lining of my stomach.' Furtively she placed the bun on the carpet, pushing it under the table with her foot. 'Somebody's dog will find it sooner or later and have a feast. There's no way I'm going to die of a blockage by eating it.'

'Getting back to Charles,' I couldn't leave the subject alone. 'I don't believe it...he's far too masculine and, well, sexy. You only have to look at his mouth. He's the sort who's probably terrific in bed.'

'But with whom, that's the question? Not all such types mince around with handbags, you know...and remember, you told me ages

49

ago that he was the only man you'd met who didn't do the old stripper act with his eyes!'

'So that makes him sexually dubious, does it?' I scoffed, 'I wouldn't trust Josh's opinion on any good-looking male. He probably doesn't fancy him as a rival.'

In spite of my dismissal, as the days passed I found myself observing Charles de la Tour rather more closely than before. Certainly he didn't flirt, even when blatantly encouraged to by Kate, who had it down to a fine art, nor was there any sign or mention of a woman in his life, either in France or England. He was courteous and friendly but apparently blind to the obvious possibility for lechery in being closeted for part of each day with three not entirely unattractive females. None of which made him what Josh and Jenny believed, but still it *was* odd.

* * * * *

Christmas was suddenly upon us, with its painful memories of my last one spent with Stefan. Now I couldn't bear to think about him at all, pushing away the inevitable pain and anger that would still flood through me. Instead I flung myself into a round of dances and parties, driving myself to exhaustion and blotting out all thought of the might have been.

Josh and I partied as far away as Helston and Lands End, rolling home at all hours to work the following day on autopilot. We grew quarrelsome from lack of sleep then made it up in bed when the opportunity arose, which activity only briefly aided our mutual hangovers and subsequent bad temper. I spent hours upbraiding myself for being a weak, immoral tart, ending up predictably irritable and short tempered with everyone. Fortunately the Trewlyns' working year effectively ended for a week or two after the pre-Christmas rush, affording me at least the chance to recuperate from our excesses.

I was restless and edgy, the frantic round of activities masking the hollowness of my present purposeless existence. I knew in my heart that I was using Josh, that he cared for me more than I ever could for him, but although I found pleasure and release in his bed it did little to ease the nagging, buried pain of loss. I felt guilty about Josh and even guiltier about trying to blot Stefan from my memory.

I had worked myself into a corner; my emotional and bodily needs at war with each other. I was aware of Matthew's compassionate regard. I realised my hectic round of partying wasn't fooling him in the least and sometimes his unspoken sympathy was hard to bear.

'Try to live life a little less frantically, darling.' He said gently one morning, when I had refused breakfast and was sitting at the table with my head in my hands, nursing a hangover of epic proportions. 'You can't go on like this.'

'It's better than having time to think.'

'You can't push thought away for ever.'

'No?' I snapped, 'I can have a bloody good try.' then felt angry guilt at the hurt in his eyes.

But it's not just *my* problems, I wanted to rage, it's you and whoever you're larking about with and being so secretive about. You can be a pal to Jenny and help her because you're not her father. You can't help me because you are – and no father should go behind his daughter's back and have an affair with the likes of Barbara – or anyone else he's are ashamed of, or unable to acknowledge publicly. Anyone doing the dirty like that can't expect confidences...

* * * * *

I missed the daily contact with Charles, who apparently stayed holed up at Tyndals for the entire holiday, unless he was very discreet about finding his amusements elsewhere, dodging all the festivities except for joining us at Trewlyns for Christmas dinner. I wished he would show himself a little less of a recluse. I wasn't looking for romance, but there was something in his calm manner and general air of quiet authority that made me feel he would be a very safe and restful person to lean on, once in a while.

'You see,' Jenny reminded me relentlessly over coffee one morning. 'Josh was right, no parties, no women, no boozing – apparently he doesn't even dance; not with girls, anyway. He probably slipped off quietly when no one was looking and got himself a bit of rough in Falmouth. With all those sex-starved sailors milling around looking for a good time, he shouldn't have found any difficulty doing that.'

'Well hush ma mouth!' I did my Hattie McDaniel's 'Yo' just stop talkin' dirty Miz Scarlet, else I'll snap yo' stays!'

But I was cross with her for putting voice to my own thoughts.

* * * * *

Wrapped up as I was in my own problems I totally missed what was happening right under my nose. All the clues were there, but my preconceived notions about the people around me meant that I just

51

hadn't seen them. Possibly I never would have until told in words of one syllable, if shortly after Christmas Charles de la Tour hadn't been invited to lunch at Trewlyns one Saturday and still been there when Jenny and I returned from a late afternoon visit to the cinema.

'Grace has a rotten cold and has gone to bed.' Matthew looked up as we came in, wrapped to the eyebrows in duffel coats and scarves. 'Better come over to the fire and warm up or you'll both be in the same boat.'

While Matthew took Jenny's coat, Charles stood helping me unwind my scarf, smiling at its inordinate length. 'Grace knitted it for me,' I said defensively, 'I think she forgot to stop in the right place!'

'It is magnificent. I should perhaps ask her to make such another for when I go home…winter in Normandy can be fierce.'

'I'll make some coffee.' Matthew started for the kitchen. 'That will warm you up, Charles and I could do with one ourselves – we've been talking for hours.'

'I'll give you a hand.' Jenny dropped her coat onto a chair and followed him. 'Better make it quick, I can't stay too long. Work tomorrow and all that…'

I sank into an easy chair as Charles stoked up the fire. We sat before it, chatting about this and that. Ten minutes passed. I glanced at the clock then got to my feet. 'About time we got that coffee.' I commented, adding facetiously, 'they must be grinding each bean separately!'

'I should give them a few minutes more.'

There was a most odd inflection in his voice. I stopped and turned to look at him. 'You would, would you?'

He looked up with the blandest most non-committal expression I had ever seen and smiled his slow smile. 'Oh, I think so.'

That did it. I'd had enough. Months of being excluded, of catching snippets of conversation, of being lied to and patronised as though I were some senile old bag two sandwiches short of a picnic was about to come to an explosive end. I gave him one searing look of pure dislike and stormed across the living room.

Under my forceful hand the kitchen door opened with a loud 'clunk' of the heavy latch, but Hannibal could probably have ridden his elephant through it for all the two occupants might have noticed. They were on the far side of the room, locked in each other's arms, two fair heads mingling and bent to each other, fast in a kiss that clearly took them out of space and time.

I closed the door again and leaned back against it in a state of temporary paralysis, while the blood pounded in my ears.

Charles's face was comical with dismay; very slowly he spread his hands in silent supplication. Galvanised into sudden action I grabbed my coat from the hooks by the door, babbling 'Out, out – quick!' and urging a bewildered but delighted Brahms and Liszt out of the house before me.

Charles followed in a maddeningly leisurely fashion, stopping in the porch to shrug himself into his coat and light a Gauloises.

'Might I have one of those?' My hand was shaking as I took the cigarette. He snapped his lighter and I bent my head to the flame, avoiding the old trick of looking into his eyes. This was no time for such shenanigans.

We began walking toward the cove. There was a long silence. He broke it, asking quietly, 'Were they...?'

'Yes!' I said tersely.

He ventured, 'They are, I think, much in love.'

'You don't say!'

'And you...do you mind – your father and your friend?'

'Mind? Of course I mind; I'm bloody furious, but only because they didn't tell me.' I shook my head, the image of those two still imprinted on my brain. I looked up at him demanding, 'and just how long have *you* known, you low-lifer?'

'A few weeks only before you came, I was out with my camera on the beach. They were sitting behind some rocks...' he tailed off and for the first time something like embarrassment showed in the lifting of his shoulders. 'I am so sorry, but...how could I tell you?'

'It could have been worse.' I managed a smile of sorts. 'At least, they were only sitting. They're obviously sleeping together, though...and what an odd euphemism for having sex, *that* is. I must say all the hanging around in Penzance dad's been doing all these past months must have been damned exhausting. I suppose they were getting worried about the cat getting out of the bag here so he had to start going to her rather than *vice versa*!'

'Will you tell Matthew that you know?'

'I shall have to. I wouldn't be able to carry on as though nothing had happened; unlike him, the devious, two-faced bastard!'

He put up a hand to cover his mouth and I glared at him.

'You bloody laugh and I'll never speak to you again.'

He shook his head reprovingly. 'Mademoiselle, with such a ravishing voice, you should not use such words.'

'I can't help it. Oh, *God,*' I sat down with a thump on a stile. 'Barbara; I've just remembered Barbara...she'll blow her top when she finds out. She's been trying to get Matthew's pants off since she first laid eyes on him.'

He pulled me to my feet, his shoulders shaking with suppressed mirth. 'In the end, all will be well.'

'Charles, if you believe that, you'll believe anything!'

I didn't know whether to laugh or cry. I just wanted to curl up in a ball and pretend it wasn't all happening. That any minute I would wake up and find Grace standing by the bed with my cup of tea...And that was another one, I thought who would be mad as a wet hen when she knew...

The more I mulled over the situation, the more complications began looming on the horizon. For a start, I couldn't for the life of me see how I could continue to live at Trewlyns; to have Jenny as a friend was one thing, to have her as my stepmother and living under the same roof was quite another.

* * * * *

When we returned, my car had gone, a note on the table announced, 'Taken Jenny home, coffee on range. M.'

Charles left for Tyndals some twenty minutes later, leaving me time to think about my next move. The last thing I wanted was any kind of confrontation; that might only lead to another tiff between us and there had been more than enough of those lately.

It was at least an hour before my father reappeared; not bad going I thought sourly, for a ten-minute journey. He looked surprised to see me sitting by the fire. 'Not gone up yet, then?' he asked, taking the chair opposite me.

'I don't know what time-scale you are on, but eleven o'clock is not my idea of late.'

He looked vague. 'Is that all it is?'

He began humming one of those irritating non-tunes just under his breath. I asked, 'Did you see Paul?'

'What? Oh, no. He was out.'

'And Barbara?'

'She was out, too.'

'They seem to be doing rather a lot of that lately. Stayed for a cup of cocoa then, did you?' I asked silkily.

That really did catch his attention. He gave me a distinctly wary look. 'You know I can't stand cocoa!'

I sighed. 'I may not have the quickest brain in the universe, in fact I've been remarkably slow in seeing what's been right under my nose ever since I came home, but I do know a spot of good unleashed

54

passion when I see it. I wonder the pair of you didn't curdle the milk out there in the kitchen.'

'Oh, you saw us.' He hunched his shoulders, but didn't appear particularly put out. 'Jenny said she thought she heard something.'

'Jesus, I should think she did – I made enough noise coming into the kitchen to wake the dead! Why didn't you trust me enough to tell me outright?'

He frowned. 'I...that is, we, thought you might hate the idea. Do you mind very much? I didn't plan it, you know. I would never do that. She just came home again after so long, and well...' He gestured helplessly. 'It was a bit of a runaway train for both of us.'

'It's your life.' I poked moodily at the fire. 'Mind you, if she thinks I'm going to call her Mother, she's got another think coming.'

He gave a faint smile at this. 'You're going to have to keep it all under your hat for a while longer, Caro. If it were just up to me the whole thing would have been out in the open and settled months ago, but I said I'd leave the final decision over telling her parents to Jenny – that's only fair.'

'But if I've spotted what's going on, and Charles has – and I bet my life Grace has more than just a suspicion – how long d'you think it will be before everyone tumbles to it?'

'Jenny has the day off on Monday. We'll spend it together and talk things over,' he promised. 'She doesn't mind telling Paul, but has an absolute thing about telling Barbara...she seems to think she'll run amok, or something.'

'She could be right. After all she knows her better than you, and Barbara will be mad you know. She's had her eye on you for years.'

I didn't know whether to laugh or cry. The thought of the spirited, damn-your-eyes Jenny and my straightforward father tip-toeing around trying to keep their affair secret, while screwing up their courage to tell his daughter and her parents was about the most ludicrous situation one could possibly imagine. A less likely pair for such dissembling was scarcely conceivable, so it was little wonder they hadn't proved all that good at it.

I looked at my father where he lay back in his chair, gazing into the fire. After all the months of most spectacularly barking up the wrong tree I was beginning to feel rather more than a mere fool. If only I hadn't been so obsessed by the idea that he was spending all his time with Barbara, I might have saved myself an awful lot of speculative agonising over their imagined affair and seen what was under my nose much sooner.

Suppose when Josh heard the news he thought it all funny enough to tell Matthew my ridiculous suspicions? I went hot all over. That would be just too humiliating; I couldn't possibly have him find out that way...I counted to twenty; ten not being sufficient for me to work up the necessary amount of nerve then took the plunge.

'Dad, I think you ought to know why I've been such a pain in the neck for so long.' He looked up and my nerve almost failed me, but I had to tell him. I shut my eyes and took a deep breath. 'Ever since I came home I thought you were screw...Oh, shit! Sorry! That you were having it off with Barbara!' I opened one eye and shut it again hastily at the look on his face. 'Please don't yell at me; I know it sounds crazy, but that was all I could think of...'

'You thought I'd do *that*?'

My face flamed and I nodded and sat up, hugging my knees, watching the salt in the logs shoot little spurts of blue and yellow flame through the fire. 'If you hadn't said you were playing cards with Paul, then I found out he wasn't even *at* the rectory those evenings, it would never have occurred to me to think any such thing. On the other hand not in a million years could I imagine it would be Jenny you were with.'

'I shouldn't have thought even you'd be daft enough to picture me getting my leg over her mother....for God's sake, Caro, you haven't been spreading that around, have you?'

'Only to Josh.'

'Oh, great...you might as well have announced it in the local pub at chucking out time.' He gave a sudden strangled snort of laughter. 'Oh, Caro, *what* an ass – if only you could see your face!'

'It isn't that funny,' I returned sulkily, 'and Josh hasn't told anyone because he didn't believe it.'

'Then the man has more sense than I gave him credit for.' He stretched out his hand. 'Come here, idiot,' and when I'd crossed to sit on the arm of his chair and take the offered hand, he squeezed mine gently. 'We have rather got off on the wrong foot, haven't we – and most of it is my fault. No more old horse, Caro...everything straight and up front from now on, from both of us. Is that a bargain?'

'Sounds all right to me, 'though I think I'll steer clear of Barbara for a while. She did do that "Tell your future for sixpence" act as Gypsy something-or-other at the Church fete one year and I'd hate her to read what's on *my* mind right now!'

But any chance of keeping out of Barbara's path was dashed the following day.

* * * * *

56

'It's a slack time, thanks to everyone working so hard this last week, so I thought I'd spend the day in Penzance tomorrow if Caro will hold the fort.' Matthew looked at Grace, 'Anything you need whilst I'm there?'

'I don't think so.'

'Caroline?' His eye drooped in a brief wink. 'Can I fetch you anything?'

'Nothing I'm likely to want,' I answered, thinking privately that it would be a good idea if he and Jenny just buggered off to the Penzance Registry Office and got married: a *fait accompli* that might have Barbara chewing the carpet but would at least get the whole ridiculous business settled once and for all.

Grace looked at me hopefully. 'I promised to take over all our junk last Saturday for the W.I. Jumble Sale, but felt too rotten with that cold. If I get it ready would you run it over to Barbara in the morning? As usual, she's organising everything and driving everyone dotty...the less I see of her the better.' She looked around the table, eyes bright as a Christmas Robin. 'Come to think of it, I haven't actually seen much of her since Caroline came home.'

I swore quietly to myself, knowing any excuse I might make to get out of taking the jumble would sound lame. I said, 'I can't imagine why not; I'm hardly likely to savage her ankles, am I?'

She gave one of her familiar snorts of laughter. 'She'll get something savaged before long now she's taken up with that Amateur Theatre lot in Poltreven...reckons herself as Juliet, I dare say, with Denny Austell from the bank as her Romeo! Still, it's seems to be keeping her away from here and off your father's tail.'

Matthew's mouth twitched and he avoided looking at me. 'Denny Austell couldn't savage a gnat, poor bugger,' he observed mordantly. 'He'd best watch out though for he'll have a job keeping his tackle safe for his wife with Barbara helping him into his tights!'

'*Matthew*!' Grace's tone was scandalised, but her eyes danced with mischief as she added: 'Well, you should know, shouldn't you?'

'Grace, you have a lewd streak in that Chapel-trained mind of yours.' He grinned. 'As it happens, I wouldn't. I feel much too sorry for Paul.'

'I could show him a bit of high-life when I take the jumble over,' I offered, trying for a lightness of tone I didn't feel. 'You know...wear my sexy red dress and take him slumming in the Piskey Tea Rooms!'

Of all the things I didn't need, a visit to the rectory was right at the top of my list. I'd absolutely no desire to see either Barbara or Paul until they were both *au fait* with the Jenny/Matthew situation, but I could hardly tell Grace that.

The following afternoon with the car sagging under the weight of boxes of old clothes, thankfully got-rid-of sundry jugs, basins and similar hideous items of bric-a-brac I set off on my mission, bowling through a typical Cornish drizzle and wondering morosely if Matthew was having a nice day in Penzance with Jenny. Knowing, despite all my protestations to myself to the contrary, that I was beginning to reach the stage when I most desperately needed to feel I could look forward to some kind of settled future. True, Josh mentioned marriage with increasing persistence each time we met but I didn't love him enough for that, and to marry for anything less than love would be a betrayal of Stefan and all that we had been to each other.

* * * * *

There was no answer to my bang on the door, but I could see a light in the church, and leaving the shelter of the porch ran across the wet grass to the west door. As I entered, Paul was walking down the aisle toward me, a pile of prayer books in his arms, his cassock swishing on the paved floor.

'Hello, Caroline: how very nice to see you. I was beginning to think you had deserted us for good.' Putting down his burden he caught both my hands with genuine warmth. Immediately I felt guilty for keeping away. I had last seen him, and then only briefly, at Christmas when Matthew had dragged me to midnight mass.

'I've been pretty busy.' I excused myself, adding, 'Jenny and I manage to see something of each other from time to time...mostly in Penzance in her off-duty breaks.'

'Yes. She said. She isn't on duty today, but she has so much on...' *or more likely so much off!*' I thought ...'that she couldn't get home. We hardly see her for five minutes at a time these days. Ah, well,' he smiled, and released my hands, 'you youngsters can't be expected to spend all your free time with us old fogies.'

Anxious to end this conversation I said, 'I came over with the W.I. jumble for Barbara but she isn't there. Shall I just unload it in the porch?'

'No, my dear, she will be back at any moment and the door is open; I can't come for a few minutes as I'm getting ready for Evensong. Just pop the boxes into the hall...I dare say she'll have returned before you finish.'

Not if I'm quick enough, I thought, hurrying back to the house, but my heart sank when I saw her car drawn up before mine, cutting off all hope of sneaking the stuff in quietly and making my escape. Giving the door a perfunctory rap I entered the lighted hall.

An unnatural silence hung over the building. I knew Barbara must be somewhere in the house but there wasn't a sound to be heard; then as I stood hesitating there was a sudden, nerve-jangling crash, the door at the far end of the hall was flung open and she came swooping down the long passageway towards me, a rain-cape flapping from her shoulders, looking to my startled eyes like something out of a Bella Lugosi shocker. Wild-eyed, clutching a piece of paper in one upheld hand she began screeching obscenities like a demented parrot.

'That bastard! That bloody, *effing* man!' She slammed to a halt before me, flapping the paper beneath my nose, demanding, 'what do you to say to this then, Caroline sodding Penrose? What do you effing say to *this*?'

For a moment I was just plain scared. I'd seen men go off their trolley after being shot up on bombing missions, but a Vicar's lady effing and blinding and gibbering like a maniac was way beyond my experience. Barbara was normally the most controlled of women, even her monumental flirtations being conducted with panache. Getting ready to defend myself I took a couple of steps backward.

'Hang on, will you – and stop waving that flaming paper about; how can I read anything that's half an inch from my nose, and going up and down like a tart's drawers!'

'Don't try to smart-arse *me*!' was the unladylike reply. She started in again with the paper waving. 'Read it, you blasted idiot!'

I started to giggle. It was only a nervous reaction, but she looked so much like some brothel Madam haggling over the bill that I couldn't help myself.

'You little bitch,' she hissed, coming uncomfortably close and backing me right up against the wall. 'I'll bet you are in this with him…some example *he* is as a father!'

Suddenly, I was coldly sober and alert with the realisation that whatever was on that piece of paper it had definitely blown the gaff on the star-crossed lovers. Concealing my fright and sounding as though I were ripping off some luckless ACW2 late back from leave I snapped, 'Stop screaming like a blasted fishwife and let me see.' To my relief she thrust the paper into my hand, although still keeping me pinned with her wild gaze.

I scanned it quickly. Leigh Hunt's immortal words, in Matthew's writing *and* on our best notepaper, no less…it was headed: '*To my own darling girl, who lights up my life.'*

> Jenny kissed my when we met
> Jumping from the chair she sat in.
> Time, you thief who love to get
> Sweets into your list, put that in.
> Say I'm weary; say I'm sad,
> Say that health and wealth have missed me,
> Say I'm growing old, but add:
> Jenny kissed me.

'Well...there it is!' I said helplessly and put the offending paper down on the hall table. 'That's what you get for looking through other folks belongings.'

'I didn't have to.' Even with her angry, blotched face and dishevelled hair she was impressive, like the Lady of the Manor in a strop with the parlour maid, and I quailed slightly under her glare. 'I borrowed her rain cape and it was in the pocket.'

'So of course you had to open and read it.' I flicked a disdainful finger at the note, adding bitchily, 'my father would never stoop to such a thing.'

'No?' she sneered, 'But he's stooped to seducing a young girl, hasn't he?'

I exploded. 'For God's sake,' I yelled, remembering all too clearly some of her daughter's past confidences to me. 'You must be wearing blinkers if you think she's still pure as the driven snow...Jenny is nearly twenty-four and has been around a bit. You don't nurse a load of randy servicemen through a war and remain forever a dewy-eyed innocent! Anyway, you don't know it's gone that far.'

'How dare you!' she spat, '...defaming my little girl! And of course it's gone that far! A mother senses these things. I knew something was going on...one of the hospital doctors, I thought. Not *Matthew!*'

'Why should you feel that going to bed with a doctor was preferable to going with Matthew?' I asked, suddenly weary and sick to death of the whole business. 'I can't think why you're getting your knickers in a twist. After all, leaving Dad's morals aside, you've set Jenny a bloody good example all these years, haven't you?'

Silenced for the moment she sat down hard on a chair, her mouth open with shock at my temerity. Remembering all the times she'd smarmed around Matthew, fluttering her eyelashes, touching him, gazing into his eyes, I could have hit her stupid face. The opportunity to vent my feelings still further was too good to miss.

'Jenny asked me only a few weeks ago if I thought you actually got into anyone's trousers,' I informed her recklessly and with relish, 'but I lied and said 'no' because she's my friend, and I knew that saying what I really thought about you would hurt. Just for the record I don't give a damn how many of the men you've chased have managed to get a leg over...' I looked at her in sudden disgust. 'You didn't succeed with Matthew, although I know bloody well that it wasn't for want of trying. He's too decent and values Paul's friendship too much to take what you offered on a plate...and he didn't seduce your daughter; when people love as they do, seduction doesn't come into it.'

At this she found her voice again, sneering, 'You'd know all about that then, would you?'

'Yes.' I said, 'I'd know all about that.'

I felt the anger draining out of me, wanting now just to get away from this obnoxious woman. You poor old sod Matthew, I thought as I turned to leave, you certainly are getting yourself one hell of a mother-in-law!

'Just a moment, Caro...' the quiet voice brought me up short.

Paul stood in the shadow of the porch, the look on his face eloquent witness he had been there for some time. 'Oh, hell...' I breathed, and felt my heart plummet like a shot partridge. Too weary and drained to even try to defend my outburst, sick at heart that Barbara had taken away Matthew and Jenny's chance to speak sanely and decently for themselves, I met his eyes, spreading my hands in apology.

'I'm so terribly sorry, Paul...but cats do have a way of coming out of bags, don't they?'

He sighed. 'Yes, Caro, they do indeed.'

* * * * *

He was very nice about it, all things considered. Gently leading Barbara away to cool down; returning to help me unload my boxes before moving her car out of the way so that I could turn mine. Finally he leaned on my open car window to lay his hand on my arm.

'It's all right, Caro...I understand; and you can hardly be blamed for going over the top.'

'I'm truly sorry, Paul and I blame myself even if you don't.' I felt simply awful. 'Honestly, if you really want to bawl me out, please do, and if coming to mass every Sunday for the next year will make up

61

for it, I'll even do that.'

'Now for you that would be a little extreme,' he smiled, adding, 'and I had guessed about Matthew and Jenny. Who could miss the shine about them?'

'I could,' I admitted honestly, 'but then they only shone the once for me.'

'Barbara will be all right. Eventually.' He gave a wry little smile. 'Soon be back to normal, I dare say.'

Wonderingly, I looked into those clear grey eyes behind the steel-rimmed spectacles. 'Don't you mind?'

'Oh, yes, but the things one cannot change one learns to live with, look the other way and love just the same. And Caro, I think you might stop now and again to reflect that nothing ever is quite black and white where human nature is concerned; that people and their relationships are not always what they seem.' He straightened, and tapped on the car roof. 'Just go and keep watch on the coast road will you, and warn Matthew that his plan to come straight over here to evensong, and a *real* game of cards afterwards are unavoidably cancelled.'

I nodded. Keeping my head down to hide my hot, embarrassed flush I let in the clutch. 'Goodnight, Paul; I really am sorry.'

'Goodnight, Caroline, and God bless...'

I drove out of the gates, guilt sitting upon my shoulders like a great black dog.

* * * * *

Matthew was stunned and exasperated by turns; relieved that everything was out in the open at last, but very uptight that Paul had been left to bear the brunt of the row between Barbara and myself. I was feeling increasingly apprehensive; knowing I had gone much, much too far with Barbara and had probably made a perfectly awful situation even worse. It went against the grain to grovel, but I supposed I did owe him an apology...

'You made a real pig's ear of that, didn't you?' I could hear the repressed anger in his voice. 'So you'd better do something about it, hadn't you? Make things a little easier for me...and Jenny.'

'Of course,' I said hastily, 'anything you say.'

'Then go and see Barbara tomorrow and make your peace.'

'*What*!' I was outraged. All thought of atoning for my sins and grovelling to him with a humble apology took instant flight. 'After calling you an effing bloody man, and me a bitch?'

'Yes, even after that. Come on, Caro, you were by your own account well over the top, and if I know you, you probably haven't even told me the half of it...' he put up a warning hand. 'Don't call me what you were just about to, or look at me like that! You know it's true, so just calm down and admit it. All I'm asking is that you help make life easier for all of us.'

'*Me*?' I was very nearly speechless, 'Just who the hell started all this?'

His face darkened. 'It's not about who started it, it's about what you did to make matters worse.' I opened my mouth to protest then shut it again at his ferocious glare. 'Barbara will feel absolutely ghastly when this all hits her again in the morning and she remembers the things she said. She may be a pain in the neck from time to time but she's not normally given to using that sort of language, even if you are...and I'm not asking, I'm *telling* you, to get over there tomorrow and start putting things right.'

I gritted my teeth, then let fly. 'Sod that! It's all right for you to talk; you weren't there. Considering that you're the cause of all the trouble it's a bit bloody rich trying come out of it whiter than white.'

His temper flared and he shouted, 'She can't help what she is, any more than you can. God knows you've plenty of room for improvement and she does have a heart, even if it is well hidden! If we're all soon to be related – God help us – *one* of you has got to seize the bull by the horns and I rather think the ball is in your court.'

'You're mixing your metaphors worse than Grace!' I got back into my car, slamming the door so furiously that the handle came off in my hand. I swore horribly: real low-down, barrack-room stuff and crashed the gears, snarling, 'There are times, father, dear father, when you are an absolute fucking louse – you got me into all this, now *I* have to get *you* out!'

And I roared off, bellowing 'Effing bloody man!' at the top of my voice as his grim face receded in my rear view mirror.

5

No one ever procrastinated as I did the following day. I hung around, hoping there would be some last minute rush order that meant all hands on deck, but it was a particularly slack morning. I was finally driven out by Grace's impatience with my hanging around the house and Matthew's black looks when I ventured to appear in the sheds. I knew he'd already spoken on the 'phone with Paul, but had offered no information other than a terse: 'I'll be at the rectory for supper.'

Obviously, I though miserably, the little matter of my having created mayhem the previous evening had not exactly endeared me to him, and my parting shot must have been the last straw.

I walked slowly into the village and after dawdling along the street, finally fetched up at my destination as Paul's car was turning out of the gate.

'Looking for me, Caro?'

'Wish I were, but no...Barbara, actually.'

He raised his brows. 'Is that wise?'

'Probably not, but Matthew insisted, as only Matthew can.'

He warned, 'She is not a happy lady this morning.'

'Then that gives us something in common.'

He gave a resigned shrug. 'Well, that has to be a first. I'm on my way now to see Jenny and bring her back later. It will give us a chance to talk before Matthew gets here this evening. I'm bound to say I think there's little chance of Barbara giving her blessing.'

'She doesn't have to, does she?' I retorted shortly. 'Jenny's a big girl now. She needs nobody's blessing, *or* permission, to get married.'

'Perhaps not, but there are other ways...'

Brooding over his parting words I walked up the drive. 'Too bloody right, there are other ways!' I muttered aloud, plying the knocker with unnecessary vigour, 'a bout of hysterical tantrums or tearful maternal blackmail for a start.'

* * * * *

Barbara looked awful. Although having obviously taken care with her make-up, her face was puffy and her hair all anyhow, as though she had been running her fingers through it. The rather nice blue eyes looked washed-out and pale. Much against my will I found myself feeling sorry for her and a lot guiltier than I'd expected.

'Oh...it's you!' Her hand went to her hair, pushing back the straggling blonde strands. She looked at me blankly 'You've just missed Paul.'

'I know, but I came to see you.' I was alarmed to hear my voice wobble slightly. 'May I come in?'

'Yes...yes. Of course.' She led the way to the warm kitchen, asking with automatic but strained politeness: 'Would you like some coffee?'

'No thanks.' I wasn't going to be treated like an inopportune parish visitor. Judging this to be no time for polite chitchat and trying to control a nervous grimace I took the first jump head on. 'Barbara, I've come to apologise for yesterday.'

She flushed a dull red. 'Caroline, if you are being impertinent I wish you would just go away; I've had more than any woman can stand in the last few hours.'

I'd never seen her like this before. Generally she had only two *modus operandi:* Vicar's Lady and Opportunist Tart. Now she was dignified and oddly touching in her vulnerability and it was my turn to blush.

'Look, I lost my temper and was bloody rude and I really am sorry. I know you've never liked me much and that yesterday just about confirmed your opinion. I didn't want to come today but Matthew got me into a corner...I gave him a blow by blow account of our meeting and now he's giving me hell...' She made no answer and I spread my hands. 'So that's why I came.' I finished lamely. 'Sorry, again; I'll go now.'

'Sit down.' She turned to move the kettle onto the hot plate. 'We'll have that coffee after all, I think.' She paused to glance in the mirror above the mantle. 'God, what a sight, no wonder Paul couldn't wait to get out this morning.'

I gaped. Was this really Barbara sounding actually human? Surely not.

She sat down and propping her chin on her hand watched me with a peculiarly unnerving appraisal. Suddenly I could see Jenny in that pose and look. More than once over the years I had observed that same steely light of well-bred battle in her daughter's eyes. My stomach churned. She wasn't as empty headed as she appeared, nor was she stupid. If she wanted to put a spoke in the wheel for Matthew and Jenny she just might succeed.

'I'm on their side.' I had to make my stand. 'Whatever you think, Barbara, they really love each other. I'm apologising for my rudeness and language, not for the general gist of my remarks.' *Oh, God,* I almost groaned aloud. *Matthew is going to slaughter me for this...*

'That's much more like it; Caroline Penrose eating humble pie is even barely believable.' Her expression didn't alter. 'For your information and to clarify a little matter that seems to have been bothering you, out of all the men I've chased over the past twenty-five years of marriage to the sweetest, but quite the dullest man on earth, only two ever actually, as you so elegantly put it, got their legs over!'

I closed my eyes briefly. This conversation is completely cockeyed, I thought. Maybe she's flipped, gone totally barmy. Perhaps any minute now she'll go for the kitchen knife...

She got heavily to her feet and began to spoon coffee into a jug, then stood with the jug clasped in her hands, waiting for the kettle to boil. I gave her a good, hard look and returned to the attack. 'Are you going to try and stop them because you fancied Matthew, or because she's twenty-four and he is forty-five?'

She didn't answer my questions directly, just stood holding the pot and gazing out of the window. When she spoke it was in a calm conversational tone.

'When I was very young: even younger than Jenny, I loved someone like Matthew. He was years older than me, experienced and fun and wholly immoral and dangerous, but I had the sense to leave him and marry Paul instead, who was safe and not in the least dangerous. That hasn't been the success of all time but the other would have been total disaster. I don't want to see Jenny make the mistake I avoided.'

'If you avoided it how do you know it would have been a mistake, let alone a disaster?'

She smiled faintly. 'Ever the logical one – when it suits you. I *don't* know, but it's reasonable when viewed from this distance to be pretty sure it would have been.'

'But Jenny isn't viewing it from a distance and Matthew is Matthew, not some randy old man from your past...and he loves her very much. You can make their lives a misery, give Jenny a load of guilt that might, in time, drive a wedge between them, but Barbara, you can't stop them marrying – even you can't do that.'

'No? Would you want to make a bet on that?' She made the coffee, and fetched milk and crockery to the table before seating herself again. 'I'll say one thing: you're Matthew's daughter all right. Your mother wouldn't have faced me out as you have today; *she* would have been much more devastatingly diplomatic and persuasive!' Pushing a coffee towards me she gave me a look full of irony.

'Perhaps it's a pity I didn't take after her then I wouldn't be up to my neck in it now.' I began to rise. 'D'you mind if I go?'

'I do, actually.'

I subsided. Putting it crudely, she had me over a barrel. I couldn't show myself to Matthew again and tell him I'd walked out without trying a lot harder than I had so far.

'So...what am I supposed to do?' she asked, nursing her cup in both hands. 'Just turn a blind eye to the fact that my daughter has been sleeping with a man twice her age and calmly give in without a fight? Give her my blessing to throw her life away? *You* tell *me*...you seem to know all the answers.'

'Don't ask me to sort out other people's problems. I can't even sort out my own.' I pushed my fingers through my hair, wishing I were anywhere else on God's earth but here. 'I just think they should be allowed to get on with their lives and live them any way they wish. Life's too bloody short to waste a minute of it in waffling about asking should we or shouldn't we,' I said bitterly, 'do that and that the chances are you'll end up alone then spend every day you have left crying for the moon you didn't have the guts to grab when it was offered.' I looked up at her impassive face. 'That's what I think, and if Matthew doesn't kill me for this I'll start believing in miracles!'

'Perhaps that would be no bad thing to do.' She put down her cup, resting her head again on one hand and I felt suddenly, gut-wrenchingly sorry for her. I said impulsively, 'I'm sorry, Barbara...for yesterday and for today, but I love my father and I love Jenny; she is my oldest friend. I don't want her as a stepmother any more than you want Matthew for a son-in-law, but they are so much in love. I couldn't bear to see either of them unhappy because of anything I've said or done.'

She picked up her cup again. 'Well then, we'll just have to wait and see which holds water won't we? My no doubt warped hopes and expectations for my daughter's future, or your philosophy of life and living.'

'But it isn't only what *we* think important, is it? What makes you so sure that Jenny would be happier if she didn't take a gamble on her future with my father, but did as you and chose second best because it was safe?'

She shrugged but didn't answer. I pressed on. 'I don't think your argument holds water. What about Paul? He's too good to be another man's substitute; he's one of the kindest and most understanding men I know. I don't believe anyone is born dull; they're only made that way by people who don't take the trouble to really know them...'

I tailed away and swore under my breath. *You stupid cow, you are supposed to be pouring oil on troubled waters, not stirring a hornet's nest.* I was shaken by an appallingly strong subterranean giggle at my own clash of metaphors. I looked down at the table, struggling for self-control and when I finally looked up again found her watching me with a calm almost amused expression.

'One day, Caroline, you must tell me how it feels to be quite so devastatingly honest while someone is holding a sword over your neck!'

I stood up. 'It feels...uncomfortable.' I answered and left, still not sure whether battle was about to be waged in earnest, or a truce waiting just over the horizon.

* * * * *

Rattled and disorientated; unwilling yet to face my father, almost without thinking I turned down the sunken lane to Tyndals and the one sane person left in this madhouse.

Charles opened the door to my hesitant knock, looking relaxed and comfortable in a thick white roll-neck jersey and old brown cords. Smiling he opening the door wide in welcome. 'Caro! Come in. We shall drink the coffee together.'

Not more, I thought, but only said 'Please. Thanks,' and followed him along the hallway.

The big square living room was comfortably if sparsely furnished, with a plank gate-leg table and four wheel-backed chairs, a couple of big leather armchairs either side of the brick hearth, a coffee table by a long deep sofa before the fire, the only notable items a beautifully polished piano, and in the far corner a tilted draughtsman's table and high stool. The whole place was in contrast to Trewlyns quite remarkably tidy. A lively fire of sweet-smelling apple wood burned in the grate, mingling pleasantly with the aroma of fresh-made coffee.

Gratefully I sank onto the couch. Stretching my toes to the warmth of the fire I let a small, relieved sigh escape as he placed a large mug of coffee in my hands. Seating himself in one of the armchairs he regarded me with calm dark eyes. 'It is most nice to be visited by a lady at this time of day, but I ask myself: why?'

'Oh,' I waved a vague hand, 'I'm feeling too fragile to plunge straight into the day's work.'

'You are ill?'

'No.' I looked down into my coffee. 'Actually, and to be *quite* truthful, Barbara and I had an almighty up-and-downer last evening after she found out about dad and Jenny. When I told Matthew about it he tore into me and we had a hell of a row. He insisted that I try to repair the situation this morning and I don't think I've handled it terribly well.'

His mouth twitched. 'If you were as fierce as once you were with me, I think, had I been Barbara, that I would have been frightened to find you on *my* doorstep!'

'Nothing frightens that woman.' Gloomily I sipped my coffee. 'But this morning she didn't react quite as I expected and I've ended up very confused.'

I gave him a brief resume of the previous evening: Matthew's bullying me to play the peacemaker, then my extraordinary second meeting with Barbara. 'Now I don't know whether I like her or hate her.' I ended. 'I honestly don't think I've ever taken a good look at her before...to see what she was really like beneath the façade. I've just thought of her as a pain in the backside because I knew she fancied my father. I suppose as an adolescent I found that threatening and she made me jealous as hell. Then, after I came back I sort of just took up where I left off. If I've got up her nose even more this morning and given her further ammunition to fire at dad tonight, he'll be so mad he'll probably sling me out of the house. '

'You *have* had a bad morning. Poor Caroline!'

'Oh, it could have been worse, I suppose.'

'I think you should be awarded the *Legion d'honneur* for going in the first place!' his eyes were dancing with laughter, 'but I think also: 'Poor Barbara.' She perhaps cannot help how she is and would much rather see her daughter married to someone younger.'

'Well, that bothers me a bit. Matthew's forty-five, for Pete's sake, and almost twice Jenny's age, but neither of them appears to find that a problem; they are the ones who matter, after all.'

'Yes, and they are the ones who must sort it out. You have tried to do your part and I shall not let Matthew beat you for failing to smooth over the trouble that he has got himself into.' He laughed outright and stood up. Taking hold of my hands he pulled me to my feet. 'Come, we will have a good walk along the cliffs and let the wind blow all your sadness away.'

For a moment we stood close together. With a shock I felt a stirring of my senses more subtle but no less powerful than those aroused by Josh. A remembered feeling, piercingly sweet and warm...and dangerous.

Momentarily his hands tightened on mine and I wondered if he had felt it too; then I stepped back, both physically and mentally. Never again, I vowed silently would I ever allow anyone to come close enough to touch that cord buried deep within me, no matter how much I might long to feel something more tender and lasting than the affectionately carnal liaison I had with Josh. Soon this man would return to France, stepping out of my life for good, and if Jenny and Josh were right in their assessment of his sexual preferences, that was just as well. I wasn't mentally equipped to do unrequited love.

If he noticed my withdrawal, he made no comment and we walked, chatting companionably for a half a mile or so, between the high grass banks of the sunken lane, before eventually turning to face the morning sun for the walk back to Trewlyns. Arrived there he pushed open the field gate, looking back at me over his shoulder. 'Now that I am here I may as well stay and work.'

I smiled wanly, relieved that he had hadn't attempted to touch me again; had kept a distance between us. I said, 'If you can just stick by me today while Matthew is around I'll be eternally grateful, because I'm keeping right out of it for now and leaving *him* to take all the flack later!

* * * * *

I awaited my father's return from the rectory that evening with more than a little anxiety. Unsure as I was whether my meeting with Barbara had made matters better or worse, I was on tenterhooks all evening and Grace kept giving me odd looks as I sat pretending to be engrossed in my book.

When he came back a little before eleven, after just the briefest, cryptic glance at me he went straight to Grace and squatting down beside her chair, took both her hands in his.

'Grace. I have something to ask you…Do you think you could, with some outside help, manage the catering for a wedding next month?'

* * * * *

The dust settled around midnight. Grace, having started off by being particularly old-maidish and difficult, came around slowly to a more reasonable and kindly view of Matthew's plans for his future.

I was so hugely relieved that somehow he and Jenny had managed to win the day and thus let me off the hook, that I got very celebratory and poured all three of us several immoderately large gins. Grace had eventually to be pushed up the stairs to her bed, showering blessings on all and sundry and being narrowly diverted from singing: 'Here comes the Bride.'

''S'trewth!' Matthew subsided into his armchair, looking tired and drawn. 'Playing the diplomat with Grace at this ungodly hour has made me feel too ancient and exhausted to go to bed with anyone ever again, let alone Barbara's twenty-four-year old imaginary virgin!'

I topped up his glass. 'What happened this evening?' I asked tentatively, 'was Barbara absolutely horrendous? Did you have to fight her tooth and nail to get her to agree?'

'No.' He sat forward, turning his glass in his hands and looking at me with a puzzled, thoughtful expression in his eyes. 'I don't know how she was with you this morning, but the whole thing was surreal. I just couldn't believe it...had I not known of her reaction yesterday: how worried Paul was that she would be hostile, I'd have sworn she was actually enjoying watching us getting uptight over what proved to be nothing to get uptight about.' He scratched his head in a bemused fashion. 'Oh, she hummed and hawed and faffed around a bit, but in a sort of half-hearted way, then before we quite grasped that it was all over bar the shouting, she'd taken charge and was setting the wedding date!'

I studied my nails and tried to repress a smirk. He looked at me hard for a very long half-minute, then said softly, 'Don't tell me I have to thank you for all this – that just for once God put the right words into your mouth this morning.'

'Don't lay on me, or God, the fact that you've had the chance to see Barbara can be human after all.' I was embarrassed and made a great business of poking the fire. Backhanded compliments of that calibre from Matthew were rare.

He gave a rueful grin. 'Now I really am sorry I ripped into you as I did yesterday, after you'd already walked into all the flack.'

'That's OK; it wasn't as if you'd never done it before, was it?' I affected a yawn, feeling that if I didn't get out of the room fairly quickly I might disgrace myself yet again. 'All this booze, on top of everything else...I'm for bed. Bye the way,' I was casual, 'I'm riding with Josh tomorrow. Do you want me to drop a word in his ear? Then he can tell Amelia and that way the whole neighbourhood will know in a couple of hours. I really think I'd much prefer that to having to dodge questions from every nosy old bat I meet.'

'Fine. Great idea.'

I stopped, my foot on the bottom stair, turning to give him a last look. He grinned back at me and sketched a salute: 'Sweet dreams, my

71

very dear, very devious daughter.'

There was a sudden pricking at the backs of my eyes. Soon this easy, comfortable intimacy of thought and feeling that he and I had, despite the odd setback, begun to build as adults must slip into the past. Jenny already held first place in his heart; soon she would hold first place in his home and I must take a back seat.

'I'm sorry I stirred it all up for you, dad. I didn't mean to.'

'Having the courage to be honest isn't a crime darling...you just have a surfeit of it from time to time, that's all. Sleep well.'

I continued up the stairs. Perhaps tomorrow I would start thinking about my future. Tonight I was just too tired, and frankly too drunk to do more than have a perfunctory wash before falling into bed.

In fact, I was feeling so low and weary that before I could stop myself, I'd slipped back into an old habit.

So here we go again, Stefan. Nothing ever stays the same for five minutes, does it? How many more people will leave me, or I them, before I can find some kind of stability in my life again?

I thumped my pillow, wishing that someone, anyone, could be here to put warm arms about me: not in passion, nor even in love, but just to hold me and be with me through the night. For once, no dreams came to haunt my sleep; only an overwhelming feeling of sadness at my losses, both past and future, when I awoke again to another day.

* * * * *

Jenny and I had our own meeting one evening in Poltreven, enjoying a meal at the Anchor and talking over plans for the wedding.

'We thought sometime towards the end of next month. Trewlyns is so busy now and Matthew doesn't want to dump it all in your lap when we toddle off to Italy for a couple of weeks.' She regarded me earnestly. 'Caro, are you sure you're all right about all this? We've had such great times together for so many years. I'm afraid of it spoiling things.'

'It won't. Stop nagging, mummy!'

She blushed, looking around furtively at the other diners. 'I wish you wouldn't say that in public...makes me feel about fifty.'

'Serves you right, you trollop, for having it off with my daddy.'

We giggled together.

'Grace always said you had a low mind, ever since you swore the minister at the chapel was after getting her skirt over her head.'

'So he was...inviting her to fire-watch with him on the chapel roof; he had his bed up in the loft, you know, ready, so he said to deal with any incendiary's that might rain down upon Poltreven. I bet he'd have had to scramble into his pants first if they had!' I paused to muse on the strangeness of life. 'Matthew said he pulled that fire-watch routine with every old biddy that'd fall for it. I often wondered why he preferred them old and stringy to young and pneumatic.'

She snickered. 'He was no oil painting himself so perhaps he thought the older they were the more grateful they'd be.'

'Odd, isn't it,' I ruminated, 'how life revolves around sex? Who would ever imagine such things went on in this quiet corner of old England?'

'Oh, I dunno; I think more of it goes on in the country,' she was thoughtful, 'fewer distractions, so more time for hanky-panky.'

That was true I thought. Certainly everyone seemed to be at it like rabbits of late...apart from Charles de la Tour.

'Matthew says you won't stay at Trewlyns after we're married.' Jenny cut across my thoughts, 'at least not in the house. I understand, but where on earth will you go? There aren't any empty cottages around that I know off. Unless,' she added mischievously, 'you move in with Charles!'

'And don't think I wouldn't.' I joked, 'After all, according to you and Josh he should be the last man to take advantage of poor little old me.'

All at once it didn't seem such a bad idea. Matthew had said Charles would be gone by early March. If I were to move into Tyndals when they returned from their Italian honeymoon it would be at the most only a couple of weeks before I could have the place to myself.

Since that morning when I had called at the cottage, I'd managed to convince myself that I must have imagined the brief tightening of his hands on mine – and the effect that his touch had on me. Although I had to admit I found him attractive, with so short a time to go and no likelihood of him doing anything so uncharacteristic as pouncing upon my person, I felt that side of things would be well taken care of. Really, all I need do was to pluck up my courage and broach the matter with the gentleman in question.

Jenny sipped her tea, the light of mischief stirring again in her eyes. 'Caro! You wouldn't...would you?'

'Want to bet?'

'Josh will be livid!'

I grinned. 'Won't he just!'

* * * * *

73

'Why do you look at me so…and with such sad thoughts behind your eyes?'

Charles sprung his question while we were sitting side by side at the bench, filling a last box with the posies so popular in far away Covent Garden. I looked up in surprise.

'What? I wasn't even looking at you unless my eyes have just figured out how to pop out and look around corners.'

He laughed. 'Not at this moment, but you do, Caro, and I think: you must be feeling unhappy or worried.'

'I am nothing of the sort. If you see sad thoughts there, they are probably because I shall be living elsewhere other than Trewlyns in a few short weeks.'

'I too have been thinking about this; now that we are alone it is a good opportunity to talk.' Heavy rain clouds were threatening and Matthew had sent the younger workers home early, leaving us to finish up while he loaded the completed boxes on the van. 'I should not be at the cottage…it would be the right place for you.' Charles avoided looking directly at me. 'I want to tell you that I am finding soon somewhere to stay until I return to France; so you do not need to worry.'

'That's a kind thought but it may not be necessary.' I paused then dived in before I lost my nerve. 'As a matter of fact, I was thinking of asking if you'd mind sharing for the last couple of weeks before you go home. I simply can't stay at Trewlyns when Jenny and Dad get back. I'm OK up until the end of the month so you wouldn't have to put up with my invasion of your privacy for long…' I looked at him hopefully. 'Would you?'

He asked solemnly, but with a glint of laughter in his eyes, 'Do you trust me so much that you would share a house with me?'

I shrugged. 'Is there any reason why I shouldn't trust you?'

'No…' now he was both teasing and provocative and I began to wonder if I might be moving from frying pan to fire. 'But what will your father say – and such a scandal for the village.'

I flushed scarlet and avoided his eyes. 'Dad won't think anything, and I don't see why he should have a monopoly on scandal. As for everybody else, the place is right off the beaten track so that no one in the village is ever likely to have any idea we're sharing …unless of course you start inviting hoards of them to tea.'

This last assertion wasn't strictly true. I hadn't yet said anything to Josh but knew he would cut up rough when I did tell him my plans, and he was unlikely to keep his mouth shut. Once tattling old Amelia

Bird got wind of the arrangement it would be all around the village like wildfire; I should have to run the gauntlet every time I needed to shop locally for groceries or buy the odd packet of cigarettes. 'It's simple really,' I took care to keep my tone light and amused, 'you have an empty bedroom; I need one and we don't have to get in each other's way. I'm out quite a lot and promise not to hold any wild parties if you're busy working in the evenings.'

He held out his hand. 'Very well; this is how we make the agreement, is it not?'

We shook hands gravely just as Matthew came limping back into the shed, entreating us to 'cut the cackle and give me the rest of the boxes quickly, for God's sake; the rain is on its way.'

By the time we were through the heavens had opened and we three ran for the house, our coats held over our heads. 'Damned if I'm going in this,' Matthew grumbled as we stood in the porch, dripping all over the mat, 'I prefer to get up at four o'clock in the morning...you'd best stay until it lets up, Charles. There's plenty of grub as usual. Come on up and dry off and I'll lend you a jacket.'

'Is now is a good time to tell your papa of our arrangement?' whispered Charles as we climbed the stairs behind him.

'No time is a good time...'

'I think we should not delay.'

'OK, so *you* tell him,' I hissed.

'*Non, non* – you do so!'

My father paused on the landing inquiring: 'Tell who what?'

I grasped the nettle. 'That I'm moving in with Charles when you and Jenny come back from Italy,' I answered and stepping into my room shut the door firmly on his startled face.

* * * * *

'I sometimes think you do things just to stir people up and watch what happens,' Grace complained, dishing up apple crumble with a forceful hand. 'You've been like it ever since I've been in this house; never satisfied with things as other folk are...a proper contrary madam.' She waved an agitated serving spoon and we all ducked as bits of crumble flew about the table. 'Matthew, how can you just sit there and let her do what she wants when it suits her!'

'Because for once she's being perfectly reasonable.' He scraped a blob of pudding from the cloth with his finger, and tasted it appreciatively. 'Umm. Smashing! I'll have an extra spoonful, please,' he smiled angelically and she gave an exasperated sigh, as pride in her cooking and annoyance with me struggled for supremacy.

'See Grace, we shall live our own two lives quite separately,' Charles hastened to smooth her feelings, 'Caro and I, we work happily together so why should we not share the cottage – and for such a short time?'

'Well, I'm sure nothing I say will make any difference...all I *can* say is that you don't know madam here very well or you wouldn't be so anxious to have her under your roof!' She tossed her head dramatically and a couple of hairpins shot across the table.

Before she came into our lives I had always thought that head-tossing was an invention of romantic lady novelists, and had never ceased to be fascinated by her ability to perform this strange action which sent hairpins flying in all directions. God alone knew how she went through life without blinding someone. Absently retrieving the pins and skewering them back into place she continued her litany of complaint: 'Not that I expect Caroline to bother about what I, or anyone else might say or think.'

'Oh, come on, Grace...She's nothing like as bad as she used to be,' Matthew winked at me and put a hand over hers. 'Don't be angry because she's flying the nest again so soon...dearest Grace, how she will miss you.'

You old fox, I thought as she smiled back at him with eyes that were suddenly very bright. How you can almost always find the right words at the right moment. Something of a lump came into my throat as I realised just how much I *would* miss her, and my father and this place they had both made so happy and safe for my growing years.

* * * * *

Over the days that followed, when the demand for orders again slackened off for a short while. Charles spent less time at Trewlyns and more on his own work, presumably sitting at his drawing board as I had seen him on the odd occasions when had walked the dogs past the cottage in the evenings.

A week or two before the wedding I began gradually to move some of my belongings into the large empty bedroom at Tyndals, in readiness for my move from home. Once again I found myself overcome by the old wartime sense of impermanence, the feeling that I was just marking time and waiting for the next order to move on. Although my days were filled with work I felt out of sorts and restless, and not only because of the impending move. Try as I might to keep the affair with Josh light and casual, he had started to make

76

that impossible. What had begun as a kind of light-hearted sexual romp had gradually turned into something much more serious and intense, at least for him. I tried to pull back and keep our affair on its old footing, but a fear of sliding again in that awful sterile limbo that followed Stefan's death made me close my eyes to the fact that that the previously fickle and shallow Josh Milton was falling in love. Moreover, that he was doing it with me.

I said nothing to him about my move to Tyndals and for a short time, flattered by his ardour, and battered by his persistence, I allowed myself to be worn down to the point where I seriously considered his proposal. I had to admit the sex was great and that our present relationship had its drawbacks: getting out of a warm bed and going out into a freezing cold night being a major one.

'Tying the knot will solve the problem of where you'll live once Matthew and Jenny are married and settled,' he coaxed as we lay together one evening.

Rain spattered the windows and the last thing I wanted to do was leave his bed and get into a cold car for the journey home. I said, just for the hell of it, 'I could always get resident rates for a room at the Penmarrion Arms.'

'You'd still have to get up and go out into the cold, cold night...' he wrapped his arms around me like a great, warm, sexy bear. He nuzzled my neck. 'Marry me, marry me, marry me...'

Suddenly I was tired of this fragmented, bed-hopping existence and gave in. Pulling him close I kissed him. 'Yes, Josh, I will marry you!'

His response was rather like that of a well-meaning but overcharged puppy on being shown a juicy bone and by the time I had finally extricated myself from his bed it was almost dawn.

That day, with typical Josh impatience he made a dash to see the vicar of the largest church in Poltreven, breaking the news to me as we sat at supper in Logan Cottage.

'Then you can just go back and tell him it's off.' I was horrified to find myself on the dangerous roller coaster of his enthusiasm, 'I couldn't think of being married anywhere but Penmarrion, or by anyone but Paul.'

'No problem,' he said airily. 'We can see *him* tomorrow and set the matrimonial wheels rolling right away.'

'We *can't*.' I was aghast at all the impetuosity that my rash agreement had unleashed. I seized on the first certain delaying tactic I could think of. 'Matthew and Jenny's wedding is in *two weeks*,' I reminded him. 'We simply cannot steal their thunder. Don't you dare to utter a word about this to anyone; not until those two are back from honeymoon and everything has settled down again.'

'OK, but no later than the end of next month.' He jumped up and enveloped me in a huge bear hug. 'Caro, forget supper and come to bed right now – just think: all night and every night like this!'

I hugged him back. 'What more could a girl ask.'

It sounded all right. I'd have to settle down sometime and why not with Josh, who was friend as well as lover? But even as we tumbled into his bed I think I knew even then that I could never go through with it.

* * * * *

Matters came to a head a few evenings later, when I made the journey to Logan Cottage to break the news that I would be moving into Tyndals when the newlywed's returned. I guessed there might be a row, but never envisaged one of quite such epic proportions.

For a few seconds after I finished speaking he simply stared; then his face flushed crimson. 'Are you mad?' he demanded incredulously. 'You can't move in with that bloody man, you're going to marry *me,* for Christ's sake! What would people say?'

'Any damn' thing they like – come off it, Josh. I have to go somewhere. I refuse to stay at the house and play gooseberry with Dad and Jenny. They'll need their space.'

'The whole idea is bloody ridiculous. Apart from anything else you'll be bored to tears in no time. The man is so solitary down there he's almost a hermit.'

'What's being a hermit got to do with anything?' I snapped irritably. 'He can be a Trappist monk for all I care. And since when, Josh Milton, have I needed to bother about what people say or think? I'll lay evens the whole neighbourhood knows I'm doing a damned sight more than warming *your* slippers! Amelia will doubtless have informed her cronies of the state of your bed some mornings – '

Enraged, he shouted, 'It's not just that. Don't be so bloody obtuse, Caro, we've already discussed de la Tour's peculiarities. You've knocked around a bit; you know there could be complications...he can't be a complete celibate; no man can. What if he brings his boyfriends back on the quiet? What will you do then: offer them both a drink and retire gracefully to bed with cotton wool in your ears?'

It was a seminal moment in our relationship and for a few tense seconds we faced each other in silence. He looked furious and utterly confused and I was sick with the guilty knowledge that I was about to cause him even more pain and unhappiness.

'I have not, as you so delicately put it "knocked around a bit",' I answered eventually, striving to keep my voice even and reasonable. 'If he lives like a hermit he won't be doing much entertaining will he? And if he doesn't need a woman in his bed I shall be quite safe, shan't I?' I tried to grin. 'Anyway, I bet you a fiver that he's neither a hermit nor a fag!'

He exploded into anger. 'Done, you stupid bitch,' he roared, 'that's five quid you'll be short. You'll see: *he* won't be doing anything to keep you warm on a cold night, and if he does I'll kick his arse through his ears...' Rampant with fury and lust he grabbed at my wrist, pulling me hard against him. 'Let's see if I can persuade you that a good fuck with me is better than anything you might get from that bloody pansy – '

Using all my strength I pushed him away. 'Are you crazy? I'd rather fuck a gorilla!' I yelled back. 'If I'd thought you'd suddenly turn into a rabidly jealous cave-man I wouldn't have come within a mile of you.'

For a moment we stood panting, eyeball to eyeball, both struggling for control over the other then he grabbed at me again shouting, 'You'll do as you fucking want won't you – you've an unbroken record for that...well it's about time the record was broken!'

Furious I fought him, and if there were such things as the Marquis of Queensbury rules in wrestling, he fought back without benefit of them. Round the room we racketed, sending coffee cups, various ornaments, papers and books crashing to the floor, until finally he cornered me, slamming me back, pinning my arms above my head with one hand and trapping me between the wall and his powerfully muscled torso. 'Got you, you bitch!' Dragging at the waist of my slacks with his free hand he ground his mouth violently down onto mine.

Panicked and furious I sank my teeth into his lower lip and with a howl of pain and rage he let go his grip on my wrists. Seizing the moment, I shoved him away from me and shaking with anger and fright, ran from the cottage and towards home as fast as my trembling legs would take me.

I hadn't expected that explosion of fury from the amiable Josh. You never could tell, I thought slowing to a trot as I reached the cliff path and realised there was no pursuit, however well you might think you knew a person, you simply had no idea what they might have locked away inside them until you put your finger on the one thing that turned the key. *For God's sake*, I blenched. *I really believe he would have raped me...*

I knew I had been incredibly unkind. He still excited me physically and I'd shamelessly taken his increasingly passionate and tender lovemaking without giving more than the response of my satisfied body in return. But I could never really love him; never give a hundredth of what I'd felt for Stefan. I'd stupidly allowed what had started as a light-hearted occasional romp to develop into what Josh saw as a serious commitment. Ashamed, I faced the fact that I had led him on then let him down badly, when letting anyone down was not normally one of my failings; certainly not when I cared for a person as much as I cared for Josh.

I sat on the stile above the lighthouse to catch my breath, knowing with a sick, sinking feeling that I couldn't leave him like that. I should have to go back.

* * * * *

I stood in the doorway, my heart thumping at the angry, hurt face he turned towards me. The place looked as though it had been trashed by a crazed gorilla: the floor littered with debris, pictures hanging askew and thin trickles of coffee from our smashed cups staining the wall: a horrible, shaming testimony to the depths of our anger and violence.

I hesitated for a moment, then crossed the room swiftly to put my hands over his where they lay clasped before him on the table. 'Josh, dear Josh, I am so sorry, but it won't do, you know...I wish I could love you. I do, but not in the way you need, or deserve. If I did marry you, we'd only fight; we always have done – '

He interrupted, 'Not like *that* we don't; I'm not a fucking rapist.'

I said tartly, 'You could have fooled me,' then banged my head with my fist. 'There I go again – Josh, can't you see, it won't *work*. I'm sorry. It was my fault. I'm carrying too much baggage in my head. I'm not fit to live peacefully with anyone.'

He wouldn't look at me. 'I want you, Caro. Not just for sex, but here, married to me and sharing my life...all the time, with or without the baggage. Not down at Tyndals playing house with de la Tour.' Suddenly, he raised his eyes to mine, and they were very clear and straight. 'I've watched you, Caroline Penrose; I know you better than you might imagine. You may enjoy going to bed with me; might honestly have thought you could marry me and be happy, but your face gets a different look when you talk about *him*.' He lifted his shoulders in defeat. 'Whether you realise it or not, I'm telling you

80

now that you're half in love with that bloody French pansy, blast you, and *that's* what hurts!'

My face flamed and I snatched my hands away. 'How *dare* you! I've never heard such absolute rubbish. I like him and we get on splendidly but I have no love interest in him whatsoever. What is it with you that suddenly you can play at taking my head apart? You just stick to your blasted sheep and cattle and go psychoanalyse old Lady Fry's sodding Pekinese!'

'All *right,*' he jumped up, sending his chair toppling again, banging his open hand down on the table he roared, '*don't* listen to me. Go your own pig-headed way and get hurt...keep batting your head against a brick wall – '

Not waiting to hear more I flung out of the cottage, as Grace would have put it, spitting nails. How dare he throw my apology back in my face? I raged impotently as I strode through the black night again. He'd try every trick in the book to keep me from moving into Tyndals. Now wild horses wouldn't keep me from throwing in my lot with Charles...

'Oh, *bugger!*' Standing on the cliff-top above the Cove, feeling the salt spray whipping my face I threw my fury into the wind. 'Damn and blast your hide, Josh Milton! *Now* where am I going to get a riding companion...I haven't even got a horse!'

And I wept angry tears for the loss of Josh and Nero and Blondie, and for all the lovely carefree hours we had spent in the saddle before flying over the meadows back to Logan Cottage to make uncomplicated love on his awful lumpy old bed.

Why hadn't I seen this coming? And why the *hell* did men always have to make life so difficult?

6

The flood of relatives arriving for the wedding almost sent me to Tyndals ahead of time; Penrose Aunts and uncles and an assorted bunch of spotty young cousins appeared out of the woodwork as if by magic to fill the Inns and Hotels of Poltreven with the overflow from the farm. Similarly the Rectory bulged at the seams with languid Debs, Hooray Henrys and look-alike Barbara's trailing large bluff spouses. The house, Jenny complained, was like the village pub ten minutes before closing time but nothing like so much fun.

With Paul officiating a hearty moustachioed uncle did the giving away bit, while Matthew's old friend Henry Trevellyan came over from nearby Tregenick to stand up for him as best man. It was a lovely ceremony and there was a happy, relaxed atmosphere in the old church as Jenny and my father took their vows, only spoiled for me by the consciousness that Josh's eyes were boring between my shoulder blades from three pews back.

Since that terrible night we had avoided meeting and now I stuck close to Charles for safety, grateful to him for giving my hand the odd squeeze when I started sniffing, hoping to God that Josh didn't see and telling myself the warmth spreading through me each time I felt the pressure of that hand was just comforting and not really the least bit sexy...

'You look a little peaky, my dear.' Henry Trevellyan caught up with me outside the church while the photographer was busy with the happy pair, 'Matthew been overworking you, has he?'

'No,' I took his arm. I liked Henry. He was a talented artist and had painted a treasured picture of Trewlyns for my twenty-first, besides which he was old and easy to talk to. 'It's been the blasted relatives who've turned me into this old hag. Thank God the rest of the family stayed north of the County when Granda moved here. I should never have survived my childhood if I'd had to put up with them on a regular basis.'

'My dear, you *must* ask them all back again for your own wedding,' his blue eyes twinkled and he put up a hand to stroke his neat silver beard, 'but no chance of that yet, I gather?'

'Don't you think the Penrose's have caused enough trouble around here for now?' I parried.

'Oh, like that, is it?' he answered. 'I can see I shall just have to return to Tregenick and watch the goings-on between Pascoe's lass and young Lindsey…amazingly, my dear, you must be the only young woman of my acquaintance who isn't at it like knives with someone.' He glanced across to where Josh stood by the porch in conversation with Barbara and cocked his head enquiringly. 'Now there's a pretty pair – the vet and the vicar's lady – although rumour has it that Mr Milton has been rather busy elsewhere of late.'

I wasn't to be drawn, 'I think Josh is quite safe. Barbara is at present, thank heaven, sublimating her urges within the Poltreven Amateur Dramatic Society, or the PADS as they are so quaintly named…and aren't we all pleased about *that*.'

He sighed. 'Well, thank the good Lord I'm too old to bother now with such things. If memory serves me correctly it was a pretty tiring business, which may be why young Josh is looking so washed-out these days. I met him recently in Tregenick and he appeared to have had a few very rough nights!'

'I'm sure I wouldn't know about that,' I said airily. 'Rough nights are not my style,'

Undoubtedly, I thought, rattle-patted old Amelia Bird had been busy spreading the word of our affair and explosive parting well beyond Penmarrion.

I should, I mused gloomily, have taken that job in the office full of bright young things when I had the chance.

* * * * *

'For goodness sakes, stop fidgeting around,' Grace was exasperated, looking at me over the top of her reading spectacles as I wandered about the room that evening, straightening papers and fiddling with everything my restless fingers lighted upon. 'I should think you could just sit still and rest now everyone's cleared off. I know I'm glad to take the weight off my feet for the first time in weeks.'

'Well, it's *too* damned peaceful for me.' I dropped into a chair, stretching my legs out for a moment then sat forward to give the fire an unnecessary prod.

'Why don't you get on over to see Josh like you used to a while back.'

'Why should I do that – he's only just gone home,' I scowled at her, 'in case you hadn't noticed, he was one of the last to leave.'

She laid her knitting aside and gave me a severe look. 'Have you been leading that poor boy on?'

I gave an outraged squeal. '*Me*? Lead *him* on? When did you last

83

get your eyes tested? That "poor boy" is a sexual predator, and whilst I'm not saying he isn't fun, it's not my fault he's finally got his fingers burned.'

'Caroline Penrose!' She was red as a turkey cock. 'Are you telling me that you have been...' she choked over the word, '*sleeping* with him?'

'Certainly not,' I snapped, 'we were too busy doing much better things to find time for sleeping – and besides, his bed's too bloody uncomfortable for that.'

She snatched up her needles again and began to knit furiously. I knew I shouldn't be doing this to Grace but the whole day had been a nightmare and my nerves were in shreds; bad enough to have said goodbye to Matthew and Jenny, even worse to have endured Josh's stone-faced looks for hours. Life, I brooded, was a bitch, and the knowledge that it was my own fault I was now so downright miserable didn't help one little bit.

Considering I'd spent five years caught up in a war, when one lived for the day and morals rather flew out of the window, I'd never been even remotely promiscuous. Stefan had been my first and only lover before Josh. Now I was suffering a two-fold guilt: for sullying Stefan's memory and allowing Josh to think I would marry him, then letting him down in such a rotten manner.

'Oh, Grace,' I burst out suddenly, 'I've got myself into the most God-awful mess and I don't know what to do!'

With an exasperated sigh she put down her knitting again. 'Come on over here and tell me about it then, even if it's something I don't want to hear. I simply can't be doing with you mooning about like a sick cow one minute, and taking my head off the next. Much better get it all off your chest right now!'

So I sat on the floor beside her chair and leaving out all reference to Charles de la Tour, told her as much about my affair with Josh as I could without sending her into a dead faint. I even managed to tell her about Stefan and me and my reasons now for feeling both angry and guilty.

'Dear, dear,' she said from time to time, and 'my poor little lass...what a pickle!' and when I'd finished spent a few minutes in ruminative silence.

'First love is always the best, or so they tell me,' she said at last. 'That doesn't mean you'll never love again, or that it won't be as good. But now you know it isn't so with Josh, don't you?'

'I knew it right from the beginning, Grace. That's what makes it so awful.'

'Well, you've made a mess of things,' she answered firmly, 'but there's no putting the clock back and you can't just keep dodging each other forever. I suggest that on Monday morning you get yourself down into Poltreven and clear the air between you. Catch Josh when his surgery finishes and before he starts his rounds. It will be best to see him there and not at the cottage...more impersonal.'

'Actually, I'd rather go through another war, but I suppose you'll only nag until I do it.'

'And gently.' She peered at me over her glasses. 'Make sure you do it very gently. Men are such great babies and I know you. Just keep that tongue of yours under control and think how he must feel – and don't tell me he's got his come-uppance at last,' she added, as I made to open my mouth, 'I'm not daft, y'know. I understand fine how many lasses he's left high and dry. But you can't play tit-for-tat now. You're too old for it.'

'All right, Grace. I'll leave Willi to hold the fort for an hour and get it over with. First Matthew gets me creeping to Barbara, now you're at it as well with Josh,' I grumbled. You're a bit of an old witch, aren't you? I bet there isn't much you miss of all our going's-on.'

'Well,' her eyes twinkled, 'I see a lot although I don't always get all the details right. But you don't shock me nearly as much as you think you do, or as much as I sometimes make out. I was in the Women's Auxiliary Army Corps in nineteen-sixteen, you know and had no end of a good time at a certain base camp at Arras!'

'Why Grace,' I looked at her with new eyes, 'and I thought you were respectability incarnate.'

'So I am – now.' She chuckled mischievously, ramming her needles into the ball of wool with an air of finality. 'I'm for my bed, Miss, before I tell you anything else that you'll later be able to hold me to ransom for...Goodnight, my lamb.' She bent to kiss my cheek. 'God bless you.'

I watched her climb the staircase before moving back to my chair by the fire. I sat quietly, feeling peaceful and calm, then after a while I did what I had never yet allowed myself to do: let my thoughts drift back, to how it had been for the times that Stefan and I had been together.

Like a series of snapshots the scenes passed in my mind's eye...stolen days of summer in the countryside around Oxford. A magic afternoon in an old meadow near Cricklade, when we found the ground carpeted as far as the eye could see with the delicate mauve bells of fritillaries; peddling on borrowed bicycles to picnic beside the

Thames; walking through the colleges in the quiet hush of evening, eating supper at an old inn before climbing a wide oak staircase to a chintz-curtained room under the eaves. Sinking into the feather bed and making love until, sated with pleasure and passion temporarily assuaged, we slept until the morning light roused us again to each other's arms.

Almost I could see the sleek blonde head and the mouth that had a funny little sideways quirk when he smiled; feel the tender hands that had coaxed and caressed me and taught me to love...

'Where are you?' I whispered. 'Why did you leave me to go on alone?'

Darling Caro, I am always here...

For a few moments I thought I really could feel his presence here in the quiet room. I said aloud, 'Well that's not how it feels when I wake in the night...'

You have been too angry to notice me.

'Don't leave me again, Stefan.'

No, not until you are ready to let me go.

I held my breath. Was this just wish-fulfilment – that illusion of company I had derided all those months ago, or was he really still 'walking beside me' as Matthew had said?

For the first time since his death I began, cautiously at first, to let slip the pain and anger, make space instead for the loving. Perhaps, I thought drowsily, Matthew had been right about sharing my sadness. That there was truth after all in the saying that time heals, and that just maybe some day the loving might come back for someone else.

* * * * *

I awoke at daybreak to a cold hearth and the sound of Grace moving about on the floor above. Brahms and Liszt were draped across my lap and legs, islands of warmth on my chilled limbs. I should have felt gritty and stiff and out-of-sorts after such a night, but instead was full of hope and determination and ready to meet the new day. Even the memory of Josh's preposterous accusation about my being half in love with Charles caused me no more than a momentary passing irritation.

Gently, I slid the two warm bodies to the floor. I would light the fire then walk them to the cove and back before taking a much-needed hot bath and starting the day refreshed, although how far my tranquil mood would last into Monday morning and the meeting with Josh remained to be seen.

86

* * * * *

At the surgery, wearing his white coat and smelling more strongly of antiseptic than horse, Josh was much easier to deal with than he had been at the cottage. The sight of him looking tired but fanciable as he invited me into his office caused a momentary twinge of regret over the end to our term as lovers. What was it about a white coat I wondered, that gave even Josh such an air of dependable maturity? Perhaps I should have got him to wear it in bed.

He beat me to the apology

'Sorry about being such a bastard the other week...not to mention behaving like a sulky kid at the wedding,' he said abruptly. Unlocking the drug cupboard he took out a bottle of whisky. 'I was going to ring and apologise when I'd worked up enough courage...' He waved the bottle, his grin a little lop-sided. 'Want any water with it – for purely medicinal purposes of course: your nerves and my broken heart!'

'No water – I came to say sorry to *you*...and hearts don't break, only bruise. Or so Matthew tells me.'

'Was yours bruised, then? Is that what it was all about?'

'Yes, but that's no excuse. I have got a conscience and I'm terribly sorry I hurt you.'

I took the glass from him, looking down into my drink for a moment and swirling it around. I didn't want to sound like a Dear John letter, but the words had to be said. I took a deep breath. 'Look, I don't regret one minute of these past few months, and I want you to know, and believe, that quite apart from your being very sexy and very good in bed, that I care for you, just for yourself. Although you didn't know it, you helped me over a very bad patch. But I wasn't just using you...no, that's not true. I was, some of the time.' I looked up. 'I do wish I could love you in your way, Josh, but I can't. I should, however, like it very much if you could love me in mine.'

'Stay pals, you mean? That depends.' He gave me a considering look. 'Would you still let me make a pass, now and again? Just for old time's sake?'

'That wasn't a roaring success last time, was it?' I met his eyes and was reassured by the look of mischief in their depths. 'Be honest, Josh. You aren't really in love with me, are you?'

He sighed. 'Lord, I don't know; I'm fonder of you than I've been of any other woman and I'd like to be married to you. Settle down a bit...have some kids. I just think we go well together, even if we do fight and you want your own way too much.' He grinned and scratched his head. 'It isn't all lust, you know. I was never just after getting your knickers off: I like you a lot, and yes, dammit, right now I love you as well…and whatever you say I'd rather de la Tour wasn't in the offing.'

'Sorry, but I have to live somewhere and he'll be away back home in less than a month.' I finished my drink and rose to leave. 'I like him and enjoy his company and he appears to quite enjoy mine. I neither know, nor care if he's homo, or heterosexual or both.' That was bending the truth just a little, but anything for a quiet life. 'Honestly Josh, there was no reason for you to get so bloody stroppy, accuse me of falling for him, then threaten to beat him up.'

'All right, I won't say another word I promise; but only if you'll still ride when time and weather permits and save me from myself!'

'What d'you think I am? The whole Salvation Army would be hard put to manage that.' I shook my head. 'God help the poor cow who eventually gets you to the altar. She'll certainly have a job for life keeping you tied down.'

'Oh, I dunno I quite fancy a spot of bondage.' He grinned then raised inviting brows. 'How about trying some now? I've plenty of bandages!'

* * * * *

I drove back to Penmarrion, laughing a little at his parting shot, feeling both relieved and sad. So that was that. Whatever had I been thinking of to go to bed with him just to try and blot out what I hadn't had the courage to face?

The belated coming to terms with grief, and the breaking down of the self-erected barrier to my remembrance of Stefan had left me feeling very vulnerable and unsure of myself. All the hard won confidence and independence so painfully acquired during the war seemed to be seeping away, leaving me a prey to every kind of insecurity and much too much in need of comfort of a certain kind. Difficult now after all this time, to just shut off my physical needs and exist in some kind of a sexual vacuum. The affair with Josh was over, but how long would it be before loneliness and need led me into another potentially disastrous relationship?

I stopped the car outside the village store, overcome by the sudden need for a cigarette. I was only an occasional smoker …dummies Josh called those little tubes of pleasure and comfort. Perhaps he was right I thought, tucking the packet in my pocket as I left the shop, but as soon as I got home I should simply have to light up and stop the empty ache that kept whacking in somewhere around the region of my lower abdomen.

'Caroline!' Paul barred my way as I left the shop. He was looking amiable and pleased with himself. 'I'm glad to see you. The chemist in Poltreven did a rush job for me on the photographs Barbara took at the wedding. If you've time, you could come back with me now and we'll look at them together.'

I hesitated; I wasn't ready to risk being caught again in a *tête-à-tête* with Barbara should he be suddenly called away, but he was looking so kind and anxious to share his spoils that I couldn't refuse.

'I should love to, Paul. I'll leave the car here and walk with you.'

Barbara's car was nowhere in sight when we reached the rectory and I allowed myself to relax as I followed him into the big kitchen. He made a pot of tea then sat with me at the table to go through a half dozen packs of photographs. I skimmed over several where Charles and I were together: one with a scowling Josh in the background, and we both laughed at some of the hats and wondered why so many people always managed to close their eyes just as the shutter clicked.

When we had finished and Paul was tucking the pictures back into their wallets he asked, 'How is it at Trewlyns without Matthew? You and Grace must find it very strange on your own.'

'Umm...it doesn't feel quite right. I won't be all that sorry to leave. You know I'm moving into Tyndals, don't you?'

'Everyone does, thanks to Josh – whatever did you do to make him so cross?'

I shrugged. 'Nothing much.'

He smiled. 'It is a very good job that Charles will soon be gone. That should stop the gossip pretty quickly.'

'There's nothing for them to gossip about, Paul.' I felt myself flushing from neck to hairline. 'It's purely a matter of convenience.'

'Of course *I* know that.' He poured a second cup of tea. 'I'm sure you are much too level-headed a young woman to get yourself into any casual affair.'

I gulped at the cup he handed me, burning my mouth and just stopping myself in the nick of time from uttering the distinctly earthy words that rose to my lips; knowing from his searching look that he knew that I knew that he knew, all about Josh. Hell's teeth I thought, why am I always left getting the mucky end of the stick? Damn and blast that tattling old biddy Amelia Bird!

'I should have one of those cigarettes of yours now, if I were you.' Paul took off his glasses to polish them on his cassock before putting them back on his nose. He leaned forward, folding his arms on the table-top. 'Tell me,' he said conversationally, 'how someone as intelligent as yourself manages to make quite such a complete pig's ear of everything, and cause utter mayhem all round when you haven't even been back here above a few months?'

'Look...I've already said I'm sorry about the other week.' I attempted to defend myself. 'Quite honestly, *Father* Paul, I can't see anything else is anybody's business but my own.'

Put that in your pipe and smoke it, I thought nastily, we're not in church now.

'Temper!' he raised his eyebrows. 'As both your parish priest and I had hoped, friend, and as you appear to be making such an abysmally poor job of everything yourself, I thought I might be of some help'

'Well, it's all over now with Josh, if that's what's worrying you... and he wasn't the first!' I added sulkily.

'Really?' He was unperturbed. 'What a pity. Who's next?'

How could Barbara think him dull, for God's sake? Once again I felt the ground shift under my feet. Beneath that abstracted, benign air he was as sharp as a bloody razor. First Barbara had caused me to revise my opinion of her, now he was turning the tables and making me look at him with fresh eyes.

Give me the flaming WAAF any day of the week, I thought bitterly, nothing had ever changed there and nobody tried searching my soul in that establishment ...for two pins I'd ruddy well join up again...

'Matthew is worried about you.' He eventually ended a silence that had begun to stretch to an uncomfortable length. 'He didn't break any confidences; only said you were unhappy and that he was worried about where you were heading.'

I lit a cigarette with hands that shook, took a deep lung-full of smoke, coughed and put my head in my hands. '*He's* worried? Paul, *I* don't even know where I'm heading, but wherever it is I don't think I want to go. I doubt if I'll ever be able to think straight again. I'm even having quite lucid conversations with somebody who no longer exists!' Once started I was unable to stop and I gabbled on, 'I've spent the past five years as a perfectly sane, reasonable, grown-up person with duties and responsibilities that I never thought twice about fulfilling with competence and integrity. Now I've come back home and in no time at all I'm up to my ears in shit and acting like a fucking moron – Oh, *Paul*!' Horrified, I put my hand over my mouth. 'Did I really say that? I'm sorry!'

'I think,' he said, flinching slightly, 'that as Barbara is due back shortly you and I had better go over to the church, find a nice dark corner where we can't be overheard and have a good long, talk.'

* * * * *

I returned to Trewlyns more than an hour later and after creeping quietly upstairs to give my face a good wash I went out onto the cliff meadows to begin banking up the early potatoes and checking for any tell-tale signs of blight.

When I heard the sound of Grace's bell announcing lunch I stood for a few moments to watch the far off streaks of grey rain staining down onto the horizon from a dull sky, then carrying my fork, the tines heavy with soil, I walked back towards the house, musing that as potatoes and flowers needed constant care and nurture, so did people and relationships. Perhaps it was time to take stock of just what was important in my life and how I might achieve some kind of balance and harmony within my circle of family and friends.

I wasn't gullible enough to think this small oasis of peace was likely to last, but while it did I might as well have a nice little wallow in being a reformed character. During my father's absence I would make Trewlyns my business, and its people my first concern, so that I might hand them, and it, back to him, blooming on all fronts.

* * * * *

In the second week of the newlywed's absence business became brisk again and we were kept hard at work. The mild wet weather brought the meadow daffodils threatening to burst out of their tight buds into golden trumpets. Betty and Willi volunteered for the backbreaking task of picking, while Kate, Charles and I bunched packed and loaded, breaking only for lunch and the odd tea and coffee.

'It'll be a bit of a shock for your dad coming back off his honeymoon to this madhouse.' commented Kate, up to her ears in posies. She was far and away the best hand at these and could turn them out in a stunning variety of patterns, preferring that task to the easier but less interesting one of bunching. 'You know,' she went on, 'now Matthew won't need to keep dashing into Penzance to meet Jenny, when I've passed my test I could start driving these into the station each evening.'

'Yeah,' I commented cynically, 'then *you* could keep the van half the night and get up to all kinds of mischief that your pa wouldn't approve of at all.'

91

'Oh, well, it was worth a try.' She grinned. 'I can dream, can't I? It would have been right nice to have that old van on a wet an' windy night.'

'As tonight will be.' Charles looked up. 'Did you hear the weather forecast this morning, Caro? There is a gale forecast.'

'Yes. I hadn't forgotten.' Already the wind was rising and I glanced through the window at the darkening sky. 'I think I'll drive the van to Penzance now. We have enough packed already for the London train and the ones Betty and Willi are cutting now can stand in water overnight and be ready for the hotel orders in the morning.'

Both young people came in at that moment looking tousled and damp. Setting down the big baskets on the bench Willi stretched and rubbed his back. 'There are some heavy scuds of rain coming off the sea, Caro and a rare wind getting up. Shall I go now and lock the shed and glasshouse doors?'

'Please...and will you check the hens are away for the night? Grace is busy baking today and might have left them.' I wasn't unduly bothered. Storms came and went fairly frequently, although so far this winter they had been relatively light and short-lived. Still, if there was a gale warning...

'Hang on a minute,' I halted his move toward the door, 'when you've done that I think you'd better take my car and get yourself, and the girls, home. I don't like the idea of that old horse and a couple of bicycles on the cliff path when it's getting dark and with a gale brewing. You can leave Tommy in the stable tonight, Betty, there's plenty of hay on the rack'

'OK. Thanks...I'll go and sort him out now.'

A sudden swirl of wind snatched at the door as Kate opened it. I looked enquiringly at Charles. 'Shouldn't you go with them? Willi can drop you off.'

'Better finish up here then I will help you load.' He was unperturbed. 'I have only such a short way to go and the lane is sheltered. I shall be home quickly.'

We were finished within a half-hour; he stood irresolute by the van as I fired the engine. 'You will be all right?' he asked doubtfully,

I nodded. 'It's gusty, but won't be that bad away from the headland. Make sure you batten down all your doors and windows when you get back. The front of that cottage always gets a pasting when it really blows.'

I drove through the gate into the black and fairly noisome night, watching in my wing mirror as he closed the gate behind me with a last lift of his hand in farewell.

7

It was the crash of breaking glass that awakened me.

I was on my feet in seconds, reaching for my clothes as the house shuddered under the assault of a sudden deafening wind that shrieked around the building, howling down my chimney and slamming great black sooty lumps across the hearth. As Grace and I arrived simultaneously on the landing, each of us struggling into trousers and jerseys over our nightclothes, lightning forked across the sky and seconds later a thunderclap exploded directly overhead with an ear-splitting crash.

I shouted above the din, 'Ring Charles. Ask him if he can make it down here...I'll see what's happening outside. I can manage the glasshouses. You stay in the house and be ready to board up any windows if they get blown in.' Not waiting for her reply I raced downstairs, grabbed an oilskin and sou'wester from behind the kitchen door. Thrusting my arms into the sleeves and buttoning it tightly I opened the door and stepped into the yard and in seconds water was tricking down inside my slicker and soaking my jersey.

The noise was deafening. In the brick stable next to the house Betty's pony whinnied shrilly as he plunged and kicked at the door. I pulled the top half of the stable door shut, securing it with both bolts before turning into the wind and making for the glasshouses. Plant pots, torn branches and pieces of wood from the wrecked fruit cage hurtled toward me as I slipped and slithered on the paved courtyard. Head down and clinging to walls, trees, sheds and anything else to hand, I battled my way through the torrential rain toward the two glasshouses at the far end of the long gravel path. The willow by the pond was lying almost horizontal to the water and above the howl of the storm came the ominous repeated crack of falling branches from the windbreak of trees alongside the farm buildings.

The smaller glasshouse, packed at this time of year with hundreds of delicate blooms for the posies, was built at a right angle to the larger one and taking the full force of the wind. It was by no means the first time it had suffered storm damage, although I couldn't remember a gale as bad as this.

Although I knew what to do I had never had to tackle such a mammoth job alone and unless Charles could make it from the cottage I knew I was facing an almost impossible task. Even so, I prayed that

Grace would stay put in the house; having a most horribly vivid vision of her tiny form being caught by the wind and tossed through the sky like Dorothy in The Wizard of Oz.

Reaching the smaller glasshouse I found the door wrenched off one hinge and hanging loose from the other. Lightning tore the sky apart every few seconds, illuminating briefly the heartbreaking sight of ruined plants. Broken glass crunched beneath my feet as I made my way towards the plywood panels kept stacked at the end of each house for just such an emergency. Above them on a wide shelf was a metal box holding hammers and nails and two Tilley lamps, filled and ready to prime, with matches wrapped securely in a piece of oilskin.

Already shaking with cold I fumbled with wet fingers; striking match after match, cupping my hands around the flame, only to have it immediately blown out. Eventually one burned long enough to light first one lamp, then the other. Hoisting these to hang on the metal struts above the shelving where they swung crazily in the wind, I was able at last to look around and judge the full extent of the damage.

I saw there were already a couple of dozen broken panes, and even as I watched a whole section of roof shattered and glass and broken pieces of branch landed on the tightly packed flowers. For a few moments I stood dithering, wondering where to begin. The door was banging on its broken hinge and pulling myself together I made for that first, struggling to get it upright in order to hammer a couple of large nails to temporarily secure the broken hinge, but each time I hauled it onto the frame it was wrenched from my hands before I could hammer a single nail into place. I was fighting back tears of frustration when I felt a hand laid on my arm and heard Charles's voice, raised against the howl of the storm.

'All right: hold it to the frame and give me the hammer.'

'That was quick!' I was weak with relief. 'Grace called you, then?'

'Ah, no…the line to the cottage is down.' He was busy with hammer and nails, fixing the door firmly in place, bracing it on the inside with a strut of wood. He gave me a brief smile. 'I was on my way as soon as the storm awakened me. Now we shall get the panels over this door then fetch the ladder and see to the roof.'

The house was built low on a three-foot brick base, making the roof panes relatively easy to reach with a short ladder. Clearing a small space under each broken section in turn, we moved slowly along the length of the building. I stood on the staging and hammered the nails into place whilst Charles stood on the ladder holding the wood panels steady against the wind and streaming rain.

Drenched to the skin, our hands covered in cuts and jabs from broken glass we worked on in a kind of controlled frenzy, sometimes on the edge of despair, barely able to keep pace with the damage, securing one pane only to have another smashed within seconds.

I lost all sense of time, scarcely aware of the pain of my bleeding hands and the state of my saturated clothes as the rain poured through the damaged roof to find its remorseless way under my oilskins, chilling me to the bone. I could only imagine what Charles was suffering. He had thrown off his bulky rain-cape when it hampered his movements and wore only in an old Army battle-dress, now so sodden that the rain ran off it as though it were made of rubber.

He swore spasmodically in French and with a quiet preoccupied intensity. Awful and dangerous as our situation was I couldn't help but laugh silently to myself now and again. I'd loathed French lessons at school and my French conversation was minimal, but during the war I had in one way or another picked up a surprising amount of Gallic curses. What I was now hearing from Charles's lips might in any other situation have been viewed as positively obscene.

'Listen…' he paused in the act of lifting another piece of wood, balancing on the ladder he cocked his head attentively. 'The wind I think is a little less.'

We stood for a long minute straining, our ears, waiting for another pane of glass to break, then letting out simultaneous breaths of relief when nothing happened. The gusts were definitely lessening and although the pounding of the sea on the rocky cliffs still beat a resounding tattoo, the thunder was rumbling away and the lightning an only occasional flicker in the heavy sky.

'I hope Grace has got the coffee on and the whisky open,' I wiped a hand across my rain soaked face and he laughed.

'You look like a pirate…all that blood now on your face from those poor hands will frighten her to death. Better not go into the house looking so.'

'The other glasshouse must be a mess.' I said, as we returned to our task with renewed energy, 'but that only has the newly planted seed boxes and can wait until the morning.'

Charles grinned, his teeth showing white in his mud streaked face. 'It is the morning…see, the sky lightens already.'

Half an hour later and the repairs completed we stepped cautiously out of the glasshouse, wedging the door firmly behind us, then stood together looking out over the meadows to the sea. I could hear the waves breaking along the bay with a sullen rumble, sucking at the flung shingle. The fields sloping away towards the cove were waterlogged and littered with the debris of the storm and the rain still fell, although lighter now. But I knew the weather of that particular coast as only someone born to it can and there was an ominous sighing note to the diminishing wind. Seized by a sudden premonition of danger I caught Charles' arm, urging him toward the distant house where I could see Grace standing outlined against the light from the open door. 'It isn't over yet. Get in! Get in!'

Typically he didn't stop to ask questions but began to run beside me along the path, both of us making as much speed as we could, hampered as we were by exhaustion and the dragging weight of our drenched clothing. We had just reached the courtyard and were within a few feet of the welcoming rectangle of light when it happened. The wind gathered and with a deafening shriek, flung a last mighty gust across the branches of the elm that stood tall beside the old house.

I heard Charles' warning shout. Felt the strength of his hands as he flung me toward the door. Heard the great *whoosh* of a branch descending, then he was lying sprawled on the ground with blood gushing from a long gash across his forehead; the splintered branch leaping and breaking on the cobbles beside him in a series of explosive cracks.

Before I had staggered to my feet, Grace was out of the door. Dropping to her knees in the debris strewn and waterlogged yard, she put out her hands to lift his head. I screamed at her. 'Leave it! Don't move him!'

Feverishly I concentrated on trying to remember the first-aid lectures, only half-listened to years before and delivered by an earnest young nursing sister to a hut full of bored aircraftwomen. Shouting that I would get something to lift him onto I raced into the house. Grabbing the broom and mop from behind the scullery door then struggling out of my oilskins, I buttoned them and thrust the wooden handles through arms and hem to make a crude stretcher.

He was no lightweight, but between us we lifted him onto it and carried him awkwardly between us to the living room couch.

He was deathly pale, the deep gash on his forehead still bleeding copiously. Grace fetched water, cloths and bandages and I cleaned the wound, pressing a thick pad of cloth to it until the flow of blood stopped, then turned my attention to his lacerated hands.

Grace was white-faced and shaken. Staggering in under a pile of blankets she stood over me for a moment, indecisive. 'We must get a doctor. He may have concussion or a fractured skull ... anything. I'll ring Poltreven Hospital. You get his wet clothes off and wrap him in these,' and she dumped her burden on the floor beside the couch. I blinked at her retreating back. She must be rattled, I thought, with a hysterical giggle, to leave me alone with a man and tell me to get his clothes off!

I struggled grimly with the saturated battle-dress straps and buckles, cursing as the cuts on my own fingers opened further and bled again with the effort, then ruthlessly hacked at the cloth with the kitchen scissors. It was only when I'd completely removed the thick jersey beneath his jacket that I understood something of the agony he must have endured while we battled to save the glasshouse.

The whole of his left side from shoulder to waist and spreading across his ribs and back was a mass of red and blue healed wounds, some deep pits in the livid scars that criss-crossed the brown flesh like crazy tramlines where the shrapnel had torn into his body. When I eased off the sodden trousers I could see his left leg was in much the same state, the scars running from the back of his knee to the ankle. When I pulled the clothes from his shoulders I saw where the branch had struck. Across one shoulder a long red weal traversed the scars and was beginning to darken and swell even as I watched. By the time Grace returned I'd rolled him onto his undamaged side, wrapping one blanket about him and piling the others on top. 'Is someone coming?' I demanded, 'he's still unconscious...I don't know what to do next.'

Helplessly she shook her head. 'I couldn't get through to Poltreven; the line must be down there. I tried Dr Hesketh in Tregenick...that line's all right but his housekeeper says he's out to a farmer with a broken leg. We'll have to get Charles into the van and drive him to the hospital.'

'I don't know...it could make things worse if we try moving him again. Let me think.' I rested my aching head on my hand. 'Who else is there?' We looked blankly at each other for a moment then I jumped up, scattering the dogs huddled in sympathy close around my feet. 'I know! If the Tregenick line is OK, try Pascoes...I saw Elizabeth getting off the bus in Poltreven on Friday, maybe she's still at home.'

'She's not yet half a doctor.' Grace sniffed. 'Not a real one at all!'

'Well for my money half a doctor is better than none – just *do* it Grace, will you.'

Please, I begged silently as she scuttled away, *please* let Elizabeth be there. I sat holding Charles' torn hands as the tears ran down my face and splashed on the snowy-white of Grace's clean blankets, staining them with great spreading blobs of grey and pink. 'Don't you dare,' I snivelled to his unconscious form, 'wake up and see me looking like this!'

* * * * *

'She's there, and she's coming,' announced Grace, returning to my side, 'so just you get upstairs, out of those clothes and into a bath. I'll re-heat the coffee and keep an eye on this lad. You'll be down with pneumonia next and I don't have any time to nurse invalids!'

'God knows if Elizabeth will get through. The roads must be littered with rubbish and there will be trees down...' Reluctantly, I relinquished Charles' hand and stood up, lingering still to look down at his unconscious face. 'Jim Pascoe will have a fit if she wrecks his van.'

Grace gave me a push. 'Upstairs, and stop worrying; she's getting young Perc from the garage in Tregenick to bring her in his station wagon. Like its owner it's built like a tank and will get through anything!'

When I reached the top of the stairs reaction set in and I was overcome by shaking limbs and a desperate urge to fall on my bed to seek oblivion in sleep. But setting my teeth I ran a deep bath and slid into it, letting the water close over my head, feeling the heat bite at my cuts and bruises and bring blessed warmth and relief to my cold, aching limbs.

Ten minutes later I was downstairs again, swathed in an old towelling robe of Matthew's, my damp curls already beginning to spring into independent life.

'That's better,' Grace's tone was approving as she pressed a cup of steaming coffee, fragrant with a generous measure of whisky into my hands. 'Just get that down you.'

I sniffed at it and grinned feebly. 'If I put this under Charles' nose it would either bring him round or finish him off altogether.'

She threw more wood on the fire. 'What a thing to happen with your father away and only the two of you to deal with it...Do you realise you were out there over five *hours*?' She shook her head. 'It'll be some time before that young man does any more work, that's for sure, or yourself with those hands.'

'Dad's due back on Sunday. How on earth are we going to get it all cleared up before then?' Dejectedly I stared into the fire, nursing my split and throbbing hands. 'So much for my looking after Trewlyns and handing it back all in one piece; even with the girls and Willi we'll never clear it all in time.'

'We'll worry about that tomorrow – 'she broke off at the sound of car tyres scrunching across the littered yard and ran to open the door.

98

The next moment Elizabeth Pascoe was in the room, peeling off her duffle and rolling up her sleeves in a business-like manner.

"You always were a rough girl, Caro – what did you do to him?' she asked breezily, 'and for God's sake get that mountain of blankets of the poor chap and let the dog see the rabbit!'

She hadn't, I registered, changed one little bit over the past six years.

With gentle hands she lifted the dressing from his head, said 'Hmm...nasty,' then pulled back the blanket, uttering an involuntary unprofessional '*Shit!*' at the sight of his scars. 'He's had quite a war, hasn't he...where did he get this little lot?'

'In Normandy: some time after D Day.'

'He could have done without all this then, couldn't he? He's taken one hell of a wallop across that shoulder. I should think he'll be *hors de combat* for a good long time.' Replacing the blanket, she turned to Grace. 'We have to get this chap into hospital, Miss Brendon. Could you have a look at Perc for me? He just fell into a chair in your kitchen and I suspect went straight back to sleep. I dragged him out of his bed and he drove here more or less on auto-pilot, but I'd prefer him wide-awake for the journey back.'

'What d'you think – is he going to be all right?' I pressed as Grace left the room with a promise to brew strong coffee for the weary Perc. 'He's been unconscious for over an hour now.'

'Well, he's almost certainly got concussion, which isn't necessarily serious although it can be. The wound is clean but will need stitching. I imagine he got that when he hit the ground as he'd have been most unlikely to have survived a socking great tree branch falling on his head.'

I shuddered.

'Don't; I feel bad enough as it is...he pushed me out of the way, you know, or it could have been me lying there.'

She eyed me curiously. 'Is he your chap?'

'No,' I hesitated, adding in a rush of confidence, 'My chap's dead.'

'So's mine.' she looked into the fire. 'Shot down over Bremen. Bomber pilot...what about yours?'

'Same thing: Fighter pilot...over the beaches on D Day.' We were silent for a few minutes, busy with our own thoughts, then: 'Henry Trevelyan told me you had someone.' I ventured.

'So I have.' her face cleared and she gave a cheerful grin, 'Henry's artistic protégé, Francis Lindsey. You may remember him from ages back; although perhaps not as he's almost three years

99

younger than either of us. We've had a bit of a thing going since school.' She giggled, 'I still blush when I remember I once showed him my knickers when we were kids. Trouble is, he's still in the Army and we only get the odd week-end together.'

'Oh, serious is it?'

She waggled her hand. 'So-so. He's had a bad time. He was an interpreter in one of those ghastly German camps and met a girl...she died a few months later. I suppose, one day he'll recover.' She gave a sudden, brilliant smile. 'He doesn't know it yet, but when I think the time is right I'm going to marry Francis Lindsey and make him a very, very, happy man!'

The solid bulk of Perc appeared in the doorway, grinning cheerfully through his pirate beard, demanding, 'Are you going to sit there chatting or do we get the poor lad to the hospital? 'Tis near daylight already an' will be safe for I to drive a sight faster going than coming.'

She stood up, handing me her cup. 'Never mind about fast, Perc, just make it smooth!'

Under her direction he lifted Charles as easily as though he were no heavier than a creel of fish, stowing him gently in the back of the station wagon, well wrapped and protected with pillows and blankets, then they were away, Elizabeth promising to ring as soon as she had any news.

* * * * *

I slept the sleep of total exhaustion, awakening with a heart-stopping jump as the dogs set up a cacophony of frenzied barking beneath the window. Sitting up I reached for my watch. Eleven o'clock...grief! I'd meant to be out and clearing some of the wreckage by now...damn Grace for letting me sleep so long. I went swiftly to the window, pushing it wide to shout at the dogs. Wincing with pain as my swollen hands met the woodwork I stared in amazement at the extraordinary sight greeting my jaded eyes.

Along the narrow lane leading to Trewlyns appeared a motley collection of people, all of them carrying an assortment of farming implements. At their head, surging forward like Moses sighting the Promised Land strode Barbara, green-wellied, tweed-hatted and flanked on either side by Willi and Betty.

Spotting me at the window the pair broke into wide grins and waved energetically.

'It's Barbara's Army come to clear up the mess!' yelled Willi,

100

above the ear-splitting howls and shrieks of Brahms and Liszt. He laughed delightedly, waving a fearsome-looking hacksaw. 'We didn't wake you, did we?'

'Not at all!' I screamed back, 'I've been up for hours!' For pity's sake, I thought, as I scrambled into my clothes, Lewis Carol would have had a field day in this place...I hurtled down the stairs to the kitchen and yelled at Grace. 'Why didn't you wake me? Have you heard from Elizabeth? Charles...is he all right?'

'You needed your sleep. Elizabeth 'phoned an hour ago, and Charles is back in the land of the living again.' She dumped a mug of tea onto the table. Jerking out a chair she ordered, 'Now sit down, stop bawling at me, and drink that!'

'Oh, God, thank God.' I slumped into the chair, put my head on my arms and burst into tears just as Barbara erupted into the room. Pausing, she struck a dramatic pose in the doorway.

'Overwrought; I knew you would be. Don't worry about a thing...' she made a sweeping motion with her hand to encompass the throng filling the courtyard, 'Lady Fry's head gardener is here and will direct us!'

Sounds like the bloody Am Dram Society I thought sourly, as Grace came to my rescue, politely ushering Barbara back through the door, thanking everyone profusely and promising mugs of tea all round as soon as the kettle boiled again. 'Awful woman.' she opined, coming back to the kitchen, 'but I suppose she does mean well. Young Willi Fischer has done all the hard work you know, rounding up all the really useful people. But he's the sense to let her take over and organise them. You can safely leave them to do a good job.' She stood back, placing her hands on her hips and giving me a look of extreme disapproval. 'You can just stop snivelling, miss and make yourself useful elsewhere. As soon as you've had breakfast get yourself over to the hospital and see if that poor lad needs anything. Your car's outside, Willi brought it over an hour ago.'

'Oh, Grace, I love you, you nasty, bullying old woman...but don't be so hard on Barbara. She's not nearly as bad as we thought.'

'Well,' she gave me one of her bright, inquisitive looks, 'now just what can have made *you* change your tune, eh?'

I grinned. 'Nothing I'm going to tell you about.'

Suddenly ravenous, I demolished a pile of toast and downed cup after cup of scalding tea before going out into the new day.

It was as though the nightmare of the storm had never been. The sun shone in a high blue sky, a strong but benign sea breeze ruffled the hedgerows whilst the usual flights of black-backed gulls drifted lazily overhead. Only the beaten, shattered hen run and fruit cage, the debris littered yard and the boarded panes in the glasshouse were proof of the savage fury of the past hours. From the hen house came an insistent low complaint from the outraged birds, imprisoned but safe in their stout wooden hut. I could see Betty and Willi leading several men armed with spades and forks toward the cliff meadows and as I watched, the unmistakable figure of Kate went scuttling after them.

I gestured toward them and smiled at Grace. 'Trewlyns is in good hands,' I said and I made my way across the yard to my car, waving to Barbara and her minions as they worked amid the tangle of wood and wire.

Later, I would join them, but first things first, as Grace would say; and for me on this perfectly splendid morning that meant the road to Poltreven and Charles de la Tour.

* * * * *

'What am I doing?' I asked aloud as I left the village and turned onto the main road toward the town, 'bawling my eyes out and rushing off to see someone, who according to Jenny and Josh would much rather have an attractive young man to soothe his fevered brow.'

To be honest, I didn't know what I felt about him, or what he felt about me, if anything. For weeks we had worked together, shared meals and taken occasional walks: friendly, and all completely impersonal. But I had trusted and relied upon him without question at the height of the storm, much as I would have trusted and relied on my father. Even now I could feel the strength of his hands as he'd pushed me from the path of the falling branch.

I remembered my talk with Paul and the promises made; I told myself now that my tears over Charles had just been of gratitude and relief that he was not seriously injured; nothing more than that. Anyone would feel the same, wouldn't they?

Oh yeah? A small voice inside me jeered, *you're heading for trouble my girl...you're heading for trouble*! 'Balls!' I answered, and turned smartly into the hospital forecourt.

Slotting my car into a space marked 'Consultants only' I shoved beneath my windscreen wiper the handy card proclaiming, USAAF. MEDICAL STAFF – PRIORITY, which had been left on the shelf beneath the dash by its previous owner, then went in search of a certain French gentleman with one very nice side to his powerful brown body, even if the other half left something to be desired.

102

* * * * *

'Open visiting is not until 2.30 p.m. whom do you wish to see?'

A large bosom crackling with starch barred my way; I gave it my "you scruffy little aircraftwoman" look before snapping: 'Monsieur de la Tour.'

The bosom swelled. 'Are you a relative?'

'Yes. His mother!' I spied Paul through the glass partition of a small side ward and waved my hand, gushing: 'Coo-ee, darrleeng! 'Ow ez our leetle boy zis morrning?' and swept past the bosom with a fulsome smile.

The PADS would have been proud of me.

He was propped up on pillows looking terribly pale, long lines of pain about his mouth, but wide-awake, the thick hair a startled halo above the white bandage. He grinned faintly as I shut the door firmly on the bosom. 'How did you get past that so frightening one?' he asked.

'Said I was your mother and, by God – saving your presence, Paul, I feel old enough after last night for it to be true!' I flopped into a chair and gave the rector a reproving look. 'I trust you have not already given him the last rites. I should hate to have missed his dying confession.'

Paul put his hands on my shoulders and kissed my cheek. 'My dear Caroline, even if you had, it would hardly have been on a par with your own!' Our eyes met, and we both laughed.

Charles looked up curiously; then one lazy eyelid drooped fleetingly in a wink before he said, straight-faced: 'Yes, do you not think you also should confess to removing all the clothing from an unconscious and defenceless man?'

'How did you know it was me if you were unconscious...or were you just putting on an act?' I parried, rather wishing I hadn't started this conversation, 'Anyway, you can blame Grace for that; she told me to get your clothes off and I always do as Grace tells me.'

Awkwardly he put out his bandaged hand and took one of mine, examining it carefully. 'And with these poor hands...that was most brave.' He gave a rueful smile. 'What imbeciles we were not to have worn gloves!'

I sat very still, suddenly tongue-tied and light-headed while he continued to hold my hand. There was a long silence, broken eventually by Paul, who coughed discreetly. 'Time to go; Sister said only ten minutes.'

103

'And Sister must be obeyed!' Charles relinquished my hand.

I shook my head. 'You may have had your ten minutes Paul, but I've only just started mine and Sisters, even when they're built like Hermann Goering, don't frighten me.'

He smiled at me, giving a very slight, cautionary shake of his own head, but departed gracefully, closing the door with exaggerated care before giving a farewell wave through the glass panel.

There was another silence and I began to think I should have gone with him. The invalid was looking at me expressionlessly and showing no signs of helping me out. At that moment he reminded me of Matthew at his most irritating. I made an effort to pull myself together; a few moments of grateful hand holding between friends meant nothing.

I studied his face. 'It must be hell lying on your back.' I ventured at length.

'I have been more comfortable.' The dark eyes were suddenly veiled. 'Caroline, I am so sorry that you had to attend to my not so beautiful body.'

'No need for an apology.' I looked around vaguely, avoiding his eyes. 'I didn't expect you to be unblemished and the rest of you didn't exactly come as a surprise.'

He gave a sleepy-eyed smile, '*C'est dommage!*'

'Yes, well.' I sought to change the subject. 'I should have brought some grapes or something...I'm a lousy sick visitor.'

He laughed, breaking the tension. 'Not grapes, I beg; all those pips!'

'OK. I'll smuggle you in a bottle of whisky next time.'

'It must be a very small bottle. There are few hiding places here. But you must not spend time away from Trewlyns, there must be much to do – and your father, he is back in two days now, is he not?'

'Of *course*! You don't know about Barbara's Army, do you?'

Relieved to find a safe topic of conversation I gave him a blow-by-blow account of the arrival of reinforcement's to the farm. '...Willi gathered everyone together in the first place,' I finished, 'but by the time they arrived at Trewlyns, Barbara was right up there in the front, green wellies flashing as she parted the Red Sea and rallied the Israelites.' I did my Barbara impression, and he lay back on the pillows chuckling, his eyes alight with laughter.

'Oh, but I wish I could have been there...what an awakening for you! Poor Caroline.'

'Time for *Mother* to leave!' Starched bosom stood in the doorway, disapproval of our laughter in every crackle of her apron.

'The patient needs rest and quiet.'

'It was the Vicar's fault,' I explained, brightly, 'I've been trying to calm him down ever since he left!' and I made a more-or-less dignified exit, Charles' laugh following me all the way down the long corridor.

* * * * *

You managed that rather well, I congratulated myself as I drove home through the winter sunshine, but it had been a close thing. It was clear that it would be a lot longer than two weeks before Charles would be ready to return to France and if we were to share Tyndals together for an unspecified amount of time, I must avoid like the plague any further holding of hands. Although it appeared not to have caused *him* any undue shortness of breath, it had certainly had its effect upon me.

And I had at last to acknowledge, most unwillingly and with an ache in my heart, that Josh had been far, far too close for comfort to the truth when he had said that I was half in love. I just wished I knew if he had also been right in his opinion of Charles de la Tour's sexual preferences; knowing, with a bitter certainty that pride would most probably forever prevent me from putting *that* judgement to the test.

8

On my way back I made a diversion to Tregenick in order to thank Elizabeth for her help and moral support, perhaps stand her a lunch at the Mermaid, but found her packed and ready to return to London.

'You must let me give you a lift into Penzance.' I insisted. 'It's the least I can do after dragging you from your bed last night.'

She accepted with alacrity. 'Well, thank you kindly. Dad's not back with the van yet and I didn't want to ask Perc again after wrecking his sleep last night.'

'Give you time to have a nice chat.' Nellie Pascoe popped two warm pasties into a paper bag and handed them to me. 'You can see she eats one of these on the way, m'dear...always in too much of a hurry to have a proper meal, she is!'

Elizabeth rolled her eyes, kissed her mother and made her escape. 'Why the hell do mothers always start stuffing one with food every time they set eyes on one?' she complained. 'If she had her way I'd end up with an arse like a bus-horse.' She handed me one of the pasties, pushing the other into her bag. 'This one's for Francis tonight. He positively drools over them...stop here and change over. I'll drive and you can stuff your face.'

'I wondered why you were in such a hurry to get away.' I settled back to take a huge bite out of my delicacy. 'God, but I'm starving still.' I glanced at her profile, alight with happiness and anticipation. 'How do you manage things – in town, I mean? You must have an accommodating landlady.'

'Like hell I have,' she gave a snort of laughter. 'I live in a student hostel – no hanky-panky allowed. But we're lucky: Francis' C.O. lets him use his house in Manchester Square. It's unoccupied except for when the Colonel's there on leave himself – nice that neither of us has to get dressed and go home afterward.'

I felt a pang of envy and fell silent, concentrating on my pasty. She glanced at me quickly then asked, 'How's our French friend this morning? I had to leave him about six to get some sleep in before I was off again.'

'Sitting up and taking notice. It was difficult getting to him though. I had to fight my way past an acre and a half of starched bosom first!'

'Umm...that would be Big-Tits Bostock. She runs that bloody

ward like a barracks. The nurses have spread a rumour that she's a leftover German parachutist with hormone problems, which could be true...did you see the size of her feet?'

We both roared with laughter then she sobered suddenly and drove for a few moments in silence before asking: 'You do know how serious his injuries are, don't you?'

'What?' I was confused. 'How d'you mean? He seemed to be reasonably all right, all things considered.'

'Oh, I'm not talking about last night, although that hasn't exactly improved matters, but the mess he's in generally. It must have taken him one hell of a long time and a lot of sheer bloody-minded determination to recover as well as he has, but wounds like that mean he'll never be really fit again; will probably always be in pain.' She gave me a swift glance. 'Sometimes the old libido takes a bashing along with everything else.'

'You mean he might not be able to, you know, get to first base, as our American friends might put it?' My insides did a sickening sideways lurch. Was *that* the reason for the lack of a woman in his life?

'Not necessarily, for all I know he may be a raging sex maniac, but men who've been that badly scarred can be difficult to live with: moody; at times just plain bloody impossible. But of course,' she paused, for a few moments to concentrate on the Penzance traffic, 'as he isn't your chap I don't really need to tell you all this.'

'No-o,' I said slowly, 'I suppose not.'

'They've all got scars, you know: those who came back: on their bodies or minds, or both. It's tough when we have our scars too.' She swung into the station yard and I got out to move into the driver's seat while she pulled her case from the car. Pausing, she gave me a wry grin across the roof.

'I must fly; God love you – and the best of luck with him!' She disappeared into the station, waving energetically, blonde hair flying, off to her lover and a weekend of which Grace would most certainly not approve.

I envied her with all my heart.

* * * * *

Returning to Trewlyns, ready to pitch in and work alongside everyone else, I was flapped away by Barbara with a dismissive: 'No use to anyone with those hands. Better you get down to the cliff meadows and oversee those young things. They're probably doing everything wrong!' I ground my teeth a bit. Leopards couldn't be expected to change all their spots in one go, I supposed, and she was working as hard, or harder, than anyone.

'It's all right, Barbara,' I did my best to be charitable. 'I trust those "young things" absolutely to do what needs doing without any supervision from me.'

I went into the house where Grace worked Comfrey ointment into my sore hands whilst I told her about my morning. 'You go to your room and have a rest now,' she bullied me gently, wrapping a crepe bandage around each hand, ignoring my protest that they were healing quite nicely all on their own, 'then you'll perhaps feel like helping me get some tea and sandwiches for these good people later this afternoon. They were so determined to get things back to normal for when Matthew and Jenny come home that all they'd stop for was soup and bread.'

'You seem to have forgotten that you had scarcely any sleep last night either.' Firmly, I pushed her down into a chair. 'Now you can just sit still while *I* make a pot of tea before we both get our heads down for an hour or two.'

With a great deal of protest she allowed me to make the tea and shoo her to bed. When I peeped in minutes later she was fast asleep, the untouched cup of tea still steaming faintly on the bedside table. Thankfully I crawled beneath my own eiderdown and lay for a long time reliving the events of the day. Uppermost in my mind being the feel of Charles's bandaged hand on mine and the look on Elizabeth's face as she hastened toward the train that would take her to London and her love.

* * * * *

By the following afternoon the work was done. The boarded panels replaced with glass and the fruit cage and hen run restored to their former glory. Less than a third of the soft fruits were damaged beyond recall and Willi and his helpers had done wonders with the meadows. Although a fair amount of the young daffodils had been wrecked, only one day's full deliveries to London had been lost, Betty and Kate working through the afternoon of the second day in order that Willi might rush several dozen boxes of blooms to the flower train.

Barbara and her army departed at dusk, loudly cheered on their way, leaving the five of us to relax at last around the big kitchen table, to talk and eat and generally unwind after all the tensions and hard work of the past forty-eight hours, secure now in the knowledge that Matthew would return the next day to a slightly battered but operational business.

Looking around at the three young faces flushed with the knowledge of a job well done, I vowed to myself that I would in the very near future reward them all with the best slap-up dinner and dance that Penzance could offer.

* * * * *

As Matthew and Jenny were not due back until late in the afternoon, I spent that Sunday morning moving the remainder of my belongings to Tyndals, then after a quick lunch drove again to the hospital, half-annoyed half-relieved, to find Barbara already in residence at Charles' bedside.

'I have been hearing more about Operation Trewlyns!' he said, the mutual greetings over. 'I wish I could have been there to help.'

'You've done more than enough. Quite apart from battling the gale so heroically you saved Caroline's life.' Barbara looked at me with a rare, slightly sarcastic grin as though hinting there'd been a bit of a blunder there. She switched her attention back to the patient adding: 'and very nearly got yourself killed instead, you poor dear!'

Behind her back I made sick motions.

'Oh, my goodness!' she leaped back in alarm as the poor dear's snort of laughter became a paroxysm of coughing, 'Quickly, Caroline...call a doctor!'

'No...no,' he was gasped weakly, the tears running from his eyes, 'please, it is nothing; just one of your delicious grapes finding the wrong channel perhaps!'

'Grapes? How thoughtful of you Barbara,' I gave her my very nicest smile, 'I do wish I'd thought of bringing some.'

'Well, of course, I'm used to visiting the sick, one of the many joys of being a rectory wife,' she replied with an oblique look, pulling on her gloves with the air of a respectable matron. 'Now that you are here I shall go to visit old Mr. Bolitho on Alderman Mellion Ward...such a thoughtful old gentleman. Do you know that when I left him the last time I visited he actually begged me not to come all this way again to see him! Now that was thoughtful of him, was it not?'

'Heroic.' I agreed, holding open the door; keeping a straight face with great difficulty. No, she hadn't changed all that much. 'Do give him my deepest sympathy...for being unfortunate enough to be in hospital of course.'

I watched until she disappeared around a corner of the corridor then turned to Charles, who was wiping a pyjama sleeve across his eyes.

'Now what's the matter with you, you poor dear?' I asked solicitously, slipping a quarter bottle of whisky under his pillows, 'Another grape gone down the wrong way?'

'Are you going to continue in this so dreadful a manner at the cottage?' he asked pitifully, 'because if so, I shall insist to stay here for my own safety.'

'It's that woman,' I said gloomily, 'she still has that effect on me, but so long as you lock me in the shed if she comes visiting, I promise you you'll be quite safe.'

'But she means to be so kind.'

'I know and she's not really such a bad old bat.' I sat down and helped myself to a grape. 'She worked damned hard on the clearing-up...and she was quite right, you know, you probably did save my life.'

He looked embarrassed. 'Please, it was...' he paused, 'Tsch! What is the word?'

''Heroic'?' I suggested, 'like old Mr. Bolitho?'

''Instinctive!'' he laughed again, 'you would have done the same for me, *n'est-ce pas?*'

'Very likely, but saving you from She of the big what's-it's is more my style.' I stood up and prowled to the end of the bed to read his chart. 'How much longer are you going to be here, you fraud,' I demanded, 'you've no sign of a temperature – '

The door was pushed open suddenly and I turned, expecting to do battle with Big Tits Bostock, but it was Josh who stood in the doorway, beaming all over his face, his arm around a fragile ethereal creature, with tumbling golden curls and eyes the colour of over-ripe gooseberries.

I was highly gratified by his classic double take when he spotted me at the bedside.

'Hi, Penrose! Didn't expect to see you; thought you'd still be in bed.'

'No, Mister Milton,' I answered silkily, 'these days I only use my bed at night – for sleeping.'

His grin slipped momentarily and he looked embarrassed, his glance moving to gooseberry eyes who was now tittering girlishly and clinging to his arm like a leech that had just found its breakfast. 'Jolly good, er...um, I'm just taking Nurse Harris to...er, tea.

Thought I'd pop in to say hello to de la Tour here.'

'My, you are having a busy afternoon, Charles – first Barbara then *moi*, now the Vet. Sure you've got the right place, Josh? There are only two legged animals here.' I popped another grape into my mouth and turned inquiring eyes on his companion, 'Tea, is it, nurse? Make sure he warms the pot properly first before he puts in the tea; he can be a bit slapdash sometimes about the preliminaries!'

Josh glared and Charles blinked, but she only emitted a frightful tinkling laugh and clung even tighter. Much more, I thought, and gangrene will set in. 'He's going to show me his surgery!' she trilled.

'How very nice,' I said approvingly, 'just the place to have afternoon tea.'

The look I got from Josh was designed to freeze blood at twenty paces.

* * * * *

'They went rather quickly.' Charles's face was a study in interested speculation.

'Yes, didn't they? It can't have been to see his etchings because he keeps those miles away at the cottage!' I took another grape and nibbled delicately. 'I expect the man's in a hurry to get his kettle boiling – I dare say they'll have tea on the operating table. I reckon it's big enough to take a fair-sized cow, you know.'

We looked at each other for a moment in silence.

'Caroline, *tu es un enfant terrible*!' he said severely, then his mouth began to twitch at the corners, and in seconds we exploded into laughter.

Altogether it seemed a good moment to leave. Keep things on this level, I thought as I drove home, and he would return to France in a few short weeks without any likelihood of an embarrassing situation having developed.

That he knew now if he hadn't before about my previous involvement with Josh would make it easier to steer clear of any messy entanglement. If he was happy to accept me at face value as a friend, I could go along with that in the short term, and if I had to put my feelings for him into cold storage, that shouldn't be too difficult either. I'd done that once before and I could do it again.

Practice, I hoped, would make perfect.

* * * * *

I stood in the silent cottage, listening to the slow tick-tock of the clock on the wall, the brass pendulum swinging to and fro with measured stroke. I was feeling distinctly strange: stranger even than when I left home to join the WAAF. Then I had been just out of school and going away an adventure. Now, after five months of settling into back life at Trewlyns as an independent adult it felt more like deportation.

My father and Jenny had arrived home in the early evening, radiating a happiness which couldn't be shaken, even by the news of our near disasters and the loss of a large amount of young plants, although Matthew was deeply concerned by Charles' accident and his daughter's battered hands. Jenny's immediate reaction to the news that Charles was in the hospital was that he must be rescued at the earliest possible moment from the clutches of Big Tits Bostock.

I did my part in keeping the atmosphere light and as normal as possible, recounting Barbara's marshalling of her troops, the quick change to rector's wife visiting the sick and her elevation of Charles to hero of the hour. But every now and again my glance would stray around the table as I surreptitiously stored away the familiar faces and voices of Matthew and Grace as they argued, teased and reminisced. It all appeared so normal and ordinary, with Jenny fitting seamlessly into the household.

Once or twice I caught my father's watchful eyes upon me and managed to return a carefree smile. It was harder to meet Grace's sharp gaze and maintain the usual verbal banter between us. Jenny too, fell quiet from time to time and I wondered dismally just who was fooling whom.

When the time came for me to leave for Tyndals I did so in the way I had learned from Matthew at an early age. "Never say goodbye more than once and never linger in doorways" had been his maxim, and it stood me in good stead tonight. I had been away from the house swiftly and smoothly but with an awful great lump in my throat as Brahms and Liszt sat in the gateway, watching and whining as I drove away from my home.

Tyndals had a hollow, empty air about it as I wandered shivering through the rooms, tentatively asking the eternal question of the empty air.

'Are you here?' I strained my ears.

Yes...can you not tell?

'And will you stay?'

Of course, for as long as you need me.

'I shall need you forever...'

You think that now – but remember:
"Winter's broken and earth has woken
And the small birds cry again."

'Yes, but I can play that game too...you've only quoted the best bit. Remember, it goes on...

"'And the hawthorn hedge puts forth its buds,
And my heart puts forth its pain."

Which it does still, my love, every single day.'

The clock ticked on. I shook myself out of the dream: it had to be a dream, didn't it? Going into the tidy kitchen I raided Charles' Johnny Walker and put a match to the laid fire in the grate. I raised a glass to my reflection in the mirror over the oak mantle. 'Life is what you make it, cock!' I said solemnly, then smiled, hearing an echo of Grace voicing one of her many favourite clichés: "When one door closes, another opens."

I sighed and thought, that's all very well to say Grace, if one could only be certain of what was behind that opening door...

Ten days later, Charles de la Tour came back to Tyndals, and my troubles really began.

* * * * *

'What d'you bet Little Miss Gooseberry Eyes is setting to marry our Josh?' I asked Charles as he sat bent over his drawing board.

He looked around over his shoulder. 'Why should you care if she does marry him? You do not, I think, want him for yourself...now.' he ended meaningfully.

I flushed. 'Mind your own business.'

He shrugged, smiling to himself in a most irritating fashion. 'Oh, la, *la*!'

'Perhaps,' I returned nastily, 'she is more your type.'

'Not for *un million de francs Français* – and stop trying to annoy me. I am busy.'

I turned away, biting my lip. I supposed that living as we were in this rather bizarre *ménage au deux*, there had to be a definite line of demarcation between us and since his return from hospital Charles was all too clearly making it. Once back he had continued to spend part of his time in the office at Trewlyns, the rest presumably at his drawing board or wandering the beaches. At the cottage we had settled into a routine of shared living: taking turn and turn about at cooking the meals and keeping the house clean.

It was domesticity incarnate, marriage without the fun.

113

I still rode most weekends with Josh, Gooseberry eyes not being keen on that sort of thing. But the price of my ride was to listen to him eulogising the lady in the most fatuous tones. This was quite unlike the old Josh and made me feel both cross and protective of him, although, as I confided to Jenny it kept him getting randy with me again.

'She must be fantastic in bed, because she's bloody awful out of it!' Jenny observed one morning when we were in Ye Piskey Tearooms. 'I never imagined old Josh going for that clingy type, did you? I suppose he might get fed up with it in time.'

'Strangely enough and going by a few of Josh's typically indiscreet remarks, she isn't exactly a tigress in bed.' Gloomily I poked a fork into the café tablecloth. 'After me he's probably tickled pink with someone who'll lay supine and willing so that he can jump up and down on her being masterful, whilst she just gives out the occasional mouse-like shriek to spur him on.'

She giggled. 'Honestly, Caro, sometimes you're such a bitch.'

'I mean it. I think Josh has finally found the sort of woman he needs, although not necessarily the one he wants. One to hang on his every word, who thinks him wonderful, will let him get her knickers off whenever he's in the mood, fake her orgasms like mad and never talk back.' I chopped viciously at my aptly named rock cake. 'She'll probably have a brood of nice, uncomplicated compliant children, who are always clean and never ask awkward questions like: 'What's oral sex?' or 'Why is that doggie trying to give the other doggy a pick-a-back, mummy?' I've absolutely no doubt she'll look ravishing in a maternity smock, completely by-pass morning sickness and produce children as easily as shelling peas. What could be more perfect?'

I stood now, covertly watching Charles handling pencil and T Square with those long, sensitive hands, wondering if perhaps I should have settled for Josh and left being in love to others. At least I wouldn't then have found myself loving a man who so far had shown not the slightest interest in me as a woman.

All very well to have been so sure that I could put my feelings on ice. He was there to invade my every waking moment and each hour spent with him became progressively more painful, the need to be in his arms nearing an obsession, and keeping up my self-imposed front of smart-arse camaraderie more difficult by the day. My heart took up what was beginning to be a more or less permanent uneven thud so that I had to get up and walk out of the room under the pretence of making a pot of tea that I didn't want.

Leaning against the old stone sink I stared through the window at a dreary March landscape, wondering how best to get through the few remaining weeks until he was recovered enough to leave, and how I should endure my loss when he had gone.

A more immediate problem looming ever nearer was the dinner and dance I had booked at the Queens Hotel in Penzance, for what Grace had dubbed my Orphans of the Storm evening. Kate was bringing her current swain, a stocky, ginger-hair amiable young engineering student, and with Betty and Willi very much a couple, I'd realised much too late that I would inevitably find myself paired with Charles for most of the evening.

I hoped most fervently that I should be able to maintain the status quo in the unlikely event that he might wish to indulge in a spot of dancing cheek-to-cheek.

* * * * *

Never the less I dressed with care for the evening, scouring my far from extensive wardrobe for a suitable garment. Discarding the backless and very sexy red gown from my late adolescent vamping days that left nothing to the imagination, and tossing aside a little number in black chiffon which left rather too much, I finally chose the full-length jade green silk that clung very satisfactorily to the curves and sported a neckline plunging more-or-less just this side of decent.

Fortified by the knowledge that at the very least I would show up with all flags flying, even if no one wanted to engage me in combat, I gave a last glance in the mirror before sallying forth with mixed feelings of pleasure and dread.

* * * * *

'I think I could manage at least one dance, if Mam'zelle would do me the honour.'

The dark eyes were half-teasing, half-inviting; I dithered, tempted for a moment to plead exhaustion after a fast whirl around the floor with an energetic Willi who, duty done, had now gathered Betty into his arms for a slow smooching waltz. Charles raised his brows at my hesitation. 'You have that 'no' look on your face!'

'Not at all, I was just wondering if I shall stay the course after all that food.'

'Anyone who could do as you in the storm can manage a dance

with a wounded hero.' He put out a hand, drawing me to my feet. 'See, it is easy: I hold you like this; you put your hand in mine...so, and now we dance.'

Suddenly tired of the painful pretence of the last weeks I gave up, gave in and let myself relax in his arms. Just for now, just for tonight in this most public and anonymous place, I would lower my guard and have myself an evening to remember.

He was, I quickly discovered, a wonderful dancer, obviously finding his battered body no barrier to dancing if not cheek-to-cheek, at least head to head. As there was nothing whatsoever that I could do to change my feelings at this late stage I let myself go with the music, dancing as I'd not danced since that last night with Stefan; knowing that with anyone else but Charles I would have dreamed myself back to that dingy Air Force mess.

I passed the entire evening high as a kite, able to laugh and talk with my companions, drink rather too much and even manage a dance or two with the other young men without returning completely to earth; thankful beyond measure that Willi, who did not drink would be driving us home.

Such a mundane task, I was sure, would have been beyond me, even without the wine.

* * * * *

It was well past midnight when Willi left us at the door. Charles went straight into the kitchen to make coffee whilst I checked the sitting room fire. Shivering I crossed the room to throw more a few small tinder dry logs on the glowing embers then stood before the flames, remembering how it had felt to be held in Charles' arms.

The room was very still. I could hear him moving about in the kitchen, the sound of the tap being turned and water running. I stared at my reflection in the oval mirror above the mantle. 'Are you still there?' I whispered. I strained my ears but the only sound breaking the silence now was the measured ticking of the clock.

Cautiously I tested my feelings. Did I feel sad that my dream lover was gone? I examined my face for signs of grief or pain, but the past few hours were too warm, too clear in my mind for me to feel more than a tender, rather sad peace. I sighed and turned away from trying to look into my soul. That was it, then; Stefan was gone at last, but perhaps in some way his presence was, and always would be there; that he would as my father had said, still walk beside me.

I said 'Goodbye' aloud then dreamily, crossing my arms, hands hugging my shoulders, I did a little waltz around the room, gathering the memories of the evening; keeping them close. With Stefan gone and Charles a million miles away from me in spirit they would have to last a long time.

'You should put up your feet.' Charles entered quietly, catching me in mid-whirl. He slid the tray with our coffee onto the low table. 'Mine are aching, and I was not dancing all evening in those so elegant shoes.'

Embarrassed, I sat down quickly on the sofa. 'Females get used to that sort of agony; after a time it ceases even to hurt.' I kicked off the offending items, stretching out and propping my feet against the sagging end of the couch to gaze at my toes, examining the ladders in each foot and trying desperately for a light-hearted, amused tone. 'That's another pair of nylons gone for a Burton!'

'But worth it, I hope?'

'Oh, yes,' I took my cup, nursing it in both hands, still hopelessly caught up in the rosy glow of the evening. 'It was that all right!'

It must have been a full minute before I became aware that he was still standing over me, his own drink untouched. I looked up to find him gazing down on me and felt the breath leave my body with an almost audible *whoosh*.

He looked so incredibly handsome and powerful and sexy that a bolt of pure lust shot through me with the speed of a bullet. But he made no move, only continued to watch me, his eyes giving nothing away. Suddenly conscious that he might think my position on the couch was an open and possibly unwelcome invitation, I blushed scarlet and made to sit up.

Silently he shook his head. Taking my cup he returned it to the table, then seating himself beside me pushed both hands into my hair and brought his mouth down onto mine in a kiss that was both gently exploratory but unquestionably the prelude to something much more earthy and demanding. A long snake of heat crawled up my belly, desire swamped me again like a warm wave and I slipped my hands behind his neck and let myself sink.

Still keeping his mouth on mine he slid the straps of my dress from my shoulders and pressing me back into the cushions his hand found my breast, setting every nerve end jangling and shock waves racing through to my very toes. In the split second between surprise and total surrender came the thought that I had been absolutely right about that mouth...and that Josh and Jenny couldn't have been more wrong about everything else.

All the pent-up emotions and desires of these last painful weeks were released in a totally unashamed response to the seeking mouth and knowledgeable hands. When eventual shortage of breath forced us to stop, I was as much at a loss for words as I had been at fourteen, when the art master had made a pass at me in the paint cupboard.

Why, and after all this time?

He stroked my hair with an unsteady hand. 'Ah, but I have wanted almost five months to do that!'

'Then what kept you?'

He began to laugh. 'Only you could make such an answer – Caro, *why* have you made it so difficult; always making the jokes so that I do not know how you are feeling?'

'Well, you've not exactly been very forthcoming yourself,' I hedged and felt my heart plummet as he sat back from me the laughter fading, his face suddenly serious. There was the most awful silence. I propped myself up on one elbow, scarcely daring to breathe. Surely, I thought with an involuntary shiver, I'm not about to hear that what just happened was as good as it was going to get; even worse, that it had been a momentary aberration and there really was a boy friend around somewhere.

'I had – have, a reason but I fear you may be angry with what I must tell you.' He took my hand to sit gazing down at it before looking up again with steady eyes.

'Charles,' my voice wavered. 'You can't do what you have just done then stop to chat about your reasons for not doing it before!'

'But I am afraid I must. I have not been honest with you.' He hunched his shoulders. 'Oh, I have not told lies, just not quite told the truth. I wanted so much to make love to you, but Caroline, I have no right to do these things. I am married!'

'Oh, my *God*,' I was weak with relief. 'Is that all?'

A whole host of emotions chased across his face: incredulity, amazement, relief, 'But...what could be worse?'

'You'd be surprised – no –' I held up a hand, 'don't, for pity's sake ask me now; I'll tell you one day when I know you better; much better. All you need to know is that I love you; have done for weeks but I thought this was all a platonic thing between you and me – '

'*Pfft*! Between a Frenchman and a woman there is no such thing.'

'Then just kiss me again and convince me, damn you!'

'But if I do so I shall not stop and shall want to do more than kiss.'

118

I glanced down to where my dress nestled in folds around my waist. 'I thought you already had.'

'But not as much as I wish.' He leaned forward to lift the straps of my dress back into place then held my shoulders with both hands. 'I want you, Caro; I want you now, but when you hear what I have to say you may not want me.' I made to interrupt, but he shook his head again. 'No; you will listen Caro, not interrupting or saying no, no, this does not matter. You will promise?'

I found this ability to step back from such a powerful emotion as he had just unleashed in us both very disconcerting. It spoke either of a formidable self-control or something quite different. But I smiled, pushing aside the niggling remembrance of Elizabeth's warning. Reaching for his hand I said. 'You have my word; but please, may I ask questions when I need?'

He looked at me gravely. 'Oh, certainly questions.'

'May I ask one now?'

He nodded.

'Does Paul know you are married?'

'Yes. We have talked of it...a long time ago, when I was staying with him.'

'I see.'

So that had been the meaning of his look when he left me at Charles's bedside in the hospital: reminding me that I'd promised to examine carefully both my own motives and those of any future man who came into my life before making another rash leap into another bed. I couldn't, he had said sternly but reasonably, continue to hop into bed how and when the mood took me, or simply because someone asked at the right moment...but this was different. This was Charles.

'You are wishing this had not happened?' his voice cut across my thoughts, and I shook my head.

'No, never that.'

He put his hand out to touch my cheek. 'Then of what are you thinking?'

But I wasn't yet ready to tell him that, so just smiled again and said, 'That one kiss, even one that lasted so long, isn't enough to keep me quiet for an unspecified length of time.'

'You are a bad girl, Caroline Penrose!'

As his mouth again found mine I slid my hands under his jacket, holding him to me for a long minute before he broke away and sat back to lay a finger across my lips.

'Enough. Remember...until I finish; only the questions!'

119

Part 2

9

'As once I told you, Architecture was my profession.' He held my hand, every now and then turning it between his own and speaking slowly. 'At the war's beginning I was living and working in Paris, sharing a small house with Joseph Kremmer, an old school friend who was then teaching at the *Lycée d'Art*. The Army seemed in no great hurry for my services. I had been ill with pleurisy the past winter and my lungs were still not strong, so I was sent back after my medical to wait for a few months. Joseph also was rejected due to a lame foot from an accident in boyhood, so I stayed on with him in Paris until I passed the army medical and was able to join-up.

'Joseph promised to stay and see that the house and my belongings, save my Leica camera that I took with me, were kept safe until after the war. I can see him now; so cheerful, waving me goodbye at the station. He was a Jew and I heard they took him to Belsen. I never saw him again.

'At this time my mother was unwell and I was granted a week to travel to my home in Carentan, after which I was to join a unit of Infantry stationed at St Malo.

'Everywhere was chaos. The trains were very full and disorganised, although the troops took precedence and I was in uniform, it was two days before I reached my mother's side. My Uncle Claude, who lived nearby had written that he was worried about her; she had complained of pains in the chest and was spending most of her time in bed, with only old Marie-Therese to look after her. None of this sounded at all like my mother and I grew increasingly anxious at every delay. When I finally arrived home I could see immediately that she was very sick.'

He paused for a while, clasping my hand tightly. 'She died a few days later and I stayed with her until the end. By then the German advance had become a route. On the day of her funeral they began sweeping down towards Normandy with the allied armies in retreat before them. I wanted to make my way to find my unit and at least be able to stand and fight, but Marie-Therese was distraught, weeping and begging me to stay and I waited too long. When the Germans over-ran Normandy, I was trapped in Carentan with her, my Aunt and Uncle and my young cousin Lise.

'The morning that they marched into my town, Lise came running

123

to the house in a state of terror. They had told her father he must take down the Tricolour and fly the Swastika...everyone must, or they would be shot. Uncle Claude, who had fought them in the last war and still despised everything German, told the officer that if he wanted it down he could do it himself. They dragged him out of the house; my aunt went after him, and...they shot them both, in the square, before everyone. After this, what could I do? My Uncle's property was confiscated and I took Lise to live in my house, promising that I would look after her and see that she was kept safe.'

Getting to his feet he began to pace up and down. 'I didn't keep that promise. She was fourteen, I was twenty-four. I left her to old Marie-Therese who had little liking for or patience with such a young girl, whilst I joined my friends in writing and printing an underground newspaper. We carried out hare-brained and ill-thought out acts of minor sabotage...Oh, we were having a high old time, we young men; heroes we thought ourselves, until reprisals began in earnest and we realised for the first time what sort of people these Germans really were.'

I interrupted him then, his voice had roughened and there was a sheen of sweat on his forehead. 'Please stop for a moment. You're going too fast ...there's plenty of time.' I left the couch to fetch whisky and glasses from the kitchen, pouring us both a measure, making him drink before he went on with his story.

'People, any people...young, old, sick, were taken to be shot or hanged, singly or in groups, for every act of sabotage, however minor; it was terrible, sickening, we had to stop. Later, when the British agents began to arrive to arm and train us, a proper disciplined Resistance was formed, a Secret Army...planning and preparing for the time when we should be liberated.'

He paused again, turning his glass in his hands. 'Then at last I became useful.' He looked at me steadily, smiling a little, watching my face. 'They wanted me to infiltrate the submarine base nearby. I was a good photographer so I posing as a simpleton I pestered the garrison soldiers to let me take their photographs to send back home, and they did: leaning against their guns and trucks, so pleased to pose as our conquerors. Eventually, after I had found out all there was to know about the U Boats at harbour there I travelled along the Normandy coast on forged papers, compiling detailed maps of the German defences to send back to England...I had a code name.' His smile deepened. 'I think you may have come across it...it was Orion.'

'*Orion*!' For a few moments I was speechless, utterly dumbfounded. 'But I worked on dozens of your maps at Combined

Ops at Oxford…and you were there weren't you – you came late in 'forty-three and up until Overlord? I remember you and a British chap coded Nimrod escaped by crossing over the Pyrenees into Spain.'

'Yes, and were locked up in the Miranda Prison when we arrived.' He started to laugh 'All that way, with the Gestapo at our heels and they locked us up for weeks before sending us to this country like so much unwanted baggage!'

'That wasn't all, was it? You kept going back to France, to bring out other Resistance people the Gestapo were after. And there were other things…' I hesitated, remembering whispers linking him to more than one covert operation that had ended in assassination. 'You lied to Matthew and me, didn't you? You were with the SOE…I always wondered about the Army photographer story!'

'I am sorry. One must say something when people ask.'

I was silent again. Tapping into my memory, remembering the medals won…the *Legion d'Honneur*, the *Croix de Guerre,* the British Military Cross… he had been something of a legend to many of us. 'I don't know how you remembered me from Oxford because I only heard about you from others; I'm positive we never met. I wouldn't have forgotten you.'

'Your eyes I think were elsewhere, but that first time we met face to face here at Penmarrion I recognised you at once. For a short while my office was in a third floor room opposite your headquarters. I watched you sometimes. You would run down the steps…' He raised inquiring brows. 'There was a young man with fair hair, a pilot, and you would look at him so…' he put out his hands to cup my face and look down into my eyes, 'then I would think: "This so lucky young man!"'

My eyes misted, and I looked away, but he persisted, drawing my face back to his. 'Tell me about him, Caro, this man you loved so much and of whom you never speak.'

And suddenly, it wasn't difficult any more. The words came easily. I said, 'His name was Stefan Maric and he died above Sword beach on D Day…'

* * * * *

We sat for what seemed like hours on the old sofa, Charles's arms about me as I talked calmly and easily of Stefan and all the plans and the dreams that never were fulfilled, and he heard me out without interruption, or meaningless words of consolation, only when I had finished, said a quiet, 'Thank you' and laid his lips against my hair.

'I want you to be quite sure of something,' I said then, 'and understand that tonight, when I first danced with you, I knew without any shadow of doubt that I could let him go.'

And that was true. Now Stefan was with the past. Always to be loved and remembered, but no longer a needed presence.

But Charles...what had he been doing all that time ago, footloose in Oxford with all its parties and flirting and intrigues? Married or not, no man with those looks was likely to have gone without female company for long.

I asked him and he gave a crooked little smile. 'Ah, yes; there were a few enjoyable interludes...once there was someone with whom I walked and talked who could have been special to me. I think perhaps I loved her a little, but she was, like you, a woman for a lifetime, not an interlude of any kind. Then, because of my marriage I could not speak...and I felt that *her* heart was elsewhere.'

The clock on the wall gave its familiar *whirr* before striking four measured strokes. We looked at each other.

'So late already, and there is much still to say.'

I laughed at his alarmed expression.

'We have the rest of the night. Tomorrow is for sleeping...or something.'

He shook his head. 'Not so fast. Now I must go on and make my confession, which is by far the most difficult part.'

I reached to pull a rug from the end of the couch, wrapping it around us, making us snug in an intimate, warm cocoon. His arms around me felt safe and strong. Sleepily content and half-mesmerised by his voice I laid my head against his shoulder and let him finish, this time without interruption.

* * * * *

'One evening, I returned to the house very late, on the alert for any patrols, although the journey was made less hazardous because the armoured division which had occupied the town for so long was moving out, to be replaced with a division of infantry. That night there was the confusion of those going and those taking their place so that the patrols were less vigilant than was usual.

'When I reached the alley leading to our back door I saw Lise. She was leaning against the wall, shaking and sobbing and making a dreadful noise. I was alarmed and told her to get inside quickly; that it was dangerous to be out after curfew. I pushed her before me into the scullery. 'Stop that noise, you will wake Marie-Therese; what is it?' I

126

asked her, 'why do you cry?'

'At first she would not tell me then began to beat her hands together and cry even more hysterically, saying that she couldn't bear it and wanted to die.

'By now I was so angry that I seized her and shook and slapped her hard, thinking of the girls in our group, some little older than her, but so level-headed and brave. I shouted at her to stop snivelling and talking such rubbish and I shook her again harder until she cried out with pain.

'They are going...they are going tonight!' she spat the words at me. '*That* is why I wish I were dead. What can I do all alone and with a baby...you are no use. You have no time for me!' and she burst into another storm of weeping.

'I thought I had not heard right, but she repeated: 'What shall I do with a baby?' I demanded to know the father, and she screamed at me saying 'Why should *you* care? It is nothing to you. *I* am nothing to you!'

'Then I struck her and said terrible things, called her a dirty whore, a stupid bitch; that if she needed a roll that badly she should have found herself a Frenchman and not a filthy *boche* pig... ah, Caro,' his arms tightened around me, 'how could I have been so cruel; she was not yet sixteen and I should have cared for her, shown her that she was not alone, that she didn't need to couple with *Wehrmacht* swine in alleyways to feel wanted and loved.

'There was only one thing to be done. I couldn't let her be shamed and branded as a collaborator. The women of the town would have made her life hell, hounded her as the mother of a German bastard. I went to our priest, told him the child was mine and asked him to marry us as soon as possible, which he did on her sixteenth birthday. You must know I never went into her bed, never touched her, never even saw the child.

'When Lise was five months pregnant the Gestapo arrived in the town and set up headquarters in the square. To keep attention away from my house I went underground with the Resistance, continuing my liaison with your Intelligence right up until the time they raided the farm in which Nimrod and I were staying...the rest you know.

'I came to England to join the Free French Army but soon found myself with the French division of SOE. I returned to France several times, but for more important matters than to look for Lise. Only one letter had reached me from Marie-Therese before I escaped, to say Lise had a son, Dominic. Since then...' he hunched his shoulders, 'nothing. I have made many inquiries. Of the army, my embassy, the town authorities in Carentan, but with little result, although from them I discovered Marie-Therese had been killed in the bombardment, so that one more hope was gone. This is why I must return soon.

'Because without Lise, there can be no annulment to my marriage, and without that, I cannot, as I would wish, make you my wife.'

* * * * *

The fire had sunk to a red glow and room grown cold. I was stiff and cramped and leaned forward to throw more wood onto the fire. I longed to go straight into his arms again, but this time I needed to be sure. The silence deepened while he remained still and watchful, making no attempt to touch me. Really, I thought, we could sit here forever playing who goes first...

Eventually, I broke the silence.

'And to think Grace always warned me about married men. What are we to *do*?'

'What do you want to do?'

'I'm not sure, except that I want to make love with you so badly that it hurts.' I shook my head, laughing uncertainly. 'But you see, I've had the 'let's live for today, for tomorrow we die" kind of love, when it was difficult to think of anything *but* going to bed. I don't want to suffer that again with all its uncertainties – and then of course, there was Josh.'

I looked at him straight, trying not to flinch. 'I didn't love him; I only needed to have sex with someone. At first I told myself I wasn't using him, but I was. It was supposed to be one of those clever no-strings, no-commitment things, but he got serious and I hurt him. I'm ashamed of that.'

'Darling, you do not need to tell me these things.'

'Oh, but I do; it's only fair now that you have told me everything. For all I know you may like your women pure and unsullied, and whilst there may still be a few genuine virgins left in this corner of Cornwall, I'm very much afraid I don't happen to be one of them. Stefan and I were lovers because we couldn't help ourselves and because we knew time was short, but I let Josh take me to bed because I was lonely and I needed a man to make love to me. It was a rotten thing to do and in the end I didn't even finish it decently.'

'Caro, will you please stop telling me what I already know and come here!' I slid along the couch and he put his arm about me. 'You must stop blaming yourself for everything. Josh is not an angel and what you did or did not do is over now, so we must look at the facts, those so boring things that are most important for our future. I am a Catholic, although perhaps not such a good one. I was married according to the rites of my church and the only way for me to be free completely is for the marriage to be annulled. This may take a long time, but I want you to have no doubt about my love and my wish that we should be married as soon as it becomes possible.' He kissed the back of my neck. 'So, *ma chère* Caroline, I care nothing for anything that has gone before. Now I am asking...will you marry me?'

All the doubts and uncertainties fled away; it was as though a door had opened somewhere, ready for me to reach it and step through.

'Yes.' I took his hand, held it, turned it and kissed the palm. 'However long it takes.'

He smiled, closing his hand around mine, touching it to his lips. 'If you wish to wait; to make sure you want to be with me – to be my lover; then I too can wait until we become used to being as we are tonight, each getting to know the other better. For all that we have shared this house for these weeks, Caro, you do not yet know me well.'

'And do you know me?'

'I think perhaps quite well. Because you are always so honest your face is able to hide very little.'

'That's unfair because you're so good at hiding *your* thoughts; and Charles...' I leaned closer into the warmth of him. 'I really don't think I can wait, you know, even until we know each other better!'

I could feel against my shoulder the rumble of laughter in his chest.

'Perhaps I should be quite, quite sober and wide awake the next time that you remove my clothes. Tonight we are both a little drunk and sleepy, and in the morning you may say this was not such a good idea.'

'Well, right now it seems a bloody marvellous idea, so will you *please* stop being so stuffy and reasonable and make love to me again?'

'You are really quite a *mauvaise* young woman, aren't you?' His mouth folded into a disapproving line but the eyes teased, 'Do you always get your own way?'

'Quite often,'

'That will have to change...sometimes you may make me do as you wish, but not always, and probably not even very often. So for now if *I* say we should perhaps doze together here like good friends until the day is properly arrived, then go to see Matthew and Jenny

129

and the good, but so disapproving, Grace, that is how it will be.'

'Just as you say, Charles,' I acquiesced meekly, 'if you will do one more thing...'

He looked suspicious at my capitulation. 'Which is?'

'Kiss me again as you did hours ago!' I put my arms about his neck and after a moment's hesitation his mouth closed on mine. I kissed him back with a fierce bruising passion, feeling with a surge of joyous delight its immediate and unmistakable effect on this wonderful, devious, aggravating man, who seemed determined to show me who was boss.

'Ah, *Mon Dieu*,' breathing heavily he pulled back to eye me sternly. 'Where did you learn to do that?'

'Well, here and there...'

'Oh, la, *la*,' he groaned, 'now we are at the point of no return ...' Fiercely he pulled me down with him onto the couch and as the straps of my gown were once more thrust from my shoulders I began with shaking fingers to pull the ends of his tie and undo his shirt buttons, barely managing to ask from between chattering teeth: 'Your place or mine?'

'Holy Mother, what a question – neither; waiting is not possible now and that so comfortable rug must do!'

We knelt before the fire, undressing each other, trading garment for garment, but when he took my last piece of clothing and sent it flying to join the others on the floor I was still only halfway towards laying all of him bare.

'Why are you smiling like that?' he asked.

'Undressing a man when he's wearing evening dress – it's like playing pass the parcel – so many layers to unwrap.'

'This is a problem?' He stood, peeled off his socks, sent trousers and pants after my underwear then pulled me to the ground. 'Now,' he knelt above me. '*Now* we begin to know each other better!'

* * * * *

Much later, when we lay, our arms still tight about each other, he lifted his head, and kissing my eyes and throat asked huskily, 'Can you with your beautiful body really love so perfectly this imperfect man?'

I smiled and passed my hand gently over his scars and when he flinched and would have pulled away, I drew him closer. 'Don't,' I kissed his mouth. 'Don't ever ask that again; to me you are, and always will be without flaw.'

He sighed. 'Caro, *ma chère amour,* not so: I fear I am only human.'

I pulled the rug from the couch over us then burrowed my tired head into his shoulder. 'I know,' I murmured sleepily, 'but all the human bits I felt tonight were perfect. *Bravo, Charles, mon parfit gentil knight...*'

He shook with laughter and gently mimicked me. '*Bravo, Caro, ma belle dame sans merci!*'

* * * * *

In the late afternoon sunlight of a mild April day we walked slowly along the lane to Trewlyns. I was deliciously, languorously tired, loving the feel of his hand in mine, the body I now knew so well moving beside me, my face warm with the remembrance of the past hours. Nothing that had ever happened before had prepared me for the fulfilment found in the arms of this man. Truly he was the other half of my being. Now I was totally committed, completely sure of my love; which was just as well, for as Charles had pointed out in one of his saner and more lucid moments during our hours of lovemaking, given his unprepared state for my unladylike precipitation of events, the taking of any precautions had not been an option.

'I shall not be so foolish again until we are married' he promised, then grinned unrepentantly, 'but to be foolish just this once was perhaps permissible and we have to keep crossed the fingers that all will be well *n'est-ce pas?*'

'If my calculations are right we should be good and married long before any little de la Tours might arrive to spoil the fun.' I comforted him.

'But it will not always be fun – we shall sometimes fight, you know, and I shall annoy you and you will call me rude names...but always we shall love. Not just as we have in this bed, in which I am at last glad you allow me to rest my poor, abused back, but every hour of every day of every year that God will grant us together.'

* * * * *

It would be impossible now to keep from Matthew, Jenny and Grace that we were lovers. We had to face them not only with what I hoped would be the good news of our love, but also the bad news of Charles' marriage.

I was nervous about this meeting, sensing confrontation yet again with my father. Grace would say we were heading for hell-fire and damnation but she would eventually come around. Jenny I knew without doubt would be staunchly on our side, but about Matthew I wasn't so sure.

He had been understanding about Stefan and tolerant over my affair with Josh, but a third liaison so soon, particularly when it meant a serious involvement and commitment to someone with quite such a dubious past and shaky future, might bring forth a very different reaction.

Charles voiced his own doubts as we drew near to the farm. 'I think your father may not be so delighted as we might hope to find his only daughter has spent the night and most of this day in the arms of an unemployed, extremely battle-scarred and married Frenchman, with little to offer her but a tangled past and an uncertain future!'

At first it appeared that he might be right. Matthew looked at us long and hard when we first stepped into the living room, holding hands in what was most probably an obvious state of smug, post-coital euphoria.

'What brings you both here on a Sunday evening?' he inquired sardonically, 'Not looking for work, are you?'

Charles shook his head. 'No. That is the very last thing on this particular day.'

Seating himself on the couch, keeping my hand in his as I sat close by his side, he very clearly and concisely put Matthew, Jenny and Grace in the picture about our present relationship, and the reasons for uncertainty about our future.

I realised that once started Charles did not exactly beat about the bush.

When he'd finished, Matthew took his pipe from the mantle and begin to fill it in silence. I stole a glance at Grace, who was red-faced, knitting industriously and refusing to look at us. Jenny, perched on the arm of Matthew's chair was beaming and making encouraging faces. I couldn't help smirking and silently mouthing: '*See, smart arse...you were wrong!*' then blushed when I caught Charles watching me, a bemused inquiring look in his eyes.

His pipe going to his satisfaction, Matthew sat down, stretching his long legs toward the fire. 'It would seem, Charles that you have something of an – ah, serious problem. I don't need to ask, I suppose, if you have done everything possible to trace your wife?'

His voice was flat, non-committal, with the emphasis ever so slightly on the *have*.

My heart sank. He wasn't going to make it easy.

'I thought perhaps you knew me better than to ask that.' Charles was unruffled. 'But yes, as I have already told Caroline: I have written to the authorities in Carentan; badgered my Embassy; asked for help from the Army, but without success. Of course, had it not been for the storm I should by now be in France and pursuing the matter at first hand,' he smiled at me, 'but then without the storm I should not be here still, and such a happy man.'

'Yes? I'm glad you are happy, but it seems to me you've both gone from working colleagues and not particularly close friends to lovers in a remarkably short space of time.'

'"I didn't go looking for it...it was a bit of a runaway train!"' I quoted daringly.

'You can just stop that.' My father turned his attention sharply on me. 'Perhaps you'll enlighten us about what *you* plan to do whilst Charles here is chasing around France looking for a needle in a haystack?'

'Go with him of course and try to find Lise. What else would you expect? That's what you'd do in similar circumstances, isn't it?' I challenged, staring him out. For a few moments we battled silently then Jenny poked him impatiently in the back.

'For God's sake, Matthew stop acting the heavy father, it doesn't suit you – and really, Grace, what are you being so po-faced about?'

'And why shouldn't I, miss?'

I risked a grin at my father, who in turn gave me a wry, defeated smile. In Grace's eyes Jenny had obviously slipped into the gap left by my departure from this household. 'I never did approve of them sharing that cottage,' Grace continued, 'and now, when they're...' she flushed an even deeper red and began to knit even more furiously, 'when they're...'

'So ravingly larky and happy that you are thrilled to bits for them!' Jenny laughed and crossed the room to hug her, dislodging several hairpins and squashing the knitting. Grace tutted and bridled, but coaxed and teased by Jenny eventually managed a smile.

Still in heavy father mode Matthew stood suddenly and crossed to the kitchen, tossing over his shoulder, 'I suppose you think this calls for a celebration, though what exactly there is to celebrate, God only knows.'

'Gins all around,' Jenny followed him, giving Charles an outrageous wink in passing, and murmuring sotto voce: 'that was almost as good as putting one over on Big-Tits Bostock, wasn't it, Charlie boy?'

133

* * * * *

'I do hope,' said my father as he kissed me just before we left, 'that this is the last time I shall have to worry about the men in your life!'

'Positively the last; there is no room now for anyone else.'

'Thank the Lord for that. I've suffered enough.'

'Cheeky bugger,' muttered Jenny, 'at least she didn't like you, seduce an unsullied virgin...'

We could hear their laughter all the way to the gate.

* * * * *

'You do not know me well.' Charles had said.

Now when I shared his life and his bed I began to understand the truth of that statement. If not overtly moody, he was given to periods of varying lengths when he would work silently at his drawing board, or sit at the piano quietly playing Charlie Parker-type jazz. On occasions and if the weather was fine, he'd lean for an hour or more on the garden gate, chain-smoking and staring silently at the horizon. If at such times I spoke it would take a moment for him to come out of his reverie and return to the present. I began to feel as though he lived his life in two parts, one with me, the other in some unknown far-away place.

And his insomnia worried me. Although I'd had my share of sleepless nights, to share a bed with a man who seldom managed more than an hour or two of unbroken sleep, was as disturbing as living with someone with a mysterious illness.

I had known that he slept badly. Over the weeks we'd shared Tyndals I'd often heard him moving about in the small hours, sometimes hearing the piano played softly in the room below mine. Now I found that he seldom slept for more than a few hours each night, sometimes slipping quietly from our bed so that I woke alone at daybreak. At other times he might wake with a cry, or a sudden violent movement, startling me awake. When this happened he would whisper his apologies, stroking and soothing me back to sleep.

Once, waking in the deepest part of the night and finding him gone, I went quietly downstairs to discover him seated with elbows on the table, his hands covering his face, a glass of whisky and half-empty bottle before him.

There was something so private, so remote about the still figure that I turned soundlessly and made my way back to bed, to lie staring at the window almost until dawn. When he returned he slid carefully

134

in beside me and fell into a deep exhausted sleep until the alarm sounded, heralding another day.

'Have you always slept so little?' I asked one morning, after a particularly bad night when he was looking gaunt and ravaged for want of rest.

'No. Not always.'

'What are you dreaming about when you shout and wake me?'

'It is nothing.' his face was closed and blank. 'I am sorry I disturb you.'

It was as though he was holding me at arms' length and I was hurt. I wanted to question him: to ask why the hunger that drove him night after night into my arms wasn't sufficient. Why he had to go away from me and shut me out; why he didn't trust me enough to tell me the reason he needed to sit alone in the dead of night, with shoulders bowed and despair in every line of his body. Why sometimes he seemed more a stranger than a lover.

But I had already discovered that when Charles wanted to keep his own counsel, no power on earth would make him allow anyone, even me, to invade his private place.

* * * * *

'You worry too much.' Unexpectedly, he smiled at me one morning when I risked a rebuff by rather sarcastically congratulating him on sleeping better than usual. 'I can do without you also losing sleep worrying about *my* insomnia!'

'Well, it's not much of a compliment to me.' I looked at him over my coffee cup. 'After I've spent a considerable time and a great deal of physical exertion giving my all, I expect a chap to at least be tired enough to be zonked-out for longer than a couple of hours.'

'Perhaps *you* are the problem,' he mocked, 'such aching you cause my poor battered body to have.'

Later, as we walked to Tyndals I comforted myself with the thought that for the first time he'd responded positively to a reference about his sleeplessness. Perhaps in time I could breach that barrier as I already had another.

In the beginning, terribly self-conscious of the constant ugly reminder that his body was less than perfect, he had still flinched and drawn back if I touched his scars when we made love. But eventually he had allowed me to touch and kiss, then finally to massage and ease the tight skin and damaged muscles that sometimes made it difficult for him to even lie down without pain.

135

'Not too far down.' he would murmur, as on occasions he lay tense with pain after making love, while my hands moved gently and soothingly over his body, 'or very soon you may cause me to exert myself so that it will be necessary for you to do this all over again!'

And sometimes it was.

10

We left for France just after Easter, making the long crossing on the night ferry from Weymouth to St Malo. Until we were actually on board I hadn't been aware of how much I needed the break from Trewlyns and work. Leaning on the after-rail to watch the phosphorescence sparkling in our wake, Charles's arm reassuringly around me, I felt a great relaxation and release of tension.

'You are tired.' He kissed me gently. 'I'm sorry we must spend time in doing not such enjoyable things. The next time we make this journey, my darling, it shall be to Paris and we shall have no cares, and spend a great deal of money, and drink too much wine, and behave very badly in night clubs...you will like that?'

'I will like that very much indeed!'

It was strange to sleep alone again, even after such a short time. Curled up on the narrow bunk I lay awake, listening to the quiet thrum of the engines; feeling the ship lifting on the swell of a calm sea, aware of Charles pretending to sleep in the upper berth. But I was tired and eventually drifted off, waking at first light to find him already shaved and dressed, seated in a chair reading a book and looking as though he had been there most of the night.

'Hello, nice man.' I greeted sleepily, and he leaned over to kiss my cheek.

'You are like the dormouse, all curled up and drowsy. Would you like me to ring for a steward to fetch you some tea?'

'No, I think I'll try that peculiar looking shower in the corner there and wake myself up properly before we dock. How much time do I have?'

'About forty minutes; I think we will have our breakfast in France and not start today with the bacon and eggs!'

'I can't believe you're so wide awake,' yawning, I put my arms around his neck, breathing in the special, clean-skin morning smell of him. 'Did you sleep at all?'

'Enough.' his brow furrowed. 'I hope today we can find a car to hire without we do too much searching.'

I stood, lifting my arms for him to slide my nightdress over my head then still yawning, stepped into the shower and twiddled with the unfamiliar taps. A blast of cold water made me gasp and leap back into the cabin exclaiming crossly: 'God Almighty, Charles; have *you* tried this bloody thing?'

'Patience, patience,' he reached in a long arm, adjusting the taps and clicking his tongue reprovingly, 'such language, and so early in the day!' He returned to his chair. 'When we land I shall see if Arnaud is still at *Le Coq d'Or*... he knows, or always did know, where one could get anything in the town. I am sure he will find us some kind of transport.'

It wasn't the sort of shower to linger under. I stepped out, towelling my hair and padded over to the bunk. He let his eyes rove over my wet nakedness, and grinned. 'Very nice, such a pity to cover it with clothes, but hurry, *ma petite*...they will not allow you to disembark looking so!'

* * * * *

It was still very early when we left the ferry and walked up through the battered town, marvelling that even at this hour men were already hard at work rebuilding and restoring shattered buildings. Cement mixers roared, drills stuttered and hammers rang on stone; the sound of clattering machinery was everywhere, voices were raised above the din in shouted instructions, argument and laughter.

'No so peaceful as I remember,' Charles made a wry face, 'we should need the ear-plugs to stay here!'

The *Boulangerie* of course was open, even at such an hour. We bought a bag of warm crusty baguettes and bottled water, then sat to eat this early breakfast on top of the walls above the harbour, while we waited for the door of *Le Coq d'Or* to open.

Charles gestured toward the bar.

'That is where myself and Joseph would come when we were grown boys pretending to be men of the world; to spend a few days away from the prying eyes of our parents, who thought we were on fishing trips!'

I raised my brows.

'And what else did you do, apart from fish?'

'All manner of naughty things' His eyes sparkled. 'Arnaud's chambermaid seduced me in the laundry when I was just fifteen and she at least fifty! *Merde,* but I scarcely knew what was happening until it was all over... you see, I was so polite I didn't like to say no!' Laughing, he put his arm around my shoulders. 'I didn't have the sense to keep quiet about it but had to brag to Marie-Therese, who of course, gave me away. My mother took a stick to my manly backside and sent me to the priest for a scolding. It was quite some time before

I tried again.'

I edged him on to tell more, watching his face liven as he recounted stories of his boyhood and youth, the friends he had, the games played and the 'naughty things' he and Joseph had done. Eventually the door of the bar opened and a tall, immensely stout figure emerged and began to open the shutters. Charles rose to his feet. 'It is Arnaud. He is still here. Come.' he pulled me to my feet. 'Now we shall have some trouble to stay sober for the rest of the day!'

As we neared the bar, the proprietor saw us and advanced with loud voluble cries and outstretched hands. 'English, Arnaud, if you please,' begged Charles. 'Mademoiselle knows only the rude words of our language!'

'My friend...but of course – and is it you back and in one whole piece? Never did I expect to see you again. They said the Gestapo captured you years ago, but here you are, come to see Arnaud...and with a most beautiful lady!' and he swooped to take my hand, raising it to his lips, taking his time before he let go.

'Watch him!' Charles warned as we were ushered inside. 'He is a big, bad wolf!'

We spent an hour or more in the bar, making short work of plates of most delicious prawns and lobster claws washed down with glasses of Dubonnet, which did nothing to settle my early morning stomach. To my relief and for my benefit, Arnaud continued to converse in his fluent, if fractured, English. He also patted my knee a great deal with a warm hand and flirted outrageously with his eyes.

The fighting for Carentan, he said, had been fierce and the casualties terrible; Charles would not know the town, it was devastated, although work was in progress to rebuild it. We should go to *l'hôtel de ville* and see for ourselves the records; although the clerks were overworked and would have little time to attend us with so many inquiring about friends and relatives after the long years of Occupation. People had just disappeared, records had been lost, and the retreating Germans in no mood to be gentle with any fleeing refugees who might be blocking the roads. He shrugged, spreading his hands.

We hadn't expected good news, but I think it was only then that I began to comprehend the enormity of our task.

Before we left home Charles had telephoned to his cousin Alain in Orléans, who had been less than encouraging: If Lise and her child had died on the roadside and the tide of war rolled over them, how, he had demanded, would anyone know? There must have been hundreds of such unrecorded deaths.

Now here was Arnaud telling us much the same thing. It was a depressing beginning. But he arranged a car for us; a battered Citroën so small that by the time our cases were loaded there was scarcely room for us to squeeze inside. With Charles directing, I drove the rattling, coughing heap of rusting metal to Dinan, where we had coffee, then across to Avranches where we stopped for and upset the *Patrone* by refusing the wine list. Several glasses of Dubonnet for breakfast, Charles observed, went a long way and he didn't intend that we should go looking for trouble.

We reached Carentan in late afternoon. He drew in a sharp breath as we drove through streets familiar to him since boyhood but now so laid waste by the fighting that he shook his head in bewilderment. 'Everything looks alike...just rubble. No, wait! There was the school, now turn right here where they are re-building those houses by the church. My house is around that corner.'

Only the Church of Notre Dame stood relatively undamaged and majestic, rising above the surrounding rubble and the roofs of new buildings. Close by the right hand side of the church we found what was left of his house: two partial walls and a mound of brick and wood.

He left the car to stand with hands in pockets, staring in sad disbelief.

'It was always so smart,' he said eventually. 'With the stone white, the shutters and doors painted green. Three stories, and up under the gable was my room. Marie-Therese below at the back, where she could hear any cats in the garden and empty her water jug – and worse – over them...she hated cats. At the front, below mine, my mother's room: over on this side a little tower room made ready for when Lise's baby would be born.' Abruptly he turned away. 'There is nothing to be gained here. We must try the town hall.'

We poured over documents and the lists of names for the killed, injured and missing until the office closed, finding only Charles's marriage certificate, the registration of birth for the child Dominic, and Marie-Therese's death certificate.

My heart ached for him as we stood in the doorway of the hall, sheltering from a sudden rainstorm and wondering what to do next. It was too late that day to begin our plan to travel over the possible routes Lise might have taken in her attempt to reach Alain in Orléans. By now we were tired and hungry and stopped at a small bar on the outskirts of the town to make a supper of bread and cheese, washed down with rough red wine.

'If we find somewhere to sleep tonight, tomorrow morning early I

140

shall go first to the church and if Father Pierre is still there, see if he knows anything of Lise. If he cannot help we must search the town for anyone else I knew and try to find which route she may have taken.' Charles rubbed a weary hand over his face. 'She may have asked help of Fabrice, or Lucien, who were in my group and they might have passed her along through the underground...I know they were still here in 'forty-four when she would have left, because I was to link up with them after the landings.'

'Perhaps they can help. Where do they live?'

His mouth twisted bitterly. 'Both are dead...Fabrice slowly at the hands of the Gestapo, Lucien more fortunate in being hanged by the *Wehrmacht.*'

Instinct told me Charles needed to leave Carentan and its memories behind that night, and when we had eaten we drove west until we found a room over a bar a mile or so from the equally devastated town of St Lô. It was clean and comfortable and after a supper of thick soup and bread we were grateful to wash in soft water from the courtyard well before climbing onto the vast bed that almost filled the small room, too tired to make love, or even talk.

I lay between the coarse sheets with my arms about him, my hands smoothing his back, rejoicing that for once he had fallen quickly into a deep, exhausted sleep. I felt myself swept by powerful, but gentle emotions. Of love and pity and possession, a deep, stirring maternal protectiveness, as though he were a beloved child who had been hurt then sought comfort with his face against the warmth of my breast. Fighting sleep, not wanting to give him up to the night, I lay for hours, holding him closely to me, filled, not with desire, but with an overwhelming tenderness that was almost pain.

I vowed that night that no matter what happened, or how hard the road we must travel, I would never leave his side. Never let him down in any way; never give up until we had done the thing we set out to do. Little knowing then just how hard the road would be or how close I would come to breaking that vow.

* * * * *

'I am going to Mass then afterward will see the priest.' Charles bent almost double before the wall mirror, knotting his tie and smoothing down his hair.

'If you'll move over and let a girl powder her nose I'll come with you,'

Giving up his place at the glass he grinned wickedly. 'Are you sure that you will manage? Your French is so bad that I can't imagine your Latin will be any better.'

'You forget I had years of Paul's particular brand of High Church goings-on. Yours can't be all that much different. I dare say I shall recognise where to bob up and down!'

'Very well, then...but you will behave and not give me any of your looks.'

'Certainly not; I shall be a model of moral rectitude.'

* * * * *

'Father Pierre,' he said, as we neared the town, 'had me on my knees for half an hour back in 'forty-two, praying for forgiveness for getting Lise pregnant.'

'Sounds a bit much to me, even if you had...which you hadn't!'

He laughed at my indignation. 'But I think quite reasonable, given he didn't know the truth and that I was old enough to know better.'

He was so relaxed this morning after his long sleep. I crossed my fingers, hoping the mood would stay with him through what would almost certainly be a trying and tiring day. We were only at the very beginning and privately I doubted that even I would be able to end each succeeding day with hope, should they be as bleak and discouraging as the one just passed.

'I'll wait in the car.' I offered as the Mass over we stood on the pavement outside the church. 'Better you don't appear with a strange doxy on your arm while you inquire about the whereabouts of your wife.'

'*Ma chère*, you think of everything.'

'Don't I just.' I straightened his tie. 'Now off you go; mind your P's and Q's and don't forget to say 'thank you' nicely before you leave.'

He made a face and turned back into the church, leaving me to settle into the car and pretend to read a book, my thoughts with him, and not on the printed page.

It was almost an hour before he returned, coming briskly down the steps, opening the door and ducking into the car, letting out his breath in a sigh of relief. 'One more thing out of the way!' he leaned back, closing his eyes. 'Take me somewhere and find me a drink, please, *ma chère Caro*. Then we will get out our maps.' He opened his eyes at my involuntary squeak of excitement. 'No, I do not know where she is, but I know how she left and with whom, and where she was headed, but first, that drink.'

142

'All right: you've got your drink, now tell me what happened.' I leaned my elbows on the table, giving him a mean look. 'You were gone so long I thought you'd taken the veil.'

'That is for nuns, darling.'

'Well, whatever…just get on with it.'

We were back in the little bar of the previous day, a bottle of wine between us, our map spread on the table. I reflected that by the time we had found Lise, or not as the case may be, we should most likely both have become raging alcoholics.

'First, she tried to leave the child with Marie-Therese and go on her own, but the old lady would have none of that, so she and the boy left with Gerard Duval, one of the younger ones in the group. He wanted to join with the Americans along the Normandy coast.' Charles hunched over the map, tracing a route with his pencil. 'He did not manage it, of course; it was too dangerous. He returned later and eventually went to live with his uncle in the south. He told Father Pierre that he had taken them as far as St-Lô before leaving them with two Resistance women from another group. He didn't know who they were, only that they all planned to leave by the following day. Lise was provided with forged papers identifying her as a nurse travelling to the hospital at Orléans and taking the boy for treatment. All were to travel by horse and cart openly and in daylight, keeping to the main roads. That is the last Father Pierre heard of her.'

'So we do at least know the roads she would have been travelling.' This sounded a bit more promising.

'Ye-es…but,' his mouth turned down, 'obviously all the main roads were filled with troops and equipment being rushed to back up the retreating *Wehrmacht*. So, assuming they left St Lô before the British reached the town they must have cut off across country, possibly on foot and sticking to the small towns and villages. Perhaps just sleeping and hiding in barns and outhouses during the day and travelling by night, keeping away from anywhere there may have been any large movements of troops.'

'Hell's teeth!' I propped my face on both hands, staring into his eyes, which were, I thought, rather more cheerful than the occasion warranted. 'It'll be like looking for a needle in a whole field of haystacks.'

'No, no, not so difficult: see, if we trace a line all along the route they should have taken from St-Lô to Orléans, then draw a grid, say,

143

ten to fifteen kilometres either side of it we shall then work through each section, one at a time. It will take time and patience, but we have a chance.'

'There must be hundreds of small villages, not to mention isolated houses and farms.' I didn't want to dampen his hopes, but it all looked pretty dodgy to me.

'Well, we must try.' He began to fold the map. 'Father Pierre says that if she is found and I bring her straight to him, he will help us apply for the annulment.' He turned his mouth down again. 'He was not, I think, very pleased to hear the truth about our marriage, and was very severe with me, but is at least willing to help. I hope Lise if we find her will be ready to co-operate and not cause us any further problem.'

* * * * *

Returning to the bar at St-Lô later that day we spent a long time after our evening meal planning our route, drawing up a meticulous grid and marking each area to be searched with a code letter. Stopping at one point to laugh together when we realised we had dropped back into our wartime role of mapmakers; planning the whole thing as though it were a military operation.

'We're good, you know.' I looked with satisfaction at our handiwork as he emptied the last of the wine into his glass. 'It just shows what can be done by harnessing the combined brains of Britain and France...if you're as brilliant as an architect we should soon be rolling in dough.'

'Dough? What is dough?'

'Spondulicks...bread, cash, money...you know; the stuff we buy food with.'

'Oh, *that*.' He laughed. 'I am not short of the dough!'

'I had noticed.' I looked at him curiously. 'D'you realise we've never even discussed how we pay for all this jaunting around.'

He looked surprised. 'But we do not need. My mother was no fool. She transferred some cash and all her bonds to Switzerland in nineteen thirty-eight. We shall never starve.'

If I had occasionally wondered where his money came from I'd just presumed he must have a whopping great Army pension. Now I pursed my lips primly and eyed him with assumed disapproval. 'Dear me; I hope that doesn't mean I shall have a moneyed lay-about for a husband. I don't think I should at all care for that.'

He laughed. 'But not a chance. I have the bread and the butter but

144

must earn the meat to put between the slices! In June I go to London and meet with some very rich gentlemen to see if I am good enough to design a Country Club for them. I have been working on plans for some time.' He smirked infuriatingly at my startled expression. 'You see, I do not only play jazz in the night ... sometimes I work then as well. I am most industrious!'

'Also very underhand and secretive and quite disgustingly smug,' I narrowed my eyes at him, 'and don't think you're jaunting off to the Sinful City on your own. I'll be coming with you.' I wasn't having him wandering around Soho on his tod.

'Would I dare to leave you behind with the so sexy M'sieur Milton close at hand?' Beneath the table his hand caressed my knee.

'Hmm, you said you wouldn't bring that subject up again.'

He looked at me through half closed eyes. 'I was jealous; I still am. I could have murdered him – and you – several times over.'

I said provocatively, 'Well, you had your chance and missed it. If you hadn't spent so long doing your noble bit I'd probably have been in bed with you long before Josh had a chance to get his leg over!.

He leaned forward and said softly, '*Vous salope!* Come upstairs and say that again.' His hand gripped my knee hard. I fluttered my eyelashes.

'Flatterer; how can I refuse?'

* * * * *

Day two was much like day one. We returned to Carentan and Charles hunted through the town in search of anyone who might add to the information the priest had given him. A few people remembered Lise's departure and confirmed her plans to contact the cousin Alain and his wife in Rouen, but added nothing to what we already had learned. Later we went again to the bar near St-Lô, where we had reserved a room for another night to work at fine-honing our plans; carefully charting the route and calculating how much ground we could cover in a day. By the time we had finished supper and a second bottle of wine and folded the map away, we were both tired and bleary-eyed and glad to climb the rickety staircase to our room.

'Did we really drink both bottles between us?' asked Charles, bringing his face close to the mirror and holding his eyes open with his fingers

I gave a sarcastic snort. 'No, *you* managed the second one practically single-handed.'

'Am I becoming a drunken pig?' He looked at me solemnly.

145

'Not yet.' I patted the bed invitingly. 'Better come and sleep it off.'

He sighed and sat on the edge of the bed trailing his hand slowly from my collarbone to my feet and back again. 'Sometime I should like to make babies as well as love.'

'Yes, but not tonight.'

'No, not tonight, because I am too tired and it would be too soon and later making love would be spoilt by big cries and small feet to come and interrupt ...and no more before the fire on winter afternoons.'

'Or down in the cove in summer.'

'And it would be only for the night time and in bed.'

'With the lights out,' I giggled, 'and I *must* have a flannel nightdress!'

'Yes, certainly flannel, and to make love perhaps only on Saturday nights?'

'Of course, and strictly missionary and only if I don't have a headache.'

He looked at me with sad eyes. 'Surely you would not do that to me?'

'No, darling, I would *not* do that you''

He rolled into bed with a groan and pulled the sheet over his head. 'Do not expect a repeat of last night, Caro – *je tombe de fatigue; je n'en peux plus!'*

I snuggled against his back. 'Me too,' I agreed, 'whatever it means.'

11

Early the next morning we began our search in a mood of light-hearted optimism that soon faded in the face of the enormity of the task before us. As the day lengthened and dusk began to fall, I thought privately that we must have been completely mad to begin it at all.

We were already exhausted from the miles covered in the uncomfortable car; from jumping in and out at every small village and remote farm; from asking the same questions and receiving the same answers.

'Does anyone know any members of the Resistance who would have helped a young woman and child get to Orléans – anyone who might have sheltered them?' Charles would enquire and there would be the Gallic shrug I was beginning to know so well. No, no one remembered a young girl and child. Hands would be spread and heads shaken.

'The Resistance here, *m'sieur*, were too busy harassing the enemy…'

'There were so many trying to escape the fighting *m'sieur* – and so many perished…'

'*M'sieur* could look over by those trees – that is where we buried some, but not all the names are there…'

'*M'sieur* may look in the churchyard, but our records are few…'

And so it went on.

Once we went wildly off our planned course, following directions from a toothless old sage in some village bar who swore before all the saints that the lady we sought had lived in Alençon since nineteen forty-four; was now married to a rich farmer and again a mother. After we had finally tracked down a very puzzled thirty-year old with a ten-year old son it was with great difficulty that I restrained Charles from driving straight back to throttle the toothless old sage. The fact that I couldn't help finding it funny didn't exactly improve matters and by the time we returned to our original route we were barely on speaking terms.

We found a hotel for the night. I had a crashing headache and he was grey with fatigue and pain. We picked at our meal, Charles turning with a shudder from the wine. There was nothing more to do than go to bed and lie restless under the covers.

Full of remorse now for being unable to hide my laughter, even if it had been slightly hysterical, I fretted, my head spinning; torturing myself with the thought that he might be unable to stand the sheer physical strain of it and if he were to fall ill, then where would we be?

Stranded in the middle of bloody France, I thought, that's where: up the creek without a frigging paddle.

'Caro, I can hear you thinking. Stop it!' he spoke suddenly out of the darkness.

I jumped. 'Don't *do* that!'

'Then stop worrying about me: I shall not fall in pieces.'

I snapped on the bedside lamp. 'Since when did you have the second sight?'

'I do not need it. You always worry about me at the first moment you see me walk like the old man. Better stop, for I shall be walking so for a long time.'

I turned off the light and lay down again, my head on his shoulder. 'I do no such thing.'

'Do not argue with me. Sleep, tomorrow we rest. There is no hurry and we both shall need all our strength before we are through.'

But we were driven, and after a morning when we rose late, took our time over breakfast and pretended that we were enjoying the respite, we set off once more, stopping only for bread and cheese at noon before moving on our carefully planned route.

* * * * *

Ten days later we were less than five miles from Orléans. It was raining again, long, driven sheets that streamed down the windows in an endless cascade as we sat in a village bar over cups of black coffee and reviewed our progress so far.

'Well, we've now been over the one half of our grid; if you want to see your cousin Alain we could do that today, then start back tomorrow and begin trawling the other side.' I injected a note of optimism into my voice. 'After all, we've a lot more ground to cover yet. Anything could happen any day.'

He frowned. 'She wouldn't have got so far without contacting Alain, and he swore to me that he knew nothing of her.'

'If you're right about her travelling across country we've a chance still of picking up the trail.' I stared into space, trying to imagine what I would have done in the circumstance in which Lise had found herself. 'You must be right. You know how the Resistance women would have coped, no matter how difficult the situation may have become. She must have stayed with them; she couldn't have got through the fighting without their help, could she?'

He shrugged. "She was very young and not so bright. She may have decided at some point to stay in a safe place and not bother to go so far as Orléans – or maybe something happened to the other women and she thought she could make it on her own. Only God knows what she may have done.'

'Did she ever talk about going away anywhere? I mean, before you left? Anyone else she might have gone to?'

He gave a short laugh. 'Oh, she was full of such ideas…going to Paris, to America, being a film-star…'

Hardly the most responsible type to be clarting around a war zone with a small child on tow, I thought gloomily. Surely the sensible thing would have been to seek shelter in some isolated farm where they might have been relatively safe, then finish the journey when the fighting was over. I was getting a headache trying to imagine what she might have done. But it was no use attempting to put myself in her shoes. Although no heroine, I liked to think that even at eighteen I would have stayed put, preferably with a machine gun and tried a spot of target practice on the enemy. I most certainly would not have gone haring off across France in some cock-eyed attempt to reach cousin Alain in Orléans. Sod the girl I thought sourly, she couldn't have caused more trouble if she'd won medals for trying.

When I met Alain later that day I felt she might have saved herself the journey, for if she was hoping for help from him she'd have been doomed to disappointment; I doubted if I would even have crossed the road to reach him.

He was a suave, urbane type to whom I took an instant dislike, his wife a pencil-thin peroxide blonde sporting a great deal of fashionably sculpted hair and the highly predictable name of Hortense. Both were adamant that they had neither seen nor heard from Lise; didn't even know she'd been trying to reach them until Charles had written from hospital in England to inquire after her.

'Are you sure that no one from the Resistance tried to contact you about that time?' Charles persisted.

Alain gave an indifferent shrug. 'Positively not, I had no wish to die before my time at the end of a rope and had no dealings with such people. Perhaps, Charles, had you stayed and kept *your* nose clean you would not now be scouring France for your wife and child.'

Charles looked pointedly around at the large, expensively furnished room in which we were seated. 'Really?' his mouth set in a thin, hard line. 'I'm sure you are right, but for some of us, collaboration was not an option.'

The self-satisfied pair before him didn't offer so much as blush between them. Hortense gave a brittle smile. 'For us dear cousin, it was the *only* option. Herr Oberführer Meikel made his headquarters here, allowing us to retain some rooms for ourselves in return for our co-operation.'

'Which I'm sure you both gave very quickly!' Abruptly Charles rose to his feet, observing ironically: 'Herr Oberführer at Carentan had Lise's parents shot when he didn't immediately get theirs.' He gave a stiff bow. 'We shall not trouble you again.'

'*Salaud*!' He spat as he slammed the door behind us. '*Salope*!' Leaning his shoulder against the wall he kicked back viciously at a large stone effigy of a cat, neatly removing its head. '*Bâtard* – for such scum good men died!'

'Steady on.' I said soothingly, 'Come away before you wreck anything else.' I had never seen him lose his temper and was glad all that pent-up fury was directed at his cousins and not me. I held out my hand and after a moment's hesitation, he took it and began to walk rapidly away from the house, practically dragging me in his wake.

'I am sorry.'

'Well you don't sound it...or look it. That poor bloody cat hadn't done a thing to deserve you kicking its head off like that.'

Reluctantly, he began to smile and slowed his angry stride, giving my hand a reassuring squeeze. 'You are right. It was childish. I am very sorry.'

'All right, but remember you're a big boy now. If I'd done anything that childish when I was a *child* Matthew would have sorted me out pretty damned quick.'

'And rightly so: did you ever?'

'Certainly not, I was a very sweet little girl.'

'Humn.' he looked cynical, 'then how you have changed. Caro, your language is *a terrible...atroce.*'

'I know,' I said cheerfully, 'but I'd have to go a long way to beat yours when you were being so heroic during the storm.'

'*Touché,*' smiling, he tucked my arm in his, 'now, I shall not be bad-tempered any more, I promise, so shall we eat, and drink and forget all this searching for today? Tomorrow is Sunday and we shall go to Mass, then rest and pretend we are really on holiday.'

* * * * *

We seemed to be spending an inordinate amount of our free time in bars. After leaving Orléans Charles suggested that we carry out our search in a less frantic fashion, and in France bars appeared to be the places one stopped for rest and refreshment.

By this time I had grown used to coffee with cognac in the mornings, Pernod in the afternoons and wine at absolutely anytime. During the war the Poles at a Fighter Station near our unit had been credited with being able to drink anyone in the mess under the table. After two weeks travelling around France with Charles, I felt that this particular one of de Gaul's boys could probably have run them a close second.

But even with the frequent breaks he was visibly tiring, although stubbornly refusing to acknowledge the fact, daring me with frowning looks to comment, even when he was once more reduced to walking with a stick.

Covertly I rejoiced to see the squares on our grid dwindle. By the time we were half way back to Carentan I had ceased to care whether or not we found Lise. I would rather, I snapped at him one evening as we were preparing for bed, live in sin for the rest of my life than watch him pushing himself harder every day of this wild-goose chase just to stay on his feet.

'Well I do not wish to live in sin. I wish you to be my wife not forever a – a *paramour*!'

He scowled as I shrieked with laughter and sprayed toothpaste all over the hotel mirror. 'What is wrong with you?' he demanded. 'It is funny to be an adulterer?'

'You're the married, adulterous one, not me, but I absolutely adore the thought of being a paramour...I've never been one of those before!' I mopped toothpaste and tears of laughter from my face. 'Oh, I do love you when you're being all stuffy and correct and pretending it matters, when you know quite well that as soon as we get into bed you'll adulterate like mad half the night.'

'Yes, and that is why I am having the lines all over my face and must walk with a stick. This is all your fault; come here!'

'Not likely; I'm not taking the blame because you are a grumpy old man.'

I was learning the ropes of relationship now: when to be serious, when to tease, when to show compassion, when to be a mother, a sister, a lover or just a friend. It was important to make him laugh when he was down and discouraged, imperative to keep his masculine pride from being swamped by his physical limitations.

From time to time I surprised even myself by what I was becoming for love of Charles de la Tour, sometimes with a small niggle of regret tempered with apprehension that whilst old smart-arse

151

Penrose was slowly fading, I was not yet entirely comfortable with, or sure of, the person taking her place.

* * * * *

It was because we'd stopped to stretch our legs just outside a small village near Dreux that we found the church. I saw it as we crossed a narrow lane to reach the river we could see through the trees; sparkling in the afternoon heat, the water looking invitingly cool.

'Look, what a strange place for a church.' I veered away from the river and began to walk along the path toward the small lichen covered grey stone building that seemed to stand alone in woodland. 'Oh, I see...' I stopped at the end of the track, 'there is a little hamlet here...just a few houses. The church is probably no longer in use.'

'The grass is cut and it all looks very tidy.' He joined me at the foot of the low stone wall surrounding the churchyard. 'See, those headstones are quite new. You forget, here people still use all their churches, unlike your hard-to-fill mausoleums in England that are left to crumble away, or made into houses for rich people.'

I scrambled over the wall and walked between old weathered gravestones and statues of angels and Madonna's to where a few low, recently set white stones nestled under the spreading branches of a pine As Charles reached my side I bent to read the one nearest to me.

At first the words didn't register. Then I read the inscription again. The air left my lungs as though I had been punched hard, and I leaned against the tree to steady myself.

'*Ah, Mon Dieu!*'

Charles was staring down at the grave as though hypnotised, his face palling beneath the tan, his hands gripping his stick so hard the knuckles stood chalky white.

The inscription on the stone was heartbreaking in its brief simplicity.

Lise de la Tour
Décédée de Juillet 22
1944

I was quite literally rooted to the spot, almost paralysed with shock, scarcely able to believe that our search was over; my first thought that Charles was free at last followed hard by a feeling of overwhelming sadness for the young life scarcely begun.

Crossing himself Charles went down on his knees by the grave.

152

After a few moments he sat back in his heels and looked up at me, his eyes bleak and sad. 'Poor little Lise, so this is where it all ended. We might have passed by and never known.' The ghost of a smile lifted the corners of his mouth. 'But for your insatiable curiosity that is just what would have happened.'

With an effort he struggled to his feet; knowing better than to offer help at this particular moment I stayed where I was. He said quietly, 'We must find *M'sieur le Curé* and discover how she came to die here.'

* * * * *

The priest was a young man, very kind and sympathetic, but with no first-hand knowledge about Lise. Father Sebastian, he said, had died a year ago, just after he himself had come to the church, but the gravedigger might know more. If we cared to wait he would fetch him.

We sat on a wooden bench beside the church and the priest's old housekeeper brought us lemonade, only too eager to give her own confused and rambling version of Lise's death.

'A young thing she was, almost dead and scarcely able to speak…we do not know where she came from, but she was pretty…The Father thought she was a child…so small…and all alone…'

It was a relief when the young priest returned with a grizzled old countryman. The new arrival wore a dirty blue smock, tattered corduroys stuffed into army boots and held an evil-smelling pipe clutched between broken brown teeth. Charles stood to greet him and I sat listening to his slow measured explanations, Charles translating for my benefit.

'Yes, I found her on the roadside when I cycled from my home early one morning. The *Boche* had retreated through here a few days previously and left me plenty of work so there were many graves to be dug and I began early.' He spat contemptuously in the grass, knocking his pipe out upon a gravestone then immediately refilling it, stuffing the tobacco with soil-ingrained fingers.

'I left my bicycle and carried her here and the father sent me back for a doctor, but when *he* came he was drunk and useless. He did not know what was wrong, except that she would die soon, the old fool! She had a fever…we thought perhaps pneumonia from lack of food and no shelter at nights. It had first been hot *m'sieur*, but then very cold and wet for a week past. Such rain…terrible! Then, when

Clothilde here washed her and brushed her hair we found this great wound behind her ear. She had been struck a blow, like with a rifle butt. Or perhaps kicked...' he paused, shaking his head, 'poor little one; poor little one.'

'What did she say?' Charles demanded impatiently. 'She must have spoken. You knew her name.'

'Only her name, *m'sieur* and even then we were not sure if we heard right. Nothing else, as you see, not even her birth-date is on the stone.'

'We passed through a town about a mile back, would her death be recorded there?'

He shrugged, 'Father Sebastian was old and at the time very confused, he might not have registered it with the authorities. Possibly the church register has the only record.'

Charles turned to the young priest.

'*Monsieur le Curé*, all I need is proof of her death – can you give that in writing?'

'Certainly, *m'sieur*; come with me,' the young priest, eager to be of use got to his feet.

'Excuse me,' I interrupted as Charles made to follow the younger man. Three pairs of eyes swivelled to stare at me. I looked directly at Charles and cleared my throat. 'You seem to have forgotten something.'

He asked impatiently, 'And what is that?'

'Isn't it obvious? Where is the child, where is Dominic?'

The most extraordinary change came over him then. It was as though a shutter had come down over that handsome face, leaving a total blank. Then in an instance the blankness was gone, replaced by a hard, dark look. He swung back to the old man and there was a terse, rapid exchange of question and answer, before he again faced me.

'There is no child,' he reported coldly and again made to turn away.

I felt my temper begin to bubble. How dare he dismiss anything so important in that manner? I was not about to do battle before this uncomprehending audience, but he wasn't getting away with just that bald statement. I spoke quietly but forcefully. 'But there must be: if not here, then somewhere else. For God's sake, Charles, don't let them put you off like that. We can't leave without finding what happened to him. We have to go on looking.'

He said with icy dismissal. 'No, we do not.'

It was like a slap in the face. For a long moment I confronted him and he glared back, his hostility palpable as a wall and with an emotion I didn't want to put a name to blazing in his eyes.

I turned and walked away across the churchyard, heading back towards our parked car. Once there I leaned my folded arms on the roof, staring blindly across the deserted dusty road, battling with the dreadful hollow sickness deep inside me.

I must have been mistaken. He could surely never be so hard, so uncaring. This was a small child we were talking about, not some grown man capable of surviving alone. Charles, my husband, my beloved, would come at any moment and make his apologies. Say he was tired and overwrought, had been taken off guard. Then I remembered that look, a look devoid even of humanity let alone compassion, a look almost of hate. But hate for whom – for me because I had challenged him, or the child for daring to exist?

* * * * *

He came at last, walking very slowly, watching me all the way. Halting on the other side of the car he met my eyes with his dark and unfathomable gaze. 'Caro, I am sorry.' He was stiff and formal. 'How you must hate me.'

'Don't be so stupid,' miserably I rubbed my fingers over the hot metal of the car's roof. 'I don't hate you. I just don't understand.'

He sighed. 'I am not sure I understand myself that I could treat you so. I think we must talk.'

'Must we...now?'

His eyes were still troubled. 'Yes, we must.'

'I thought I knew you but I don't.' I fought the tears. 'You can go away from me in a second...like *that*,' and I snapped my fingers. 'I don't do that to you. I couldn't. I love you too much.'

'You think that I do not love you?'

'Don't ask me that. I don't know any more.'

'Will you come with me; now?' He held out his hand across the roof of the car. 'Come down to the river where it is quiet and cool and I will try to explain, probably not very well, because it is difficult for me, and you being the impetuous, impatient Caro that I love, may make of it all the wrong conclusions.'

Blinking hard, I took the offered hand.

'Your grammar,' I said, 'is abso-bloody-lutely *awful*!'

* * * * *

'I know how it is hard for you to understand,' he kept my hand in his

155

as we sat on the bank above the slowly moving river, 'although we have both been through the same war, your view of it must always be different from mine. Your country was bombed, as was mine, and your family, friends and lovers died, as did many of my people, but your country was never occupied; mine was, and that is the difference. You want to understand why I cannot sleep and leave our bed at night, why I shout sometimes and wake you? And you worry about these things, yes?' He looked at me with gentle inquiry and I nodded wordlessly.

He was silent for a time, staring at the river. 'There are things that one shuts away because it is the only way to go on living,' he said eventually. 'For me, not sleeping is an acquired habit. For years I found it safer not to sleep. Now I cannot. Lying awake, one can hear the car in the street and the footsteps on the stairs. To sleep is not to know they are there until the door is smashed down, they have you by the arms and there is no escape. No way to avoid the journey through the night to the room with the high windows and the bright lights and the men without pity. To remain awake and alert means one may have a chance to escape that room; escape the things that happen there to make men pray for death, and embrace it when it comes as a friend. For years, Caro, I lived with that fear. All the time I was an agent for your Intelligence Service I knew that every day may be my last; that some eagle-eyed S.S. man would see through my forged papers, or someone like that *collaborateur* Alain would point the finger and talk, and that would be the end. And so every night I sat awake, listening.' His mouth twisted. 'The Germans were our conquerors; they taught us the meaning of fear, of terror; but most of all they taught us to hate.' He turned bleak, questioning eyes upon me. 'Can you understand that I still hate, and always will?'

'Even a little boy who did none of these things?'

'Even so; his father, whoever he was, may have been for me the foot on the stair.'

'But he bears your name, doesn't that mean anything? How can you deny that...and he is Lise's son.' I couldn't bear to look at him.

'Lisa's child was fathered by a German and that is enough. My name is all he has of me. I cannot, and will not, acknowledge him in any way. If he is dead, and that is most likely so or why should Lise have been wounded and alone, then that is probably best for him.'

I gave a long shuddering sigh. 'I can't think like that.'

'Caro, if I could change how I feel, I would...for you, as for no other, but I cannot.'

'Will you, please, not say anything else at all,' I withdrew my

156

hand from his. 'I love you, Charles, but at this moment I don't think I like you very much.' I looked at his stricken face then turned my back. 'Leave me alone. Please. Just *go.*'

Only when I could no longer hear his footsteps did I put my head down and weep.

* * * * *

When the storm was over I lay down on the river's edge to plunge my whole head into the water then sat back, letting the cold rivulets run down under my shirt and cool my hot body. The awful thing about it all was that I did understand, after a fashion, and thought I could see why he felt as he did. At the church I had reacted purely on instinct, outraged that a child could be rejected so violently, whatever the reason. Now plain common sense told me that there were many hundreds of children in that same situation; that if he was still alive he was not out there alone. The war had been over now for more than two years and no six year-old would still be wandering the countryside with nowhere to lay his head. Someone would be caring for him.

All this I knew, but still my heart ached for Lisa's child.

I stared down into the sunlit water until the sparkling eddies merged into one bright silver-green mass and my head began to spin. Pushing my hands through my wet hair I told myself it was time to go back and face a possibly very angry and hostile Charles.

But still I stayed on.

We should have been together in some bar rejoicing that at last he was free and we could be married. But now the shock and reality of that young death seemed too high a price to pay. Over and over I thought about the rifle-butt or the boot driving into her head, and her desperate journey to find sanctuary. Had she left a small dead body behind her? Surely if the little Dominic had been alive she would never have abandoned him? Or had she had found somewhere safe for him to be hidden before she went on alone to her death?

In time perhaps I could accept that, could live with it. But I knew that the memory of Charles's face when I had asked that fatal question would be with me for a long, long time, perhaps forever.

That was far more difficult to accept and live with and not let it come between us.

My throat ached as it had when I was a child and been ticked-off by Grace, or chastised by Matthew for some misdemeanour or another, afterwards facing them out, refusing to cry or say sorry, no matter how much I hurt. Was that what I was doing now? Charles had said he was sorry, had opened his heart to me, said the things he would rather have left unsaid. And I...what had I done? Turned my back on him; told him to go away because I wouldn't let him see me weep and could not, would not, accept his anger and pain.

I loved him; couldn't possibly imagine life now without him, but if we were to go on together I knew that over this it would have to be on his terms, not mine. If I accepted that, and I knew in my heart that I must, there was no reason for continuing to sit alone on this riverbank.

I stood up and began to climb the bank onto the path leading back to the road.

I would put all thought of that small boy out of my head. I would marry Charles and love him and live with him and in time have children with him, forgetting everything that had happened on this day.

I could do that, couldn't I?

I should have known myself better.

* * * * *

He was sitting on the running board of the car, elbows on knees hands loosely clasped before him. As he saw me he stood, straightening his back, his mouth and jaw set in uncompromising lines; only the sad, questioning eyes betraying his pain and uncertainty.

There was no way that I could hold out against that look. I felt my heart turn in my breast and put my arms about him. His heart pounded against mine as for a few moments we stood clasped closely together, swaying gently in each other's arms.

'*Ma pauvre petit.*'

His lips were on my eyes; my cheek; my mouth. '*Caro, ma pauvre petit!*'

I laid my head against his. 'Take me home.' I said.

* * * * *

We were very quiet, neither finding much to say as we drove back to St-Malo after spending the night in a quiet *pension;* returning the car to the hire garage we made our way to *Le Coq d'Or* to stay overnight and await the morning ferry to Weymouth.

Arnaud, delighted to see us back ushered us with great ceremony into the best bedroom, displaying with pride the adjoining bathroom tiled in direst yellow, with a bath the size of Wembley Stadium and sporting a plug large enough to stop the drain in a swimming pool.

When he left us Charles began to unpack our bags. 'Do you want to rest before dinner?'

It was the sort of question he might have asked a maiden aunt and I eyed him cautiously, still not at ease with him at the end of this confusing day with all its emotional highs and lows. 'No thank you, I think I shall bathe now.'

'Very well, I'll change in a minute then wait here for you.' Picking up a book he seated himself in the cushioned wicker chair by the bed. 'If I go down now Arnaud will soon have me intoxicated so that I cannot eat.'

I lay in the bath for ages, going over and over the events of the day, letting my thoughts range further back to when we had first made love: to Elizabeth Pascoe and her sombre warning that a future with Charles might not be plain sailing: to the storm: to the day we had first met and I had looked up to find him watching me as I sat on the cliffs above the cove and mourned for Stefan.

I told myself that he was still the same man, and yet...there had been that moment in Orléans when his control had slipped; and the barely restrained fury directed at me when I'd challenged him in the churchyard. I stared unblinking at the yellow walls. No, not quite the same Charles: today I had seen another. One shaped by the vigilant, sleepless nights listening for the feet on the stairs and the men without pity, by brutality fear and hate. Shaped too, I guessed, by the secret pitiless acts that he also had carried out in cold blood, now buried deep, surfacing only in dreams or an unwary moment of passionate anger.

Reaching for a towel I stepped from the cooling water then stood watching as it swirled and disappeared down the vast hole with a rushing, gurgling roar.

Whichever, or whatever, man was on the other side of the door didn't really matter. Charles was still Charles and I was still me: a combination that had worked so far, even so frightening a thing as seeing a man's soul stripped bare couldn't change that.

* * * * *

He was still seated in the chair, reading, one leg crossed over the other, but now he wore his dressing gown and his hair was damp. As I stood in the doorway irresolute and still wrapped in the towel, he put a finger between the pages to keep his place and looked up at me with dark enquiring eyes.

'I thought you were changing.' I swallowed hard at the lump lodged in my throat. 'We shall be late for dinner. You take even longer than I do to get dressed.'

'I found a shower down the hall. Better, I thought to be clean, and dinner can wait a little.'

His voice was mild, his look tranquil, just as he usually was. I crossed the room and knelt, laying my arms across his knees. I could feel him naked under the robe and suddenly I wanted him so desperately that my legs began to shake. 'I haven't told you yet that I'm sorry...and I am, most dreadfully, dreadfully sorry.'

'For what are you sorry?'

'For telling you to go away. For not trusting you. For not trying to understand.' I laid my head against his knee.

Putting the book aside, he uncrossed his legs and drew me to him. 'It has been a hard day and we both have much to be sorry for.' He raised my head, cupping my face in his hands. 'Ah, Caro, but you are crying.'

And I was; the cool healing tears trickling down my face. I gulped. 'It's your flaming fault, I make it a rule not to bawl in front of people.'

'But I am not people. You should not hide your tears from me.'

I mopped my face on a corner of the towel. 'I should have taken more notice when you warned me you wouldn't always do as I wished.'

He smiled. 'Although I seem to remember on that occasion you made sure that I *did* do as you wished; by very underhand means.'

'Would that be a good idea now?' I raised myself, bringing my face up to his level, my heart beginning to race.

'Oh, I think so,' with one smooth movement he rose, loosed my towel, his robe followed it to the floor and he lifted me onto the bed, 'a very good idea.'

'What about Arnaud and his dinner?' I asked. He smiled

'First, we satisfy *this* hunger then we eat Arnaud's dinner.' He browsed his lips down my body murmuring, 'He is a Frenchman...he will understand!'

* * * * *

We ate at ten o'clock; Arnaud, Charles and me, sitting in the small courtyard at the back of the bar; we two holding hands between courses, Arnaud giving us knowing glances, heaping our plates and keeping our glasses filled.

'When one is in love, one must eat well.' His look was sly; the epitome, I thought, of the *louche* Frenchman beloved of English playwrights. 'The strength must be kept up at all times, or nothing else will be!'

'Oh, I don't think we have to worry too much about that tonight – or anytime do we?' Charles raised lazy eyes to mine, one eye drooping in a wink and I was instantly reminded of him smiling at me from the hospital bed, belatedly aware that even then he had been flirting with me and I, fool that I was, hadn't seen it.

I fluttered my lashes in return. *'Je suis d'accord...venez a n'importe quelle heure, il n'y a pas de quoi toujours, m'sieur!'*

His eyes sparkled. 'Who has been teaching you behind my back?'

'No one, only you – you know what they say: the best way to learn a language is with one's head on a pillow – and we do spend quite a lot of our time in bed.'

* * * * *

We reached Tyndals late the following evening, collecting the Standard from the front of the Penzance garage where we had left it almost three weeks before, then drove home through a fine Cornish drizzle.

We were expected and someone, doubtless Grace or Jenny, had left a rabbit stew simmering at the back of the range and the house was fragrant with the aroma of herbs and garlic.

I stood in the familiar welcoming room, listening as Charles moved about upstairs, opening cases, putting clothes on hangers. Little, ordinary sounds that now meant so much.

We had never been away, I told myself. Never made all those journeys, never come almost to the brink of parting. Our life was here, in this quiet house and we should live it together with nothing to disturb our peace and tranquillity.

'Ahh! Mon Dieu!' An anguished cry came from above followed by a volley of curses as he hit his head on the beam he always forgot was there.

I grinned. Well, almost nothing!

161

12

'Where is Charles this morning?' Matthew looked up from his paper as I reached over his shoulder for a piece of toast. He smacked my hand away. 'Leave my breakfast alone. Haven't you eaten yet?'

'Gone over to Tregenick to see someone called Father Con about the wedding; don't be so damn' mean, and yes, but I'm still hungry, in that order…and good morning to you, too!'

He laughed and took a swipe at me with his paper.

'Jenny,' he raised his voice, 'better get down here quickly. Caro's scoffing your breakfast.'

She came, pinning up her hair looking, as usual, absolutely ravishing.

'Hi, Caro; take no notice. Sometimes he can be hell in the mornings…as if I need to tell *you* that. Have you come to work?'

'Of course; if Charles and I are taking off for another two weeks after our wedding I feel duty-bound to put in my penn'orth whilst I'm around.'

'Mind telling me why you're being married in Tregenick and not Poltreven?' Matthew beheaded his egg neatly with his knife. 'The church there is bigger and better than old Con's stone hut.'

'I know. But we don't want masses of people and Elizabeth says that the little chapel is nice and plain and unpretentious and the old priest is a perfect duck.' I buttered more toast then turned to Grace as she entered with a plate of bacon. 'You'll come, won't you, Grace, to see me properly married at last? But no shouting 'Down with the Pope' and setting fire to the pews!'

She sniffed. 'I suppose I must. Anything is better than having you two living in sin.'

'Isn't she wonderfully old-fashioned?' Jenny winked at me and dropped a kiss on Grace's head.

'Yeah, if there were more like Grace in this world we'd all be perfect.'

'All but you,' Matthew looked at me over the top of his paper, 'You'll like Father Con, although I don't think I'd describe him as a perfect duck; a wily old bird maybe nearer the mark. His name's O'Connor, but it's OK to call him Con, he prefers that. Barbara always refers to him as 'that lovely man'; which is praise indeed…and you could just ask Willi about him. He's been a good friend to him for the past six years.'

'Well, I'll let you know my opinion when we've met.' I stood up. 'Now I'm off. What do you want me to start on this morning?'

'There are a stack of buds been standing overnight, if you'll bunch and crate them. I'll be with you soon.'

But as it happened he decided to rotavate in the big field and I spent the morning with Willi in the packing shed, while the two girls worked in the glasshouses. I asked him what he thought of Father Con over in Tregenick, and was promptly treated to a eulogy that went on for about ten minutes.

I was a bit sceptical. 'I must say I'm constitutionally allergic to saints.'

'Oh, he's no saint...he likes his whisky and his cards too much,' he laughed then looked suddenly serious. 'But, you see, he doesn't care who or what you are, he just treats everyone the same. I'm a Jew, and that makes a difference to some people, but not him.'

'Tell me, Willi.' Carefully, I began to pack a box. 'What do *you* feel about the Germans?'

'The Germans or the Nazis?' he asked.

'Is there a difference?'

He gave me a puzzled frown. 'Well, yes...I mean, I grew up with ordinary Germans. Hell, I *was* one! In my village there were only a few Jewish families so we all went to school together and played together: my family weren't orthodox anyway. When the National Socialists Party came to power some of them changed and turned against us. But not all.' He shrugged. 'People are what they are, good and bad. Although all my family, every one, died in Concentration camps, except my father, who was hanged, I still remember those who didn't turn against us better than those who did.'

'So you don't hate all Germans?'

'I don't think I hate anyone, but then I never was in Dachau or Belsen as my family were. Perhaps if I had been, I would hate.' He paused in his work for a moment, and gave me a direct look. 'But the Nazis I never forgive. You should talk to Francis Lindsey some time if you want to know about hating *them*. He went into the camps.'

'Charles hates them, all of them.'

'I know. We talk sometimes; he has what Rabbi Emmanuel used to call "the dark places of the soul."'

'You put me to shame, Willi, talking so wise.'

He grinned. 'Jews and Irishmen, we are the same: born with long memories and we talk too much. Frenchmen, now, they *think* too much!'

163

I looked at him with a new respect. 'Perhaps you should be a Rabbi.'

'No, all I want is to one day manage, or even own for myself, a flower farm like Trewlyns.' He grinned again. 'Do you think that likely?'

'No, I think it's a dead cert,' I answered, and we laughed together and went on packing companionably through the morning.

It was only much later that I became aware I had taken one small, tentative step on the forbidden path.

* * * * *

Father Con I was relieved to discover was not as saintly as I had been led to believe. The mouth in the wrinkled brown monkey face was too humorous; the bright blue eyes too lively. He was very small and old and Irish and wore a black *soutane*. His curate, introduced as Tim, was a tall, thickset young Scot, informally attired in disgraceful cords and an open-necked shirt. The pair of them together performed a kind of clerical double-act reminiscent of Laurel and Hardy, with little Stan on the whole coming off rather better than big Ollie.

We sat, not as I expected in some dim parlour surrounded by saintly objects but on the harbour wall below the little chapel, in the peace of a evening in June; the early summer visitors all gone to their fish and chip suppers. The long rays of the sun lay over the water as we chatted of this and that while Charles smoked his Gauloise and they both smoked their pipes.

'A grand evening for the fishing.' observed the old man, folding his arms and puffing contentedly.

'But a better one for the close of a good game o' football.' countered the other.

I exchanged glances with Charles who was having some difficulty with keeping his mouth under control, and waggled my eyebrows, wondering what any of this had to do with getting married. So far, in a full ten minutes of amiable chat, neither of them had mentioned the reason for our visit.

''Tis a good month for a weddin', June.' Father Con again.

This was better; I looked expectantly at Father Tim.

'Ma mother married in February.' He looked skyward. 'She said it was a lucky month to be wed.'

'Ach.' the blue eyes snapped with sudden devilment. 'People always say that, when everyone knows 'tis mostly the result of too much wine drunk at Christmas, with a stampede to the altar a month

164

or two after!'

'I'll have you know ma mother was wed many a year before I was born.'

The old man made tutting noises, 'So I should hope.' The bright eyes switched to my face. 'The end of the month it is then? Your man has agreed to that an' not a day more. He's not tryin' to hustle you, is he?'

Charles gave a strangled, sarcastic snort and I pinched his thigh. Hard.

'No.' I shook my head, 'in fact, you couldn't, I suppose, manage it any earlier?'

'I cannot...an' if you can't wait three weeks I don't give much for your chances of makin' it last.' He looked disapproving. 'When you join up with our lot it's for life, y'know...and I'll be needing a word or two with ye on that matter before these three weeks are up!'

'I could,' I said with some asperity, 'wait three *years* if you insist, but I'd rather not, and if it wasn't for life, it wouldn't be worth having, would it?'

He grinned, his monkey grin. 'Three weeks it is then,' he leaned forward to peer at Charles over his crooked wire-framed spectacles. 'Knows what she wants, doesn't she? Ye'll have to watch her. Puts me in mind of Pascoe's lass, and *she's* a handful all right.'

Charles bent tranquil eyes on him. 'Oh, I know that, Father.'

'So you're sure you'll not change your mind at all, are you?'

'Quite sure.'

'Take no notice of me,' I muttered, 'much more of this all boy's together lark and I could just change *mine*.'

The old man smiled, taking his pipe out of his mouth to blow a perfect smoke ring into the still air before giving me a very mischievous wink. 'I shouldn't do that, young Caroline, for 'tis already in the diary in red ink an' would be the very devil to alter!'

* * * * *

'That's the oddest half-hour I've ever spent. He's a bit Alice in Wonderland, isn't he?'

Charles looked thoughtful, 'Perhaps more Brer Fox than Alice.'

I looked at his profile, bronzed and lit by the setting sun, then at the strong, capable hands on the steering wheel and tried not to start getting ideas this early in the evening.

'Does he know we are living together?'

'Yes.'

'I wonder we didn't get a lecture then.'

'Perhaps he is saving it for you when he has his word or two!'

'Better not.' I narrowed my eyes at him, but he was laughing.

'I only pull your leg, Caro. I don't think he is the lecturing kind. Yesterday he asked me outright and when I told him 'Yes,' he just nodded and said, 'Well you would be, wouldn't you, but you shouldn't be, should you? Then said that if that was the lie of the land we'd better get married as soon as possible and three weeks was the earliest. He asked then would I be interested in an afternoon's fishing some time when the novelty of being married had worn off.'

'Brer Fox is about right,' muttered, 'but you're not going to sleep in the spare room for the next three weeks, are you?'

'Only if you are also.'

'Not likely, anyway, I never did see the sense in bolting the stable door etc, etc...'

* * * * *

Our wedding was perfect. No simpering bridesmaids or cute little pageboys or hoards of relations, but calm and quiet and beautiful, the tiny chapel filled with just our friends, a wonderful air of peace and tranquillity over the whole. It would have been nice, observed Charles as we drove back to Trewlyns, to do it all over again so that we could catch up on any bits we might have missed.

I had some unfinished business with Josh and when he reached Trewlyns hot on our heels, grabbed him while Charles was talking to Matthew and the clinging vine powdering her nose, to remind him I'd won our bet.

'What? You want your fiver right here and now? You've got a nerve, Caro!'

'Shhh...you don't have to tell the world – and stop moaning, you should have coughed up weeks ago.'

He took a crisp white five pound note out his wallet and waved it tantalisingly in the air. 'It's all right. I had it ready for you...but I *do* sometimes wish I'd been right!'

'Josh Milton,' I snatched the note from his hand and tucked it in my bra, then went on tiptoe to kiss him, 'just control your eyes will you? I have a strong suspicion that you could tell me what colour my undies are and you shouldn't be doing that when a girl's just got married.'

'Old habits die hard.' he grinned wickedly, 'something blue, are they? I won't tell anyone if you don't.'

'Caro, look who was lurking at the back of the church.'

I spun around at the sound of Charles' voice and blushed guiltily to discover he had come up behind us with Elizabeth Pascoe on his arm.

'I missed my train last night and had to come first thing this morning,' she explained, 'but congratulations anyway.' She raised an eyebrow at Charles, 'Was it the biff on the head that did the trick?' she asked.

He grinned at me, his eyes dancing. 'Either that or the celebrations a few weeks later.'

'If it isn't Pascoe's lass...did that heathen Francie not make it then?'

Father Con had joined us and Elizabeth turned to him smiling. 'No, he's still in Rennes but he'll be on leave for a week next month. I spoke to him on the 'phone yesterday and he says to have the rods and bait ready.'

'That I will. I'll tell Perc an' he'll see the Linnet is spick an' span an' ready for the water.'

Elizabeth made a face at me. 'I stay in London when Francis is in Cornwall. All he does is paint with Henry or fish with Father Con. I don't get a look in.' She glanced across the courtyard to where Henry was pinned in a corner by Barbara and took the little priest's arm. 'I think our help may be needed, Father,' she hissed in a conspiratorial whisper. 'Henry looks as though he's waiting for the cavalry to arrive and save him from the Squaw Woman!'

Charles watched them go then said pensively, 'I am enjoying our wedding but how soon do you think we may leave?'

'Our train isn't due for another three hours and all our bags are packed. We only have to pick them up from Tyndals.' I looked at him innocently. 'The ferry leaves Weymouth at midnight, so we should get a reasonable amount of sleep on the way over.'

'Ah, yes but there is only room for one on those so small bunks.' He slipped his arm about my waist. 'Another hour, then we shall steal away to the cottage, and how you say, "make the hay" for an hour. Everyone will have drunk so much wine that they will not notice we are no longer there.'

But we said goodbye to Matthew and Jenny, and Grace who, and I could scarcely believe my eyes, was chatting amiably to Father Con without actually holding up the sign of the crossed fingers.

And I kissed and hugged her very hard, partly for throwing her Low Church principals to the wind for my sake, but mostly because I loved her so much and realised this late in the day that I had never

167

actually told her so before.

'Thank you, Grace...and I love you for all the years you've put up with me and been so wise and always so infuriatingly right!'

Charles took my hand. I turned to leave, quickly, Matthew fashion, and caught a grin from the little priest.

He closed one eye in a brief, bright wink. 'Ach, you'll do!' he said.

13

We were quite back to our old selves, I thought, standing high above the city. Charles's arms were about my waist and with the whole of Paris spread beneath us it seemed impossible that so recently there had been bitterness and dissension threatening to tear us apart. Now we were easy again with each other. He was even beginning to sleep a little better, although conversely, I now tended to lie awake, just for the pleasure of watching his sleeping face.

Lulled into a sense of safety and security I peered down from the dizzying height from the top of the Eiffel Tower. Tightening my hands on the arms he had wrapped around my waist I leaned back against him. 'It's worse than being in a 'plane; up here *everything* moves.'

'Are you feeling very insecure and easily frightened?' he asked, holding me closer.

'Very. Please move back, Charles.'

'I will when you tell me something that has made me most curious. Caroline, why did Josh give you five pounds at our wedding?'

I gave a nervous laugh. 'He owed me that fiver and just remembered to pay it back.'

'Caro, I do not believe you. What has been going on between the pair of you that you must hide it from me?'

'Will you *please* let me step back from the edge?'

'Why? You are in no danger of falling.'

'Maybe, but I don't want you flinging me over the side when I tell you.'

'It is that bad?'

'You'd better believe it!'

I was silent for a moment, marshalling my thoughts. I had hoped this little bit of the past might stay buried. Damn Josh! Why had he made it so obvious? 'Look,' I began, 'the night of the dance when you finally got around to kissing me, I told you then that I'd got the wrong idea about you in the beginning. Remember?'

'Yes. So as Kate might say, 'Spill the beans!''

'Easier said than done, but here goes...' I took a deep breath. 'Shortly after we first met, I thought you and Jenny were having a fling together.' I scowled repressively at his quick snort of laughter.

169

'*Don't*! Or my lips will forever be sealed!'

'Sorry.' He got right down the back of my collar to kiss my neck and my heart turned over very slowly before beginning to jiggle around in a cosy, sexy sort of way. Maybe I could just about manage to tell him.

'I told Josh about it and he nearly laughed himself sick and said...and said...' Momentarily I closed my eyes. I couldn't, I just couldn't get the words out. The whole thing now was too ridiculous; he would either laugh like a drain or be quite incredibly angry. I wasn't sure which.

A couple of American tourists, huge cameras hung about them like eccentric necklaces, were lingering, pretending not to eavesdrop. Charles glanced from them to my scarlet face in amused perplexity then drew me away from the rail and into a quiet space by the inner wall.

'If you would rather, I could arrange for you to do this in the confessional!' His voice was not quite steady.

'Charles, if you laugh at me, I'll never forgive you.'

'Then I shall not laugh. Continue: Josh said?'

'That he was sure that because you didn't go whoring about the countryside like a randy mongrel, never went dancing or seemed to take the very slightest interest in women that you were a...a French pixie!' I paused to draw breath, saw he hadn't understood and was sickeningly aware I'd have to take the fence again.

'He said you were...' I hissed the word '*homosexual*!'

I couldn't have silenced him more effectively if I'd hit him with a brick.

I gabbled on, trying to delay the expected explosion: 'We had an almighty row about it and I bet him a fiver you weren't, although the way you carried on – or rather *didn't* carry on – made me think he was probably right. And if you are absolutely furious and want to push me over the side I'd say you were being perfectly reasonable, considering that you're quite the sexiest man I've ever been to bed with!'

All at once I registered that the two Americans were back and listening openly with expressions of outrage plastered across their faces. I glared at them. 'Would you,' I asked icily, 'like a recording of all this to take back home? I should hate to think you'd missed anything.'

'*Caroline*!' Charles grabbed my arm and made for the stairs. 'Come with me. Now!'

I dug in my heels. 'I'm not walking down all those bloody stairs.'

'No, but we shall sit on them for a moment, away from those poor

170

people. Caroline, how *could* you?'

'Quite easily,' I was hopping mad, 'their bloody ears were out on stalks, the nosy buggers.'

'You are only cross because you had to tell me such things. Do not be so two-faced. Had you been in their place you would have climbed onto their shoulders to hear!' He dragged me through the doorway and sat, pulling me down onto the steps beside him. 'What am I to do with you? Matthew should have beaten such naughtiness out of you when you were young enough to be corrected. Now I must suffer.'

'Don't think he didn't try from time to time,' I sulked. 'I didn't have to tell *you*, let alone them. I could have lied.'

'No you could not, not to me. You do not lie well.' He sat back, looking at me from under drawn brows. 'Caro, did you really think I was *une pensée*? The truth, please.'

'Yes, I did...and you've no one but yourself to blame! It was you who kept the distance between us, you who never touched me except by accident. What was I supposed to think? Living in the same house together and you not even behaving like a moderately affectionate brother ...and I said don't laugh.' I felt my eyes beginning to prickle. 'I suppose you think it's all bloody hilarious?'

'Yes I do, but why does it upset you so?'

'Because I loved you and wanted you so much and you wouldn't love *me*!' I began to cry in earnest, remembering all the frustration, all the doubts and fears, the sleepless nights, the longing to be in his arms. 'While you were being all noble and keeping your distance, you tore me apart, you rotten, secretive bastard!'

He took me in his arms then, rocking and soothing me until I was quiet. Reduced to long shuddering sighs and the odd hiccup I sat, hot with shame at having burst into tears yet again. If that was what love did to you, I thought miserably, you could keep it. The old Caroline would have died before bawling her eyes out all over a chap.

He wiped my face with his handkerchief and took both my hands in his. 'Is it over?'

I nodded. 'Yes.'

He raised my hands to his lips and kissed them very thoroughly, one finger at a time and my whole spine goose-pimpled.

'I brought you to Paris to be happy, and now you are sad. I only can tell you again that I too wanted and loved you. Right from the beginning, even, I think in Oxford when I would watch you, all cool and correct in your uniform, running down those steps...Truly, I only tried to do what I thought was the best.'

171

'Well, don't try so hard another time,' I answered crossly, 'because you are turning me into an absolute snivelling, spineless wimp.'

He grinned wickedly. 'I rather like having you fling yourself into my arms to wash my shirt fronts.'

'That,' I said, 'is because you are a sadist.' I pulled myself together. 'Come along, I want to buy you something really nice with Josh's fiver to cheer myself up. I can't wait to see his face when I tell him that I've told you! How about a new shirt?' I snickered. 'A pink one, perhaps.'

'Not even for you will I wear pink. You wish to do this now?'

'Yes, because if we stay here any longer I refuse to be held responsible for what may happen next. I'm absolutely sure there must be a notice somewhere saying "No sex on these stairs."'

He laughed, pulling me to my feet and we returned to the promenade. The Americans were still there, eyes glued to the doorway.

'Please, Caroline, you will apologise.' Charles pinched my bottom rather hard.

I yelped then bared my teeth at them. 'Sorry if I upset you,' I said sweetly, 'you should have followed us out there…you would have got some pictures even a Yank Magazine wouldn't print!'

'Mother of God,' Charles practically threw me into the lift, shouting: 'Not one more word…not one!' then collapsed against the wall, laughing helplessly as we were borne downward to where the street lamps were lighting up all over Paris, under an evening sky studded with stars.

* * * * *

After that, it was a time of pure joy. We ate and drank too much, spent far more than was proper or that Grace would have approved on as many forms of gambling that we could find, rejoicing loudly when we won and being philosophical about our losses. We toured the Louvre and Notre Dame and went to Fontainebleau; wandered Montmartre; explored the Latin Quarter and brought pictures from thin men with straggling beards and dried paint under their fingernails; spent our evenings in smoky clubs, listening enraptured while women wearing skimpy black dresses sang throatily of lust and unrequited love; afterward drinking coffee at midnight at pavement cafés. In fact, we behaved as generations of lovers had before us.

Only on the last day did I return to earth with a bump, over something that Charles didn't even notice, and most probably would not have thought twice about if he had.

* * * * *

We were on the banks of the Seine: Charles leaning on the parapet smoking and watching the river, while I faced the street, playing the game of picking out the tourists from the native Parisians and trying to guess their nationalities. Suddenly, along the opposite side of the street came a nun. Wearing a huge white winged head dress and voluminous grey habit she sailed along like a stately galleon while behind her, holding hands and walking two by two, straggled a long line of small boys: hair cut painfully short, all dressed in identical blue belted smocks, absurdly short trousers, and laced boots on their small feet.

Beside me, a little girl tugged her father's hand and pointed: '*Regardez, Papa – les pauvre orphelins!*'

All at once the day was less bright, as silently and with a terrible tug at my heart, I watched the forlorn crocodile disappear down the street, while Charles watched the river unaware of the little scene played out behind his back.

'I thought we might go to the Moulin Rouge this evening to see once more all the naked ladies,' he turned around suddenly, 'but only if you would like to see the show again – ' he broke off, his face full of concern. 'Why, what is the matter? You are so pale. Are you ill?'

'No. Yes …I have a headache.' God help me I thought, *that* old chestnut – the last refuge of a shameless woman! 'Can we go and find a drink? I must have overdone the sightseeing.'

'Would you not rather return to the hotel and lie down?' He was anxious, watching me with a worried frown.

The last thing I wanted at that moment was to be alone with him. "You do not lie well," he had said. I didn't want to put that statement to the test away from the distraction of other people around us. I smiled brightly and assured him that a small cognac would set me right, and then of course I would love to go to the Moulin Rouge again.

He looked as though he was about to question me further, then appeared to think better of it. Steering me towards the nearest café and seating me at a quiet corner table he went to the bar. I sat watching him order the drinks then walk across to join me. He had a disconcerting habit of keeping his eyes on mine, even at a distance. Now, summoning all the guile I could manage I tried hard to meet that

173

steady regard.

He sat down, his gaze unwavering. 'You look,' he said accusingly, 'exactly like your father when he expects someone to ask him a question that he does not wish to answer.'

'You're quite an expert on the Penrose family, aren't you?'

'No. But I am beginning to read the face of Madame de la Tour rather well.'

I laid my hand over his. 'You mustn't think that every time I feel a little tired, or have a headache that there is something monumentally wrong...after all, sometimes one is *triste* with out any real reason.'

'You are sure?'

'I am sure.' I took up the glass the waiter placed on the table before me, '*Salut*; to us, the naked ladies and a quiet, smooth crossing home in the morning.'

* * * * *

That night, after we had made love I lay beside him feigning sleep, my head aching from the pressure of all the images racing through my brain.

He might have been there, might have been that blonde, round-headed one at the end. That was how Charles would expect him to look. How he probably would look. His unknown father in miniature, complete with pale blue eyes...

I tried to still the hurdy-gurdy turning around and around in my head. Stupid to let the sight of those few small children stir again the feelings I had so carefully buried by the river all those months ago. It was dangerous to our love and our future even to think such thoughts. I wanted to stretch my limbs, turn the hot pillow, get up and walk about; do anything but lay tense and silent with my painful thoughts.

When we got back I should have to talk to someone or go crazy trying to put all these conflicting thoughts and feelings into order. But who could I talk to? It would have to be someone not too close; someone who was really down to earth and who would understand...not my family, not even Paul. Bad enough that I should deceive Charles, without placing this burden on any of their shoulders...

Elizabeth! That was the one. I almost sighed aloud my relief, Elizabeth Pascoe, of *course*. Why hadn't I thought of her before? Of all the people I knew she was the most likely to give forthright, considered advice. As soon as possible I would go to see her.

'Caro,' Charles spoke in the darkness. Laying his lips on the crown of my head and sliding his hand from my waist to cup my breast he murmured. 'I can hear you thinking – again. It is deafening; what is wrong?'

I turned to him, buried my head in his shoulder. 'Nothing, just hold me.' I dug my fingers into his back as the ache in my head reached a crescendo. 'Hold me,' I repeated fiercely. 'I have to sleep; I really have to sleep and I can't.'

He wrapped his arms around me, 'Darling Caro, I have you; you can let go; just let go and you will sleep.'

Soothing and familiar his hands moved over me, smoothing and calming; he kissed me, his mouth gentle on mine. 'Let go,' he repeated, 'and you will sleep.'

The pain in my head began to lessen, my taut and tortured muscles relaxed beneath his touch and I slipped away, marvelling sleepily that one small boy I had never met could be the cause of so much trouble.

14

'Darling, do you still want to come to London with me?' Charles looked up from the letter he was reading. 'I shall need to spend most of Thursday with these people, then on Friday...' he consulted it again, 'we go to the site at a place in Epping ...you know of this place?'

'Only that it has a forest.'

'Yes, that is where they want the club built. Very ambitious, a swimming pool, tennis courts, and now a hall for squash.' His brow was furrowed. 'What is squash?'

'A very fast ball game played against a wall.'

'*Pfft!* Why do so stupid a thing when there is a swimming pool!'

'I shouldn't tell them that, darling.' I dropped a kiss on his head as I brought a rack of toast to the table. 'But if you get the commission, isn't it going to be rather difficult later on when work starts? Surely you'll need to be nearer at hand than Cornwall?'

'What is it that Grace is so fond of saying – "We cross the bridge when we come to it"?' He took my hand. 'What will you do when I am meeting with them for two days? Go sightseeing?'

'Yes, there is that, but I'll probably find out if Elizabeth has some free time. We can have a good gossip and do some shopping.'

'Ah, my good angel – you will give her my love?'

'I will not. She gets enough of that from her own chap.'

He laughed. 'Lucky chap, she is so very pretty.'

'Yes. I noticed you noticing!'

As we sat over our meal, laughing and talking together I wondered how I could be so deceitful with the man I loved. I had many faults, but being dishonest wasn't one of them. When I allowed myself to think of the harm I might be doing I went cold with fear. But driven as I was to know if Lise's child was alive or dead, until I had at least tried to discover what had happened to him there would be no turning back.

Quite how Elizabeth could help I didn't know, but at least I'd be able to share my thoughts and feelings with someone else.

* * * * *

'Are you taking up day-dreaming as a profession, or is it just your latest hobby?'

Matthew's voice cut across my reverie and I started guiltily.

'Sorry. Am I lagging behind?'

'Not exactly, you've barely started.' He gave me a look, the blue eyes keen and searching. 'Anything wrong?'

'No. Just thinking that I shall be leaving the rest of you to slog it without me again tomorrow. I'm not being much use to you lately, am I?'

'I wasn't expecting you to work here forever – you have your own life to lead. In any case, now that I have Willi and Betty and Kate have both decided to stay on, things are much easier. Not that I don't miss you when you're away.' He reached for a new hank of raffia. 'But that's something all fathers have to face eventually. At least, the next time it happens I shall be more used to the idea.'

'The next time?' I looked at the slow smile spreading across his face. '*Dad*! You haven't? Jenny isn't...?'

'We have and she is. You don't have to look so stunned. I'm not *that* old!'

'I think it's just lovely!'

I hugged him, feeling very emotional and sad and happy all at once. But of course they would both have wanted a child. I sniffed a bit and hugged him again. 'What a relief,' I said, 'Someone else I can shove the work onto when you're in your dotage!'

'That's better; much more like my Caroline...full of daughterly reverence.' He smiled and waved me away. 'Go on up and see Jenny for a while because you're no use to me here this morning.' Then as I passed him he asked quietly, 'Caro, is every thing all right between you and Charles?'

'Every thing is fine, dad. I'm still a bit punch-drunk from Paris and now we have to go off again.' I lied glibly. 'It takes a bit of getting used to. All this rushing about, it's a bit like joining up all over again.'

* * * * *

Jenny and I danced a little jig in the kitchen.

'Does Grace know yet?'

'No, you're the first...isn't it great? Now Josh's brat and ours can grow up together. I hope his doesn't take after Gooseberry eyes!'

'God Almighty, Jenny!' I sat down hard. 'How? I mean Josh and *thing*...Cynthia?'

'How? The usual way, I imagine, it's hardly likely to have been

177

an Immaculate Conception with Josh around, is it?' She giggled. 'You'd think that as a nurse she'd have been a bit more careful before the knot was tied, I know I was! They're getting married next month. I hope she's got enough coupons left for all the tulle she'll need to cover the bump!'

We clutched each other and howled.

'We could make her a very large bouquet...' I mopped my eyes. 'We shouldn't laugh. Poor Josh; but he always was inclined to be careless when he got the bit between his teeth.'

'Which bit?' She gave another shriek of laughter. 'Serves him right, the randy swine.'

'How did you know? Did he tell you?'

'No. Fa told me last night after Josh came to see him about putting up the banns. Apparently old Amelia let it out in the village shop this morning and Madge Tregorran got such a shock she dropped a two-pound bag of sugar on the cat and nearly brained the poor thing; it's been walking sideways ever since. Of course by now it will be all around the Parish...the news, not the cat!' She rolled her eyes. 'Josh is so proud of himself you'd think it was the first time he'd ever shot his bolt.'

We howled again.

Well, I thought, as I returned to help Matthew. I just hope no one expects me to join this fecund throng.

I had quite enough problems as it was.

* * * * *

'This is a treat for me,' Elizabeth said when we met in a café on the Waterloo Road. 'I'm going hairless over being on Wards, fitting in lectures, trying to study and romping with Francis, who at the moment is well-in with some RAF types who give him a lift over almost every other weekend. Just sitting in a café with nothing to do but chat to another female is bliss!' She looked at me expectantly. 'Well, come on...give! I can see the cork is about to fly out of the bottle. Has Charles been laying Barbara or something?'

I laughed. 'I doubt she'd object if he did. No, I just need to bend an ear...'

She heard me out, sipping her coffee, watching me over the rim, then sat in silence for a few minutes when I'd finished. 'Well,' she said at last. 'I wouldn't fancy being in *your* shoes! He's a bit formidable, isn't he, your bloke? Beneath all that charm I spy a wicked bit of temper; all the more lethal for being kept under such tight control.'

'That's the understatement of the century.' I said, dryly. 'The thing is I have to know. I've tried, I really have, to put the whole business of Dominic out of my mind, but since I saw those pathetic kids in Paris I just can't do that any more.'

'Have you tried talking to him again? Now that a few months have passed he might be prepared to give a little.'

'I could try, I suppose, but I can't imagine him giving an inch. You should have seen him. He hates, he really does, in a way that I doubt you or I ever could.'

'Yes, well, I've got one of those types to cope with myself.' She propped her chin on her hand, the deep blue eyes thoughtful. 'I guess you'll have to go it alone, won't you? Tell you what, though: Francis will be here by tomorrow mid-day. Why not come to Manchester Square and talk to him? After all, he spends his life roaming around Europe and knows all kinds of people. I'm almost sure he'd know the best way to go about making inquiries. Mind you, I won't guarantee you'll get an easy ride. He'll dig for every one of your reasons for wanting to do this and dissect them minutely before he'll commit himself, or you, to anything.'

'I've nothing to hide and if you think he might help I'll take my chances. Quite honestly, I don't have the faintest idea of how to even begin. My French is lousy, and I can't just bunk off over there and start looking.'

'For someone who's just got married, and to a character like Charles, you're taking a hell of a risk.' She gave me an appraising look and asked frankly, 'Are you sure you're not just being stroppy and bloody-minded? You always were, you know!'

'Quite possibly, but what would *you* do if you were me?' I countered.

'I've no idea. I can't imagine ever being in that position. Although I don't know…sometimes I wonder if I was to put a ruddy great stick into Francis' head and stir *him* up, just what would pop out and cause me all kinds of problems; but then I don't really think I'd want to deal with whatever came roaring to the surface.'

She ferreted in her shoulder bag and produced an old envelope. Tearing off a piece she scribbled an address and passed it to me. 'Come around about two-thirty. He'll definitely be there by then. What time will Charles be back to your hotel?'

'Not until late afternoon at least.'

'Good, that gives us plenty of time. Now I must fly. Have yourself a good day. And don't worry so much, it simply isn't you and it'll give you wrinkles!'

After she'd gone I walked over the bridge and along the Strand to the National Gallery, where I spent a couple of hours wandering the galleries before going in search of lunch. When I'd finished my coffee and sandwich in one of the ghastly chrome and plastic coffee bars that were springing up all over London, I did my tourist bit by walking under Admiralty Arch and down the Mall to gawk at Buck House. Hot and footsore I finally returned to our hotel to find Charles waiting for me, freshly bathed and dressed and looking enviably cool.

'Did you have a successful day?' I kissed him and he pulled me into his arms.

'Very good indeed, we shall do business...and you? You also have had a good day?'

'Yes, but tiring and I'm all hot and sticky...come and talk to me while I bathe.'

He was enthusiastic about the proposed club, telling me at length about his day, sitting on the edge of the bath and rolling up his sleeve to soap my back, which was one husbandly chore I much appreciated. Sliding down to rinse off I asked casually how late he expected to be returning the next day, trying not to show my relief when he replied he thought it would be about seven.

'What will *you* do with yourself...perhaps see Elizabeth again?' He held out the towel as I stepped out, wrapping it around me and planting a kiss on my shoulder.

'Umm, yes, her chap's home this week-end and I'm meeting them both in the afternoon.'

'Good. So I need not feel guilty at leaving you so long alone.'

No, I was the one feeling guilty I thought a few minutes later, as I sat on the edge of the bed beginning to dress, because I'm deceiving you and about to do something I know will hurt and anger you if you ever find out. Should that happen, the shutter will come down again as it did before and behind it will be a terrible, passionate outrage against me that I could do such a thing...

'*Triste* again?'

He had come to stand before me, hands in pockets, rocking back a little on his heels. I looked up. 'No, tired again!' I smiled and kept my voice light. 'I've tramped half of London today. I think that tomorrow morning I shall sit in a chair as you do and read, then go to see Elizabeth after lunch. I do love London and want to see more; it's just that my feet aren't so keen.'

'Could you ever leave Cornwall – not for ever, just for a time?' He squatted down on his heels before me, his gaze inquiring.

'Why do you ask that?' I stopped buttoning my blouse and he slid his hands beneath the silk to move them gently over my back.

'Because I think I may have to stay here soon. Perhaps for some months: six...eight, perhaps.' He looked me straight in the eyes. 'You in Cornwall and me in London would not be a good idea unless of course, you would be glad to be rid of me for a while.'

'No. Never that.' I put my hand on the back of his head, smoothing his hair with the other. 'And I should quite like to live here for as long as needed, but not in a hotel. We should have to find a house to lease, or a flat.'

'They will give me an office to work in at Putney...that is near here?'

I laughed, 'Not terribly, but near enough.'

'They say it is pretty and Geddes, the senior partner has a garden flat we could rent. I do not know what is a garden flat, but it is by the river. Will you do it Caro? Will you come and live away from your home?'

'My home is with *you*. Don't you know that by now?'

'Yes? But sometimes now I feel you go away from me. Inside here.' And he tapped his head.

'I'm not brave enough to do that, even in my mind, even supposing I wanted to, which I don't.'

And that was true. Not go away, just hide a little, keep a space for thoughts and feelings that I doubted, knew, he wouldn't understand. I bent my head over his, pushing my fingers through the thick dark hair and as his hands continued to move lightly across my back, felt desire begin to quicken. I stirred, pulling him closer into my arms.

He looked up into my eyes and gave his slow smile. 'I thought you were tired.'

'There is tired, and then again, there is tired.'

'Such riddles – and you will make us late for dinner.'

'That is a gift we two have,' I observed, 'that we seem to be making into a kind of art!'

* * * * *

I consulted Elizabeth's piece of paper, checked the number then climbed the shallow steps to a dark green door. It had a heavy brass knocker in the shape of a Dolphin. I lifted then let it fall and it made a satisfyingly solid thud.

There were quick footsteps, the door opened and I found myself looking up at a tall, whipcord thin but broad-shouldered and quite

181

stunningly good-looking man, who stared at me for moment with eyes so dark as to be almost black.

He had about him that indefinable air of the man who doesn't have to make any effort to be attractive. With sudden blush-making awareness I was conscious my clothes were being lazily but expertly removed by those dark eyes, and had a sudden definite sense of *déjà vu*.

I'd seen him somewhere before.

As I raked my memory for the where and when, his firm mouth broke into a broad grin. 'As I live and breathe,' he said, 'it really *is* Pink 'un's Penrose!''

Then I remembered exactly who he was and pinned him with an icy glare. '*You* were the rotten little tyke who hung over the school wall at King James when I rode my bike to school one windy day; you shouted 'pink knickers' so loudly that I fell off and bled all over the road.'

He gave a mocking bow. 'Guilty as charged!'

I smarted at the remembered indignity of that day. 'You were an absolute swine...capering on the wall shouting 'Look – pink frilly ones!' and encouraging all your beastly friends to howl with laughter and scream "pink 'un's, pink 'un's" like a load of demented parrots...God, but you were the *pits*. I was fifteen and being barracked by a shower of snotty-nosed first formers! It was the most embarrassing moment of my life.'

He laughed and took my hand, drawing me into the hallway. 'Well you were avenged. I was well and truly thrashed by the Head for my sins.'

He continued to hold my hand, standing looking down on me, his mouth still curved into a smile. 'Strewth, I thought, if I were Elizabeth I'd put a ball and chain on this one; aloud I said: 'Don't expect me to feel guilty for storming into the school demanding justice and creating hell, because you deserved all you got – was it very painful?'

'I still bear the scars: on my mind if not my backside. The old man once played cricket for Somerset and had a powerful forward drive.'

'Good,' I said with feeling, 'I shouldn't like to think you'd got off lightly.'

Elizabeth appeared through a door at the end of the hall and grinned at us. 'All right Linney put her down. She's already spoken for.'

He laughed and let go of my hand then turned to close the door. Elizabeth beckoned me into a large airy kitchen, pulling out a chair at the round central table. 'You'll get used to him. He's a hopeless flirt, half the time he swears he doesn't know he's doing it – I gather you've remembered him from the dim and distant past?'

'Have I not,' I replied feelingly. As I sat I saw his uniform jacket hung over the back of his chair; noted the Captain's pips and did a quick mental calculation. He couldn't be more than twenty-one at most and I wondered what he had done to earn the rank.

He saw me looking and winked. 'First in the NAAFI queue for two years!' he said, and looked reprovingly at Elizabeth as she laughed. 'Just stop sniggering, woman or Madame de la Tour and I will take ourselves off elsewhere to talk.'

'Well, you'd better have some refreshment first.' She turned to set out mugs for the coffee percolating on the stove and he moved behind her, placing his hands on her waist and whispering softly close to her ear. She flushed and smiled and I thought then that openly inviting as he was, Elizabeth was probably the only one on the receiving end of any seriously romantic attentions.

When we sat around the table to talk, I quickly became aware that there was most certainly a great deal more to Francis Lindsey than just good looks and a possible habit of flirting with every woman he met.

The dark eyes became disconcertingly steadfast; never leaving my face as I told my story, the air of dégagé good-humour replaced by a keen-faced, intent watchfulness. When I finished speaking and he continued to sit unmoving, pinning me with the same steady cogitative look, I began to get some inkling of how he might have attained his rank and that being first in the queue for the NAAFI had nothing to do with it.

A multi-linguist interrogator with the War Crimes Commission, Elizabeth had told me, and as he continued his unblinking stare I could well believe there were people, perhaps some of them Charles's men without pity, who would not care to meet those eyes.

He took out a packet of French cigarettes, offering them silently and when I shook my head, lit one and sat smoking quietly for a few moments. 'If this child is dead,' he said eventually, 'and he met his death on the road, then you would only discover that by chance, as you did with Lise, and I wouldn't recommend you waste your time looking for graves; there are far too many of those. If he is still alive, then there are several possibilities.'

He held up his hand, counting them off with a long, artist's finger. 'One, the State Orphanages, of which there are many. Two, possibly several hundred of the small Convents and homes run by the Church...and these could be the most difficult because they would

183

have taken in any and every wandering child, not knowing from where it came or anything about it. By now some of those places will have been closed or moved and not necessarily anywhere in France. How old would he have been? Two? Three?'

'Going on three by then.'

He was silent again for a few moments, before continuing: 'Thirdly, there are the *mere adoptives*…foster homes, some of which will have actually led to adoptions…and God only knows how many of those there may be, also if shocked and frightened he may not even have remembered his name let alone where he came from. So as I said, it will be difficult.'

'Looked at logically, it sounds impossible.' I wrapped my hands around my coffee mug, shivering and feeling in need of warmth on this hot summer's day.

He smiled, and his face softened. 'I said difficult,' he pointed out, suddenly gentle, 'not impossible. Nothing is ever impossible for those who care enough.'

I felt a hard lump come into my throat that someone I scarcely knew could understand how I felt and be willing to help, when the person I most loved and was closest to could do neither of those things. I dug my nails into my palms, unable for a few moments to speak.

He said, 'I have a friend…Victor Lestoc, he's a Burgundian but practised as a Solicitor in Tours before the war. He's with the Commission in Nuremberg at present but I think he'll be our man.' He stood up. 'Back in a minute – I'll just make a call.'

I looked at Elizabeth as he left the room. 'Does he often switch personalities like that?'

She laughed. 'All the time; sometimes his job shows and it's never a good idea to take him at face value.'

I said dryly, 'I had worked that out for myself.'

'He is the easiest person in the world to love, but sometimes quite the most impossible one to understand.' She pushed her fingers through her hair, rumpling it, looking rueful. 'It shouldn't be difficult, we've known each other more than ten years, but you see he went away a boy then came back so *old,* and with that look…'

There was a sudden laugh and a volley of rapid French from the direction of the hallway; I looked at her inquiringly. She shrugged her shoulders. 'Don't ask me,' she said. 'I haven't a clue!'

He came back after some minutes, running his fingers through his thick black curling hair in a gesture almost identical to Elizabeth's, then seating himself again, clasped his hands in front of him; bringing them up to rest against his mouth he watched me with quiet, considering eyes.

'If you should find him what would you do then?'

The question was unexpected. I looked at him warily. 'Do? Why, go and see him; do what I could to help.'

'On your own?'

'Of course.'

'And your Charles, you wouldn't consult him?'

'Francis,' Elizabeth warned him, 'you're on very thin ice.'

With only the slightest movement of his head he turned his eyes on her and I was aware that perhaps the most unnerving thing about him was his stillness. Particularly unnerving to me because it was so reminiscent of Charles. They both could convey a quite extraordinary amount of bland and controlled disapproval without as much as a blink of the eyelid.

'It's all right,' I put in quickly as Elizabeth flushed and looked as though she might throw something. 'I know there are two sides, but all the same...'

'In a minute,' he put in quietly, 'you are not going to like me at all.'

'You think so?'

He nodded. 'Yes, I do. So shall we get it over with? You see, although I've never met your husband I probably know quite a lot about him that you may not. I understand some of the things he has seen...and done. Things he has been afraid of and things done of which he is perhaps still ashamed – and I understand why he didn't wish to be dragged into finding out about this child. If you go through with this and he *is* found, you'll not be content just to see him, will you? You'll want more than that, and for your man that could be the end of his peace of mind for ever.'

'So what you are saying is, don't do it!' I sat back, frowning. 'Well to me that sounds like a case of the boys sticking together and a typical male reaction! What about *my* peace of mind?'

His eyes never wavered. 'I said you wouldn't like me.'

'Caro.' Elizabeth put her hand on my arm. 'Much as I hate to say it, he's right. You have to be honest and think really hard about what may happen. It will be three lives you know.'

'I should do. I've had enough bloody sleepless nights thinking about it already.' I looked at Francis Lindsey accusingly. 'I thought you were going to help. What was the point of the 'phone call if you're going back on it all?'

He contemplated the glowing end of his cigarette in silence for a

185

moment then raised one eyebrow and gave me another of his dark, inimical looks. Suddenly I was close to tears again; he was duelling with me, using a rapier against my blunt cutlass and I didn't like it much, but if I was to have any chance of finding Dominic I needed him on my side. I swallowed my pride and said, 'I seem to spend my life saying sorry.'

'How very uncomfortable for you!' He gave a tight smile, looked at the table for a moment, then up again at my face. His eyes were like a camera lens, I thought, clicking and recording, missing nothing. 'I *will* help you find him. Not,' he added with brutal honesty, 'because it's the sensible thing to do, or because I think it right. I don't. I'll do it because you care so much. In my book anyone who cares enough to risk their own happiness, even though they are too plain bloody-minded and stubborn to take into account anyone else's, merits that at least.'

'Excuse me?' I was stung. 'As a back-handed compliment I reckon that just about takes the biscuit.'

He smiled again and his tone was faintly sarcastic. 'You look like a girl who can handle any amount of compliments, backhanded or otherwise.'

I rested my head on my hands and gave in. 'OK. You win...I'm a bloody minded, marriage and home-wrecking idiot. Just stop needling my brain and tell me what to do and where to start.'

* * * * *

'You can take this letter and use it as copy...it's quite short and to the point and in the form of a questionnaire, so that you'll have no trouble in seeing where they have answered *Oui* or *Non*. The English translation is on the back for your use.' He looked up briefly, a hint of mischief in his eyes. 'You can manage that, yes?' He finished writing then passed the page of foolscap across the table. 'Send a copy to every foster home that has taken in a male child under the age of four since nineteen forty-two. Victor will let you have the list within the next ten days. Also, he'll contact by 'phone all the State Orphanages while I scour the countryside for the Church homes, that way we'll cover a lot of ground in a relatively short time. Mind you,' his eyes suddenly sparked wickedly, 'God help me if my Colonel catches me at it. If that happens I shall immediately put the blame on you, so just watch out if a man with eyes like gimlets and a shocking turn of language appears on your doorstep.'

'I can't begin to thank you...and Elizabeth.' I could hardly grasp what was happening it had all come about so quickly. 'I didn't intend or expect you to go out of your way like this. I really only came to talk and get rid of some of the fog from my brain.'

He leaned forward to put a hand over mine. 'Do one thing for me, will you, pink 'un's Penrose?'

'What's that?'

'If you do find the child tell that man of yours, even if you have to duck very quickly and make a run for it! Mostly because you will at least owe him that, and also because without his co-operation you'll be able to do precious little but just look at the boy, then turn and walk away.'

'If Charles didn't hate as he does I wouldn't need to go behind his back like this, would I?' I looked at him curiously. 'I find it odd that *you've* made absolutely no comment about Dominic being German, because when I asked Willi Fischer if he hated them as Charles does he said no, but that if I really wanted to know about hating I should ask you.'

He raised his eyebrows, saying coldly: 'Did he now?'

'The war is over...' I felt anger and despair rising and demanded passionately, 'Do feelings like that have to go on forever wrecking people's lives and making them miserable? Do you, deep down, feel the same about every last one of them as Charles: guilty or not guilty, grown man or little child, but are just too bloody smart or practised to show it? '

For a fraction of a second, his eyes blanked. Suddenly, I remembered the girl in the camp that he had loved and lost and knew that now I'd put my own foot on some very thin ice. I held my breath.

The hand on mine was very still. After a moment he gave his tight, bleak smile. 'Ask me again how I feel,' he said softly, 'when I've finished sorting the sheep from the goats and seen the last of the guilty bastards on their way to the gallows.'

I had never seen eyes so cold and knew then that Charles was not the only one who could hate with such single-minded intensity; that Elizabeth was quite right in not wanting to see what a good stirring-up might bring to the surface of Captain Francis Lindsey's mind. Such dark thoughts and memories were best left undisturbed.

* * * * *

'Give my address for all the replies,' instructed Elizabeth as I left later that afternoon. 'That way you won't have to keep beating your man to the post every morning. I'll find a way to get them to you somehow.'

187

Had we remained in Cornwall it would have been a daunting task to keep my letter writing from Charles, but apart from the list of foster homes, which I managed to grab before he saw the post had arrived, we'd left Tyndals and were settled into the Putney flat by the time I had really begun my inquiries. Once there it was a simple matter to meet Elizabeth every few days and collect any replies.

'What will you do with yourself for these months?' Charles asked as we strolled along the towpath at the end of our first week at Kingdom Cottage. 'You are so used to being busy that I am afraid you will soon become bored.'

'I thought that once we were properly settled and I'd hidden all the furniture and *Objets d'Art* we don't like in the cellar, I might start going to French classes.' I swung his hand gently. 'Then the next time we go to Paris I shan't feel such a dim-wit...and I shall also know what you say when you talk in your sleep!'

'My last small privacy gone,' he laughed then suddenly held up my hand. 'Darling, why have you ink on your finger here...and here? You must be writing many letters.'

I cursed myself silently. I had meant to pumice off the telltale stains.

'I'm keeping a diary.'

He lifted his brows. 'May one read it?'

'No, one may not.' I gave what I hoped was an innocent smile. 'It is all about your love-making technique and when it's complete I shall sell it for a vast sum of money to the News of the World!'

He laughed. 'Remind me then to buy a copy...and take a plain brown paper bag in which to carry it home.'

'You just do that small thing!' He raised his brows again. 'Air Force slang,' I said. 'Come on, let's walk across the bridge and spit on the boats as they go under!'

'*Caroline!*'

'It's all right. I wouldn't really, although it would be fun. I'm going to like living here, you know.'

'You must go down to Cornwall whenever you miss the sea too much.' He smiled and gestured at the river beneath us. 'Very pretty, but not like the waves breaking against the rocks in Penmarrion Cove.'

'And what would you do while I was in Cornwall and you here?'

'Oh...have lots of beautiful women to stay.'

'What – all at the same time? That's an orgy!'

'But I *like* an orgy, once in a while.' He put his arm about me as we leaned over the bridge, slipping his free hand inside my jacket to curve over my breast. 'Have you ever,' he whispered, caressing me with his thumb, 'heard of an orgy with just two?'

'Heard of it? I've done it...but not in the middle of Putney Bridge!'

As we laughed and strolled on I pushed to the back of my consciousness, and conscience, the nagging thought of my deceit, telling myself that it was only a case of the end justifying the means and that somehow, someday, and in some miraculous fashion, Dominic would be found, Charles would change his mind and all the soul-searching and deception and lies would have been worth while.

* * * * *

Kingdom Cottage, our temporary home was delightful. We had the ground floor and basement of what was in fact a narrow three-story house, tucked away behind two sweet chestnut trees and surrounded by a stone wall with a wrought iron gate leading to the tow-path beyond. There were two bedrooms and a new, rather posh bath and shower room on the ground floor. At the back in the basement was a big square living room with French windows opening onto the prettiest small walled garden; at the front of the apartment a kitchen with a half-moon window looking out onto a wall covered in clematis and honeysuckle. As birds, bees and a myriad of other small flying things constantly flitted in and around the foliage, even washing-up became a pleasure.

A strange little lady, who wore many trailing garments and floating scarves and went by the entirely appropriate name of Miss Remnant, lived on the floor above while right at the top under the eaves dwelt a rather wild-looking young man with a great deal of uncontrolled hair, who cooked delicious Oriental-smelling dishes at all hours and earned a precarious living by drawing horoscopes and reading the Tarot. We called him Stir-fry because of the Oriental cooking. Miss Remnant whispered to me one day that he was also Amelia Honeywell, who did the agony column in True Tales Magazine and I was inclined to believe her. One morning when we met at the gate he told me in a high, fluting voice that he could see my aura and that it was green. I was intrigued and flattered until he informed me distantly that a green aura meant trouble and when I laughed he went off muttering. Later when I relayed this conversation to Charles he said that he knew all about the trouble, but perhaps I should see a doctor about the green aura as it might be something catching.

I did miss the sea on my doorstep, and the farm and everyone at home, sometimes most dreadfully, but the fascination of watching the endless river traffic and walking across the vast reaches of the common made up a little for the temporary loss of my life in far-off Cornwall.

Each weekday morning Charles left the house at about nine to walk the mile or so to his workplace, not returning until the late afternoons. Regular, absorbing work seemed to improve his health and energy. He slept better and began leaving his stick behind more often. As his body strengthened and he tired less easily, we walked together along the towpath most evenings, ate out often, went to concerts and the theatre and spent our week-ends tending the small garden or going by river to visit Kew, or Richmond or Hampton Court.

True to my word I enrolled at the local Polytechnic and buckled down to improve my meagre French, not only in readiness for our next trip to Paris but also for the time I may have need of it should the little Dominic be found.

But as the weeks passed and only negative replies came to my letters hope began to fade. Victor Lestoc had drawn a blank on the State Orphanages, whilst Francis Lindsey's progress with the Church homes was slow, steady, but so far unrewarding.

By the time autumn came in earnest and our chestnut trees began to drop first their conkers and then their leaves, I knew I was facing defeat. Not one of my letters had produced news of any child who bore the slightest resemblance to the now six year old Dominic de la Tour, who had gone missing somewhere between Carentan and Dreux in July nineteen forty-four.

* * * * *

'Francis has reached the end of the line.' Elizabeth told me sadly one cold, crisp October morning, 'and now there's no place that between you three that hasn't been investigated. He's very down in the mouth about it, and blames himself for getting up your hopes then dashing them again.'

'But he mustn't...I can cope with the disappointment; it was not *trying* that I found so impossible. I'm just sorry because he's worked so hard on something he didn't really approve of, only to come up against the same blank wall.'

We were in a cosy workman's cafe near her hospital. Although it was ten-thirty in the morning all around us large men were still tucking into the huge stodgy fry-ups that passed for a cooked breakfast. Meat and eggs still being in such short supply, I wondered aloud what else was padding out the bubble-and-squeak and fried bread; Elizabeth averted her eyes.

'Don't ask; they'll most likely all be in Casualty with perfectly disgusting bowel disorders in a few months time and I'll be the muggins doing my stuff there when they arrive.'

'A good job we can still laugh about something.' I lifted my tannin-loaded cup, 'and please don't tell me what this is doing to my kidneys, I couldn't bear to know.'

'So will you ever tell Charles what you've been up to all these weeks?'

'I don't think I'm brave enough, and anyway, it's all over now. No point in stirring muddy puddles is there?'

'I don't think I could ever have kept such a thing from Francis. He can smell deception a mile off.' She stirred her tea absently. 'D'you like him?' she asked, 'Francis, I mean.'

'I wasn't sure at first,' I said honestly, 'but yes, I do, and when he isn't being good at his job I should think he's probably a very restful sort of person to have around. He's so still inside, isn't he?'

'Umm. He's such a calm, reasonable bastard…I could brain him sometimes!' she looked gloomy, 'Me, I like a good blow-up every now and again to clear the air but I doubt I'll ever get that from Linney. When I lose my rag he either shuts up tight like a clam, or just laughs and says 'Let's go to bed' which we usually do…and who can have a row when you're both having such a good time'

'Not me, that's for sure.'

'Oh, well, I suppose I must be getting back to the factory.' She laughed and reached for her coat. 'London suits you, you know. It's given you quite a bounce in your step.'

'I love it, although Trewlyns will always call…'

'Will you go back there for good d'you think?'

'I don't know.' I stood in the street, wrapping my long wool coat about me. 'I'll go where Charles goes; I don't mind as long as I'm with him. So long as I can return to Trewlyns and Tyndals from time to time any place will do me. What about you?'

'Oh, like you I go with my chap…but not until I'm sure *he's* sure! Then it will be most definitely and irrevocably to Cornwall. He will paint and flirt with every woman who crosses his path, I will doctor and yell at him and he will still laugh and say 'Come to bed' because he is how he is…' She threw back the corn-coloured hair, her blue eyes sparkling, 'and what could be better than that?'

'Smug tart,' I said, and watched as she ran laughing across the street, pausing on the other side to wave before swinging on her way, leaving me to wish that I could say the same, and be so sure, about my own beloved chap.

* * * * *

When Charles came home that afternoon, I went into his arms and held him even tighter than usual, needing the closeness of him to help exorcise the feeling of sadness and disappointment at my failure to find Dominic.

'What have I done to deserve this?' he asked, but I couldn't answer him. Because now I should never know if he would have remained hard and unforgiving and filled with hate. If he would have said, 'He is nothing to me', and looked as he had in the churchyard near Dreux.

There was relief that our love was safe, but an ineffable sadness that for me the question mark would always be there. Would he ever have accepted Dominic for my sake, or would he have turned his back and walked away from us both?

Better not to know. Better to just forget.

15

Although my main reason for learning French had been dealt as it were, a mortal blow, I continued to attend the classes, enjoying the company of the other students, many of whom like me were ex-Service. To my surprise I found it not so difficult once I'd managed to master the complexities of gender and verbs, my early struggles with which gave Charles many an uproarious moment as I practised on him what I had learned each day. At such times he would frequently take his teasing revenge for all the times I had corrected *him*.

'I had a better excuse than you,' he said one evening, 'because I must learn my English very quickly, and not have such an easy time of it...but I had a good teacher.'

'Someone fat and ugly with a beard, I hope?'

I was sitting curled on his knees before the fire and felt the rumble of laughter begin in his chest. 'Ah...but not quite!'

'No beard?' I asked. He shook his head. 'Not fat and ugly either?' I pursued.

He laughed outright. 'She was that someone in Oxford that I might once have loved...and beautiful, like a golden reed standing alone in the muddy creek of war; but not for me...' he kissed my neck. 'I told you; even then I think I must have been waiting for you.'

I was intrigued. 'Didn't you even make a pass?'

'No, she too was waiting, I think, for someone she had lost. Someone she loved very much...a quarrel, or a misunderstanding... perhaps something she had cause to regret.'

'I hope it all came right for her.'

'I think perhaps it did; I saw her once when I went with your father to take flowers to Porthcurnow, she was with an older, but so big and handsome a man. They walked close and hand in hand.'

'You really are an old romantic, aren't you?' I grinned. 'It was probably her father.'

He shook his head reprovingly. 'He was not so very old and I do not think this woman would look so at her father! Also, he and I had already met, after a fashion. He was an MTB commander and I was picked up two times from France by his gun-boat.'

'Twice, not two times,' I corrected smugly, 'and I reckon you had it easy, learning English from some gorgeous piece.' I snuggled down into his arms. 'Because my tutor *is* fat and ugly, has a beard, galloping halitosis and looks like Ernest Hemmingway on a bad day!'

He laughed again. 'That is good, but my poor Caro, let me console you...' Which he did, and it turned out to be very nice and cosy and sexy and a lovely way to spend a winter's afternoon.

However, something he said about the girl who was like a golden reed stayed in my mind.

A misunderstanding, perhaps something she had cause to regret...

The next morning when Charles had left the house, I took from the wooden box in my securely suitcase all the letters that had come from France, tearing each in its envelope into small pieces and putting them all into the dustbin.

That way that episode at least, would not furnish *me* with any cause for regret.

* * * * *

A few days later I met Francis Lindsey again early one evening as I waited for a taxi.

Charles was dining in town that night with a half-dozen of the shareholders in the Club project. He had been tense and on edge for the past week, but when he had neatly fielded my concerned inquiries and grumpily dodged any explanation, I'd left him to work off his moodiness in his own time.

We were going to Cornwall for Christmas and what with shopping for presents and Charles's funny mood, I was quite pleased to have time to myself. After taking in a late afternoon performance at the Studio One cinema near Oxford Circus I'd planned afterwards to walk as far as the Piccadilly tube, but when it began to drizzle, flagging down a taxi suddenly seemed a much better idea.

'*Bonsoir, Madame de la Tour.*'

I looked around from the door of the cab I had just snatched from under the nose of a disgruntled floozy, to find Elizabeth's chap saluting me. He grinned sympathetically at the floozy, who immediately smoothed down her dress and gave him the eye. As he was looking particularly devastatingly handsome and sexy I couldn't exactly blame her for that.

'Are you are going Knightsbridge way in this?' he asked and I gave a nod. 'Then may I scrounge a lift? I was supposed to be meeting Liz for a meal in a dive near the Nat. Histmus ten minutes ago, but got delayed by my colonel giving me a bollocking over the 'phone.' He grinned unrepentantly. 'I, er, 'forgot' he needed me to go with him tonight to some Embassy do.'

'You're welcome to share. I'm a temporary grass widow and being a sociable girl, only too pleased to have company.'

'I must remember that.' He ducked his head and slid in beside me, then sat back casting an appreciative eye over the new coat I had stolen Charles's coupons to buy, before letting his glance pass to my legs.

'Very nice,' he said, having taken his time to examine them thoroughly, 'no wonder Izaac let you beat one of his regular fares back there!'

'Who's Izaac?'

'Your driver.'

The cabby turned around and let loose a stream of unintelligible chatter. My companion hitched himself forward on the seat to engage in what was clearly a hilarious spot of repartee before sitting back and pushing his cap up his forehead with his cane.

'He says not to worry…it will give her time to pick up another client before he gets back, so she'll probably be grateful to you and so will her old mum who lives in Paddington and takes in washing to make ends meet.'

'What was he speaking? Hindustani?'

'What, with a name like Izaac…have a heart; that was your genuine East End Yiddish!'

'And I suppose you also know the name, antecedents and patios of the bloke who sells flowers outside Waterloo station as well?' I queried sarcastically.

'If it's the one to the right of the steps, yes…the one on the left is a spiv from the Edgware Road down on his luck. He's been pinched by the Law five times and doesn't *have* any antecedents. Not legitimate ones, anyway. Well, here we are…God love you!' and he was out of the door, bending down to salute me again through the window, then pushing money into Izaac's hand before leaping across the Cromwell road, dodging the traffic as he ran.

'Is alvays in the hurry…he nice bastard though, but *Meshugana*, yeah?' Izaac swung his cab out again into the stream of traffic. 'An' he got very naughty flirty-flirty eyes for the ladies, yeah?'

'Yeah,' I said, 'you're damn' right he has.'

I leaned back on my seat thinking it was a good job I hadn't met *that* one when we were both footloose and fancy-free. Elizabeth might be able to handle him, but I was damned sure that coping with Francis Lindsey's 'flirty-flirty eyes' would have been way beyond my ability.

195

* * * * *

"'I'll be seeing you, in all the old familiar places...'" crooned
Charles, as I half unbuttoned the front of my dress, kicked off my
shoes and flopped down onto the sofa.

I looked at him in some surprise. Perhaps it was the effect of all
the wine he and Matthew had put away during the evening that had
dispersed the vaguely abstracted air and general moodiness of the past
couple of weeks. I gave a mental shrug. Whatever...singing, even off
key, was better than Charles brooding over something about which I
could do nothing. I grinned and undid a couple more buttons. 'Coarse
beast; look the other way then – what a party!'

'You are pleased to be back here?'

'Oh, yes, lovely to see everyone so happy: Jenny and her big tum
and Matthew so proud. Even the clinging vine seemed almost human.'

'And Paul and Barbara,' he sprawled beside me, pulling at the
ends of his bow tie and undoing his collar. 'Did you see them do the
smooch to music? Perhaps at long last she is thinking him not such a
dull person to be with.'

'Possibly. I suppose even the Barbara's of this world must come
to a point in life when just being friends and liking each other is more
important than sex...although God save me from such a fate just yet.'
I yawned and kissed him sleepily. 'I do still feel the odd man out
amongst them all, you know. I thought I was so grown up when I
came back from the war, but tonight I realised that I'd just run back to
Matthew and Grace like a big kid because I was feeling lost and hurt
and thought they could make it all better...and so they did. A little.' I
felt wistful, but thought that was from too much wine rather than
sentiment. 'Now I'm really growing away and I shan't run back any
more.'

'Not ever again?'

I shook my head.

'Not to live here again, much as I love Trewlyns, but to visit, have
a good holiday, see everyone is OK. Somehow, since you and I have
been away things have changed. Everything, that is but Cornwall
itself and the sea and the sky.'

'Most wise Caroline,' he put his arm about my shoulders, 'to
know when to let go, of places, and people. Although sometimes,' He
began to wind a lock of my hair around his fingers and suddenly there
was the slightest edge to his voice. 'Sometimes one can move on to
the wrong people and places, leaving the right ones behind.'

'What *do* you mean?'

He shrugged. 'Oh, nothing much, I suppose; but I wonder…'

Faintly and far off a warning bell began to ring. We have both drunk too much, I thought and in a minute one or the other, or both of us are going to say the wrong thing. Best go to bed now. Still, I couldn't help probing. 'Wonder what?'

He sighed and leaned back to stare at the ceiling then slowly turned his head to look at me. 'Why my wife writes a diary for a few weeks then stops; what was in all the torn letters with the French stamps that I see in the bin when I take out the old newspapers – and who other than myself does she ride with in taxis?'

Grabbing at the last as the only question I felt capable of answering, I attempted a laugh then saw the look in his eyes and stopped. 'Damn!' I said irritably. 'We've just had a bloody marvellous evening. For pity's sake, Charles let it go. We've only been here three days and its *Christmas*.'

'No,' he was persistent. 'Tell me.'

'What were you doing when I got into that taxi – spying on me?'

'No. I just happened to see you as I arrived at Ley Ons' with the boring businessmen. So who was the man sharing your taxi?'

'Francis Lindsey, you mutt – Elizabeth's chap; he cadged a lift.'

'Yes?'

'Yes, so no need for the green-eyed monster, OK?'

'And the mysterious diary? Also the letters?' His finger's tightened on my shoulder. 'Tell me about those.'

My stomach began to churn ominously.

'This is stupid.' I sat up away from his encircling arm, shrugging off his hand. 'What I write and who writes to me is *my* business. Do I ask you what, where, how, and to whom, or from whom, you write or receive letters?'

'There is no need because I tell you.'

'Well, bully for you!'

'Your Captain Lindsey is with the Army in France, is he not?'

'He is not *my* anything, but yes he's in the Army and sometimes in France, as are whole lot of other blokes.'

'But they do not all get into taxis with you, nor write letters.'

'Charles, will you just stop this.' I was both angry and alarmed. 'Don't you trust me?'

'I don't think so, unless you will answer truthfully what after all are some perfectly reasonable questions.'

'Why in hell have you waited until now to ask? A pretty nasty, snide way of going about things, I must say.'

I was on the defensive now, fighting a losing battle and he knew it. Relentlessly he held my reluctant gaze with his own. 'I thought that if I waited you might perhaps tell me without being asked...Caro, I *know* there are things that worry you; things that you keep from me. In a marriage, this is not good.'

'If you think for one moment that I'm having an affair with Francis Lindsey, or with anyone else for that matter, then you are out of your mind.' Distractedly, I ran my fingers through my hair. 'Just what do I have to do to convince you?'

'You could try telling me the truth...about everything...the letters, the dairy; everything.'

'Charles, please leave it for now; it's late and I'm tired, we both are. I can only say that I've never been unfaithful to you, nor am I likely to be; with Elizabeth's chap or anyone else.'

'Very well.' He stood up. 'Then we shall talk in the morning when you are less tired. Doubtless by then you will have had time to think up some good, if not entirely true answers to *all* of my questions.' He looked down at me with sombre eyes. 'When did you begin to be less than honest, Caroline – you, the most truthful of people?'

That hurt, and it hurt even more when we were in bed and he made no move to put his arms about me, but lay on his back, eyes closed and with his good arm above his head, creating both a visible and invisible barrier between us.

* * * * *

I slept fitfully, half-waking between troubled dreams, sensing him lying sleepless beside me until finally, waking with a frightened start I put out my hand and found him gone.

It was cold. I pulled on my dressing gown and went downstairs.

He was at the table, a glass in his hand as I had seen him once before. He looked up as I crossed the room to sit opposite him. His eyes were hooded and dull, but whether from drink or anger or pain I couldn't tell.

'Caro, go back to bed.'

His voice was quiet and faintly slurred. I shivered and pulled my gown about me, determined not to leave him alone with that bottle. 'Too cold without you...and can anyone get pissed or is that just your prerogative?'

He almost smiled then, pushing the bottle toward me. I fetched a glass from the kitchen and seated myself again, pouring the whisky, noting with tired detached interest that my hand was unsteady and liquid was slopping on the table. This, I thought, is where the shit really hits the fan. I said, 'You win.'

He raised his brows but made no reply.

'No lover...' I gulped on my drink, downing it fast and pouring another. 'No love letters from me to him and him to me, no clandestine meetings and kissing Francis Lindsey in taxis ...none of that. Just lots of lies and evasions and going behind your back, because you have this thing in your head that I can't deal with. Because sometimes you scare me.'

'Am I such a frightening person?'

'Yes, on occasions you are.' I propped my head on one hand, staring down into my glass, surprised to see it was empty again. I refilled it. Nothing now would do but the plain unvarnished truth. 'There isn't any way to wrap this up and make it all nice and chummy and tidy...Charles, I've been trying to find Dominic.'

His head snapped up. 'You have *what*?'

'The letters you found were replies to mine.' His eyes were blank and uncomprehending. I thought he probably was drunk and repeated carefully, 'I have been trying to find Dominic.'

'For how long?'

I looked away. 'Since soon after we came back from Paris.'

The silence stretched between us. The ticking of the clock seemed to be unbearably loud and my heart thudded along in time with its remorseless beat. I was swamped by a sudden wave of nausea. I pushed my glass away then picked it up again. 'Are you very angry?'

'Am I angry?' His voice was tight and cold. 'I am so angry that I can scarcely speak to you. Why?' he demanded bitterly, 'In the name of God, *Why*?'

'I don't know. I just had to...there were some kids in Paris...' I drank my whisky in two gulps, then pushed my hair back from my forehead with both hands, holding it, staring at the splashes on the table. 'Oh, what's the use...you wouldn't understand. Not because it's difficult, but because you wouldn't want to.'

'Kids? In Paris? What the *fuck* are you talking about?'

I risked a glance at him. He was tight-lipped and pale with anger and I quailed inside.

'On our last day...down by the Seine.' Still staring at the table I did my best to explain how it had all begun: about the nun and the orphans and Francis and Elizabeth and a man called Victor...how every area had been covered, and how I had now reached the end of the line.

'To spend all those weeks, to involve others...to go behind my back and meddle with something I had asked you to leave alone? You think that was right?' He demanded with a deadly furious calm.

'No, I think it was unforgivable, but I refuse to be full of guilt because I tried.' I met his hard, angry stare. 'Even though I didn't find him it was worth every bit of effort. I am not going to change my mind. I still think you were inhuman in the way you behaved; that you made a horrible mistake you may live to regret in turning your back and saying the things you did. You were *wrong* and nothing you say or do will ever have me believe otherwise.'

'Must I hear more of this, or are you finished?'

'Not quite.' I flinched at the cold sarcasm but I wasn't afraid of him now, my boats were burning all around me, hotter than a funeral pyre and I might as well say it all. It couldn't possibly get any worse. 'You see, I love you; I love you very much. If it came to it I think I would die for you. But there are some things I cannot do. I cannot allow you to smother my conscience...to expect me to act without integrity or compassion. I thought I could. After we found Lise I tried, I really tried my best. I thought I could do it and damn' near made it. Until I saw those kids.'

He was silent for a long time, rolling his empty glass between his hands, looking, but not looking at me. His expression was remote and his eyes unfocussed. *Please,* I begged silently, *don't let him be so pissed that he can't make sense of all this...*

Eventually he put down the glass. Spreading his hands before his face he examined them closely for a moment before laying them palms down on the table. 'You thought carefully about everything before you went ahead?'

'Yes.'

'How much I loved and needed you and you me? All that we meant to each other?'

'Yes.'

'And still you did it?'

'Yes. I had to.'

'I see.'

'Do you?'

'I see that if you had found him we may have lost everything.'

'Willi Fischer,' I said deliberately, 'doesn't hate every German, though one might say he had every reason to. Francis Lindsey hates them all right, but despite that, or because of it, spends his days sorting the sheep from the goats. For you to live a life full of hatred for the innocent as well as the guilty may also bring us dangerously close to losing everything...if it hasn't already.' Suddenly the nausea was back; wave after wave. I closed my eyes and my voice seemed to come from a long way off. 'Sorry, Charles but I think I'm going to be sick!'

I didn't hear him move, but he was beside me, turning me in the chair, placing an arm about my shoulders and holding a cool hand across my clammy forehead, saying calmly and with authority 'No, you are not.'

I made a feeble attempt to hold my ground. 'Don't bloody contradict me...it's my stomach.'

'*Tsch,* don't argue with me!'

For a few swimming moments I thought I would prove him wrong, but slowly the waves of nausea receded until I could sit up straight and take the water he fetched.

My teeth chattered against the glass; he waited until I'd emptied it then put his hand beneath my elbow. '*Nom de Dieu,* but no one can look as ill as you when you put your mind to it. Come...this is enough for tonight. I am taking you to bed.'

Too exhausted to argue I let him help me up the stairs.

'You're not going down to sit and drink again, are you?' I asked in alarm as he pulled the covers over me and turned away.

'No.' Moving a chair nearer the bed he seated himself and taking his book from under the corner of the mattress where he always slipped it at night, turned the lamp so that it lit his page and left the bed in shadow. 'I shall sit here to make sure you stay in this bed and go to sleep.'

Thankfully, I closed my heavy eyes, saying weakly, 'At times of any crisis in my life you read! We shall have to talk tomorrow, though.'

'Yes. Now sleep.'

On the edge of sleep and through a drowsy haze, I thought I felt his lips on my forehead and heard him murmur, '*Tout comprendre, c'est tout pardonner*' but couldn't be sure.

It seemed, in the circumstances, unlikely.

* * * * *

There was the rattle of china. I opened my eyes to see him placing a cup and saucer beside the bed. He stood looking down at me, his face tired and grey. I ventured a feeble grin. 'Thank you, but you don't look a bit like Grace!'

'Today, and only today, I indulge you. It is quite disgusting to drink the tea before cleaning the teeth.'

Uncertainly I reached out to touch the sleeve of his tweed jacket. 'There is cold air coming from you and you smell of the sea.'

'I have been walking while you slept, and thinking what I should say to you this morning.'

I shivered and sat up, clasping my hands about my elbows. 'Then whatever it is will you please get it over with quickly.'

'First drink your tea. You are not yet properly awake.'

He put my dressing gown around my shoulders then crossed to the window to pull back the curtains. 'We have a fine Cornish day beginning...a good day for us both to walk.'

'Christ, no; that's the last thing I want to do.' I drank the tea thirstily, watching him through half-closed eyes. 'I feel like hell.'

'You are sick again?'

'No. Just a good old-fashioned hangover from drinking too much whisky on top of too much wine...the wages of sin and all that, and arguing at four o'clock in the morning didn't exactly help. You should be delighted that even God has got it in for me.' I put down the cup and held my aching head. 'Sorry. I shouldn't have said that. I shall be all right in a minute, but please don't mention breakfast.'

'Then I shall have mine and leave you to bathe. After, we *shall* walk and talk.'

'Sadist,' I muttered, but once warm from my bath and dressed in tweed trousers, jersey and duffel coat, I was ready for the walk, if dreading the talk.

But one must, eventually, face the music.

* * * * *

'You are going to say you've had enough, aren't you?'

We had walked in silence almost as far as Lamorna; time enough for me to have gone over in my mind the previous night's debacle in minute detail, recalling the whole ghastly business with hideous clarity. Now all I wanted was to hear the bad news and get it over with, so that I might crawl into a hole somewhere and finish slitting my own throat.

'Enough of what?'

So help me, I thought, one day I'll belt him when he answers one question with another, then realised with a sick dread that there may be no other days and retreated into silence. He stopped and turned towards me, repeating: 'Enough of what, Caro?'

'Enough of me – us – all the mess, look, I cocked it up. You don't have to go on being calm and grown-up about it and you might just as

202

well have a jolly good yell at me because I don't think I'm really sorry about anything, except nearly being sick on your slippers...so *please*, Charles, don't drag it out. I just can't bear much more. I'd rather you slapped me than go on like this – '

'Caroline,' he interrupted me, pulling down his brows and frowning repressively. 'Sit down,' he pointed at a nearby outcrop of rock, 'and *shut up!*'

I stared. The words and manner were so unlike him that I felt a highly dangerous desire to giggle begin to bubble in my chest. I said factitiously, 'Well, put like that...' He made a movement towards me and I sat hastily.

'Now you listen to me – and do not dare to interrupt; why God should punish me so...' He stood before me his fists rammed deep into his jacket pockets. 'Last night we came as close as I ever wish to be to finishing everything. I realise now that much of the blame must be mine. If I had shown a little more humility – and humanity, in the beginning, all this would not have come about. Do not think that I have had a change of mind, or that now there is only peace and love in my heart for those I shall always think of as my enemies...Not so, I still can hate.'

He sat down beside me, silent a moment, looking out to sea, pulling at his lower lip with thumb and forefinger, then gave an exasperated sigh. 'This little *gosse* who has caused so much trouble, even by once existing! Because I love you, I am sorry for you that he is not found; but not sorry for me, for us. Although I should no longer visit his father's sins upon his head, it is better so.'

There was another long silence. 'Do I get to speak again?' I ventured.

He looked at me sideways. 'Can I prevent you?'

'What would you have done had I found him?'

'Probably thrown you both in the river!'

'Ungentlemanly of you, but understandable; never mind...but now, suppose he was still alive and you knew where to find him, what would you do?'

'Does that matter?'

'To me it does.'

'I don't know. How *can* I know,' his mouth set in the old, hard line. 'I should not I think, want ever to see him; would perhaps put him in a good school, see he did not starve...salve the conscience you think I do not have.' He shrugged. 'How can I say this about something that will never happen?' He stood up abruptly. 'Come. It is cold, sitting. We should go back now.'

I hesitated. Too much remained unsaid but I knew that look. So far as he was concerned, that was that and there was nothing more to be done. The matter of Lise's child could be pushed back into the cupboard and the door firmly closed.

He smiled rather bleakly at my hesitation. 'We can be friends again, yes?'

'Not more than that?'

He put his arms about me. 'Yes, much more, but carefully...we have to find our way back along some rocky paths.'

'Look, I *am* sorry, and not only about the sick.'

'I know. But not so very sorry, *n'est-ce pas*?'

'You could be right,' I admitted. 'I may do better in the fullness of time, but don't bank on it.'

* * * * *

We stayed at Tyndals until after the New Year. Most extraordinarily, Jenny and Josh's Cynthia – wouldn't you just know, I had demanded of Charles, that she would have a name like that – were rather matey together. They met frequently, in order one presumed to swap knitting patterns and pregnancy symptoms, so that I continued to feel very much out of things.

When there were just the two of us, Jenny was as warm and funny as ever but there was no doubt about it, approaching motherhood changed a person in ways both subtle and obvious. Even Matthew and Grace seemed different and more distant from me, concentrated as they both were on the impending birth of the baby soon to take his or her place in the room under the eaves vacated by my departure from the house a year since.

All of this, coupled with Charles rather obviously doing his best to paper over the rift in our marriage, was straining what was left of my nerves to breaking point. I knew I wasn't really trying to meet him even halfway. He was considerate and thoughtful in taking pains to repair the damage, but his refusal to even think, let alone talk about the fact that Dominic might be alive made it impossible for me to respond. There was still too much repressed and unresolved anger in me to allow that.

I caught Matthew's eyes upon me from time to time, but whatever he was thinking, he stopped short of asking any questions. Only Paul, meeting me one morning as I wandered alone in the village, stepped in where others wouldn't, or couldn't. Falling into step beside me he asked, 'Want to talk?'

'Nothing much to talk about,' I answered brusquely, adding rashly, 'I don't know, maybe; perhaps.'

'Well,' he looked at me encouragingly, 'That's a progression of thought in the right direction! So walk with me and let the wind blow the cobwebs from your mind.'

But I didn't want to bare my soul; it was Charles, I thought mutinously who should be doing that. If he could bottle it, so could I. 'You'll freeze without a coat.' I eyed Paul's cassock, 'and the grass is wet. You'll get your dress muddy!'

Ignoring the sarcasm he paused by the stile leading to the cliff path. 'Let me worry about that,' he climbed over and looked back. 'Well, are you coming or not?'

'If you insist, but as I said: there's really nothing in particular to talk about.'

'What you mean is that there's nothing in particular that you *want* to talk about, which is a different matter altogether.'

After a moment's hesitation I shrugged and followed him over the stile and in silence we began to walk along the headland. We had covered quite a distance before spoke.

'Charles is looking guilty, you are looking sulky and Mathew is looking worried: so what's gone wrong?'

'I'm not sure I want to answer any of that and if I did I'm damned if I can see how a short nature ramble with the vicar is going to sort anything out.'

'In that case,' he said, striding out, 'perhaps we should make it a long one.'

* * * * *

'I think that you are both quite the most stubborn and pig-headed pair I've ever come across,' he said, as an hour later we climbed back over the stile, 'For heaven's sake, if you don't shake down together pretty quickly and give way gracefully to each other when necessary, you'll spend the rest of your lives fighting about who gets to be right all the time.'

I said sulkily, 'I don't fight with Charles because he doesn't give me the chance; he simply won't discuss what he doesn't want to. He hates Germans, so *ergo*, I should hate them too.'

'Charles is wrong, very wrong, but you can't just up and tell him so to his face then expect him to back down and make all the moves towards peace, whilst you go around still nursing your grievances. Didn't you learn *anything* about diplomacy from five years of dealing with people in the forces?'

'Yes. Plenty, but it wasn't the sort to use on Charles!'

He looked sceptical. 'Put your hand on your heart and tell me you've tried.'

'I've told you, I can't. If he'd just talk, really talk I'd try, but he won't. He thinks that if he says it's all over and we can forget the past, that makes it all right. But it doesn't, it bloody *doesn't*, and I can't just smile sweetly and pretend it does.' I clenched my hands in my pockets, swamped again with misery.

'I think you've both done more than enough talking. Give yourself time to remember how much you love him and how it would feel to be without him. Because if you don't meet his peacemaking halfway and show him how much you still care, that's how you'll end up. Alone.'

'I know.'

'Then *try*, for your sake and everyone else's. You're driving poor Matthew to distraction!'

'Sorry. I'm sorry. I'm a cow. I know you're right. But Charles isn't the easiest person...'

We stepped out of the lane and there was the object of our discussion, leaning against a wall, smiling his faint, enigmatic smile as he watched us walk towards him.

'Good morning, Paul, your so sharp-eyed postmistress told me that you had gone walking with my wife.'

The rector grinned. 'In that case, my reputation is already in shreds. Better take her away, Charles, before she causes any more trouble.'

I stretched to kiss him on both cheeks, murmuring. 'You are a rat, Paul, but a nice one!'

'I'm honoured.' He squeezed my shoulder and walked away down the street. Charles looked after him for a moment then took my hand and began to pace slowly back through the village.

'You are too quiet and too thin; you do not sleep and now you have needed to walk with the discerning and so understanding Paul.' He gave me a wry smile. 'It is time I think to go home. Tomorrow, perhaps?'

'Please.' I tightened my fingers around his. 'Funny, I never thought to look upon Putney as "home"'

'Where would you like to live when my contract is finished?'

'I really hadn't thought beyond the next few weeks. It all depends doesn't it, on where any future work might be?'

'When we get back I expect we shall know more of that – if you remember about such things after all the troubles that have intervened these last days, there are other possible contracts coming up...two at least in London and one in Paris.'

'I don't mind where we live as long as we can somehow get back to being as we were.'

He smiled. 'I am missing the old Caro who is not so polite and distant but says rude things and fights with me and wishes to make love at inconvenient times! I want *her* back as she was. So, we shall go home tomorrow.' He turned into the alley behind the butchers. 'Now, I have not been idle. I have the car here. We are going on a little trip. I have something for you. A New Year gift.'

Staying infuriatingly close-mouthed he drove the Standard along the coast road to Tregenick. Parking beside the Mermaid Inn he pulled me out into the stiff sea breeze then strode alongside the harbour wall, my hand held close in his.

'Now,' he stopped before double doors at the end of a cul-de-sac backing onto the netting sheds, 'you are to close your eyes and not open them until I say, or your present will vanish into the thin air!'

'You have no idea how silly I feel.' I could hear the sound of doors being opened, the whiff of something other than fish...

'Now you may look.'

I opened my eyes.

Perc, big bearded Perc, Elizabeth's chauffeur from the night of the storm stood smiling broadly beside a beautiful little dark green Triumph with a white hood and shining chrome lamps. 'Yours,' Charles dropped a pair of keys into my hand, 'to drive around London or Paris and keep you from gentlemen in taxis!'

Speechless, I walked around the car, touching the gleaming lamps and running my fingers over the glossy paintwork. I looked at him over the hood. 'New Year's gift my foot! Perc didn't find *this* overnight. When did you ask him to start looking?' I demanded and he had the grace to blush.

'Almost two weeks ago – the day after our quarrel; I thought, a peace offering.'

I smiled, 'A big offering.'

'It was a big quarrel!'

I looked at Perc as he stood grinning at us through his beard. 'I don't wish to shock you so would you mind awfully turning your back a minute?' I asked.

He gave a wink of fearsome proportions. 'Tak yur time, m'dear, I'll be in the Mermaid when yur quite thru...'

* * * * *

With great ceremony I made Jenny a present of the Standard which, as she had been using it ever since our move to Putney, wasn't much of a gift. But she was suitably grateful and promised she wouldn't let Matthew use it to keep assignations with other women once she was anchored at home with the baby.

It had been too old to be relied upon for long journeys and too thirsty for London driving, so it was a joy now to make our way home free from the long train journey, stopping as we wished to eat and drink and stretch our legs. Required to spend long periods with his knees under his chin Charles bore the discomfort with fortitude, only groaning occasionally when the distance between stops became too protracted.

I had never, I told him at one point, really approved of husbands who bought their wives expensive presents to make up for their own failings, but in this case was prepared to waive my objections. He just laughed and said not to expect something so grand every time we fell out as it was almost always my fault and he was seldom to blame for anything.

Which blatant arrogance I thought, but didn't say, was pretty well par for the course

* * * * *

From this happier beginning to the New Year I put all my energies into the slow process of regaining and rebuilding the loving trust between us that had been so very nearly damaged beyond repair. The way back wasn't as easy as the first time we had really quarrelled, and it wasn't like the movies where the couple solve all their problems by making up with lightning rapidity, go into a big close-up passionate kiss and live happily ever after. This was hard work, with each stepping carefully around the other to avoid further damage or hurt.

In scarcely six months we had two almost disastrous clashes behind us and all because of the small Dominic. But that didn't stop me thinking about him, grieving over my failure to find him and still illogically believing he was somewhere in France, waiting to be found. But Charles and our future came first now, and I would look no further.

'When you join up with us it's for life', Father Con had said, and I now used those words as my lodestar when rash words were about to spring to my own tongue. Nothing worth having ever came easy I told myself, and barring accidents, for life was a hell of a long time.

16

Charles's design for the proposed sports complex to be built in North London was accepted and Mr. Geddes, the owner of Kingdom Cottage, suggested we continued to rent it for as long as we needed to be in London.

I had half expected and hoped that Charles would choose to go to Paris, feeling a complete change of scene might be good for both of us. But as he pointed out, drafting plans for a restaurant in the Paris suburbs or designing a new sports centre in the outskirts of London really didn't bear comparison, so for the time being we settled back in Putney.

'There is something much better to be looked forward to in France, but we must be a little patient,' he promised when we decided to stay. 'My old firm is opening business in Chartres in the early summer and already they are making overtures. But it would mean living there, certainly for some years, perhaps permanently.'

'I remember you once said that you would like to stay in England.' I teased, sitting cross-legged on the thick rug before the fire. 'What made you change your mind...too much rain and wind for you here?'

'Ah, but when I said that I thought Matthew's daughter would never leave Cornwall.'

I laughed, leaning forward to stir the fire then sat back against his knee. 'What a lie. We'd only just met.'

'For you, perhaps, but for me...not quite,' he put his arms about my shoulders. 'But you, would you really want to live in France?'

'Providing it is with you, yes; and so long as we can always go back to Trewlyns from time to time and spend holidays there.'

'Will your father mind very much?'

'At first, I imagine. I think he would have liked me to stay and eventually inherit the farm but didn't really expect it to happen. Soon he'll have another child to watch grow and perhaps this time he'll be lucky and get one rather more amenable than me.' I looked out of the window at the grey London sky, thinking how it would be now at Trewlyns with the daffodil spears green in the meadows and the posy flowers brilliant under glass. I gave an involuntary sigh. 'I hope he has a son who will make him proud and happy.'

'He will have to work hard to live up to his big sister.' He held me close. 'Your father is very proud of *you*...almost as proud as I am.'

'What a nice man you are.'

'This English word 'nice'.' He made an expression of disgust. 'It is for old ladies to say about cakes or kittens, not people! '

'OK. You are charming, discriminating, delightful...shall I go on?'

'Please,' he laughed.

'You are also lazy and idle and sitting too long by this fire...get up, we shall go for a nice brisk walk and work up an appetite for lunch which, on this far from nice day should be eaten in a nice, overheated, smoky London pub.'

He shook his head reprovingly, and settled deeper into his chair. 'If you were a proper French wife you would now be in the kitchen concocting some delicious meal, possibly with many oysters; then after you had satisfied me at the table I should then be able to satisfy you in the time honoured French fashion.'

'Which is?'

He leaned forward to whisper in my ear.

I looked thoughtfully through the window at the bare trees and wintry sky. Somehow a brisk walk and a smoky London pub seemed less inviting with every passing second. 'I don't know about the oysters,' I said eventually, 'but d'you think you could possibly manage all that after just soup and cold chicken?

* * * * *

James Matthew Penrose was born at the end of February, at a time when the Trewlyns daffodil meadows burst into golden life. We drove down to Cornwall, the car laden with the best collection of assorted fluffy animals that Hamley's had to offer, Charles grumbling intermittently that we should have brought the train set so that he would have something to grow into.

Train sets, I told him firmly, were for the end-of-the-bed pillowcase at Christmas when James would be at least five years old. Bought now, Matthew and Paul between them would wear it out long before Penrose Junior had a chance to get a look in.

He was a beautiful baby. Not the rather bland batter-pudding variety, nor the wizened old man, but a perfect little person, with Matthew's cornflower blue eyes and Jenny's golden hair.

'Do you think we will ever manage anything as lovely?' I asked Charles, touching with awe a tiny hand.

'Perhaps; if we really put our minds to it.'

211

Jenny laughed. 'Don't get too carried away. You haven't heard him cry yet.'

Charles feigned alarm. 'Is it loud enough to be heard at Tyndals?'

'Not yet, but he's working on it.' My father lifted his son and held him in the crook of his arm, smiling down on the tiny face, and I knew with a sudden shaft of pain that this little brother of mine had already usurped, partially at any rate, his sister's place in this house.

* * * * *

'You hid your feelings very well, but not from me.' Charles' hand tightened on mine as we walked back to Tyndals later that evening.

I smiled wryly. 'I got so used to being Matthew's only one for so long that it's a bit of a shock to be suddenly in second place.'

'You are, and will always be, in the first place with me.'

I stopped and faced him, needing the extra reassurance of his eyes, asking: 'Have we really made it back at last?'

'I think so…I hope so.' he smiled and touched my cheek. 'It feels so.'

'I love you.' I said and laid my face against his heart. For a moment he held me close then asked: 'Darling Caro, are you again washing my shirt?'

'I rather think I am.'

He bent his head, kissing me very gently, wiping the moisture from my cheeks with his thumb. 'It has been a long time,' he said, 'since I have been so damp.' He smiled. 'I had forgotten how very *nice* it could be!'

* * * * *

He was offered and accepted, the post with his old company to head the new business in Chartres, and it was arranged that we should move some time in late August; to give us time to find and furnish a house before the offices were ready to open.

For the remainder of the winter months I was content to spend my weekdays making noises like a housewife: shopping, cooking and cleaning; going to my French lessons and dawdling in the street markets, with an occasional meal or trip to the cinema with Elizabeth. But when spring began slipping into summer I became restless, longing for Charles's present work to finish and set us free to leave England early and look for a house; preferably somewhere outside Chartres but near enough to avoid for him a tiring daily journey to work.

As June was drawing to a close he was asked if he would go for a week to Paris for meetings. I was tempted to travel with him to start house-hunting, then thought perhaps the time would be better spent in Penmarrion, packing the things still at Tyndals that we might need and spend what might be my last holiday for some time at Trewlyns.

'Remember: no riding with gentlemen in taxies.' he teased, as we kissed goodbye in the airport departure hall.

'And no orgies at all in Paris.' I countered.

I waited to see his 'plane take off, watching until it was a mere speck in the sky, then drove out onto the Great West Road, heading back once more to my roots and the softness of the Cornish summer meadows.

17

Matthew made an effort to mask his disappointment when he realised how close we were to leaving England.

We sat talking over the remains of breakfast on my first morning, whilst Grace fed the hens and collected the eggs and Jenny dealt with James in his nursery above.

'You know Tyndals is yours and will always be ready for you,' he said, 'and I hope you'll use it as much as possible.' He gave a small, wry grin, 'I always thought you were the last person to hanker after city lights.'

'Well, we plan to live out of Chartres, not in it, and Charles says it's a beautiful city. But you know, dad, spending the war years away, living in all sorts of places, one does change. I've loved being in London because of the contrasts...the street bustle of it and the quiet, beautiful green places, but I'm always glad to recharge my batteries here.'

'I hope it's what you really want. I was afraid you might have felt, well a bit *spare* around here lately; I shouldn't like to think I was the reason.'

'It does feel rather odd.' I answered him honestly. 'But Charles is my reason for going, not anything you have done.'

Suddenly, I wanted to tell him about all the things that had so troubled us. About looking for the little Dominic and all my deception and lies; about Charles's anger and his unfounded jealousy and how, despite having weathered that storm there was still an undercurrent of things unsaid, of a problem unresolved. But that seemed disloyal and anyway, why should I burden him?

So I kept my thoughts to myself, leaving him to organise work for the day while I carried on to Tyndals to sort through and pack our possessions. As I pulled the cases from the cupboard and placed them open on the bed I mused how strange it was to be in this house without Charles. I had never lived here without him since he'd returned from hospital almost two years before, and every corner of the house was filled with his presence.

Methodically I began to sort and pack our winter clothes. Charles's army uniform still hung in the wardrobe and I folded it carefully and laid it on top of his second best suit, reflecting that he would need to visit a tailor before he took up his new, rather more prestigious position. I ran my finger over the medal ribbons on the army jacket and wondered how he had looked in uniform and if the girl he had walked and talked with in Oxford ever thought of him.

Even now there was so much of his past of which I knew little or nothing. The hot-headed young man who had risked his life as a saboteur, tied himself in a sham marriage, escaped death at the hands of the Gestapo, then returned to risk his life again and again for his country was aeons away from the calm and balanced man who now shared my life. Perhaps one day I would understand him, perhaps one day truly comprehend how so gentle and loving a man could still steel his heart and turn his back on Lise's son.

Leaving the half-filled cases I went to lean at the open window and look down on the sunken lane and the high bank covered with wild flowers. The soft susurration of waves breaking on the shore could be clearly heard above the cry of distant gulls and I was filled with a sudden aching sadness that soon Trewlyns and all it meant to me would be no more than a memory.

I was leaving all this to go to another country and another life with a man I still didn't completely understand.

If he really loves me I reasoned, someday he will see how important it is for me – and for him – to find what happened to Lisa's child: be able to cleanse his heart of hatred and close the book on his past. Until he could do that, despite our love and our commitment to each other, there would always remain a distance between us.

* * * * *

Grace had insisted that I should take my meals with them to save the necessity of shopping and making my own meals, so just before noon I broke off my somewhat sporadic efforts at packing to walk the familiar lane, enjoying the feel of the warm sun on my bare arms and legs and filling my lungs with sea air. I'd go down to the cove for a swim after lunch, I decided, and wondered if Jenny would leave James with Grace for a while and join me. Still busy with my own thoughts I turned in at the farm gate and saw Grace waving urgently from the doorway.

'Telephone…' she shouted, 'for you!'

Filled with sudden fear I began to run. *Not Charles, dear God, surely nothing had happened to Charles…*

She saw my face and came to meet me. 'It's all right lamb; it's only a Captain Lindsey asking for you. He 'phoned the cottage, but you must have left. He said it was urgent. Why,' she caught my arm,

215

'you're as white as a sheet!'

'It's all right.' My heart was hammering, my throat suddenly dry. I stood holding onto the lintel of the door to catch my breath. Wanting, yet not wanting to hear what he may have to say after all this time.

* * * * *

'Caroline?'

His voice, when I gathered the courage to lift the receiver, was quiet and faintly hesitant. 'Caroline...do you still want to know?'

* * * * *

Very gently, I replaced the 'phone.

Grace had prudently left me alone and could be heard rattling pans in the kitchen, while in the nursery above my head Jenny laughed and played with the baby. I sat on in Matthew's old leather-seated captain's chair, swinging slowly half round then back again. Outside the window the sea sparkled; in the distance I could hear the sound of the tractor being driven over the cliff meadows, then an abrupt silence as either Matthew or Willi cut the engine to leave work for the lunchtime break.

'Dad.' I was at the door waiting for my father as he turned into the yard. 'I have something to tell you.'

* * * * *

'Don't get your hopes up too high,' Francis had said, 'because this is all a bit muddled and hangs on rather vague intelligence at second hand. But you remember Victor Lestoc, the solicitor? He hates being beaten over anything and few weeks' back he began contacting all the hospitals around the area where Lise was found. When he turned up some rather odd and co-incidental information he delved a little deeper...so here goes...

'Latish in July 'forty-four a young girl walked into a hospital a few miles south of Argentan bringing a small child suffering from a high fever. She was travelling with some other women and left him, saying they were on the way to Orléans where she had relatives and that she would return for him when he was better. A week later there was a Panzer counter attack against the area and the hospital was heavily shelled and the survivors moved to a temporary emergency

216

hospital near Paris. With many of their records destroyed or lost in the shelling the only information on one surviving small boy came from a young nurse, one of the few staff who lived through the attack. She wasn't sure but thought he was the one left by the girl and that they'd travelled from somewhere on the Normandy coast...'

'Hang on! Didn't they ask the child his name?' I interrupted, 'He would have been almost three...most kids know their own name by then.'

'They did, and he told them he was Jean Delour – '

Disappointed I interrupted him, 'Jean? That's nothing like Dominic.'

'I know,' he was patient, 'but its possible Lise shortened his name to Dom. If he was shocked and frightened it would have been easy for them to hear Jean for Dom and Delour for de la Tour.'

My heart began to beat fast again. Yes; it was very possible.

He continued, 'Victor followed it up and found the child had been diagnosed with TB. By then Paris had been liberated and he'd been packed off to some sort of temporary sanatorium in the countryside outside the city.'

He paused for a moment, and I heard the rustling of papers before he continued. 'Now here's where it all gets a bit blurred around the edges! He couldn't have been a bad case as he seems to have recovered well and was discharged as cured to a convent orphanage in Belgium around Christmas 'forty-five. Now I spoke to the Reverend Mother there last week and according to her they had three nuns from their Order in Ireland living at the convent right through the war, who were either never rumbled by the Germans, or more likely left alone as they weren't officially British nationals – you may remember our German friends liked to keep the South sweet in order to run their U Boats off the Irish coast. These Sisters returned to Ireland early last year, and to relieve the overcrowded Belgian orphanage received permission from the French and Irish authorities to take twelve of the children back with them...our possible Dominic amongst them.'

'Oh, God,' I groaned. 'This gets more complicated by the minute.'

He laughed. 'I did warn you. I've checked with the hospital authorities in Argentan and traced a ward clerk who also remembered his arrival there. She says the girl came from the lower end of the Cherbourg Peninsular; she couldn't remember exactly where but did recall that she'd been on her way to take refuge with a cousin and his wife living on the Northern outskirts of Orléans. The boy's birth date, she thinks, was sometime in the summer of nineteen forty-one.'

'He was born August fourth.' I was positive about the exact date, as Charles had been given the Birth Certificate along with the other papers to do with his marriage to Lise.

'Well,' he said, 'it *is* a long shot, but I've the Irish address for you here and the Reverend Mother knows what's going on. So...what are you going to do about it?'

* * * * *

'What are you going to do about it?' echoed Matthew as I paused for breath.

I swept a pile of catalogues from a chair and sat down. 'What do you *think* I'm going to do?'

He looked at me sharply. 'Not without you tell Charles first.'

'Of course I shall tell him. He won't want to see him, but I shall most certainly go. I can't let this child know who I am...I may not even speak to him. I'd hate to stir things up and find he's not Dominic at all, but at least I shall get the chance to discover if he really *is* Lise's child.' I jumped up, my brain going like a millrace. 'Aer Lingus fly to Dublin from somewhere near Bristol, don't they? With luck I might get a flight tomorrow. Meanwhile, dad, may I please, *please* phone Charles in Paris and tell him before I burst!'

But it wasn't to be quite so easy.

M'sieur de la Tour, I was informed, was at present somewhere in the area around Chartres. No, they did not have a contact number but would leave a message at the new offices. Frustrated, I gave the Trewlyns number and replaced the receiver, then sat having a pensive nibble at my thumbnail.

'You're going tomorrow just the same, aren't you?' asked Matthew.

'Dad, I must. I can't wait.'

He grinned. 'I'd rather not bet on Charles being best pleased, but guess it's no more than he would expect you to do.'

'Hold the fort for me.' I put my arms around his neck and hugged him. 'If he does turn up, soothe him, smooth him; tell him anything...everything. Just keep him off my back for forty-eight hours if you can; I'll be back by Friday.'

* * * * *

By lunchtime the following day the DC10 was circling Dublin Airport and I was about to begin the last lap of my journey to the Convent of

Saint Francis of Assisi, Dunlorn, in the County of Wicklow, Southern Ireland.

18

It took me no more than an hour or so to have a snatched lunch and hire a car. I left Dublin in brilliant sunshine, driving through the great hills that lie fold upon fold around that city then through miles of peat bog stretching as far as the eye could see, the whole countryside clothed in differing shades of brown, with mounds of dark brown peat stacked alongside the biscuit coloured roads.

I map-read my way through this sombre wilderness, coming at last to the wild green grass and glens of Wicklow, passing white-painted crofts and stone-walled fields where the sharp smell of peat from the range fires hung in the still warm air like incense in a church. I remembered an Irish air-gunner I once knew laughing and saying: 'If you ever go to Ireland, it will get you!' and on this shining day as I gazed on his strange, wild country I understood the passionate pride that had lighted his eyes.

The convent when I reached it was not particularly prepossessing, made up as it was of several low grey-stone buildings clustered around a much grander chapel, the arched stained-glass window of which shone and sparked coloured fire in the rays of the afternoon sun. Inside, the house was so clean that I took a surreptitious glance behind at the polished wooden floors to see if I was leaving a trail of dusty footprints behind me, while the diminutive nun who had invited me to follow her glided silently ahead down several corridors, stopping eventually to tap on a heavy panelled door before opening it and standing aside for me to enter.

A plump, pale-cheek nun with a sweet, distant smile rose from behind a desk and offered her hand.

'Good afternoon, Madame de la Tour; I am Mother Marie Joseph. I understand from our telephone conversation yesterday that you have come to see the child we know as Jean Delour. Please sit down.'

I sat obediently, pulling my skirt over my knees and feeling as though I were twelve years old again, up before the Head for chalking a rude limerick on the blackboard. I said, 'I'm not too sure whether I should actually meet him. As I explained over the telephone, matters are rather complicated.'

'Ah, yes, we must make sure of our ground before the child is told anything that might raise his hopes. And of course, there is your husband to consider; Captain Lindsey also indicated this was a delicate area!' There was a sudden gleam of something very like mischief in her pale blue eyes. 'He is not with you, I see.'

'No. I was unable to contact him in Paris but I left a message and my father will explain where I am when he rings.' I was becoming rattled by the rarefied, polite atmosphere and feeling increasingly out of my depth.

There was silence for a moment or two and then she smiled again.

'Perhaps I should tell you something about him, this little man who may have the wrong name. If you are expecting a strong, confident child, he is not that. If you look for sparkling childish chatter, he is sadly deficient, but if you wish to spend time and look beneath the surface, which few seem to do, you will find intelligence and charm, and I think, just the right amount of mischief!'

I was cautious. 'He may not be the one I've been looking for.'

She inclined her head.

'That is so, but if you wish we can view the playroom from a window. Then you can make up your mind if you would like to see him at closer quarters and perhaps talk with him.'

As I followed her from the room and along yet another corridor, I wished Charles were with me for moral support. Even he, I reasoned, would surely want to at least look?

No he wouldn't, I answered myself. *He's told you plainly enough: he would perhaps find him a good school, ensure he doesn't starve, but that's about all.*

We stopped before a large, waist-high window.

'This is where our teaching students come first to observe. It eases them gently into their work. It can be a little daunting to go straight in with such a busy throng.'

Too damn' right, I thought, it would put me off teaching for life!

It was not that the room I looked down upon lacked the things dear to a child's heart. There were books, toys and puzzles, crayons and modelling clay in abundance, but how did the shy and the timid fare in what appeared to be a seething mass of small bodies, all hurling themselves with boundless energy into whatever occupation they chose?

It was only an illusion of course, after a minute or two I could see that the twenty or so small boys below fell into separate groups engaged in various types of play, not just one vast juvenile rugger-scrum as at first appeared. I hunted for a blonde Aryan bullet-head without success and gave up after a few moments.

The nun touched my arm. 'Over there: with the crayons and the blue paper. That is your young man.'

As if on cue the apparently absorbed artist lifted his head and stared straight up at us. I gave slightly at the knees. 'Oh!' I caught my breath. 'It isn't possible...'

I took from my wallet a favourite photograph of Charles. Seated on the low wall of the cottage, he was laughing as I struggled with the complicated mechanics of his camera, eyes lively under the straight brows.

I handed the picture to the nun, who smiled and returned it. 'Family likeness can be quite startling,' she observed, 'your husband's "son" is very like him, is he not?'

* * * * *

'He will not be surprised,' she led the way down a winding staircase to the playroom door. 'We have many visitors. People are good and often come to take one or more children to their homes, or out for the day. Some even end up fostering or adopting, but mostly only the more boldly attractive ones.' She smiled a little sadly. 'Others less immediately captivating, such as Jean, stay with us.'

'It's getting a little late today to take him out.' I ventured, 'but perhaps tomorrow...?'

'Certainly. There is an excellent small Inn in the next village where you could stay tonight and we shall have Jean ready if you wish to collect him early.'

Willing Matthew to keep Charles stalled for those precious forty-eight hours, I went to meet the child whom I was now quite certain was Dominic de la Tour.

* * * * *

'Madame is going to be an Auntie?'

His English was good, if stilted. Perched on the edge of an upright chair in the little parlour we had been allotted for our meeting, he regarded me with wary dark eyes, obviously used to summing up visitors and placing them swiftly in the right categories.

'I shouldn't think so. I've come from England, but only for a visit.'

'To visit me?'

He was sharp; his dark eyes didn't leave my face and again I was reminded of Charles. I said, 'You and others.'

'It is a long way to come for just a visit.'

'I thought you might like to come out with me tomorrow.'

'There will be time...before you go back to England?'

222

'Plenty of time if we leave early.'

I tried to see what Mother Marie-Joseph saw in him. Since being left alone with me and up until these last exchanges he had given only monosyllabic answers to my cautious questions. Thin and undersized, his resemblance to Charles was only really in the forehead and eyes. A thick mop of smooth brown hair was cut short above his ears, making them appear too large for the small pointed face; Josh's description of Charles suddenly flashed into my mind: "a French Pixie" and I laughed out loud.

He blinked, the wary look still in place for a moment, then he smiled and the charm was there, exactly like Charles when he was about to tease.

'Madame has big teeth!' he said, then covered his mouth with his hand to stifle a giggle.

* * * * *

Madame was back early the next morning, teeth and all.

He was waiting at the door, dressed in a blue shirt and shorts, with shoes that gleamed; his hair, dampened and brushed down by some zealous hand, escaped in joyous defiance in a little tuft that stuck up straight from the crown. As we descended the steps he eyed the hire-car with professional interest.

'Madame cannot be an auntie,' he said confidently. 'Ordinary auntie's do not have such shiny cars, nor come from England.'

'You don't have to keep calling me Madame.' I said as we left the convent behind. I thought it might have helped if Mother Maria Joseph had introduced me as Mrs de la Tour...but would he then have addressed me as Missus? It would hardly have been an improvement.

'What then should I say?'

'You could try Caroline.' I suggested.

'*That* would not be polite!' There was disapproval in every syllable.

My God, I thought you're just like Charles at his most stuffy...

* * * * *

'I come from France, you know,' he confided as we sped towards Dublin and the delights of baked beans on toast followed by ice cream, his choice, 'but I don't have a mama and I don't have a papa. Some people have an auntie to take them out and sometimes the auntie becomes their mama, but none of mine ever did.' He added with unconscious irony, 'for me, there have been many aunties.'

So much for his lack of conversation; there was nothing much wrong with Jean-Dominic's tongue that a willing listener wouldn't put right, I thought.

As the hours passed, I wished with all my heart that Charles could see him like this, going on seven and as bright and funny as a sunrise field of March hares. He took my hand, holding it unselfconsciously as we wandered the streets of Dublin, trekking from one bridge to another over the Liffey and craning to watch the boats pass.

He was fascinated by the water and its busy traffic, 'If I lived by this water, I would watch it all day...' he enthused and hung over the parapet, waving to the boats while I clung grimly to the band of his shorts.

I told him about Cornwall. How the sea foamed at the foot of Penmarrion Cove on the spring tides, and how I now lived by a river, the biggest in England, where boat-race crews sped under our bridge and pleasure boats took people to gardens and palaces along its banks. 'It must be nice,' he said, craning round to look at me from his position on the parapet. 'Will Madame live there for ever?'

'No, not for ever; soon I shall go to live in France near a city called Chartres.'

'You might see my house if you go to France.' His brow furrowed in a frown, 'but Sister Veronica says France is a big place so you probably could pass by it and never know. Will there be a river where you live?'

'Yes; quite near: the Loire, but I haven't seen it yet.'

'That will be nice for Madame, to still watch boats going by.'

I didn't know if such conversation was usual for a child, never really having known such natural phenomena with any degree of intimacy, but he seemed quite alarmingly grown up for his size, if not his age.

He enjoyed the museum, but was a little nonplussed by some of the pictures in the Art Gallery. Pausing before a large canvass depicting a group of very buxom nymphs wearing only minimum wisps of strategically placed gauzy draperies he observed gravely, 'Those ladies, Madame, it must be very hot where they live... hotter than summer for them to need no clothes!'

It was rather, I felt as the day progressed, like spending the time with a midget who might suddenly turn out to have a degree in Philosophy.

But when at last we had to begin the drive back, he grew quiet as the city was left behind. Back an hour before bedtime had been the request and we mustn't, I reminded him, be late.

'Why do you have to go home tomorrow?'

'Well, I have a husband, you see, and he will be coming home from France very soon.'

He was quiet for a long time. Eventually he heaved a sigh. 'I think a lot of aunties have husbands! If Madame didn't have one perhaps she would come again many more times...' his shoulders slumped, 'but if you go to France then it will be too far.'

'I should like to come back and see you before I go. It might be possible, but I don't want to promise and not be able to.'

To my horror I saw two fat tears splash down onto his bare knees. I stopped the car pulling over onto the edge of a field. Taking a handkerchief out of my pocket I begged, 'Please don't cry. I'm sorry. I really would like to stay and be an auntie. But I have to go tomorrow, d'you see?'

Oh, God, I thought, everybody else was right. I should never have started this. Now he is going to weep and I am going to die a little inside when I hand him back into the bright playroom and the rugger scrum and the forlorn hope that another auntie will come along and want him for more than a day...

He didn't howl or sniff or make any sound, just sat with downcast eyes, twin rivulets of tears running down his cheeks whilst I mopped industriously and cursed Charles de la Tour, Hitler, and the sexual incontinence of the entire German Army, with a silent heartfelt profanity sufficient to close the gates of heaven to me forever.

Eventually the torrent slowed to a trickle and the trickle to an occasional dry gulp as I sat with my arms around his thin body and planned my next trip to Ireland.

Sod Charles and sod France and sod anything that might stand in my way.

I was coming back.

* * * * *

Although the temptation to stay another day and spend extra precious hours with Dominic was almost overwhelming, my first priority was to get back at the earliest possible moment and make my own explanations, not to mention my peace, with Charles. With luck he might not have viewed the news as important enough to interrupt his plans. If this were so I may have a day or two in hand for a spot of strategic planning on what I would say and how I would explain my impulsive flight to Ireland.

By the time my return flight had landed and I'd collected my car, it was late afternoon and too tired to make the long drive back to Cornwall that night, I booked in at a small hotel near in Bristol. Although exhausted with the events of the past forty-eight hours I passed a sleepless night and left early the following morning, heavy-eyed but consumed with impatience to get back to Trewlyns.

But the nearer I drew to my destination, the more apprehensive I became. My efforts to summon the necessary courage to explain to Charles my feelings and determination to continue to see Dominic dwindled with every mile that passed. Francis Lindsey had been right. I hadn't been content just to see him. I did want more than that, and although Charles would not, I thought, be so terribly surprised or angry that I *had* seen him, try as I might I couldn't imagine him co-operating in making it easy for me to continue to keep contact with any kind of regularity. The irony that I should soon be in France and Dominic in Ireland was almost more than I could bear.

I drove fast, the miles flying beneath my wheels, feeling a rush of relief as I crossed the border into Cornwall and headed for home, not realising at first that the strange, guttural sounds I began to hear above the thrumming of the engine were coming from my own throat. Blindly, I pulled into the side of the road and leaning my head on the steering wheel gave myself up to painful, wracking, uncontrollable sobs. Why, I raged, when I had been through so much, should I be faced again with having to make a choice between the man I loved and the child who needed us both?

'Oh, Charles,' I wept, 'please put the past behind you. Don't make me choose.'

I thought of my talk with Paul, and how hard I had worked afterward to repair the damage already caused by my determination to find Lise's child. All very well in the face of Dominic's distress, to damn Charles and everyone to hell and think only of the boy. Twice already, I reminded myself, I had come to the brink of disaster and I couldn't bear even the thought of returning again to the misery and despair of those dreadful weeks.

Gradually, my sobs subsided. Charles wasn't a monster. He was my husband, my lover and my friend. He knew me better than anyone else, better even than my father did. He would be waiting for me at Penmarrion and together we would find a way around this dreadful impasse...

I scrubbed at my swollen eyes and pressed the starter button.

Please be there, darling. I'm almost home.

226

* * * * *

One look at Matthew's face when he met me at the door was enough to tell me I was too late.

'Where is he? I have to talk to him. He *must* be here.' I was sick with disappointment.

He gave an apologetic, down-turned smile.

'He was, but he's gone again, Caro!'

'*Gone*? Where? When?'

'After you...early this morning; you must have passed each other on the way.'

Silently, I took in the full implication of what he was saying. Charles had been concerned enough, or furious enough to leave his meetings in Paris and come charging after me; probably in the hope he might get to Cornwall before I'd left for Ireland. *Shit*, I thought as I followed Matthew into the sitting room, if he'd gone tearing off to Ireland after me he must be hopping mad.

Jenny got up from her chair to hug me as Grace came in bearing the inevitable tea tray. 'I heard you come.' Grace observed briskly. 'Now just sit down and drink this before you say or do anything else...there's a drop of something warming in it to steady your nerves.'

Accepting the spirit-reeking cup I sat at the table; propping my head on my hand I look bleakly at Matthew. 'Tell me all,' I invited.

'Your message didn't reach him until yesterday morning and he 'phoned from Chartres as soon as he received it. I explained briefly what had happened and he said he'd get the first flight he could from Paris, which would be late evening. He came down, driving most of the night in a hire car.'

I closed my eyes. Oh, he was mad all right. 'Go on.'

'I tried to stall him; said he must rest after tearing all the way here, but he'd have none of it.' My father's face was full of sympathy. 'Sorry, Caro, I did try, but all he wanted was the details of where you were heading then took off again and driving like a bat out of hell!'

'Oh, my God,' I slumped back in my chair. 'He'll be in absolute agony after driving all that distance then sitting in that bloody Dakota before another journey across country...hell's teeth, but I hope Mother Maria Joseph has a good right hook, because the way he'll be when he arrives she's certainly going to need it.'

'He was quite calm.' put in Jenny. 'Not raving mad or foaming at the mouth.'

'Charles is always calm until he really flips – and you wouldn't

227

have got the best of it even if he had. I suspect he's saving that for me.'

'I almost forgot,' Matthew jumped up, 'he left a letter. Grace put it on my office desk.' He hesitated. 'Perhaps you'd better go and read it in there. Just shout if you want anything: a shotgun; a rope with a noose in it; a large knife...anything like that!'

'Oh, very funny...' I wouldn't dare, I thought; Grace would complain if I made a mess on the carpet.

I stood before Matthew's desk for a full minute turning the letter in my hand, then broke open the envelope and sank into the swivel chair.

I scanned it quickly at first then read it again, slowly and carefully. It was quite short.

Caro,
Not dear Caro, I noted, or even Caro, you bitch...
As I have no doubt you will be returning to meet me with all your guns loaded and ready to fire, this is to let you know that I intend to go straight to the Convent...alone.

I have no idea when I shall return. Possibly within the next few days or it may be longer. I should like you to stay at Tyndals until I join you there.

This is my *battle. Please do as I ask and leave me to fight it in my own way.*
Charles.
Hallelujah! I thought, now what in hell do you mean by all *that,* you close-mouthed, devious sod!

* * * * *

'Perhaps,' suggested Jenny as we sat at lunch, 'he's finally seen the light and all is forgiven.'

'That I doubt. I note he signed it "Charles" not, "Love, Charles" or even "Damn-your-eyes, Charles"' I brooded over my macaroni cheese. 'He's a real bastard, isn't he?'

'I think he's been a lot more restrained than you would have been.' Grace was her usual uncompromising self. 'And we can do without that sort of language. It sets James a bad example.'

I laughed for the first time since my return. 'If he grows up in this place he'll hear a lot worse than that before he's through, but just for you, Grace, I promise never to swear again in the house.'

She sniffed. 'Pigs might fly!'

Jenny picked up the letter again to re-read it, a frown creasing her brow. 'If he thinks he might be longer than a day or two, what do you suppose he could be planning to do with the time?'

'Go back to Paris and finish his business there, do you think?' asked Matthew.

'Most probably,' I agreed wearily, 'but we could all guess until Christmas before we'd have the faintest idea of what may be going on in his head. Half the time even I don't know that and I'm married to the blasted man.'

* * * * *

It was possibly the longest day of my life. I couldn't settle to anything. When lunch was over I told Matthew that until Charles returned I would work at Trewlyns to fill the daylight hours. Then pleading the excuse of packing still to be done, I walked slowly back to Tyndals, feeling unutterably drained and dreary. For an hour or more I lay on our bed, holding Charles' pillow in my arms, breathing in the faint trace of him I thought I could discern beneath the clean, cool linen.

What was it about something, or someone "being born to trouble as the sparks fly upward"? That was me...Perhaps the hairy young man under the eaves of Kingdom Cottage had been right; maybe he could see my aura, whatever it was, and maybe it was green and bad.

Because sure as hell, I thought morosely, something wasn't feeling very pink and healthy right now.

Eventually I got up off the bed, bathed my face in cold water, changed into a fresh shirt and a pair of cotton shorts and started in again on the packing. I supposed I could take my time over that; it looked as though I would be grateful for anything that would keep me busy over the next few days...or longer. I paused for a moment, standing at the window, folding Charles's heavy Guernsey and wondering if he was in Ireland yet, and what he would do about Dominic.

If he broke his own rule and looked down as I had into that room and saw that funny little face peering up at him, perhaps recognising the little girl Lise in those eyes, would he soften at all? Be able to put hatred behind him and recognise that a good school and food for the body was not enough. That perhaps he was committing a sin of omission in not allowing himself to see what others could. Or would he sit opposite Mother Maria Joseph, polite and distant, offer the financial support that meant so little to him, then turn and walk away.

229

I could only wait and see.

Pushing myself mercilessly, I worked an ten-hour day on the farm and after an evening meal with my family at Trewlyns, walked alone each evening, until the light faded and I was forced to return to a cottage empty and bereft of his presence.

I passed the days numb with the pain of his absence, until the evening I found tucked under his side of the mattress one of his books, and sat in a chair beside the bed to read from the page where it fell open. The last few lines of verse were underlined in pencil and I had a sudden vivid recollection of seeing him marking that page the night I'd told him of my search for Dominic, when he'd sat by the bed reading until I fell asleep.

> *...And if Fate remember later, and come to claim her due,*
> *What Sorrow will be greater than the Joy I had with you?*
> *For today, lit by your laughter, between the crushing years*
> *I will chance, in the hereafter, eternities of tears...*

I closed the pages softly, the words touching a cord deep within me. All at once I felt at peace, almost as though his voice spoke the words in my ear, his arms around me, holding me close and safe against his dear, familiar body.

I had no idea of where he was, or what he was doing now, only knew, without any shadow of doubt that he would come back to me; that somehow once again and for the last time, we would pick up the pieces and go on together.

'Good to see a smile once more.' greeted Matthew as I arrived for breakfast the next morning, the fifth since Charles had left for Ireland. 'No word though, I suppose?'

'No, but that is his way, he does nothing in a hurry...unless he's caught off guard, which is when you duck...pretty smart!'

I sat down at the table, suddenly ravenous and he watched with a smile as I devoured a breakfast of bacon, eggs, tomatoes and sausage, topping it off with a mound of toast and half a pot of coffee.

'Back to normal! Caro, you pig...leave some for Jenny.'

'Nonsense, she needs building up,' Grace entered with more of the same, plonking the dish down on the table. 'Better hurry though,' she eyed me mischievously. 'Cynthia is coming over early this morning to pick up some eggs. She's bound to have little Marianne Julietta with her, and you know how you are...'

'Omigawd!' I snatched a final piece of toast and made for the door, 'I wouldn't mind. There's nothing wrong with the poor kid, apart from the fact that she has gooseberry eyes for a mother. But what a name – and frilly knickers over a *nappy* – I ask you; is that natural?'

Matthew's laughter faded behind me as I strolled down, replete and at peace. Crossing the big field I walked to the cliff edge to stand looking across the water. I could feel the heat of the day building as I stood, my hands in the pockets of my shorts, my shirt half unbuttoned to catch the faint early morning breeze. I remembered Josh libellously describing me as having my shirt unbuttoned to my navel and grinned. Dear Josh, big and sexy, still my pal and, Cynthia or no Cynthia, still greeting me when we met with a breezy, 'Hi, Penrose!' and stripping off my clothes with one expert sweep of those wicked eyes.

I should always have a soft spot for Josh Milton...

The sea was running with a slight swell; breaking along the foreshore of the cove below in small, cream-crested waves. Already the sun was warm on my face. Another lovely day, I thought, filling my eyes and ears with the myriad sights and sounds of a Cornish summer. Here I had stood with Charles on that long ago night, the dogs snuffling around our feet, the waves breaking far below with a rhythmic hiss on the sand, while the moon lay a pathway across the black water.

'Hurry up, my love.' I said aloud to the blossoming day, then turned and walked back to where Matthew waited, the first pipe of the morning in his mouth, his sleeves rolled to the elbow, ready to begin the working day.

* * * * *

Ella Fitzgerald was singing *My Happiness*. Too sad I thought, and turned off the radio, wishing I had brought Brahms and Liszt back with me. Such an evening needed dogs by one's side to walk the headland as the day came to a perfect end, a blazing sunset ready to burnish the treetops and set the grass afire with its dying rays.

I took the track up towards Porthcurnow, the setting sun in my eyes made little specks of purple and black dance across my vision as I walked. This evening I wanted to feel I had the whole world to myself and was considerably less than pleased when only a few minutes into my walk I saw a man in the distance. He was coming slowly towards me along the cliff path, swinging a stick and carrying a large pack on his back, while an even more aggravating intrusion in the shape of an empty parked car stood on the brow of the hill behind him.

'Bloody tripper,' I thought uncharitably, wondering if the car belonged to the man with the pack. The track, too narrow for a car, led only to Tyndals and the farm beyond, so there was a chance the man was on his way to seek work from Matthew. I watched him draw nearer, then suddenly stop and swing his burden to the ground before straightening again to look down the track towards me.

I screwed up my eyes, shading them with my hand against the dazzle of the sun, my heart beginning to pound wildly and erratically in my breast.

Charles!

But no...common sense took over. How could it possibly be Charles, walking home from Ireland or France with a haversack on his back? Sick with disappointment I made to turn back towards the cottage when the burden the man had set down began to move; grew two skinny legs, gathered speed, faster and faster until those legs were going like pistons as with a joyous shout of '*Madame*!' Jean-Dominic flew down the slope and into my open arms.

I knelt on the dusty pathway, holding him, his arms tight around my neck as Charles reached us to stand leaning on his stick, looking down on me as he had that first day on the cliffs above the cove. When he spoke his voice was rueful, his expression wryly self-mocking.

'We two have spent much time watching the boats on the Liffey and resolving the sort of house we think you would like in France, and the sort of boat *we* would like to sail on our river. We have talked things over and think we may both like to live there with you, and in time all be very happy and like each other very much.' Smiling, he leaned forward, holding out a hand for me to take, pulling us both up into the shelter of his arm. 'So at last we decided that it was time Jean-Dominic de la Tour left the good sisters and came home to his mama and papa!'

* * * * *

I took a last look at the small sleeping head on the pillow then closed the door softly and went quietly down the stairs. Out in the garden

Charles stood relaxed, hands in pockets, looking up at the night sky. I walked to him across the moonlit grass and leaning against his back put my arms around his waist. 'What made you change your mind?' I asked.

He laughed and turned; hitching himself onto the broad, moss-covered garden wall he pulled me towards him. 'Have you ever had to face a most determined Mother Superior?'

All about us the night closed in, velvety blue, the moon a high silver disc in the sky; yellow lamp light spilling across the grass from the open door behind us. I looked up into his face. 'Tell me.'

'Almost an hour I held out,' he admitted, 'I was determined not to be coerced into seeing him; but she beat me in the end, because all I could do to keep my mind from being washed by her was to think of you, my darling Caro, and *that* was my undoing!'

'Hmm, but I bet you were pretty mad all the same...haring back from France like that.'

'I was not pleased.'

'I thought you would understand, you see.'

'But I did. I did!' He put both arms about me, kissing my hair, my eyes my mouth. 'I understood that you were going to be hurt, that you would curse me for not wanting to be involved, and that you would pull yourself in half trying to have everything you wanted and felt was right!'

I blushed. 'You don't have to sound so pleased to have been one hundred per cent right in knowing what I'd do.'

'But I was far from being one hundred per cent sure of what *I* should do.' He looked down into my eyes, shaking his head slightly. 'Then as I watched those little ones at play I could see *they* weren't bothered about nationality or accidents of birth; they were just small boys playing – and no doubt sometimes fighting – together. I thought of our first quarrel – and of our second; the things you said that I wouldn't then listen to, and knew you were right and I was wrong.' He spread his hands and his mouth twitched at the corners. 'I fear I am not as altruistic as my wife, nor ever will be. Old memories die hard and there will always be some I shall hate; but not those who have no say in what they are.'

'You know,' I said innocently, 'this is the first time I've ever heard you admit you were wrong about anything.'

'And it is probably the last! But now...' he took my hand, spreading the fingers, counting them off with one of his. 'One, two, three, four, five...I am running out, give me the other... six, seven...*Ah, mon Dieu*! It is eight nights since we made love. This is too long!'

He slipped down off the wall, tightening his arms, pulling me hard against his warm, welcoming body, his mouth breaking into the slow, familiar smile as I locked my arms about his neck.

'Now that at last our so tired *garçonnet* is fast asleep...' he murmured against my mouth, 'perhaps Matthew's daughter will do me the honour of coming to bed with me tonight.'

A Year Out of Time

A Year Out of Time is the story of one twelve year old girl from a "nice" middle-class background and a "nice" private school (where her mother hoped she might learn to be a lady) who, in the Autumn of 1940, finds herself pitched into the totally foreign environment of a small Worcestershire hamlet.

For the space of one year her life revolves around the village school and its manic headmaster; the friends she makes, notably Georgie Little the "bad influence"; the twee but useful fellow evacuees, Mavis and Mickey Harper, whose possession of an old pigsty proves the springboard to some surprising and sometimes hilarious happenings; and Mrs 'Arris, the vast and formidable landlady of The Green Dragon Inn.

In the company of Georgie Little she awakens to the joys of a new and exhilarating world: a secret world which excludes most adults and frequently verges on the lawless.

The year comes to an explosive end and she returns unwillingly to her former life – but the joyous, anarchic influence of the Forest and Georgie remains, and sixty years on is remembered with gratitude and love.

ISBN 978-0-9555778-0-2

By the same author

Available from Sagittarius Publications
62 Jacklyns Lane, Alresford, Hampshire SO24 9LH

And All Shall Be Well

And All Shall Be Well begins Francis Lindsey's journey through childhood to middle age; from a suddenly orphaned ten year old to a carefree adolescent; through the harsh expectations of becoming a man in a world caught in war.

Set mainly against the dramatic background of the Cornish Coast, it is a story about friendships and relationships, courage and weakness, guilt and reparation. — *The first book in a Cornish trilogy.*

ISBN 978-0-9555778-1-9

By the same author

**Chosen as the runner-up
to the Society of Authors 2003 Sagittarius Prize**

"The author has succeeded to an extraordinary degree in bringing Francis to full masculine life. The storyline is always interesting and keeps the reader turning the pages. All in all it is a good novel that can be warmly recommended to anyone who enjoys a good read."
– Michael Legat

"Seldom do I get a book that simply cannot be put down. The settings and characters are so believable, the shy falling in love for the first time and the passion of forbidden liaisons written with feeling. Many of the sequences left me with a smile on my face, others to wipe a tear from my eye." – Jenny Davidson, The Society of Women Writers and Journalists Book Review

"A beautifully written novel. Eve Phillips' writing is a pure joy to read and her wonderfully graphic descriptions of the Penzance area of the Cornish Coast made me yearn to be there."
– Erica James, Author

Available from Sagittarius Publications
62 Jacklyns Lane, Alresford, Hampshire SO24 9LH